QUEEN OF SHADOWS AND ROSES

ROSES

BROTHERS OF OLYMPUS

BOOK ONE

HELENA M CRAGGS

HERMANA BOOKS
PUBLISHING

Cover design and map by Emily's World of Design

Edited by Jennifer Kay Davies (IG @jkdavieseditor)

Proofread by author, Liana Valerian (IG @liana.valaerain)

Character art by Tony Viento (IG @tonyviento)

 Formatted with Vellum

NO AI TRAINING:

DEDICATION

"To my family, this book is for you. I love you all. But maybe skip chapters 9, 16, 20, 23, 25, 27, 35, 38, 39 or 42, and if you do read them, let's never talk about it." 🤍

AUTHOR'S NOTE

Queen of Shadows and Roses is a sizzling New Adult fantasy romance rooted in the Hades and Persephone myth. Expect slow-burn intensity, enemies-to-lovers tension, mature themes, and a growing heat level that builds with every chapter. The spark starts slow—but the fire will consume you. 🌶️🌶️🌶️ You've been warned.

Queen of Shadows and Roses includes several TW/CWs. For more information, please check the book's trigger warning page in the table of contents.

PLAY LIST

MY TOP 10 SONGS

"Let the World Burn" — Chris Grey
"Don't Blame Me"— Taylor Swift
"Anxiety" — Sleepy Hallow
"Chains" — Tina Arena
"I Hate U, I Love U" — gnash
"A Thousand Years" — James Arthur (cover)
"You Should See me in a Crown" — Billie Eilish
"Tornado Warnings" — Sabrina Carpenter
"All of Me " — John Legend
"One More Night"— Maroon 5

THE GODS IN THIS BOOK:

HADES: (hay-deez) God of the dead. King of the underworld.

ZEUS: (zyoos) God of sky, lightning, and thunder. King of the gods.

POSEIDON: (puh-sai-dn) god of, storms, earthquakes and horses. King of the sea.

PERSEPHONE: (pur-seh-fuh-nee) goddess of spring; associated with growth, fertility and love.

HECATE: (heca-tee) goddess of magic, witchcraft, the night, light, ghosts, necromancy, and the moon.

HERMES: (huh-meez) the messenger of the gods, the protector of travellers, thieves, and the conductor of the dead to the underworld.

THE GODS IN THIS BOOK:

DIONYSUS: (dai-uh-nai-suhs) god of wine and pleasure.

APHRODITE: (a-fruh-dai-tee) goddess of love, beauty, and fertility, pleasure, passion, and procreation.

APOLLO: god of the sun and light, archery, music and dance, truth and prophecy, poetry, healing and diseases.

ARES: (air-eez) god of war or, more properly, the spirit of battle.

ADONIS: god of beauty and desire.

THANATOS: (than-uh-tos) god of death. Collector of souls.

CHARON: (cha-ruhn) conductor of souls; guide to the dead.

HEDONE: (hey-doh-nee) goddess of pleasure, enjoyment, and delight.

EREBUS: (eh-ruh-buhs) God, and the personification of darkness.

DEMETER: (duh-mee-tuh) Goddess of the harvest. Persephone's mother.

A TWISTED FATE

Cry, oh god of death,
For your one true love.
A soul reborn from a single flame.
A flower needs sunlight,
Like a shadow needs light.
Memories that weep—anguish runs deep.
Her loss reduces flames
To embers that no longer burn bright.
The tragic loss of abandoned brokenness.
The gods shall reap havoc.
Then, mankind will suffer.
All for the sins of witchery.
Witchcraft will be banished, and a war will rage.
The gods will again rule the mortal plane.

THE UNDERWORLD

A CRUEL CURSE

THE UNDERWORLD.

We are all slaves to fate, even the gods.

Hades, the god of the Underworld, never believed in destiny until it led him to Perse- phone—his soulmate—and his dreams became reality.

Hades and his best friend Hecate, the goddess of witchcraft, had been called upon to judge a Dunamis mage —the most powerful of magical beings.

That day, once again, destiny was afoot, and sometimes fate tests our strength and determination...

'YOU ARE HERE TO BE JUDGED.' Hades' icy voice slithered like venom through the mage's bloodstream, yet she did not flinch. A small smile twisted on her lips as she regarded the god of the Underworld.

'Hecate will not allow you harm me.' The woman's eyes shifted towards her goddess.

'Hecate has no choice. I am the god of the Underworld, and I see into your dark soul, old crone. I see your crimes and malevolence. You will be vanquished... by Hecate.'

The mage's eyes widened, and, for the first time in a long while, she felt fear. They'd ensnared her in a bubble of pure magic—Hecate's magic—from which she could not escape even if she tried. But her words could maim—she was a more powerful being than they realised. The mage laughed softly, then pointed at Hades.

'The pain of losing her
Will consume and maim.
Your dark heart will perish before
You find her again.
The thing of beauty will be such a sweet foe.
She did not feel.
She will not know.'

A crack of lightning blinded the room, and the mage's laughter echoed off the walls.

Hades felt a tug in his chest, and suddenly, it seemed hollow—a void of darkness. The dark sensation morphed into agony, yet he gritted his teeth and endured the onslaught.

'What the...' He turned to Hecate, whose eyes glowed white, her mouth twisting into a snarl. With a flick of her wrist, the crone fragmented like smoke in the wind, and particles of her were sucked towards the small golden box in Hecate's hand. Hecate snapped the lid shut.

'She is dangerous—immensely dangerous, Hades. This box must never be opened. We need to bury it in Tartarus.' Hecate's eyes widened as she whipped her head around to meet Hades' gaze, mentally recounting the nonsensical, cryptic words of the curse. 'Persephone... we need to check on her.'

'My wife,' Hades muttered. 'I shall return soon.' Shadows enveloped Hades, and with a loud pop, he vanished. Hades materialised in Zeus's kingdom to discover a party in full swing—typical of Zeus. Persephone loathed these gatherings.

Zeus swaggered towards his brother wearing his trademark conceited smirk. 'Hades, to what do we owe the pleasure? I can't recall the last time you graced us with your presence.'

Hades ground his back teeth.

Zeus... King of the gods.

King of deceit.

King of vengeance.

King of infidelity.

The manipulative king who had underhandedly bound Hades to the underworld aeons ago after Titanomachy, the ten-year war between the Olympian gods and the Titans. The only place Hades was permitted to visit was Zeus's kingdom of Naxos, which was filled with sycophants. No. Thank. You.

Hades' hatred for his brother was as consuming as wildfire, but now was not the time for bickering; he needed to find Persephone. Before her, Hades merely existed. Since Persephone, he had discovered what it meant to truly live.

At Hades' silence, tense jaw, and darting eyes, Zeus's face paled as he tilted his head. 'Brother?'

'I need to know that Persephone is safe,' Hades hissed through clenched teeth. He felt panicked; that warm glow in his chest—their soul bond—was missing. The notion of his love being no more tasted bitter on his tongue. Daggers of pain and turmoil tore at his heart.

'Of course she is.' Demeter, Persephone's mother, strode towards the man she loathed. 'She is with the gods of Olympus, where she belongs.' With a haughty smile, she raised her brow; oblivious to the mage's curse, she was typically contemptuous towards him. 'I still have three months with her, Hades,' Demeter spat.

Persephone, stifled by her mother, still loved her and had agreed to spend half of the year with each of them following Demeter's meltdown over her bonding with Hades.

'So, where is she?' Hades ground out.

They scoured and turned Zeus' kingdom in Olympus inside and out, but Persephone had disappeared—vanished—along with their bond. Hades knew he had lost her.

'What have you done?' Demeter screamed at Hades, who looked at her from between his hands. His movements were listless, and he sank to the ground, his heart in shreds.

'I judged a mage. She cursed me,' he uttered as he closed his eyes.

'Tell me everything, Brother.' Zeus placed a hand on Hades' shoulder.

Hades explained how he had judged the malevolent old crone and the curse she had placed upon him: the curse to lose his one true love... Persephone.

'Magic is a threat to us all,' Zeus bellowed as multiple forks of lightning shot through the sky. 'I decree that we, once again, take control of the mortal realm. We shall go to war! Any being with witchcraft will be destroyed,' the god of the sky yelled as Demeter sat beside Hades, both a shell of their former godly selves.

'It's all your fault,' Demeter growled through her sobs.

'I know,' he whispered, holding his bowed head.

CHAPTER
ONE

TWENTY-TWO YEARS LATER, LONDON.

PERSEPHONE

There was a Lamia demon at Starbucks.

Of course there was.

I sipped my extra-shot latte and sighed. She was glamoured, looking like a regular businesswoman heading home. Dressed in a black trouser suit, her red hair piled atop her head, she wore sunglasses—a bit out of place in the evening, but a necessity. Their crimson pupils were a bit of a giveaway and tended to freak the hell out of humans. As a witch, I could sense her true essence, and it made my skin crawl.

Double crap on a cracker. So much for a quiet evening.

The demon had eyes on a couple of youngsters—

perhaps around fifteen years old. She was clearly sussing out her next meal. Lamias didn't need to feed often, but when they did, it was grim.

Fucking demons.

After the war, everything changed.

The gods reclaimed control of the mortal world, and the battle between them and humanity was catastrophic. It raged for nearly a year—bloody, ruthless, and always tilted in their favour. Sure, some gods fell. Or maybe a few were conveniently eliminated by their own kind. I wasn't there, and honestly, I didn't care.

What mattered was the aftermath.

The chaos cracked something open, and things that should've stayed locked in the dark slipped through. Demons. Nightmares. Creatures born of shadow and blood. The Underworld had spilled over, and the world never quite healed.

This Lamia was one of them.

But her time was almost up... I was going to make damn sure of it.

Humans stayed blissfully unaware of the monsters lurking in their cities. Most attacks were blamed on deranged people—and to be fair, there were plenty of those too. The rest of the magical community—shifters, fae, and the like—had learned to blend in, carving out hidden enclaves within human society and playing nice under the watchful eye of the Council of Magic.

My brethren, witches and mages, worked tirelessly to rid cities of the problem ghouls, but we had to lie low since the gods had returned to our world. We had to be careful. The gods banished witchcraft, and the Council of Magic, along with witches, mages, and covens, went underground. And the slaughter of my people? It was history repeating itself—just like the old witch trials, only bloodier.

If you possessed magic, it equated to a death sentence. The gods were our enemies. *My* enemy.

The Lamia rose to her feet and followed the youngsters. It was time for me to play the role of bait. I may have been twenty-two, but I looked younger, and *I* was on my own. I maintained my distance as I trailed her past the British Museum and headed towards Russell Square. I walked breezily past the demon and shoulder-bumped her. I heard her hiss.

'Oh, I'm so sorry.' I flashed a broad smile and turned down a dark alleyway. She followed, about thirty paces behind. Bingo.

'Young girl,' she hummed.

I slowed, every muscle tensing. Suddenly, she was only feet away from me. I could feel her breath lifting my hair— it reeked of rotting flesh. My heart jackhammered against my ribs as I reached down, slow and silent, unclipping the thigh sheath beneath my leather duster. Nestled against my leg, my divine blade waited—sleek and deadly. Its double-edged black blade gleamed, set into a hilt of rich golden metal with a smooth grip carved from blue crystal. Ancient runes shimmered along its length, pulsing faintly with magic.

It was priceless. Beautiful. My most treasured possession.

'May I help you?' I turned slowly. My gag reflex triggered and my latte almost reappeared. She had taken her true form, and man, she was fugly. A human torso and, from the waist down, a snake—a big-ass snake. Lamias have sharp, pointed, retractable teeth that extend beyond the human teeth, as well as razor-sharp claws that could inject lethal poison. They were not to be messed with.

'You can,' her voice hissed, a smile revealing her fangs.

'Look, Medusa. I'm *so* not in the mood for this. I just need to get home. So I'm gonna kick your *ass*.' As I slipped out the divine blade, I smiled back at her. The dagger was all I needed; it could harm and kill anything supernatural, including gods, which was why so few blades remained. Most had been destroyed, along with my brethren.

She lurched forward and grasped a handful of my hair, wrenching my head to the side, but instinct propelled me into action. I was like a ninja—quick and agile. I twisted and delivered a spinning kick, which connected with her jaw, snapping her head back. She grunted and jerked backwards, ripping out several strands of hair, and pain flared across my scalp.

'Bitch!' I snarled.

I rushed at her, but her tail snapped into action as my blade arced upward, knocking it from my grasp. It went skittering across the ground.

Mother-tucker.

My eyes popped wide, and she laughed, licking her

lips. 'I can't wait to get you to my lair. You're a feisty one,' her voice slithered.

I eyed my dagger—I wasn't going down without a fight, and there was no cat in hell's chance of me returning to her place. It definitely wouldn't be a wine-and-movie girly night. When people inexplicably vanished into thin air, it was usually due to a demon attack. Demons were integrated into our community, and this one was cunning. Unease spread through me like a choking vine.

I sprang forward and used a teep—a brutal kick to the head—which caused her to howl, her head snapping back with enough force to break a neck. As she lunged at me, I flipped over her and dove for my dagger, but that tail whipped me like a bitch. It lifted me off my feet, and I collided with a wall, cracking my skull. Fiery pain exploded along my nerve endings, black spots darkening my vision.

Shit. Shit. Shitting shit.

I crawled towards my blade as she snaked towards me. I was *so* going to gut this bitch.

'I would *not* do that if I were you.' The voice cut through the air—strange, powerful, and disturbingly familiar. It held the promise of pain.

We both froze.

I looked up and saw him. He stood over twenty feet tall, a towering figure forged from shadows, shifting and crackling with restrained violence. I lunged for my blade, then held it up towards both of them as the Lamia backed away, choking on fear. Whatever he was, he wasn't mortal —and definitely not just another demon. He radiated dominance. Power. He was likely more dangerous than the Lamia.

I was so screwed.

The man of shadows turned to me, and I sucked in air. I glimpsed a flash of eyes—eyes of pure gold—and ice lodged in my throat. I *recognised* those eyes. My mind was hazy... I needed to try to summon my dark magic—but something inside me... froze.

'What mess have you got yourself into?' His voice was a dangerous purr—silken, sharp, and threaded with judgment. He tutted, almost amused. He was power made flesh, and every instinct I had screamed at me to run.

I was scared shitless.

His huge, hulking form took shape in the moonlight, reducing in size but still over six and a half feet, and my heart almost stopped beating. My eyes travelled up, up, and up. He was *big*. He was also mind-bendingly beautiful. As he gazed at me, his eyes turned cerulean blue with a ring of gold encircling the black pupils, and something flickered in those eyes—something akin to melancholy.

I felt dizzy and sick. Those eyes... sparked a memory—a memory that was like mist slipping through my fingers. I stared at him like a total creeper, unable to tear my eyes away.

He possessed a vicious beauty—a sculptured, breathtaking face, hair as black as night tied at the nape of his neck, and a covering of short, dark stubble lined his chiselled jaw. The black shirt stretched across his muscled chest, and his long, ripped legs stood slightly apart. I'd seen nothing as beautiful yet equally chilling.

A strange tugging in my chest, as if a part of me was drawn to him, sent goosebumps racing over my skin. A ball of dread in my stomach inched up my throat, threatening to suffocate me.

The pounding of my heart rang in my ears. *Maybe you're having a cardiac event?* my befuddled brain said to me.

'Are you alright?' The demon's eyes narrowed, studying me with unnerving intensity. His voice struck something inside me—strangely familiar, like a memory brushing just out of reach.

'Mhm,' I squeaked.

'And you'—he turned back to the Lamia—'have displeased me... greatly.'

'Your Highness.' The Lamia trembled, her jaw slack.

I attempted to summon my magic, the magic I wedged deep within me; I felt it bubbling, and his head whipped around as he squinted at me. 'Don't.' The magic inside me fizzled out—I was *so* gonna die.

The stranger raised his arm, and a tattoo lifted from his skin, floating through the air and dropping to the ground. It transformed into a mass—a gigantic mass—of a dog with three heads. My brain seemed to have slowed down completely. It wouldn't process what was happening.

'Oh my God,' I croaked.

'*Gods.*' A sardonic smile twisted his lips, sending a shudder through me.

The dog's heads were almost as tall as I was, and it was brutal. Its fur was the colour of obsidian, and when six blood-red eyes turned my way... I whimpered softly. My heart hammered in my ears, making my head swim with fright, but the three heads cocked to the side as they studied me, and as those crimson eyes left me and swung back to study the Lamia, I swallowed thickly. The Lamia let out a small screech, quivered, and raised her arms in surrender.

Holy fucktarts.

I took that as my cue to leave. I struggled to my feet and ran.

'Wait!' yelled the beautiful demon, but adrenaline danced through my veins, propelling me faster, leaving his curses bouncing off the alley walls.

MY DREAM that night was the recurring dream I'd had over the past year. It was always the same place—one I didn't recognise... I found myself back in the ethereal garden. The emotions I felt here were alien but good. I didn't know the garden, but I sensed a connection to it on some weird level.

The garden was a wide-open space brimming with blooms of countless colours, with black marble walkways scattered symmetrically amid the perfect flowerbeds. A copse of cypress trees encircled the garden; their fresh, woody fragrance filled the breeze. The vibrant, cheerful colours of an enormous patch of narcissus always made me smile.

As I wandered around, I trailed my fingers over the

flowers, and nature's electricity tingled through my finger-tips. Lipstick-pink peonies adorned the fringes of the garden, while honeysuckle festooned the trellises, a swarm of butterflies flitting around them, swirling in an array of exquisite colours.

Climbing roses, with clusters of abundant silken petals and green stems copiously armed with sharp thorns, infused my nose with their misty sweetness. Their paradox —the softness and beauty of the flowers, paired with the pain of the thorns—made them one of my favourite blooms.

The aroma of petrichor permeated the air—a potpourri of scents creating a sensory explosion. The full glory of the garden's colours and fragrances made my soul sing with pleasure. As the lullaby of the breeze whispered in my ears, I sighed happily, and moved to the next flowerbed, inhaling deeply.

The tinkling sound of water was pure therapy. In the centre of the beautiful garden, on a grassy expanse, sat a pond teeming with lily pads and water lilies. In the middle of the enormous circular pond rose a lovely fountain with water cascading around a large pedestal—sculpted in the shape of two giant, intricately carved serpents, their bodies entwined in a sort of slow dance.

'Hello again, Persephone,' the deep, lyrical voice I was waiting for said to me as I spun around. I imagined from his tone that he'd be like one of the swoon-worthy men from my novels.

'Why won't you reveal yourself?' I asked as I sat and lazily dipped my fingers into the water.

'We shall meet soon, my queen.'

I laughed. He always called me 'my queen'. 'That sounds nice,' I murmured. 'If you're half as sexy as your voice, I can't wait.' *Lord, have mercy; I love this dream.*

'See you soon, sweetness,' he breathed in my ear, and my heart skipped a beat.

I BLINKED awake as the world snapped into focus. My fists clenched the downy comforter, knuckles white, while the memories of last night slammed into me like a wrecking ball. The fear. The adrenaline. The utter chaos. It simmered beneath the surface now, momentarily dulled —but those eyes...

Those eyes still haunted me. And they freaked me the hell out.

My housemate Tee had been home when I'd returned. She almost had a nervous breakdown at the state of me, but as always, she poured me a generous glass of wine, magicked a red velvet cake from somewhere, and calmed me down. Obviously, I couldn't tell her the entire truth... battling a demon? Nope. So, I concocted a cock-and-bull story about some guy with weird blue and gold eyes scaring me. She gave me a perplexed look but didn't press further.

My gaze landed on my laptop and a stack of books on my desk. My forthcoming days off would be filled with reading and book blogging. Aside from nature, books were my next level of therapy—an escape into another world—and, let's face it, men are so much better in books. The tall, dark, devastatingly handsome, you-are-the-object-of-all-my-desires man of your dreams only ever happens in romance novels. Who needs spice in real life?

Releasing a long breath, I slid from my bed and made my way to the ensuite, deciding a long soak in the bath would soothe my aching muscles. I'd inherited my home from my only family member... my gran. She was as mad as a box of frogs, but *the* best person. Plus, a powerful witch and former leader of the Council of Magic.

We eventually moved to London from New York when I was fourteen, after... I tried never to think of the reason for our move. That incident was buried deep in my subconscious, along with the dark magic I couldn't control. Gran had passed away when I was seventeen, and I still missed her like crazy.

The house is lovely—a four-bedroom Victorian terraced dwelling on Milner Square in Islington. The issue was that I couldn't afford to maintain it alone—enter Tee and Matt, my housemates.

I'd known Tee for about a year. She and I had bonded —largely over wine and food—and we had become best friends. Making friends in London was almost impossible for someone like me—a demon hunter and a witch. And Matt, well, he was so laid-back he was practically horizontal. He was kind of an ex, but someone I still cared for deeply.

In my humble opinion, when the kiss doesn't burn you to the core, there's no point in going the whole way;

there had always been *something* missing... because no kiss had ever come close. I refused to succumb until it was right. Old-fashioned, I guess.

Or perhaps I was just frigid? I tried not to dwell on that one.

Walking into the kitchen, I spotted Matt slurping coffee, sitting with his latest squeeze, Elissa. She was friendly, albeit dippy.

'Morning, Sephy.' Matt gave me one of his trademark smiles, dimples and all. He was a good-looking guy, just not my guy.

'Morning. Where's Tee?'

'Dunno?' Matt shrugged. 'I've made coffee.' He pointed to the pot.

I lowered my brows as I poured my coffee. Tee worked as a PA for some influential person; she was always evasive about her job, but her hours were pretty sketchy for such a well-paid position.

'No work today?' I turned to Matt, grasping my coffee as if it were the answer to life. I took a sip and sighed contentedly. Matt came from a wealthy family, and his jobs typically revolved around bar work. He'd recently been hired at some nightclub.

'I'm on tonight, yeah,' he answered as his gaze met Elissa's.

'Where are you working now, then?' I asked, taking a seat.

Matt hesitated before speaking, and I pinned him with a glare. What was his problem?

'Well,' he muttered, 'I've been working at The Underworld for the last few weeks.' His eyes met mine, and his cheeks bloomed pink.

I almost choked as I spat out my coffee and yelled, 'What the fuck?'

'Sephy, we all know you hate the gods, but I couldn't pass it up. It's great pay and a cracking place to work.'

'The gods are dicks! They killed thousands of humans.' *And witches*, I added mentally. They had banned witchcraft, murdered countless of my brethren, forced us to hide away like a filthy little secret, and still left us vulnerable to death should we be discovered.

'Sephy, it's in the past. They rule now, and there's fuck-all we can do about it.' Matt raised his voice, then sighed. 'Look, I've got VIP tickets for tonight. Come and see me at work. Let your hair down for once.'

'Not a chance. I'm not lining the god of the Underworld's pockets with my hard-earned cash. I hate them. Hate them all!' I shrieked as I jumped up. I grabbed my helmet and bag, and as I stormed out, I gave the door a dramatic slam. Anger burned deep in my gut, but I wouldn't allow its darkness to consume me like before. I hopped onto my Kawasaki Ninja 300 and started her up. The vibrations of her throaty growl reverberated through me, easing my temper. I blew out a long breath, then pressed down on the throttle.

I loved plants, and they loved me right back, so in addition to demon hunting—which paid very well—I also worked at Boma Garden Centre a couple of half days a week. It felt like heaven on earth—a little oasis of petals and foliage, which, right at that moment, was exactly what I needed. Ten minutes later, I was at work.

'Hi, Sephy,' Colette called as I walked in.

'Hey.' I attempted to smile, but it didn't quite happen. 'What's up?'

I shrugged. 'Nothing. Don't worry.'

Colette puckered her brow. 'Okay, well, Kim wants you in the nurseries again.'

'No problem.' I stashed my bag in my locker, then made my way to the perspex tunnels, feeling the cool breeze on my face, laden with the scent of primroses, while taking in the vast array of various flowering plants as I passed. This was my favourite time of year—spring. The feel of spring whispered to me on the breeze and lightness filled me; men were jerks, but plants made up for it.

I lost myself in the joy of creating new life and hummed happily as I worked. I had the ability to make plants grow—any plant... Grandma said it was my flora magic. The tiniest burst of magic infused each seedling, invigorating their roots and turning wilted foliage green, ensuring they grew into the most incredible array of blooms. Everyone just assumed I had green fingers.

After spending four hours with my plant babies, I decided to visit Kew Gardens, one of my favourite places— a botanical garden housing the world's largest and most diverse mycological collections. It spans three hundred and thirty glorious acres, and since I only had a couple of hours, I headed for the Waterlily House, a spot brimming with an array of sprawling climbers and tropical plants.

Kew was quiet, and I needed that. I craved the fresh

air, the scent of flowers, the greenery, and the water. I wandered towards the Waterlily House, lost in thought.

Once they had retaken control of our world, many of the gods remained reclusive, however, several of them relished the attention and had become icons—bigger than movie stars.

Stupid humans.

Hades, although still reserved from the public eye, had opened classy nightclubs in all the world's major cities, while Apollo had invested in live music venues. Dionysus's exclusive wine bars sold his own wine, rumoured to contain a touch of nectar.

Aphrodite launched a chain of superstores, obliterating the likes of Ann Summers and Victoria's Secret: lingerie, sexy clothes, sex toys, and the like. Pretty on point for the freaking goddess of love. The asshole, Zeus, had a massive investment company employing Oracles. Again, they were all located in the world's most prominent cities.

The gods had promised a fairer world, and much to my chagrin, they had delivered. If you were a law-abiding citizen, life was good. If not, the punishments were pretty archaic and vicious, but no one could question or argue with them. I guessed the answer to life was to be a good person, not an asswipe. The standard of living was higher, and homelessness had become a thing of the past.

Even thinking about the gods rattled me—I could feel the darkness within, almost pounding against my chest to escape, to destroy. Thanks to Grandma, I'd learned to control that dark magic. I inhaled deeply through my nose to quell my fury and hurried to the little oasis.

Strolling inside, my thoughts evaporated, and the feeling of bitterness and anger settled. I wandered towards the water, inhaling the mingled scents of the blooms, which felt like a meditation, before sitting on the edge of the circular pond.

The water, dyed black with harmless food dye, shimmered as the glasshouse ceiling reflected off the surface, and colourful fish zipped through the darkness. The giant Victoria Boliviana water lilies were breathtaking creations, yet the flowers only bloomed for forty-eight hours. I trailed my fingers gently through the water.

'Hello, beautiful,' I whispered as I touched one of the Victorias. A ripple of water and leaves saw the plant sprout a tall stem, which emerged from beneath. A large white flower peeled open, igniting an inner warmth within me, illuminating my world. I smiled and inhaled the fragrant scent. 'Clever girl.'

'Cool ability, Sephy.' A man's voice caused me to jump up and spin around.

A blond-haired, tall, muscular guy stood six feet away from me—he had the kind of face that stops you in your tracks... It was a vaguely *familiar* face. His dark blond hair was knotted atop his head, but his eyes were bizarre—almost violet—though I was sure I saw silver flashing through them. What was going on with insanely gorgeous men and their freaky eyes?

'Who are you?' I ground out, placing my hands on my hips.

'You wouldn't believe me if I told you.' His smile transformed his face from stunning to jaw-dropping.

'How do you know my name?' I snapped, striving not to lose myself in those bewitching eyes. I *so* didn't need this. I wanted peace and plants, not stupid hot men.

'I know a great deal about you.'

Well, that wasn't weird. 'Are you stalking me?'

He laughed—a deep, rumbling, sexy sound—and I gritted my teeth as I glared at him.

'Stay away from me,' I hissed as I turned and ran. For the second time in two days, I fled from a super-sexy man.

The story of my life.

I RETURNED HOME SHAKEN and edgy.

'Sephy.' Tee's husky voice drew my gaze to the doorway leading to the kitchen. Tee is a beauty—her skin the colour of burnished copper, with her long, black hair styled in intricate braids adorned with silver beads. Her eyes are like pools of darkness—their depths seem never-ending.

'Are you okay, girlfriend? You look like you've seen a ghost. I'll pour you a wine.' Tee's answer to everything is wine or red velvet cake, and often both. I followed her into the kitchen and collapsed into a chair. 'What happened?' she asked as she handed me a glass.

'Well, there was another strange guy in Kew Gardens. He recognised me, but I've never seen him before. And his eyes...'

'What about his eyes?'

'They were almost violet and seemed to have silver flashes in them. Like, you know... lightning.' I felt my cheeks heat—Tee probably thought I was doolally-batshit crazy. When my gaze met hers, I was almost certain she blanched. 'Should I be worried? Do you think he's stalking me?'

Tee recovered immediately. 'Girlfriend, it's London. London is full of weirdos.' Before I could say anything else, she put me on the spot. 'Matt told me about your hissy-fit.'

I cringed and took a long gulp of wine. 'I lost my shit. I need to apologise.'

'Well, I promised him we'd use those VIP tickets and go tonight. What better way to apologise?'

'What? No! What if Hades is there? You freaking know I hate the gods.'

'Sephy.' Tee blew out a breath. 'What are the odds of Hades being at the club? Next to none. I *know* you loathe the gods, but you gotta let go of the past. Don't let it eat you up. You need to live... Start having some fun. Come out with me, Sephy. Please.' There was a flicker of exasperation in her voice. I attempted to speak, but the words caught in my throat. 'Come on, take your wine and have a nice relaxing bath, then I'll come in and help you get ready.'

'I've got nothing to wear.' I tried hard to object, but perhaps a night out would do me good. I wasn't back on demon-hunting duties for a week—week on, week off.

'I've got something you can wear.'

'Tee! You're nearly six feet tall, and I'm five-foot-four. Really?'

'Yep.' She grinned. 'I bought you a dress today with matching accessories.'

'What?'

'No excuses, Sephy.' She stood and picked up her wine. 'Come on.' Defeated, I gave her a pathetic smile, grabbed my glass, and followed her upstairs.

HADES

'What in Olympus, Hades?' Hecate glowered at me.

'Remember with whom you speak, Goddess.' My icy tone almost slithered.

'I believe we've been friends for too long to be calling those shots, *Your Highness*.' Hecate's voice brimmed with fury.

My shoulders dropped as I let out a resigned sigh. 'I miss her, Hecate.'

Her expression softened. 'I know, Hades. But revealing yourself to her like that? And in your true form, for gods' sake? You scared the living crap outta her.'

'The Lamia would have killed her.'

'Hades, she's a powerful goddess. She still has no idea just how powerful she truly is. I've witnessed her defeat

26

foes far greater than the Lamia. Stop fretting so much. I'm guarding her, as you requested.'

'It's been an age since Morpheus found her. I need her back, Hecate. She belongs to me.'

When that warm, velvety sensation reappeared in my chest, I knew the soul bond had reignited. I knew Persephone was alive. My hope was like a tiny bird singing even amidst the darkest storms. My only aim had been to find her again.

'Her ex-boyfriend... who lives with her'—I released a low rumble, but Hecate paid me no mind and continued —'works at your club. I've arranged for him to have VIP tickets. We're going tonight.'

'And Persephone?' I felt my eyes flicker between gold and blue as she nodded. 'Then tonight, you shall bring her here.'

'Are you sure?'

'Yes.'

'She's not the Persephone you knew. She thinks she's a witch... that she's your enemy, Hades,' Hecate said softly.

'She *is* different.' I paused, gritting my teeth. 'But she's still in there somewhere, Hecate. She will remember me. Eventually,' I said hoarsely, my gaze falling to the floor.

'She has a divine blade.'

'I know.' I released a jagged breath.

'She could kill you.'

I gave a lopsided shrug. 'I'm very difficult to kill, even with a divine blade. Anyway, I'm not sure my immortal life is worth living if I don't get her back.'

Hecate blew out a frustrated sigh. 'I've gotta go. I'm doing Persephone's hair and makeup.'

I lifted my gaze to Hecate, then closed my eyes, clenching my fists.

'Oh, and there's a slight problem you should be aware of.'

My eyes snapped open. 'What?'

'Zeus knows about her.'

My shadows exploded, whipping around me. 'Fuck!'

THREE

PERSEPHONE

As I stared at my reflection, I scarcely recognised myself.

My pale-blonde hair was styled in a half-updo, with a few stray curls brushing my bare shoulder and the rest flowing down my back. My bright green eyes popped beneath dark kohl that rimmed them, and my full lips were stained a deep, sultry red. Tee had sculpted my cheekbones with blush and highlighter.

'I look...' I whispered, voice trailing off.

'Beautiful?' Tee's laughter was warm, her eyes sparkling with mischief. 'Sephy, you've always been a natural beauty. You just didn't know it.'

I stood in front of the full-length mirror, taking myself in. The dress was a daring little red number—short, halter-necked, and tied at my throat. It left my back bare all the way to my waist, and paired with strappy matching heels and a clutch, the look was complete. I felt... beautiful. Unfamiliar, unnerving—but I decided to ride the high of it anyway.

My gaze flicked to the leather trousers and duster hanging from the wardrobe door, then back to my reflection.

'I can do this,' I breathed. 'You've outdone yourself, Tee.' I turned to her with a grin, smoothing my hands over the dress.

'It's easy with your looks, Sephy. You don't even realise how captivating you are.'

Heat crept up my neck at her words, but I didn't reply. Instead, I pulled her into a tight hug, hoping she couldn't hear how fast my heart was beating.

Tee, as always, looked like a freaking supermodel. A sleek, black leather catsuit hugged her tall, lithe frame, revealing her ample cleavage and accentuating her long, shapely legs, and her braided hair was swept into a high ponytail atop her head.

I snatched up my red clutch and made for the bathroom. 'I'll see you downstairs,' I called. Alone, I strapped my divine blade to the top of my thigh. The skirt wasn't too tight—after a few experimental bends and twirls in the mirror, I figured it would behave.

'Don't forget phones aren't allowed.' Tee handed me a glass of Malbec as I crossed into the kitchen. I nodded and took a sip.

Hades was notoriously private; he insisted on a media

lockdown whenever he attended an event, which, according to rumours, wasn't very often. Reporters were tolerated; photographers were not. But, like Tee said, the chances of him being there tonight felt slim. That was the hope, anyway.

Apparently, some of the other gods, particularly Zeus, had no such issue with notoriety. They could flaunt their power, immortality, and obscene wealth to their heart's content; I was neither interested nor impressed. I didn't even know what the asshole gods looked like. But if one of them stepped out of line, I'd happily use my blade to make an example of them.

'The limo's picking us up in ten minutes,' Tee said, pouring herself another glass of wine.

'Limo?' I squinted at her.

'Perks of having a wealthy boss.' She winked at me, grinning. 'We're gonna have a night you'll never forget.' We clinked glasses, and I hoped she was right. I was beginning to get hyped about letting loose and having a dance.

Maybe I would have a night to remember?

THE LIMO PULLED up at *The Underworld*. Because of course that's what Hades' club was called. Subtlety clearly wasn't part of his brand strategy.

The Underworld was a glass pyramidal tower, taller than any other building in London. Of course, the glass was black. In comparison to the bright buildings surrounding it, it appeared quite ominous.

'It's a fabulous sight, isn't it?' Tee said as she noticed me peeking up at it.

'Hmm, I'm not sure that's the word I'd use. I'd say more foreboding.' Tee rolled her eyes at me. As I stepped from the limo and looked up at the menacing structure, I had a weird feeling: my stomach knotted with apprehension and I hesitated.

'Come on, Sephy. You look like you're about to bolt, and that ain't happening,' Tee said as she linked her arm through mine. I took a breath as she practically dragged me towards the steps leading to the doors marked VIPs. The queues for the non-VIP entrance extended around the block.

'It's members-only and invitation-only. They'll allow a few in, but most won't stand a chance.' Tee nodded at the queue. 'But it's the hottest spot in town, and everybody wants a piece.'

Shaking my head, I climbed the wide stairs with Tee and came to an abrupt halt when I spotted the doorman.

'A Cyclops?' I whispered.

'I guess no one messes with them?' Amusement coloured her tone.

The Cyclops was massive—easily over ten feet tall and built like a war god. Dressed head-to-toe in black, his long red hair was tied back in a surprisingly neat ponytail. I had to crane my neck just to see his eye—*singular*.

And gods, that eye.

Facial symmetry? Nonexistent. Intimidation factor?

Off the charts. Was there anything more unsettling than a bodybuilder-sized bouncer with one enormous, unblinking eye? Doubtful.

As Tee gave our names, he nodded with stiff efficiency and murmured into a mic clipped to his lapel. A beat later, the double doors to The Underworld Nightclub creaked open. I stepped through, and he handed me back my clutch, but not before that freaky eye landed on my face—and *widened*.

Then he bowed. Deep. Regal. Reverent.

Tee let out an annoyed huff and shot him a glare. The Cyclops quickly dropped his gaze to the floor like a chastened puppy.

'What was that?' I whispered to Tee as I strolled over to her.

She raised a perfect brow. 'It's probably Cyclops speak for "I'd like to get into your panties".'

'Ugh. You're grim.'

She answered me with a throaty laugh and walked away. I followed her towards another set of doors—she seemed to be au fait with the place—but anxiety still clawed at my stomach. I pushed the feeling aside and blew out a long, slow breath, which hitched when we passed through the next set of doors.

We stood on a balcony overlooking a vast dance floor filled with swirling and undulating bodies. The venue was packed. The club exuded luxury—pure elegance, decked out in gold and purple, the vast expanse broken up by towering cypress trees. The cypress trees, much like the club itself, were pyramidal, their acorn-like seed cones shimmering in the strobe lights above. Black chandeliers and wall sconces—rich in detail—lined the ceiling and interior, twinkling with precious jewels, and pinprick lights threaded between them like stars stitched into the dome.

Cleverly arranged and uniquely designed furniture tastefully outfitted the club, while a rainbow of lights and bouncing tunes revved my soul.

'This place is unreal,' I breathed, taking it all in. Tee laughed squeezing my hand as we descended the sweeping staircase. The mingled scents of sweat, alcohol, perfume, and cypress hit me in a heady rush.

We wove our way toward the bar—an immense, glowing centerpiece. Rows of bottles gleamed under the flashing lights, their muted hues refracting like gemstones, while patrons held sophisticated beverages and garnishes in stylish glassware. The eclectic mix of voices and music hummed in my mind.

'Two lime daiquiris, please, Matt,' Tee called out.

Matt's head snapped around, and a grin split his handsome face. 'Sephy! Tee! Two daiquiris coming up.' He went to work as my gaze took in the surroundings.

'Ladies, allow me.'

The confident, velvety baritone made us both turn. The smile Tee was rocking faded like an old memory, and goosebumps raced over my skin as I stared into the freaky violet and silver eyes of the stunning stranger from Kew Gardens.

'You,' I whispered.

'Hey, Sephy.' He flashed me a wicked smile. '*Tee*, is it?' He turned to my friend, who narrowed her eyes at him.

'You know him?' I asked, incredulous.

'Unfortunately.' Tee jutted her chin, her glare sharp enough to cut, while the stranger's smile widened.

'Follow me,' he said smoothly, plucking our drinks from our hands before striding toward one of the VIP sections. Tee made a low growling sound and tugged on my arm as we trailed behind him.

'Who the fuck is he?' I whisper-snarled, and Tee blew out a frustrated breath in response.

'Everyone, this is Sephy and Tee.' He chuckled lightly on her name, almost mockingly, before gesturing at the circle of people waiting. A few lifted their glasses in lazy greetings.

'Pleased to meet you.' The beautiful blonde smiled warmly as I slid into the seat beside Tee and picked up my drink. 'I'm Sybil.'

'Hi.' Tee's gaze lingered on her. 'So, I guess you're an Oracle?'

Sybil's cheeks bloomed a soft pink as she nodded. 'I work for Zeus's company, yes.' Her eyes darted briefly toward the stunning stranger.

Of course she did. Oracles offered counsel and prophecy; who better to prop up Zeus's empire of wealth and power?

At the mention of Zeus, my fingers tightened on my glass. Maybe coming here hadn't been the brightest idea. My gaze caught on the narcissus arranged in a vase before us, and I bent closer, brushing the bloom with my fingertips. Its fragrance —an opulent sensation reminiscent of lush green leaves with traces of hyacinth and jasmine—soothed my nerves and anger.

Around us, conversations rose and fell, laughter mingling with the pulse of the music. I downed another three drinks, humming absently along, until movement drew my gaze back to the beautiful stranger.

'So, Sephy, would you care to dance?' the gorgeous weirdo asked.

'No.' I beamed at him sweetly. His eyes flashed again with that enthralling silver hue. 'I don't even know your name, but you seem to know me. How is that possible?' I squinted at him.

'I've heard of you,' he said, a secretive smile playing on his lips. As his gaze flicked to Tee, her lips thinned, and she glared at him. He turned back to me. 'You can call me Zee.' As he spoke, the chatter around us stuttered into silence, every eye in the VIP group ping-ponging between us.

'So—' he extended a hand, smooth as sin, 'do you want to dance or not?'

'Still a no. Come on, Tee, let's get another drink.' I stood, tipped back the rest of my daiquiri in one gulp, and set down the glass. 'Nice to meet you, Zee.'

I turned—then pivoted back, smiling brightly. 'Oh, and a word of advice? Next time you approach a strange woman, dial down the stalker vibes. It's not a good look.'

He clenched his jaw and eyeballed me as his guests gasped.

'Laters!' I spun on my heel and strode for the bar without bothering to see if Tee followed. Catching Matt's eye, I lifted a finger for another drink. Two minutes later, it was in my hand.

'You alright, Sephy?' Matt lowered his brow.

'Yeah,' I replied, downing another lime daiquiri. 'I'm freaking fabulous.' A moment later, the rum slammed into my brain with the force of a freight train, leaving me feeling buzzed. I needed to dance.

'Hey, Matt!' I screeched. 'Look after my bag.' I tossed it at him, and he caught it effortlessly. I pushed my way to the dance floor, my synapses bouncing to the music.

Dancing was freedom, and I craved that freedom. The music felt like a drug—an energising drug that made my mind hum with pure joy, and as I moved to the beat, I felt as though my soul would shine so brightly my skin would glow. Scents swirled around me, blending together like mist in the air, and I was completely lost.

I didn't know how long I'd been dancing—long enough for my muscles to ache—when a pair of strong arms wrapped around me from behind. Instincts flared, my hand flying toward my blade, but a larger hand caught mine, dragging my arms across my body, just beneath my breasts.

He held me tight, tugging me flush against him, my ass pressed firmly against the hard line of his body. It was undoubtedly a 'him'—I felt him pressing hard against my back. He wanted me... no freaking question.

I hesitated, my battle instincts screaming... but then the pulse of rum and music drowned them out. I surrendered to a feeling of desire so strong my knees nearly buckled.

'Go with it, Sephy,' I whispered to myself, leaning back into his solid chest and breathing in that heady, earthy scent. Whoever this man was, he felt good. Sinfully good.

'Sephy!' Tee's hand clamped around mine, jolting me. I stumbled and spun to face her—she was right behind me on the dance floor.

My mysterious man was gone.

Had I imagined him? Maybe. The buzzing haze in my head made it all too easy to conjure one of the tall, dark, dangerous heroes from my books. Honestly, that was fine. They were more dependable than real men, anyway.

'Tee!' I giggled like a dork. 'We need more drinks!'

'Sephy, come on.' Tee's tone was tight, but I was far too buzzed to care. By the time I staggered to the bar, I was properly hammered. She pressed a pink drink into my hand.

'Oh. Pretty!' I slurred, grinning at the glass. Tee shut her eyes briefly, her expression pinched. 'What's wrong, Tee?'

'Drink up, Sephy. I love you. I really do.'

'I love you more!' I laughed, wobbling as she steadied me. I lifted my glass in a sloppy salute. 'Cin-cin!' Then I tipped the whole thing back, gulping it down.

'And Sephy... I'm sorry.'

'What for?' I frowned as my eyes met hers.

Then everything went black.

I AWOKE GROANING and feeling groggy, a hand clutching my head. 'Ugh. I'm never drinking again,' I muttered. My poor head was pounding. I peeled my eyes open and sat up in one swift motion.

What the hell?' Purple and gold paint adorned the room, but there were no windows.

The ceiling shimmered with the brilliance of a cloudless sky, glowing as though it had been enchanted to mimic the sun. I blinked several times, disoriented, before slipping out of bed. A glance down made my stomach twist—I was dressed in white silk shorts and a matching cami. Not mine.

The room around me dripped luxury: a golden satin quilt sprawled across a bed big enough for a small army, while a velvet sofa in regal purple was plush and soft beneath my hand as I trailed it across the cushions.

I tested the doors. One was locked. Another opened to a lavish ensuite with a rainfall shower, a soaking tub, and toiletries laid out neatly in a wicker basket. A gilded mirror loomed above the vanity. I caught my reflection—hair mussed, eyes wild—and smoothed myself down. Still a hot mess.

The last door revealed a walk-in wardrobe overflowing with clothes: leather fighting gear, sharp trouser suits, glittering ballgowns. My pulse kicked. *What the actual hell?*

Feeling queasy, I sank onto the velvet sofa and pinched my arm hard. 'Ouch.'

Not dreaming. Definitely awake.

A door clicked open and Tee stepped inside, leather

pants hugging her long legs, a sleeveless top clinging to her frame. 'Sephy.' She gave me a sheepish smile.

'Where am I, Tee?'

'You're in the Underworld.'

'The nightclub?'

She hesitated for a heartbeat. 'No. The real Underworld.'

I sucked in a sharp breath. 'You're kidding, right?' I glanced at my feet, briefly wondering if that crack on my head during the Lamia fight had rendered me unconscious and this was all some elaborate coma dream. I reached out to touch her, and she took my hand.

Tee shook her head, nervously licking her lips. 'I'm not joking, babe.'

I snatched my hand back. 'What the fuck, Tee? Why am I in the Underworld?' My voice pitched higher.

'You don't remember... *anything*?'

'Remember what?' I threw my hands up and squinted at her.

'Shit,' Tee muttered, her hands curling into fists. 'Then you really do need to talk to Hades, Sephy.'

At his name, my belly cramped, and my mouth went dry. 'Hades?' I squeaked.

'He won't hurt you, Sephy,' Tee said, raising her hands like she were trying to soothe a wild animal.

'He's a god. And I'm a...' I stopped myself before I said 'witch'.

'He's a good guy, Sephy. A fair god.'

'The gods, fair?' I barked out a laugh, my fear turning

into anger. 'Selfish, overindulgent pricks would be closer to the truth.'

'Sephy.' Tee sighed and shook her head.

'Don't Sephy me! You're supposed to be my friend. Was it all lies?' My voice cracked as tears pricked my eyes.

Her eyes sparkled, lips trembling. 'Never think that. I've always been your friend. Even before.'

'What do you mean "before"?'

'Once again, a story I'm not at liberty to share.'

'God!' I shrieked.

'*Gods*. Remember?' She placed her hands on her hips.

'Tell me why I'm here,' I spat. 'What's Hades' problem with me?' My heart was racing.

Tee blew out a frustrated breath. 'Okay. His problem is you, Sephy.'

'Huh?'

'You are his Persephone. And he wants you back.'

Hysteria bubbled up, spilling into manic laughter that bordered on unhinged. I bent over, hands braced on my knees, then straightened, swiping at my tear-streaked cheeks. Tee glared at me and my laughter died abruptly.

'You're not serious?' I whispered.

'Yes. You're a goddess. You were married to Hades and... he wants you back.' Tee exhaled hard. 'I know you think this is ludicrous, but trust me, it's the truth.'

I dropped back onto the couch, my mind spinning, fatigue pulling at my brain and body. 'I was married to Hades. How? I'm twenty-two years old, and I've never been married.' I dragged in a shaky breath, but panic stopped my lungs from inflating. 'My brain is in turmoil, Tee. Please take me home.'

'I can't, I'm sorry.' A worried look crossed her beautiful face, and then she let out an enormous sigh, closing her eyes. 'You've eaten three pomegranate seeds from the Underworld orchard. You're tied to Hades for three months, or until he lets you go.'

'The drink you gave me?' Tee nodded and wrung her hands together. I jumped up and paced the bedroom. 'You bitch! A friend wouldn't do that.' I was going to murder her. I was going to be arrested for best-friend-icide.

Tee let out a resigned sigh and collapsed onto the sofa. 'I am your friend, Sephy. But I also answer to Hades. He's my friend too.'

'Hades is your friend. Seriously?' She gave a resigned nod. How could *my* best friend be associated with the god of the Underworld? 'You did trick me. You pretended to be my friend... for him?'

'No. I am your friend. That part is true, babe. Honestly.'

'Don't call me babe,' I snapped, and she flinched. 'Tell me why the fuck anyone would think I'm *the* Persephone? It's absolutely ridiculous.'

'I can't explain that to you. It's Hades' story to tell.'

A flash of anger bubbled through my exhaustion as I paced the room. I spun on my heel and jabbed a finger at Tee, my voice climbing higher and sharper. 'I've been kidnapped—ripped from my life! Told I'm the goddess Persephone, married to the god of the dead? And now I'm stuck with him for three months?'

At my words, Tee flinched again. 'What happened to Persephone, Tee? Tell me!' My breath hitched, and I sniffed. 'If she's gone, why isn't the world up top aware? I just don't understand.'

A flicker of pity flashed across Tee's face. 'Alright.' Her gaze locked onto mine. 'The gods are clever, Sephy. You've been missing for over twenty years, but the mortal world has no idea. The gods can morph into anyone they wish, and for a time Aphrodite covered for you—smiling for the reporters. But it became too painful for Hades. Eventually, he started appearing alone. And you... you were never one for publicity. Elusive. Distant. People stopped asking questions.' She shook her head, her voice softening. 'The rest... that's for Hades to tell you.'

Anxiety fluttered through me, sharp and frantic, threatening a full-blown panic attack. I couldn't be here for that long—being in a place with no outside space was my idea of actual hell. I need gardens, flowers, greenery, space, and sunlight on my skin. I inhaled deeply and thought of my gran. A twinge of pain surged through me —I missed her so much. But how would she advise me to handle this mind-boggling situation? She'd tell me to be cute. Be clever. And to bow to no one.

Fatigue and uncertainty overtook me. 'This is real, isn't it? I'm in the Underworld.' I slumped next to Tee, who nodded and took my hand. 'Fuck.' *Once he finds out I'm a witch, I'm as good as dead.* I tried for humour. 'I think I might need to develop a drug habit to get through this.'

Tee chuckled softly. 'It's going to be okay. Honestly.'

'Will it?' I whispered.

But I had no choice, did I? Freaking out and rocking in a corner would get me nowhere—I just needed to go along with it. Then get back home to my life, away from Hades and the Underworld. He'd realise I wasn't his Persephone and let me go. Hopefully before discovering what I really was.

Or maybe... just maybe... I *was* in a coma, and, eventually, I'd wake up from this nightmare.

CHAPTER
FOUR

HADES

'Highness.' Thanatos strode into my office. 'Zeus has summoned you. He wishes to see you.'

I emitted a low growl and rose to my feet. 'I will not be gone long, Thanatos.'

'And, boss...' Thanatos hesitated. 'How is Persephone?' His gaze fell to the floor. Persephone had long been a sore subject around me; it had been for over twenty years. But touching her again in my club, if only for a brief few minutes, had elicited a myriad of emotions. I missed her so much. I *needed* her back.

'I don't know, Thanatos. She is with Hecate at present. I have yet to see her. Tell Hecate I've gone to Olympus and to meet me in my office before lunch.' My shadows engulfed me, and I shadow-walked out of the room.

As I appeared, Zeus was in his throne room, seated

upon a silver and white throne sculpted from thunderbolts and clouds. He was dressed in a sharp business suit, while I preferred a more informal look—black jeans and a black shirt rolled up to my elbows.

'Brother!' Zeus stood and sauntered over to me.

'Zeus.' I offered a slight nod.

'How's the lovely Persephone?' Zeus smiled mischievously at me. I entertained the brief fantasy of kicking him in the balls—either that or strangling the ever-loving crap out of him.

'I don't know.' I held his stare, my jaw like granite. 'I haven't seen her yet. She is settling in with Hecate.'

'Ah, Tee.' A razor-sharp smile sliced across Zeus's lips. 'Quite the little trap you set to stake claim to your ex-wife.'

'Wife,' I snapped.

'Well, Brother. That's debatable, is it not? Persephone has no memory of being your wife. She is a new woman. A free woman, capable of making her own decisions this time. And I'm not so sure she will be happy about being kidnapped by you... again.'

My anger simmered beneath my skin, yet outwardly, I remained calm.

'She's still as feisty as she ever was. I can see why you like her so much,' Zeus said, winking at me; my nostrils flared, but I stayed silent.

'The gods have decided'—Zeus paused, a smug expression on his face—'that any interested parties will host a dinner, a ball, or some other event for our new guest.'

I stepped towards my brother until we were toe to toe. 'What do you mean...? Interested parties?'

'Well, some of us wish to make Persephone *our* wife this time. All's fair in love and war, Hades. You ought to know that by now.' Zeus narrowed his eyes and cocked his head. 'No?'

Rage hit me like a sledgehammer, but after an aeon of being manipulated by Zeus, I had honed the ability of control.

'You included?'

Zeus cut me off. 'She's a new woman, Brother.'

His words struck me like a speeding juggernaut. She was *still* my wife... wasn't she?

'If any god lays a hand on *my wife,* the full extent of my wrath will be unleashed upon them. And that includes you... *Brother,*' I said in a dangerously low tone.

'Then you must raise your game, Hades. Win her back the right way. Now Hera is gone'—Zeus swallowed, his face momentarily flickering with sorrow—'I need a new consort as much as you do. May the best god win.' Zeus grinned and slapped me on the back before vanishing.

'Fucking Zeus,' I snarled quietly as my shadows enveloped me.

This definitely complicated matters.

FIVE

PERSEPHONE

Tee brought a breakfast of poached eggs on sourdough toast, accompanied by coffee—lots of coffee—and my mind was mulling over everything she'd told me.

'So, on the slim chance I *am* that Persephone, I must've had sex with the god of the dead?' For the love of sweet baby alpacas everywhere—the thought made my insides shrivel.

'Well, yeah, you shared a bedroom with him, so I think it's probably a given.'

'Ugh. I think I'm gonna vomit.'

Tee chuckled sexily. 'He's not so bad. Wait until you meet him.'

'He's how old? No way, Tee. He's an ancient god. This is so not going to work. I'll just grit my teeth and behave for three months, then I'm outta here.' Tee cocked her head, but I focused on eating and ignored her, lost in my thoughts.

'Come on, Sephy. Get showered.' Tee tugged at my arm, interrupting my musings as I sipped my coffee.

I sighed and gave a wan smile when a loud knock on the door made me jump up. Was it Hades? My hand instinctively reached to my thigh—but of course, my dagger was gone. Panic swelled in my chest. 'Tee,' I squeaked nervously, 'where's my blade?'

'Safe. Don't worry. You'll get it back; I promise,' she replied, opening the door.

A young, very tall guy in dark jeans and a rock T-shirt stood in the open doorway. He was simply delectable— shaggy black hair, sparkling grey eyes, and a toothy grin that lit up his face.

'Thanatos!' Tee squealed, launching herself into his arms and giggling as he swung her around.

'I've come to tell you Hades is off seeing Zeus. He may be a while,' the man said, his voice deep and unhurried. 'He wants to see you in his office before lunch.'

At the mention of both gods' names, my heart rate sped up. As he set Tee back on her feet, his gaze snapped to me.

'Persephone!' Before I could react, he swept me up, my feet leaving the floor as his arms locked tight around me. Dark shadows rippled off his skin, curling around us like smoke. My stomach knotted and a pathetic mewling sound escaped before I could stop it. My magic surged beneath my skin, fierce and instinctive. I shoved it down hard, burying it in the dark where it belonged.

'Put her down, Thanny. You're manhandling her. And rein in those shadows,' Tee scolded as he set me back on my feet and grinned sheepishly.

'Sorry. They always get excited when I'm around you.' I felt my eyes widen and my lips tremble. He bent down and looked questioningly into my face. 'Persephone?'

'I—I don't remember you,' I whispered. A wave of unexpected melancholy rolled through me. My chest ached, and a lump rose in my throat. What the hell was wrong with me?

Sadness clouded his eyes, but his smile returned, lighting up his face. 'Well, we can become friends all over again!'

'I'm not staying.' His face dropped, and I added, 'I'm so sorry.'

'We have her for three months, Thanatos. Plenty of time to change her mind.' Tee gave me a wicked smile, and I scowled at her. 'Now get out of here. She needs to get ready for her busy day.'

My head swung towards Tee, and I squinted at her. A busy day?

'See you around, Persephone.' Thanatos gave me a small wave. 'I've missed you.'

At his words, something tugged in my chest, and I smiled, stepping forward to wrap my arms around his waist. 'Looking forward to reacquainting myself with you,' I whispered into his ear as he leaned down to me.

He placed a hand over his heart, his lips curling into a playful smile. 'Me too,' he said as he turned and sauntered down the long, wide hallway—leaving me with fading shadows, questions, and a tug in my chest I couldn't explain.

'Off to the shower. Go on.' Tee nudged me towards the bathroom. 'I'll fetch more coffee.'

'Tee,' I whispered, and she paused and turned. '*Am* I in a coma... and you're sitting by my bedside?'

An amused look crossed her face. 'No, babe. This is real.'

I curled my lip and stomped into the bathroom, turning on the shower. Stripping off my pyjamas, I stood beneath the cascading hot water and reached for the shower gel. I frowned. It was my favourite—Jo Malone, Pomegranate Noir. Shrugging it off, I lathered myself and relished the water sluicing over my body, my mind still spinning with the revelations from Tee. I tried hard to switch off; I'd get through this without revealing myself as a witch. I *could* do it. I'd be home in no time.

Once clean, I wrapped myself in a fluffy white towel, wrung out my wet hair, and then rubbed it dry. I walked into my bedroom and stopped dead. The super-hot, sexy demon was sitting on my sofa, his blue and gold eyes pinning me with a look that made my traitorous lady parts clench with desire.

For the love of sweet fuck, what was wrong with me?

'Tee!' I screeched. The look on the demon's face would have been hilarious if I weren't so freaked out.

'Persephone, I've been waiting for you,' he said in a low, smoky voice as he stood. His voice was like a shadowy caress—a voice that stoked the same feeling of familiarity. I stepped backwards; I was defenceless without my blade, and I'd have no choice but to attempt using my dark magic if he came any closer. I glanced at the door and inched to the side.

'Don't.'

My gaze flew to him, and I took an unsteady breath. 'Don't what?'

'Run from me again.'

'You can't stop me.' He'd regret it if he tried.

'I won't try to stop you, but this time, I *will* catch you.' I tensed as carnivorous butterflies chomped at my gut. 'But perhaps you'd like that?'

An unwelcome thrill heated my blood. 'No, I wouldn't. At all.'

'Are you sure about that?' His eyes narrowed on me. I was irked, but more thrilled... and extremely pissed off at the thrilled part.

'Allow me to introduce myself. I'm Hades.' He gave a slight bow, and I inhaled sharply.

This was Hades?

'You're Hades?' I squeak-whispered. He frowned and smiled at me, as if he couldn't believe I was a fully functioning human. 'Oh.' All words shrivelled in my throat as I took him in, my eyes darting down his body. His black shirt stretched tight across massive shoulders, rolled up to the elbows, showcasing ridiculously appealing muscular forearms. When did forearms become sexy? The shirt was open at the neck, revealing a smooth chest, and, with faded, ripped jeans hugging his enormous legs, he was beyond beautiful. His full lips were parted slightly as he gazed at me.

Shit! I was *ogling* the god of the dead. I was flowing with heat, embarrassment, and something else that pulsated. Holy crap. I was *totally* turned on. Dammit. My *stupid* body. That pulsating heat coiled low in my core as my gaze met his again.

'Anyway, I have much to do, so I shall take my leave.' His cheeks heated. Hades was blushing—well, who knew gods blushed? 'But I wanted to introduce myself.'

'Thank you.' I gave a small curtsey, which made his mouth twitch. I cringed and pictured punching myself in the face. Hard. Repeatedly.

I was incapable of being coherent; all known words in my vocabulary somehow escaped me. I knew my eyes were wide, and the heat in my face burned my cheeks. I made a concerted effort to focus on his nose—not his annoyingly beautiful face or that ridiculous body, which caused the beat of my heart to skip and then speed up.

As Hades vanished with a pop and swirl of dark shadows, I slumped to the floor and cradled my head in my hands. Why hadn't I kicked him in the balls or yelled at him for kidnapping me? But when my eyes met those swirling pools of blue and gold, every word in me had frozen.

You were supposedly married to him once. How was that even possible? He was the god of death and shadows, and in his true form, he was terrifying. My despicable mind flashed to what sex with him would be like. I shut the thought down immediately. Nope, not happening—but I was drawn to him. No one had ever elicited lust-filled feelings in me like he had, and that was just in his presence. I needed to ignore my pounding hormones. He may have been ludicrously attractive, but he was still a god... and as a witch, he was my enemy.

But, hellfire, this was going to be a *long* three months.

TEE and I walked down a labyrinth of hallways to the training rooms. I wore leather trousers, which clung to the curve of my hips, paired with a matching halter neck top that I'd eventually managed to squeeze my breasts into. With lightweight boots and my hair scraped into a high, messy bun, I felt as ready as I could be. I was still missing my divine blade, though, which left me feeling vulnerable.

'You're worryingly quiet, Sephy.' Tee side-eyed me, and I exhaled sharply.

'Hades visited me.' Tee stopped, her brows inching up her forehead.

'Oh. He did, did he? I thought he was letting you settle in before coming to see you.' Tee narrowed her eyes in thought, then resumed walking. 'So, what do you think of him?'

'He's the guy that freaked me out the other night,' I muttered.

'When you were battling the Lamia?'

I came to an abrupt halt, my throat squeezing with dread as icy horror drenched my veins. 'How...?' Oh, fuck. Of course they'd know. They'd know everything—that I was a demon hunter. And probably a witch.

'Come on, Sephy. Let's do some fight training.' She pushed open a door and walked through, leaving me in the hallway, my mind in tatters. I let out a long breath and followed her through the door into the training hall. It was vast, glowing with the same magical daylight as my room —looking up at the ceiling felt like gazing at a sun-filled day. Columns lined the room, giving distinct Grecian vibes, which made sense, and the walls were adorned with shelves and hooks holding all sorts of weapons. The floor was covered in a soft material that my feet sank into as I walked.

'We'll warm up first,' Tee said, smirking at me.

We faced off, both adopting an attack stance. I was well-trained in various fighting techniques: grappling, martial arts, jiu-jitsu, and Muay Thai, to name a few, alongside weapon training. However, the only weapon I truly needed was my divine blade. I felt naked without it, but I clenched my teeth and inhaled deeply through my nose.

Tee moved as swiftly as a cobra striking, but I was ready for her. I bent my knees and pushed off the ground, somersaulting over her head and seizing her in a rear-naked chokehold. Tee twisted behind me and fell backwards, taking me down with her. Quick as a shadow, she pinned me in a mount position, straddling my abdomen, and when she grinned, my temper simmered.

I planted both hands on her chest, drew my feet up towards my bottom, and lifted my hips forcefully, pushing forward to force her hands down above my head. Hooking one arm around hers, I used the other to push and roll us over. I sprang up in one fluid motion before she could grapple me again.

She was up in a flash and came at me. I threw a hook kick, which she dodged with ease. She was quick and agile. Then she executed a roundhouse kick that would have knocked out teeth and cracked bones had the floor not been so forgiving. Nevertheless, I still fell hard onto my butt.

I groaned and rose fluidly to my feet, refusing to wince at the pain in my ass.

'Right, let's do some more *interesting* training,' Tee said as she turned away, then tossed me a fighting stick, which I caught easily. It was a simple, long, slender, wooden gun staff—the grandfather of all weapons. We both stood with our feet slightly wider than shoulder-width apart. I held my stick in my right hand, over my shoulder, and my hand close to my ear. Eyeing Tee with caution, I wondered if she'd try to kill me—then gave myself a mental slap. She was my best friend. I loved her like a sister.

Damn, this was so messed up.

Tee pounced with a spring semi-forward step. We were evenly matched, both struggling to get too close to inflict any real damage. I swung my stick in an uppercut, and Tee hissed as I clouted her wrist. I stifled a squeal of triumph until she thwacked me good on my side. We remained silent throughout the sparring. I used the time to quiet my mind, avoid dwelling on my precarious predicament, and burn off some pent-up energy.

Eventually, Tee stopped and set down her stick,

crossing her arms and adopting a more relaxed stance. I wondered whether she was contemplating knocking me on my ass again or wounding me with the vast array of stabby things lining the walls. Instead, she declared we'd done enough, thank the gods. My muscles ached, and my backside and ribs were bruised.

'Let's go back, Sephy.' Tee took my hand, and there was a loud pop as I was blinded by bright, white light. My stomach dropped off the deep end—I felt like I was flying downhill on a rollercoaster until we were finally back in my room.

'Oh, my God,' I grunted.

'*Gods*, Sephy. Gods.' Tee smirked, and I curled my lip at her.

'What was that? Can't we just walk?'

'It's teleporting. Travelling through the aether. You'll get used to it; don't worry. I thought you might need a drink after I kicked your ass but good.' Tee extended the word 'good' and winked at me. I gave her my best resting bitch face, which she ignored as she walked over to a cupboard full of bottles, pulling out a golden-coloured one along with two glasses. She poured the amber liquid and handed one to me.

'Have I got wine in my room?' I asked, taking the glass. 'Yup.'

'Great, I might just end up intoxicated for the next three months.' I lifted the glass to my lips. The scent was sweet, and a mildly floral, fruity flavour filled my mouth. Warmth and strength flowed through me as I sipped the drink. My ribs and butt stopped hurting, and I felt rejuvenated. 'What *is* this?' I asked Tee as my gaze met hers, and I swallowed another gulp.

'Nectar is in the gold bottles. One glass a day is enough, so don't overindulge.'

'Mm, I like it!'

'Let's chat... We have a lot to discuss.' Tee motioned for me to follow her to the sofa, and I sank beside her with a sigh. 'I need to tell you my real name,' Tee began, eyes dropping to the glass in her hand. 'I'm actually called Hecate.'

I shot to my feet, nearly spilling the drink, and glared down at her. 'You're the goddess of magic and witchcraft?' My lip curled, teeth bared.

'Among other things, yes.' Her gaze darted to mine, lines of tension bracketing her mouth.

'And you allowed the gods to kill your brethren? My brethren!' The pitch of my voice rose, along with the blood pumping in my temples. 'I—I can't process this.' I covered my eyes with my hand.

'It's not as straightforward as you think. There was nothing I could do. I tried, believe me. I had no involvement in the war, but right or wrong, the gods had their reasons.'

I dropped my hand and glowered at her. 'Reasons?' A wild laugh escaped me, high and brittle, and Tee's shoulders stiffened. 'Why couldn't you stop them? You're a goddess!'

Her eyes hardened, voice low and cutting. 'I am a goddess. But more than that... I'm a Titan.'

The word landed like thunder, silencing the room. I

froze, staring. Titans were whispered about in myths—ancient, dangerous, *extinct*. My stomach dropped as if the floor had vanished beneath me.

Tee's mouth twisted into a bitter smile. 'Many of us stayed out of the ancient war against the gods. That's the only reason I'm still here. But Zeus loathes Titans even more than witches, Sephy. I may be powerful... but not powerful enough to take on them all.' She sighed. 'I'm sorry. Truly.'

The fight left me. This was all too much. 'How long have you known I'm a witch?' I asked as I slumped back down beside her.

Tee hesitated. 'I've known you've hunted demons since day one.'

'And *is* our friendship real, Tee?' I asked in a small voice.

'Sephy, babe, I've always loved you, and *still* do. That's never changed. You gotta believe me. When we found you again'—Tee swiped her hand across her eyes—'I was so happy.'

I clasped her hand in mine. 'I'm glad I found you,' I whispered as we hugged, cried, and laughed like two adolescents sharing a bonding moment.

Tee pulled away and ran a hand down my face. 'Zeus is a dick. Don't tell anyone I said that.' I giggled weakly. 'He fears me. Fears Hades. He knows we are both as powerful, if not more so than he is. That's why he bound Hades, Thanatos, me, and the rest of Hades' allies to the Underworld.'

'But how can you go up top if you're bound here?'

'Because Hades refused to fight with the gods unless Zeus broke the bindings that tied us all here.' Hecate showed me a tattoo of four different runes encircling her calf. 'These were the bindings that tethered me to the Underworld. When Zeus deceived us, we could go nowhere but here or Zeus's kingdom. Not that any of us wished to go to Zeus's kingdom. It's full of ass-wipes.'

'Zeus sounds like a manipulative asshole,' I mused.

'That he is. Though since Hera vanished, he's mellowed a little. He can still be an ass, though. And Sephy, when Hades lost you, well, let's just say your return has cheered up the grumpy bastard.'

I snorted a laugh. 'I find it utterly crazy... mind-numbingly so... that you genuinely believe I'm really the goddess who was married to him. Whatever happened to the real Persephone, Tee?'

Tee studied me for a beat. 'I've told you. That's Hades' story. Don't be too hard on him about the war until you hear what he has to say. Understand the reasons behind the events. Alright?'

I gave a lazy shrug, but it still rattled my brain. 'And me being a witch?'

'You're *still* Persephone.' I huffed a frustrated breath. She was utterly convinced I was *the* Persephone, so I swallowed my retort. 'Eventually, you may be able to help sort out the banishment of magic. You never know. You could be the saviour of witchcraft in the human realm.' I narrowed my eyes and tapped my forefinger against my lips. Would that be possible? 'But, oh, the irony of it.' Tee chuckled darkly. 'The crafty old crone.'

'Old crone?'

'My lips are sealed, sorry. Speak to Hades. In fact, he's eager for you to have lunch with him.'

'What?' I gasped so hard, I almost choked.

'He won't bite, Sephy. Well, not unless you want him to.' At her words, a hot, tight shiver ran through me, and my lady parts tingled. I cursed my ridiculous body. 'We can start doing some magic training if you'd like?'

My breath hitched in my throat. Magic training with *the* goddess of magic? 'I, I only have flora magic.'

She gave me a knowing smile. 'You sure about that?' I nodded emphatically. I couldn't mention the dark magic I wielded. Because it was uncontrollable. Dangerous.

'Come on, let's choose an outfit to impress.' Tee stood up.

'I have no desire to impress him.' I grimaced at her as she lifted her brows. I closed my eyes and said, 'I need some advice. Not about Hades, obviously, because there's no way I'm interested in him.' Again, Tee cocked her brow at me. 'I'm, erm... I've never had sex—like, you know—*full* sex, before.'

Tee bellowed with laughter. 'Scriously? You've never been penetrated by a penis? Or anything that resembles a penis?'

I wrinkled my nose, shifted uncomfortably, and gave a slight shrug. I'd pleasured myself if that counted; had a bit of foreplay with Matt, but maybe my vagina was broken because sex with a man just wasn't that important. Or hadn't been.

'You're a twenty-two-year-old virgin?' She choked out

the words through her laughing fit. I scowled at her, feeling rather offended. She wiped her eyes and sucked in her cheeks.

'Glad you find me so amusing,' I said with a clenched jaw. 'Why does society believe someone not wanting casual sex is a freak?' I spat. 'Just bang someone and move on. It's no biggie. But I refuse to follow society's conventional wisdom. Do what works for you, I say... And *stop* laughing at me,' I growl-hissed at her.

'Sorry.' She burst out laughing again, then sobered for a beat. 'What about Matt?'

I shook my head. 'I've never really been attracted to anyone in that way. I think I might be frigid.' My shoulders sank. *Well, unless I'm around the god of the dead.* At that thought, an involuntary shudder ran through me, but Tee cracked up laughing again.

I glared at her as she carried on with her inappropriate laughter. Eventually, she settled down from her hilarity; she cleared her throat and managed to speak.

'Sex is fun. Much more entertaining than slaying demons. You've obviously never had the right guy or girl.' She blew out a breath and shook out her arms, still trying to control her laughter. I narrowed my eyes at her. 'Come on, let's get you ready for lunch. I'll sort your hair. It looks like a rat's nest.' She snorted through her nose, which made me grit my teeth, but I ignored it. I swear to the gods, if she laughed again, I'd punch her.

'Gee, thanks,' I muttered as she shoved me towards the bathroom.

'Shower. Hurry up, you only have an hour. I'll be back soon; need to see the boss. Oh, and here's your blade.'

The divine blade, still in its sheath and with the leather straps attached, appeared in her hand. 'And keep that thing away from me.' She squinted at me.

I laughed evilly as I sauntered into the bathroom, then dramatically slammed the door shut.

CHAPTER
SIX

HADES

W hen Hecate appeared, I was brooding in my office.

Seeing Persephone in the Underworld again stirred need deep in my belly... Wrapped only in a towel, the lust in her gaze, combined with the scent of her arousal, ignited the desire I'd always felt for her; it coursed through my veins like venom. She was *mine*. She belonged to me. But it broke my heart that she didn't know me.

The emptiness within me since her disappearance had consumed my soul. It was a void that only she could fill.

But *was* she still my Persephone?

Spikes of unease gnawed at my chest—what if she left me again?

'Who made you the demon lord of downers today?' Hecate remarked as I lifted my gaze to her.

I didn't mention my concerns about Persephone. 'Fucking Zeus,' I ground out with gritted teeth.

'What's the meddlesome old bastard done now?' she huffed as she flopped into a chair.

I told her what Zeus had planned with a few other gods, her eyes widening by the minute. Then her temper flared. 'What the actual? Do they think she's a commodity to be traded to the highest bidder?'

I shrugged and stared down at the papers on my desk. 'Zeus told me to win her back the right way.'

'We need to be smart about this, Hades. You love her, unlike the other gods. And I know deep down she still loves you.'

I scoffed a laugh. 'She might be drawn to me'—I remembered the desire in her eyes as her gaze devoured me —'but what if it's not her anymore, Hecate?' I gave a resigned sigh, and Hecate's brows furrowed.

'Bollocks, Hades. It's still Persephone.'

'Is it?'

'Yes. You can't back down because of Zeus's meddling.'

'I can't endure any more heartbreak, Hecate. Having her here only deepens my longing for her... intensifies my craving. I feel vulnerable. *She* makes me vulnerable, and I don't like it. I ought to have left her in the mortal realm.' I felt as if my heart was being squeezed through a juicer... slowly.

'Oh, for fuck's sake, Hades. Grow a pair of ovaries,' Hecate vented. I glowered at her impertinence, then her expression softened. 'You *will* win her over. You will woo her and show how much you love her. You can do that, can't you? But first, you need to take the stick from up your ass.' I blinked at her. 'And stop being such a miserable git.'

'You make it sound so simple,' I replied, rolling my eyes. 'Queen of the gods, residing in beautiful Olympus, or queen of the dead, existing here with me.' I slammed my hand down on the desk.

'You're not bound here anymore, are you?' Hecate cocked her head. 'You have a life up top, as well—now you have equal access to the mortal world. You're also far sexier than Zeus.' I chuckled at the goddess and my best friend.

'There's one thing, though.' I regarded her, raising my eyebrows. 'You need to protect your heart, Hades.' I concurred with her on that point. 'And don't go in all gung-ho, arrogant god with her. She's a spitfire and doesn't take kindly to arrogance.' Hecate reached across the desk and took my hand. 'But she feels something for you. I know she does.'

'I'm not so sure.'

Hecate shook her head in frustration. 'Hades, she believes she's a witch—your sworn enemy. But she has the link to you. The soul bond. She needs to see the real you, not the arrogant son-of-a-bitch you.' I tightened my jaw at her disrespect. 'Oh, and another thing. Sort this crap out, Hades, because she's a virgin.'

I jumped up, my eyes popping.

'And put those golden eyes away,' Hecate snapped. 'Gods, you're such a typical man. Get lunch prepped. I'll have her with you in forty-five minutes.'

Hecate vanished, leaving my mind reeling. If another god laid a hand on Persephone, there'd be a second war, but this time in Olympus.

SEVEN

PERSEPHONE

I watched Tee in the mirror as she fiddled with my hair, creating one long Dutch braid, arranging it along my hairline, and pinning it in place. A few wispy strands framed my face. I wore minimal makeup—I didn't want Hades to think I was interested in him, because I wasn't. Ugh, *not* at all.

'There you go. That's what's known as a halo braid. You need to practice doing your hair, Sephy. You look like a bag of shit most of the time.'

I coughed a laugh. 'Way to go boosting a girl's confidence, bestie.'

Tee sniggered. 'When you return from lunch, we need a chat.' Hecate said as she smoothed her hands around my head.

'What about?'

'It'll wait. Come on, let's go.'

I stood and looked at my reflection. I'd insisted on staying in my leather fighting gear, refusing one of the flowing dresses in my wardrobe, and I had my divine blade strapped to my thigh. 'Can we walk, please?'

Tee looked to the sky but took the lead. The wide hallways seemed endless, shimmering with magically imbued daylight. The walls were painted a deep aubergine colour, complemented by a sumptuous grey carpet underfoot.

Tee gestured towards a pair of broad grey doors before disappearing in a flash of white light. *Damn her.*

I hesitantly pushed open the door and peeked inside. It was a spacious, light kitchen adorned with soothing shades of cream and grey. Chequerboard tiles in dark and light grey covered the floor, and a massive island was lined with leather bar stools on one side, sufficient to seat eight people. The white marble countertops appeared to shimmer as if sprinkled with stardust, glittering in the magical light, while a long table displayed a magnificent vase of narcissi. I smiled at the colours. The space seamlessly combined style and function while remaining inviting.

I quietly slipped through the door and saw him. He had his back to me, standing by the cooker—still in black jeans but this time wearing a black T-shirt. His hair hung loosely around his shoulders. As he turned around, his eyes widened, and his lips parted as though in surprise. I gulped as he held my stare—his eyes were captivating—and my mind went blank. He was utterly beautiful and completely terrifying, and my treacherous stomach did a backflip.

'Persephone.' His voice was deep and hypnotic.

He said my name as if he were tasting it on his tongue, and my stomach clenched in the most delicious way. Was he really supposed to be this hot? The fuckalicious god of the Underworld was here to suck out my godsdamned soul.

Ignoring my raging hormones, I chewed on my bottom lip as I dropped my gaze to the narcissi and muttered, 'Hi.'

He moved towards me with leopard-like grace, and my eyes shot to his face. His earthy scent swirled around him, and I tried not to breathe. A small smile twitched at his lips, causing heat to infuse my cheeks like a fever as he extended his hand for me to shake. Hesitantly, I placed my much smaller hand in his, and the buried dark magic thrummed in my chest, making my eyes snap to his again. I forced the magic back down, trying to quell my panic.

'Sephy,' I breathed.

At his touch, images flashed in my mind—me naked and his smiling face looking up at me from between my thighs; me on top of his sculpted body, riding him with my head thrown back. Vague recollections of him and me pulsed in my subconscious, as if fighting to escape. I yelped and dropped his hand. What the fuck? Heat pooled between my legs, causing my core to tingle, and I took a step back.

He must be using some sort of divine manipulation. Focus!

As we locked eyes, a slight frown marred his wonderful face. Emotions I didn't recognise surged in my chest; those memories slipped through my fingers like sand yet hammered in my mind, trying to break free. Gazing into those desperate, liquid blue pools of flaming fire, I realised once again that this man was familiar. His voice was familiar. As I closed my eyes, I broke eye contact.

He is my enemy; he has killed thousands of people... thousands of my kin.

I opened my eyes to find him still staring at me; his gaze held a look I couldn't fathom, and something tugged in my chest, but I dismissed it.

My heart thumped unsteadily as I got a grip on myself, and a maelstrom of irritation brewed within me.

'Do all gods kidnap women, or is that just *your* love language?' I snapped.

'Only the ones who threaten to unravel me.'

I rolled my eyes. 'Kidnapping is not flirting. It's a felony.'

'Gods don't commit crimes. We commit fate.'

'Try that line on someone not fantasising about stabbing you.' I blew out a breath of irritation. 'Seriously, why *have* you kidnapped me? Why didn't you simply come to see me? Talk to me. If you think I'm *the* Persephone?' I said through gritted teeth.

'Why?'

'Excuse me? What?'

'Why would I come to see you? When I know this is what you will ultimately want. You belong to me... I didn't steal you. I claimed what was always mine.'

'I'm sorry... I—I *belong* to you? You own me?' Oh, now he'd really pissed me off. 'Listen here, mister high-

and-shadowy.' I pointed my finger at him. 'I don't *belong* to anyone. I'm not a freaking pet. And what I *want*?' I coughed out a laugh. 'You can't kidnap me and not expect to piss me off.' He lowered his brows. Gods, I was on the verge of screaming. 'Because, whether you think you know it's what I ultimately want or—'

He stepped closer, voice low and dangerous. 'I could have you begging with a single word.' My mouth fell open. The audacity.

'Try it. But don't cry when I laugh.' I tilted my head and glared at him.

He stared down at me like I was the most infuriating thing he'd ever seen—and maybe I was. Good.

'I know you want me,' he murmured. 'I can *taste* your attraction. Your arousal. You want this... me.'

'You can *what now*? *Taste* my *arousal*? I stepped back, pure disbelief twisting into fury. 'Well, that's plain rude. You can stop doing that right away. You creep.' I was so close to kicking him in the balls. 'You need to learn some manners, mister. And if you wanted to take me out, all you had to do was ask. Politely. Not kidnap me.' I placed my hands on my hips, and as I glared up at him, those eyes churned more gold than blue, the line of his jaw turning brittle. He didn't speak for a long moment.

'Interesting.' He studied me like I was a riddle he couldn't quite solve, but desperately wanted to. I didn't flinch; I met his gaze, unblinking. If he thought I'd squirm under his stare, he hadn't been paying attention.'Well, I'm sorry. I would like you to spend time with me.'

'What if I don't want to?'

He paused, tension bracketing his mouth as he tilted his head. 'Then I suppose I shall respect your wishes.'

I pursed my lips. 'Will you let me go then? If you're respecting my wishes?'

'No.' He cocked his head again as I ground my teeth. 'Not yet.' The 'not yet' part sparked a flicker of hope. 'I'm making grilled cheese sandwiches... if that's alright?' His voice was slightly strained. The last part sounded awkward —like it physically hurt him to ask for permission. I almost applauded the effort. Almost. But, upon hearing his words, my anger nosedived, and a traitorous smile touched my lips. But come on... grilled cheese.

'Perfect. My favourite.'

'They always were. Take a seat.' He motioned towards the bar stools, and I huffed out a breath before settling into one as I watched him work. The aroma of grilled cheese permeated the room, and my mouth watered.

'You know,' I said, watching the cheese sizzle, 'kidnapping and sandwiches don't cancel each other out.'

He didn't look at me. 'They don't,' he agreed coolly. 'But they help.'

The muscles in his Titan-sized shoulders and arms flexed as he busied himself, his face devoid of emotion. I noticed a tattoo peeking above the edge of the V of his tee, but the one on his arm was missing.

'Where's your tattoo?' I asked, and he paused, turning to me.

'I take Cerberus into the mortal world as a tattoo.'

'Oh,' I squeaked.

'While I'm here, he roams freely. You must meet him; he's missed you.' I inhaled sharply—the demon dog of the Underworld missed me? 'He won't harm you, Persephone; he loves you.' He half-smiled, showing some teeth this time, and it transformed his face into something simply... *mouthwatering*—well, until I noticed the fang. A fucking *fang*?

'You, erm, have fangs?' I whisper-croaked as I felt the blood drain from my face.

'I do.' He ran his tongue over the sharp canines.

'Oh,' I muttered in a stunned stupor.

'It's evolution.' He shrugged, eyeing me closely.

'Evolution?'

'Well, when we relinquished the human world to humans, who then proceeded to ravage the planet out of greed, we lost worshippers. Or rather, the other gods did. It didn't impact me quite as much, being king of the dead.' His eyes met mine again, and I gulped. 'Loss of worshipper signified the loss of our life force, as it were. Blood is the essence of life; we developed fangs to counter this possibility many, many aeons ago. Thanks to Hecate...'

'Hecate?' I drew in a sharp breath.

'Indeed. Aeons ago, Hecate was rather an anomaly. Ask her about it.' A half-smile tugged at his lips. 'Drinking blood helped to preserve our life force. We don't need to do it now, obviously. However, it can still be a pleasurable experience.'

'You're vampires?' I whispered.

He released a throaty laugh that made me shiver. 'No, not at all. We are gods.'

'Oh.' I looked down at my hands. Lifting my eyes to his, I asked, 'Do you still feed?'

He shook his head. 'Not often. Not unless we are injured or weakened.'

'Weakened?'

'No being is so powerful it cannot be weakened, Persephone.' He turned away and carried on cooking, leaving my mind in a whirl.

When he served lunch, I ate slowly, my stomach in knots, and we sat in silence. The grilled cheese sandwich was divine, but with the god of the dead sitting before me, I struggled to swallow. *He has freaking fangs. Gods have fangs.* My mind couldn't keep up with this insane world. But, I needed to ask about things—about Persephone. When I met his gaze again, they swirled with golden flecks, like angel fire.

'Why do your eyes sometimes swirl with gold?' I asked, taking another bite of my sandwich.

'It's the aether in my body. Heightened emotions affect it. In my true form, my eyes are pure gold.'

'Your true form? Like in the alley? When I was fighting the Lamia?' He nodded in response. 'You're made of shadows,' I said, almost to myself.

'My shadows are my aether too.'

'I prefer your human form,' I muttered, causing his lips to twitch. Damn it—I *really* preferred it. Too much. Warmth surged between my legs.

Seriously? I needed to bleach my brain because there

was no way I should be having indecent thoughts about his stacked body and reacting to him like this.

I set my sandwich down, furious at my traitorous, tingling nipples.

'Why did the gods start the war ?' I asked as calmly as I could, raising my eyes to his. 'Why banish magic?'

He stopped eating, his gaze meeting mine again. 'That's a conversation we need at another time.'

'No!' I raised my voice, causing him to flinch. 'Tell me. Tell me why your twisted little pantheon slaughtered so many—so many witches and mages. My kin!' My voice rose with every word, pitch climbing like the storm building in my chest.. 'And what became of the real Persephone?' I felt my temper prickling as the darkness within me fought for release.

He slid off the stool and sighed, turning away from me. He raked both hands through his hair as he stared out of a towering window. Anger rose swiftly, and the last little tether on my temper snapped. I cursed under my breath, jumped down from the stool, and stalked toward him. My steps echoed like a war drum across polished marble. He turned—slowly, deliberately—as I drew my dagger, and he eyed the movement.

'Dangerous things can be kept in the prettiest of places,' he murmured, voice like smoke. He didn't flinch. He didn't move.

I raised the divine blade to his throat. Pressed.

A sharp breath. A trickle of blood bloomed—deep violet laced with gold—trailing down his neck, catching at the hollow of his collarbone before slipping beneath the V of his black shirt.

He looked down at me. Not angry. Not scared.

Resigned... and something else. Something that scared me more than the shadows ever could.

My mouth went dry.

'Do it,' he said hoarsely, an angry frown marring his flawless face.

My eyes met his, and my resolve faltered. I saw something new flash in his eyes, and my breath caught. Desperation filled me as I gazed into those bewitching eyes and that beautiful face. Slowly, I lowered the dagger, and it clattered to the floor as I lifted my hand to touch his stubbled jaw. He closed his eyes, and the sensation of his skin sent electricity firing through every nerve ending. Yearning skittered through my core.

'I know you,' I whispered. I felt as if I truly knew him —as though I'd known him for a lifetime. It seemed absurd.

He opened his golden eyes. 'And I know you.' I could hear the love in his broken voice.

'You're beautiful,' I murmured, inhaling his earthy and spicy scent. My hand journeyed down, resting on his solid chest, and his eyes flashed with hunger... lust.

'I'll always want you.' He stepped closer, pushing me backwards, then pressing me against the wall, his hands resting on either side of my head. For the love of every baby kitten on the planet, I was pretty sure my panties were close to combusting.

His voice dropped to a low rasp. 'You were the brightest star in an endless night,' he murmured as he lowered his mouth to mine. As his stubble brushed against my cheek, I contemplated the other kinds of friction I'd like to create with him, and an avalanche of shivers cascaded down my spine. 'Simply being able to touch you again...' His breath caressed my lips, and as he uttered the word 'touch' like a sin, like a promise, it sucker-punched me straight in the lady parts.

I wanted him. I wanted to grab his face and kiss the ever-loving darkness out of him. And that terrified me.

At the very last second—heart pounding, skin buzzing—I gasped and ducked under his arm. No. Absolutely not. I was not going to be one more conquest carved into the stone of his throne.

I wasn't going to kiss the goddamn fanged king of the Underworld.

I staggered back, shaking my head hard like it could fling out the desire. When I looked up... He was gone. Just—gone. Shadows and silence where his warmth had been. My stomach dropped.

You were the brightest star in an endless night.

His words echoed, wrapping around my ribs like a chain. My chest tightened, and traitorous tears blurred my vision.

Because I hated him. And I wanted him.

And that combination was lethal.

I STUMBLED down the maze of hallways, wiping the tears from my face. I had no idea where I was going. My mind was a sea of confusion. I recognised the god of the Underworld; I *knew* him. Was it because I *was* Persephone? I couldn't fathom that ridiculous notion or my inexplicable feelings for him. He was absurdly hot, and I was definitely drawn to him, but it was more than that—more than mere attraction.

I needed to get out of this place; I was suffocating.

I came to a large wooden door that I opened cautiously. It led outside to wide steps, the colour and texture reminiscent of polished obsidian. I glanced towards the sky, which glowed an ethereal amethyst and silver hues —there was no sun. Panic surged within my chest, and my hand flew to my mouth. I needed to get out of here and return home. The landscape was desolate—no greenery or flowers thrived in this godsforsaken place. I couldn't bear to be trapped here for three months. I'd wither. Die.

Far in the distance, I could see a river; as I stared at it, I wondered if it was the river Styx. Descending the steps, I knelt and picked up a handful of dirt; the inky, sand-like soil trickled through my fingers. Life... I felt the residual embers of life in the dirt, and I smiled. Wiping my hands on my trousers, I surveyed my surroundings. It was like a black desert with no oasis in sight, and something unexplainable pulled in my gut—a feeling of loss and sadness— emotions I couldn't understand at all.

My flora magic hummed beneath my skin, deep into muscle and bone, desperate to revive the life that had once thrived. I bent down and placed my hands in the soil. My magic cascaded through every nerve ending, every synapse. Grasses sprouted, flowers bloomed, and a myriad of narcissi appeared interspersed with various vibrant flora as the bare trees changed colour and broad leaves unfurled on the branches. 'That's better,' I muttered as I stood and scanned the landscape as far as my eyes could see.

Turning back, I glanced at the structure behind me. It resembled a crystal fortress—immense and oddly beautiful, crafted from the same mineral as the steps, but imbued with star-kissed sparkles. Aristocratic and imposing, the castle featured tall round towers capped with conical roofs, grand arched doorways, vast windows, and cantilevered balconies. The place was absolutely breathtaking.

As I walked towards the flowing river, more flowers and grass sprouted in my wake. The sight of this began to calm my pounding heart until an almighty *woof* almost made my ears bleed. Coming towards me as fast as a speeding freight train was Cerberus, Hades' demon hound.

'Oh, crap,' I screeched as I reached for my dagger. My sheath was empty—I'd left my blade on the kitchen floor. Rooted to the spot, my knees trembled, and my heart galloped as the hound drew closer and closer. 'He won't hurt me. He won't hurt me,' I whispered to myself.

Cerberus came to an emergency stop in front of me. He crouched on his front paws, ass in the air, and all three heads whining, tongues lolling as his six red eyes fixed on me. One head nudged me, and I toppled onto my butt. He immediately seized the opportunity, and the next moment, three long tongues were lavishing me with affection, making me screech with laughter. 'Well, hello, boy,' I said as I managed to sit up and pat each head. 'You're delightful. You're not scary at all.' I ran my fingers through the black fur on his muzzles.

'Sephy!' Tee's stern voice shattered the moment. 'What are you doing out here?'

I struggled to my feet. 'Walking,' I uttered without meeting her gaze.

'I see.' She glanced around at the meadow ablaze with colour, and a small smile played on her lips. 'Let's get you back. Come on.'

'See you soon, boy.' I kissed each of Cerberus's noses, and he nudged me towards Tee. She took my hand, and with a pop and a flash of bright white light, I found myself back in my room, my stomach lurching. 'Ugh, I wish you'd stop freaking doing that.' I walked over to the bed, flopped down on my back, and closed my eyes.

'I take it lunch was a bust?' I felt the mattress shift as Tee settled beside me.

'You could say that.'

'What happened?' She nudged my arm.

'I think he might be pissed off with me.'

'Why?'

I hesitated and covered my face with my hands. 'First, I gave him a roasting for kidnapping me. I mean, why bother asking a girl out on a date when you can simply abduct her? Plus, he's an arrogant twatwaffle.' I peeked between my fingers and had a feeling Tee was sucking in her cheeks, trying not to smile. 'Second, I tried to kill him.'

'What in the gods' names, Sephy?' Tee squealed a laugh.

'And third, I chickened out of kissing him.' My cheeks were so hot with embarrassment, I kept my hands over my face. 'His grilled cheese sandwiches were good, though, I suppose,' I mumbled.

'Well, nothing's changed there. You've always loved grilled cheese *and* your relationship has always been passionate.'

I peeled my fingers away from my eyes and wrinkled my nose. 'He wouldn't talk to me, Tee; about the war, about the other Persephone. I lost my shit.' I groaned and covered my face again.

'He will, Sephy. When the time is right, I promise. He's a good guy. Besides, the "other" Persephone is you, and you know it, right?' I flopped my hands onto the bed and scowled at her, but I had a feeling she might be speaking the truth. How? *How* was I *the* Persephone?

I was silent for a beat. 'He's the king of the Underworld. He embodies shadows and death. I love nature. I love flowers and plants, and I *need* the sun, Tee.' I sighed animatedly.

'He's not tied here all the time now. He has a life up top, too; you know that, Sephy.'

I wrinkled my forehead, still fighting with my conflicting emotions. 'He's also a freaking god. I hate the gods,' I growl-whispered.

'You don't hate me.' Tee gave me a slight shrug and a mischievous smile.

'You're a Titan.'

She chuckled with amusement and shook her head.

I sat up and stared down at my hands. 'I'm drawn to him, Tee. I've never experienced anything like it, and I can't explain it. It's so intense; it's scaring me. I'm like a freaking walking hormone in his presence. But I'm a witch; he's a god; we're enemies... It's not right.' I lifted my chin as my gaze caught hers, and she took my hand.

She hesitated as though she wanted to say something, then replied, 'Love is mysterious, Sephy. You can't fight it, no matter how hard you try.' I shook my head and scowled at her. 'There are eight different types of love. You and Hades had Philia: a deep friendship; Ludus: a playful love; and Pragma: a lasting love.'

'A playful love with that grouchy git? Seriously? This is *ridiculous*!' I exclaimed, wringing my hands together and dropping my gaze.

'And, of course, the love, Eros.'

'Eros?' My head snapped up.

Tee's eyes sparkled. 'Sexual passion, Sephy.' A tingling sensation crept down my spine, making my insides quiver at the thought of having sex with Hades.

I huffed. 'I *do not* love the king of the freaking dead, Tee! I don't even know him! Maybe it *is* just physical attraction?'

Tee cocked a brow and completely ignored me. 'You complete and balance each other. Together, you're whole. You're physically and emotionally drawn to one another, Sephy. What you're feeling is the soul bond you two share. We are ancient beings, Sephy, older than you can imagine.

We don't often love, but once we do, you're fucked, because it's forever. He loves you; you love him.'

I licked my too-dry lips as nervous energy danced in my core. Did Hades love me?

'I do not love him,' I gritted out, prompting Tee to roll her eyes. 'It's not as if I'm a guest here, is it? I'm a prisoner until Lord Grumpy and Deadly decides to release me.' I lifted my chin as nausea gripped me. 'How can I love someone who kidnaps people?' Tee puffed out a breath but remained silent, and I needed to change the subject. 'Anyway, what did you want to discuss with me?'

'It can wait until tomorrow... Don't worry. What do you want to do now?'

'I want to fetch my books... from home,' I said, giving her puppy dog eyes.

'Next best thing. Hang on to your panties,' she replied as she grasped my arm.

She flashed me out of the room again, and as I opened my eyes, I was mere seconds away from punching her until I saw where we were. I found myself in the middle of an immense library. I squealed as I looked around, wide-eyed —a circular room with thirty-foot-tall walls lined with books. A mezzanine level held even more books and was accessed by a wide staircase. When my eyes caught sight of the rolling ladders, I jumped up and down, gasping with excitement. I was in heaven. The high glass ceiling glowed with the light of a bright, sun-filled day, while plenty of sofas, tables, and chairs were arranged in cosy groupings.

'I'll be back for you in an hour. We have a dinner tonight, and you can't wear your combat garb.'

I barely heard her. I was itching to explore. 'Okay,' I grunted as I moved towards the shelves, hearing her flash of aether as she vanished. As I strolled along, I trailed my fingers over the spines of books, sighing happily. The deliciously sweet smell of old books wafted through the air; a balmy, comforting aroma of knowledge, adventures, unrealistic romances, and faraway places—it was a calming setting of endless possibilities. I climbed a ladder and rolled it down a bookcase, much like Beauty does in *Beauty and the Beast*, letting out a little whoop.

'Don't break my ladders,' a voice shouted, and I nearly tumbled off them.

'Holy crap, don't scare me like that!' I glowered down at the floor and almost tumbled off the ladder again. I hurried down and jumped the last few rungs, landing with a thud. I stared at the half-goat, half-man creature. He stood about four feet tall. His lower half was black and furry, with goat hind legs and a small tail. The fur reached his waist, and downy black hair covered his human torso. Small, pointed horns poked through his dark, curly hair, and my gaze settled on his cheeky-looking face.

'You're a Satyr?'

'No shit, Sherlock,' he said, quirking a brow at me. I ignored his rude comment.

'I'm Sephy. Pleased to meet you.' I held out a hand, and he hesitated before taking it—a quick grasp and release as if to say, *You're on my turf, bitch.*

'I'm the librarian,' he said as he turned to walk away.

'What's your name?'

'Simos. So you're the one everyone's buzzing about,

are you?' He eyed me up and down. 'Can't see what all the fuss is about.' The cheeky little shit! 'Though you've got a smoking hot body. I like a woman in leather.'

'Ugh,' I huffed, squinting at him. 'Nice to meet you, too.'

He paused for a beat. 'How old are you?'

'I'm twenty-two.' I snapped, still glaring at him.

He turned and began to walk away, muttering something about babysitting brats and not being a fucking child-care worker.

I bristled, clenching my fists. Dropping him with a roundhouse kick seemed extreme, so I inhaled a calming breath. 'How old are you?'

He stopped and turned to face me. 'Five hundred and sixty.'

I felt my eyes widen and croaked, 'Oh.'

He narrowed his eyes as if in thought, then locked eyes on me again. 'So, you like reading?'

I nodded, still wanting to punch him in his cute face. 'I do.'

'Come on, then. Let's find you some books,' he said, trotting off. 'But don't go breaking my ladders.' He offered a small smile over his shoulder, and I followed him into the sanctuary of a million books.

RETURNING to my room with Tee, I carried a stack of

books on the gods and Greek mythology and placed them on my desk.

'Simos wasn't too friendly when I first met him,' I muttered.

'Ah, he's loyal to Hades, Sephy. Everybody is worried about him. All of his people are his friends and love him.'

I creased my brow. Were the king of the Underworld's subjects his friends, who loved and cared for him?

'Worried? Why?'

'Well, your disappearance broke his heart, and the fallout was unbearable, especially at first. Mr Grumpy became Mr Insufferably Grumpy in your absence. They're worried you might break his heart again,' Tee said as she fetched two glasses and a bottle of wine.

I said nothing. Would I break his heart? How could I? I didn't even know him—not really. Crap; I was awash with confusion. 'Pour me a wine. A large one,' I said as I held out my hand.

She poured the red wine and handed me one. It smelled like sun-ripened cherries, and as I took a sizeable mouthful, it burst with notes of ripe and juicy fruits—cherries, berries, and plums. The flavour was refreshing and delightful. 'Mm,' I uttered.

'I'll come back for you in an hour. Get dressed; pick one of the dresses from your closet. Do your makeup as I taught you... Make an effort,' Tee instructed as she handed me the bottle. 'And don't get shitfaced.'

I sat for a while, my thoughts bouncing around like a butterfly in a whirlwind. I may have had this weird connection to Hades, but I couldn't spend most of my life here.

My life is in my world. If I *were* her—the Persephone—which I questioned, I wasn't that person any longer. I was a different Persephone. I had to ignore the insane infatuation I had with the god of the Underworld.

I took a sip of my second glass of wine and sighed. I needed to prepare for dinner. I was dreading seeing Hades again. Tendrils of unease clawed at my stomach at the mere idea of looking into those captivating blue-gold eyes.

'I can do this,' I whispered as I stood, and made my way to the closet.

CHAPTER

EIGHT

HADES

M y cock twitched at the thought of touching and smelling Persephone again. At last. The bond between us was growing stronger; I could feel it. I was sure she felt it, too, but she was resisting.

This Persephone made me furiously angry and impossibly turned on at the same time, and I didn't like the feeling one fucking bit.

Looking out of my window, the life Persephone had begun to create in the Underworld uplifted my mood. She was the goddess of life; the goddess of my heart. I slammed my hand down on the desk. She *belonged* to me.

Persephone's dark power was growing while she was in the Underworld—it all but purred in my presence like a siren's call. I sighed and poured myself another Scotch, downing it in one gulp. I was pouring my fourth when Tee materialised in my study. I poured another and handed it to her. It was difficult for a god to become drunk unless we drank rapidly in substantial quantities, but as I was apparently hosting a dinner this evening, I decided it would be best to avoid arriving rolling drunk.

'I hear lunch went well,' Hecate said with a straight face.

I glared at her, then looked down at my drink. 'Persephone is infuriating, yes.' I downed another Scotch. 'She's feisty and insolent, and I don't know whether I want to fuck her or send her to Tartarus.'

Hecate guffawed with laughter. 'You definitely want to fuck her, Hades.' She sank into a chair and took a sip of her Scotch. 'She's pissed off that you kidnapped her.'

I let out an exasperated sigh. 'I know. But what other choice did I have? I've messed up, haven't I? Binding her to me for three months and bringing her here?' I lifted my eyes to hers, then closed them.

'Don't behave like another Demeter, boss. Keeping her locked away like a prisoner and compelling her to fulfil your demands will extinguish her spark.' I brooded on her words. I was tempted to take the easy option—keeping her regardless of her wishes. After all, she was *mine*. But I longed for Persephone to choose me of her own free will, just as she had the first time.

Gods, this was a mess.

'Do you sense her dark power growing stronger?' I lifted my gaze to Hecate, and she nodded.

'It's like a sleeping dragon yearning to be awakened. I'm starting "magic" training with her. Would you like me to chat with her about it?'

I shook my head.

'You sure? It's simmering, fighting for release.' I tilted my head towards her. 'She needs to be able to control it.'

'Okay.' I sighed. 'Speak to her about it.'

Hecate stood, then paused and turned back to me. 'Oh, she feels the soul bond.'

My head snapped up. 'Has she told you?'

Hecate nodded. 'She's confused, Hades. Give her time to come to terms with it.'

'But Zeus wants to hold the first "event" for Persephone in fifteen days. What if she falls for another god before she "comes to terms"?' I grunted.

'That meddling asshole,' Hecate bit back. 'You'll win her heart, Hades. Stop doubting yourself. Maybe lose the attitude if you want to charm her, though.' I narrowed my eyes at the goddess. Rude. 'Come on. I'll meet you there.' She vanished, still clutching her Scotch.

I blew out a frustrated breath. 'They can wait for me,' I grumbled, finishing the last of the bottle, my heart clenching at the thought of Persephone ultimately rejecting me.

CHAPTER
NINE

PERSEPHONE

I gazed at my reflection and was pretty impressed.

I wore a strappy, plunge-neck, fitted emerald-green dress that flowed down to my ankles. The colour accentuated my green eyes, making them pop. The gold silk shift was visible through the sheer chiffon, with a wide gold belt cinching my waist.

Matching gold sandals featuring crisscrossed straps tied up my calves completed the look. My hair remained styled in a halo braid, and my makeup emphasised my eyes, cheekbones, and full lips. I grinned at myself, pleased with my first solo attempt at being a lady.

I was puckering up and adding a touch more dark berry lip colour when Tee appeared. I smiled and gave her a twirl as she raised a brow.

'You'll do.' My smile faded, and she laughed. Naturally, Tee was breathtaking in a black mid-calf leather dress, her intricately braided hair piled high on her head.

'Gee, thanks a million,' I bitched. She ignored my request to walk to dinner; instead, she flashed me there. I grunted upon arrival and swallowed thickly as the red wine I'd consumed threatened to make a reappearance.

'Stop freaking doing that,' I hissed.

She replied in a sultry murmur, 'Didn't want to be late,' before striding off.

As my eyes followed Tee's retreating form, I glanced around. People I didn't know mingled; a vast obsidian-coloured table was adorned with cutlery and cream crockery, accompanied by potted herbs scattered down the centre. The table, laden with baskets of fruit and bread, rested on a beautifully landscaped terrace.

My gaze was immediately drawn to the enormous planters, overflowing with narcissi and small cypress trees, before drifting to the view beyond the terrace—my meadow. It was soul-elevating; the sight, colour, and vitality of the plants, both outside and on the terrace, made my heart swell. I approached one planter and smiled as I ran my fingers over the tree's lush green foliage.

'Persephone!' A pair of strong hands gripped my waist, and I squealed as I was hoisted off my feet, and swung around to land in front of a man I'd never encountered. He was tall with wavy, chin-length auburn hair and a neatly trimmed beard. His topaz eyes sparkled with mirth, and his mouth twitched up at the corners as he tilted his head. Our eyes locked onto one other.

'Hermes, for gods' sake,' Tee snapped at him, slapping his shoulder.

'I'm sorry,' I whispered, looking up into his lovely face. 'I—'

'Don't remember me,' he interrupted with a kind smile. 'But I remember you, and I'm glad you're back. If only to stop your miserable bastard of a husband from being such a dismal fucker.' I let out a peal of laughter and decided I really liked Hermes—the mischievous herald of the gods. 'I see you're already making your mark again.' I squinted at him, and he nodded towards the abundance of blooms and trees outside the terrace.

I smiled coyly. 'Thanks.'

I grinned at Thanatos as he approached and stood beside Hermes, accompanied by a man I didn't recognise. The stranger was like the hero I'd envisioned from one of my romantasy novels. His Achilles-like golden hair tumbled around his shoulders, and when I lifted my gaze to him, his unfathomable honey-brown eyes flickered with curiosity.

What was with all these beautiful men?

'Lady Persephone. You look exquisite!' Thanatos took my hand and kissed my palm, making me squirm internally and blush. 'This is Charon.' He pointed at the stranger.

'Hello again, Lady Persephone. I'm glad you're home,' Charon said, then he shifted uncomfortably as I realised my smile had faltered. Was this my home? Absolutely not. I would *not* live with the shadowy god of death.

Ugh.

But I smiled brightly again and took his hand, whispering thanks.

'And I'm Dionysus,' a large man said as he squeezed between them. Dionysus was dashing, with a roguish smile, dressed in leather pants and a bright Hawaiian shirt that clung to his Corinthian shoulders. 'Not that you remember me.' He studied me for a few moments. 'But we were friends. And man, the fun we all had in the good old days.' Tee elbowed him in the stomach, making him grunt.

'Let's sit,' Tee instructed. 'Hades will be here momentarily.'

'Allow me,' Hermes said, taking my hand and leading me to the table. He pulled out my chair as I sat down, then plopped beside me. Thanatos sat on my other side, smiling happily, his gaze constantly flicking at me as though he thought I'd disappear again. It warmed my heart even more for him.

Stop it, Sephy. Don't get too attached. You're not staying.

I clenched my hands into fists beneath the table, maintaining the smile plastered on my face.

I heard the tinkling of female laughter and swung my head around to investigate. Striding alongside Hades, with an arm looped through his crooked elbow, was one of the most stunning women I'd ever seen. Her long red hair shone, like molten lava pouring over her shoulders and down to her waist; her warm beige skin glowed with opalescence, complemented by the layers of gold bangles that dangled from her arms. The woman's eyes were feline, topaz, and utterly luminous. Her short, fitted, strapless red silk dress showcased her long sexy legs. As they chatted,

Hades' leaned down to her, and his lips curled into a playful smile. That smile transformed his face from a vicious beauty to one of jaw-dropping beauty.

Jealousy seeped through my bloodstream like poison, twisting my stomach into knots and causing my breath to catch in my lungs.

*Control yourself; he's not yours. You don't want hi*m! Ugh, I was about to punch myself in the face.

'That's Minthe,' Hermes whispered to me, and I sensed Thanatos stiffen as he cleared his throat. 'She's desperate to become the queen of the Underworld. Watch your back, kiddo.'

'It's not my concern. Hades can marry whoever he pleases... even a floozy like that,' I retorted. Hermes tilted his head and raised a brow as he regarded me, while Thanatos choked on a laugh. I narrowed my eyes at him and gritted my teeth.

'Still as fierce as ever, I see.' Hermes chuckled. 'But you've always been a dreadful liar.' I shot him a death glare before turning to Thanatos, looping my arm through his and resting my head on his shoulder as I looked up at him and smiled. Thanatos widened his eyes and gulped. I followed his gaze. Hades' eyes shone gold for a fleeting moment; the expression he wore could have frozen the infernos of Tartarus. His jaw was like concrete. He pulled out a chair for Minthe and sat down beside her.

'Thank you for coming, everybody. Please enjoy your meal,' Hades' silky voice purred. He avoided making eye contact with me. When he snapped his fingers, bowls of steaming food appeared on the table, along with trays of meats and cheeses, and bottles of wine galore. I seized a bottle and filled my glass, taking a lengthy gulp of red wine. I refused to even glance at Hades. He was such a typical god: wanted 'his' Persephone back, yet eager to screw anything with a pulse. Disgust slithered through me like a viper, making me drink my wine more quickly, until Tee leaned across Thanatos and placed a hand on my arm.

'Slow down, babe. It's not what it seems,' she whispered.

I harrumphed at her and finished the wine anyway, with Thanatos refilling my glass.

Hades fixed his gaze on mine and hellfire—the way he looked at me—like a predator sighting its prey. The wine hit my chest and stomach in a warm rush, and a shivery wave of irritation and heat scorched my skin, igniting my reckless, impulsive side. I should have kept my lips sealed, but gods, when it came to this man, I had zero control over my mouth.

'So, I didn't know you and Dionysus were friends with the kidnapping god of *death* and *shadows*?' I said with vitriol in my voice, loud enough for everyone to hear as I turned to Hermes.

'Oh, I wish they had popcorn on this menu... I suppose wine will have to do,' Hermes said, tipping his glass to his lips. I jabbed him in the ribs with my elbow, eliciting a grunt-cough from him. Thanatos and Charon almost choked on their drinks while I smiled sweetly at Hermes, who then burst into laughter. My gaze flicked to Hades. His lips thinned, his nostrils flared, but the skin between his brows creased. A stab of remorse stung like a bitch, and I wanted to smack myself.

Tee swiftly rescued the situation. 'These two reprobates have been allies for years. They like hanging out with us because the Olympians suck. Or perhaps it's mostly for the wine?' Tee regarded Hermes and Dionysus with narrowed eyes and a slight smile, while both gods grinned mischievously and raised their glasses in a fake toast. I giggled and took another long sip of wine.

'Eat, Sephy,' Tee instructed in a low voice.

'Yes, Mother.' I smirked at her and selected a variety of meats, cheeses, breads, and fruits.

The remainder of the meal flew by, and I had fun chatting with everyone except Hades and fucking *Minthe*. I stood up as people left the table to mingle, drink, and chat, when I spied Minthe approaching.

'Persephone.' The sultry way she said my name made my hackles rise, and I had to exert every ounce of self-control not to punch her in the nose. I'll likely need a stepladder to reach her—the tall bitch. 'I'm Minthe. It's good to see you back.'

'Is it?' I tipped my head and smirked at her.

'Well, of course it is.' She smiled, but it didn't reach her eyes.

'Well, don't worry. I'm not staying. You can carry on shagging the god of the dead... I honestly don't give a shit.' All conversation ceased, and everyone's eyes were on me and the hoe bag. She smiled again, and this time, it reached her eyes. I'd hit the nail on the head, and my stomach plummeted to my pretty sandals. As I turned away, I caught Hades' eyes; he looked like he wanted to throttle me, or perhaps bury me in Tartarus. I smiled brightly at him, before making my way to Tee and Hermes. *That'll teach him to kidnap me, the tosser.*

'You're playing with fire.' Tee shook her head, but Hermes and Dionysus chuckled darkly.

'This is splendid entertainment,' Dionysus whispered, and Tee glowered at him. 'You're still a pocket rocket, Persephone. Poor Hades.' He and Hermes had coughing fits, and I smiled wickedly. Then, slightly tipsy and full of devilment, I went to flirt shamelessly with Thanatos and Charon.

I INSISTED that Thanatos and Charon walk me to my room, refusing Tee's attempts to take me. As I beamed at them, I linked my arms through theirs and shot Hades a haughty look.

'Come on, boys. Take me to my bed.' A muscle ticked in Hades' cheek; he appeared to be grinding his jaw so hard he might break a tooth. I hoped he did. The fucking asshole. I turned away from him, carefully trying not to wobble on my heels. The combination of far too much wine and sore feet was a miserable mix. 'Can you carry me? Please?' I batted my lashes at Thanatos, who cast Charon a worried look. Charon merely smirked in return.

'Of course, my queen.'

'Don't call me that,' I hissed. He pursed his lips but bent down, slipping an arm behind my knees as I wrapped my arms around his neck. He then walked forward, with Charon following. I peeked over his shoulder and gave Hades a small wave—he appeared as if he was about to combust.

Excellent.

Once back, the boys left me, and I sank into the soft mattress, brooding. Tee appeared in a flash of white light, hands on her hips.

'What the Fates are you playing at, Sephy?' she ground out through gritted teeth.

'Nothing,' I replied, smoothing my hand over my dress. 'He can bang Minthe all he likes. I have no doubt he will... He's that much of an arrogant prick.' I chewed on my bottom lip as I stared at my clenched fists. 'Maybe he'll let me go home. I don't want to be here, Tee.' I looked up at her, tears blurring my vision. I was *not* crying over Hades; I was crying because I was his prisoner.

Ugh. I needed to stop drinking; it was making me act like a scorned housewife.

'You're jealous!' She flashed me a smug smile.

'Am not!' I jumped up, then sighed. 'I'm confused. The attraction I feel for him is making me angry.' My irritation spiralled. 'The gods think it's perfectly fine to screw around, and that's not who I am, Tee. I refuse to be just a notch on a bedpost.' She smiled at my words, and I quickly added, 'Not for Hades or any of them.'

Tee sat on the bed, and I flopped down next to her. 'He's not screwing Minthe, Sephy, even though she's trying her hardest to seduce him.' At her words, jealousy sucker-punched me again. 'They were a couple before he met you... the first time. And when you vanished, let's just say she's been keen on taking your crown and is trying everything to achieve it.'

That made Minthe number one on my people-I-want-to-kill-slowly list. 'What a conniving cow!'

'Mmhm,' Tee said. 'Don't treat him like that, Sephy. You're killing him.'

'What? He walked in with her clinging to him like a barnacle. She's like an alley cat on ecstasy around him. Ugh. But the way he smiled at her...' I paused.

'He was being polite. He's known her for years, and like I said, they were once an item, but that was a long time ago, Sephy. Stop over-analysing things.'

'I don't care. He's like freaking unhappy Gilmore.' I pouted. Tee rolled her eyes and shook her head. 'What? I absolutely do *not* fancy the grumpy god of death!'

I brooded a little longer. Was she right about Hades and Minthe? And why the freaking hell was it affecting me so badly? I was utterly bewildered. What *did* I want? I didn't know. The only thing I knew was that something about him transfixed me, and I felt like something connected me to him. I also knew I wanted to blast Minthe with a roundhouse kick.

It's the alcohol making you think irrationally. You don't care if Hades is banging Minthe.

'Let's get you to bed. Come on.' Tee helped me to my feet, and I staggered into the bathroom, changing into a pair of pale green silk PJ shorts and a matching cami. I looked at my wild eyes in the mirror and released a heavy sigh. I couldn't think clearly. I couldn't function. I needed water, and I needed sleep.

As SOON AS my head hit the pillow, I found myself back in my otherworldly garden and everything felt right with the world. A cascade of butterflies flitted among the brightly coloured and fragrant blooms, and I inhaled deeply. I needed the scent of nature and the feeling it gave me; it was like my life force. I walked around, trailing my fingertips over the flowers, until I reached the vast patch of narcissi. I bent down and took in the scent—an opulent sensation, like wet summer lawns—intense, yet cool and floral.

'Persephone.' That low, lyrical voice jolted me from my reverie, and I stiffened. That voice—the very one that had haunted my dreams over the past twelve months—I knew who it was, and nausea gripped me. It was *his* voice. It was Hades.

I rose and turned slowly. He towered over me, about six feet away, still clad in his black jeans and black shirt—looking like a character from a steamy romance book cover. Had I imagined the mysterious man from my dreams to resemble him? To sound like him? It was a dream, so it was highly probable. It was *my* dream, after all. I had control.

'I want my dagger back.' I jutted out my chin.

'Of course, my queen.'

'Don't call me that!' I whisper-hissed, trying not to get lost in his captivating eyes.

His gaze dropped to my chest, and he shifted slightly. I felt my cheeks flush; my nipples were hard against the silk of my cami, and heat poured between my legs. I watched as his eyes ravaged me, and an ache in my core made my breath feel laboured.

'You think I'm beautiful.' His mouth quirked into a half-smile as his eyes met mine again. Wait, what? Oh, crap. I *had* told him so. But it was my dream, so I guess he'd know that.

'You're not bad.' I offered an evil grin.

'Persephone,' he said again. His voice was strained. 'I've missed you.'

'Have you?' I said, reflecting on Minthe. Why *was* I so bothered by Minthe?

'Yes. May I touch you?'

'Not until you beg.' Gods, I *loved* this dream.

'I shall never beg.' At his words, my jaw tightened. He was still an arrogant dick, even in my dream, but before I could utter a response, his eyes sparkled with delight, a sly, relaxed smile spreading across his lips. Shadows leaked from him, swirling between us.

'You think you can intimidate me with shadows?'

'No. I intend to seduce you with them,' he drawled, causing my breath to still in my lungs. As the shadows started twisting over my stomach, curling around my aching breasts and over my hard nipples, I bit back a moan.

'That's cheating... Oh, God,' I whimpered.

'*Gods.*' His smile was feral as more shadows crept down to my thighs and under my shorts. I locked eyes with him. They were full of desire, causing me to gasp, filling me with a need I'd never felt before. His shadows licked my body like a thousand tongues, teasing and stroking until my knees turned weak. When the shadows lapped at my clit, I cried out—the twisting and licking continued until I broke into a thousand pieces. My back arched as release tore through me—the vortex of pleasure enveloping me caused my core to pulse, and my thighs tightened as wave after wave of release crashed through me, and then my knees buckled.

MY EYES FLEW OPEN, and I heaved a breath. My body tingled, and a sense of bliss enveloped me. I was relaxed for the first time in ages, stretching and yawning like a contented cat. Who knew dreams could be so vivid and so freaking satisfying? I had never experienced such release. Ever. Then my mind switched to Hades. Why him? But I pushed the thought aside—it was just a dream. It meant nothing.

The magic in the ceiling glowed softly with tiny stars, which indicated it was still the middle of the night. I jumped from the bed and grabbed a bottle of water, then something caught my eye. I walked to my bedside table, and there lay my dagger. I frowned. Shrugging, I snagged the books from my desk. Settling down on the sofa, I leafed through the first book; it was time to learn more about the gods, Hades, and the Underworld.

CHAPTER
TEN

HADES

'Leave me.' I turned to Minthe, who was overstaying her welcome. I poured another whisky and settled onto the sofa.

'But Hades, the night is still young. Let's have some fun,' she purred as she knelt between my legs. As her hand moved to my belt, I grabbed it.

'It's still a no, Minthe. I'm married. Do not push me.'

Minthe laughed, and I felt my temper prickle. 'You're not married to *her*, Hades. She doesn't even know you... Not like I do. No one understands you as well as I do. We're good together.' She licked her lips, glancing up at me from beneath her lashes. 'She treated you terribly at dinner.' I glared at her; the truth stung. 'You know I truly love you, and I'll do *anything* to please you.'

I stood up and pulled her to her feet. I could have fucked her senseless and got rid of my pent-up irritation and sexual frustration, but the only person I wanted was Persephone.

Gods, I was so screwed.

'Goodnight, Minthe.' I pushed her out the door; her protests were lost as I slammed it.

'Fucking Persephone,' I grunted as I poured another drink. She *had* humiliated me at the meal, much to the delight of my old friends, Hermes and Dionysus. The look of defiance she wore so well only made me crave her more. I wanted to bend her over my knee and spank the insolence out of her, and the sight of other men touching her drove me to fury, wanting to tear their dicks from their bodies. I grimaced and knocked back my Scotch before pouring another.

Morpheus appeared. 'She is dreaming, Your Highness.' I raised my glass to him as he bowed and disappeared.

Persephone had no idea I had orchestrated her dreamscape or that I possessed the ability to dream-walk. It had been the only way to visit and converse with her. But this time, I would reveal myself.

Taking a deep breath, I willed myself to her. Looking at her, leaning over and smelling the narcissi made my cock swell. The silk shorts clung to her pert butt, and when she turned around and saw me, her nipples hardened like pebbles, and I had almost lost it. She was desperately impertinent and infuriatingly beautiful. It had demanded every ounce of self-control to refrain from bending her over and pounding my cock into the wilful enchantress.

Touching her hot, desperate body with my shadows and watching her fall apart so quickly because of me was sheer bliss. I hungered for the feel of her, the taste of her, and her moans of need.

I *had* to have her.

Afterwards, I watched her sleep for a moment, her face relaxed and sated, and then I placed her blade on the bedside table and vanished.

Her body responding to me as it always had served to lighten my melancholy. I yearned to be inside her—to fill her in all the right ways—but the time would come, and it would be she who begged for it, not I.

ELEVEN

PERSEPHONE

I was trying to keep my head above water, committed to the belief I *would* find a way out of this fuck-upery, but with each passing day, I drowned a little bit more.

I was well and truly *trapped* in the Underworld.

My favourite place became the library, and Simmy was one of my favourite people. Over the following week or so, I spent time with Simos and books, learning more about Greek mythology and the gods, particularly about Hades and Persephone. I was eager to ask Tee a million questions.

Tee was brilliant with magic, as you'd expect the goddess of magic to be, but even though she somehow knew about my dark magic, I couldn't summon it in train-ing. I was too frightened. Nevertheless, she didn't push me; she gave me breathing space, and we focused on combat training instead, often with Thanatos and Charon.

I hadn't seen Hades, which I kept telling myself was a good thing, but the pull in my chest was getting stronger; the urge to see him infuriated me. I hadn't dreamed of the garden either, which made me angsty. I was missing my ethereal oasis, and even though it was just a dream, the respite of being in that otherworldly place sated me.

I still had precisely eighty-two days before I could leave unless Hades freed me beforehand, which was unlikely. I didn't like how my heart clenched when I thought of leaving Hades, but I dismissed it as a stupid crush on the insanely beautiful hunk of arrogance.

I showered and dressed in a leather bustier, leather pants, and lightweight boots. I was enjoying a breakfast of French toast and crispy bacon when Tee appeared.

'Hey, I've got a bazillion questions for you,' I said, taking a bite of bacon.

'We need to talk first, Sephy.' She appeared agitated, prompting me to stop eating and lower my fork.

'What's up? I thought we were training?' Unease skittered through me, settling over me like a prickly blanket.

'We are. But I need to speak to you first.' Tee poured two coffees and handed me one.

'There's a problem,' she began.

'What? Something other than me being kidnapped and held here against my will by the high and mighty Lord of Shadows?' I gave her a pointed look, which caused her expression to drop.

'No. Worse. Much worse.'

My heart hammered violently against my chest. 'Worse?' I croaked.

She nodded. 'You know I mentioned what a pain in the ass Zeus is?' I gave a slow nod.

'Well, he also loves meddling, and'—she hesitated, taking a deep breath—'he's decided that Hades isn't the only one entitled to woo you and claim you as a wife.'

'You freaking what? What does that even mean?'

'They...' she whispered.

'They what?' I stood and placed my hands on my hips.

'He and several other gods have always been jealous of Hades' love for you and your relationship with him. The love you shared was boundless; you were like two halves of the same circle. You brought balance to him and the Underworld, and often kicked his grumpy ass, but he would've burned the world for you.' I narrowed my eyes at her words. Was that true? 'You were revered, Sephy... Beautiful, fiery, passionate, and immensely powerful. This time, they want a chance to win you as their wife.'

I stood speechless, staring at her, running a hand over my face as I began to pace the room, knots of tension balling in my stomach. 'So I'm like a prize in their sick little game? An object of their sexual desire and ego? That's not right, Tee!' My tone rose until I ended up screeching. 'They can't be serious?'

Tee exhaled raggedly. 'Oh, they're dead serious, Sephy.'

'No, no, no, no.' I buried my head in my hands. 'This can't be happening. How do I get out of it? Out of here?'

'Zeus knows Hades has you for three months. You must choose a husband before the ninetieth day.' I was caught between disbelief and a mess of a hundred other emotions. My stomach rolled, and a violent shudder ran through me.

'I don't want a husband. I especially don't want a god as a husband. I need to go home, Tee. Please take me home.' Tears filled my eyes and spilled down my cheeks. 'I'm trapped in a living nightmare. And it's all Hades' fault for bringing me here!'

Fury surged through my veins and poured into my chest, causing the dark magic to sizzle. The more I seethed, the closer the darkness came to boiling point. 'I'm going to destroy them all,' I gritted through clenched teeth. My rage was ready to erupt, dark magic pressing against my skin—a power I still couldn't control. For the briefest moment, I wanted to level the castle. I swallowed hard. 'They've made me a prize to be claimed. Let them learn what it means to worship a queen forged of fire and thorns.' I growled, shaking with anger.

Tee placed her hands on either side of my face, bringing me under control. I felt her power dominating mine, and I closed my eyes, panting hard.

'Calm down, babe. We'll sort something out before Zeus's deadline. I promise. But it's better Hades found you before Zeus.' My eyes snapped open. 'It's true, Sephy. Hades is a fair god. He likes structure and has a pole up his ass, but he's honourable. Just go with it for now... Play their silly little game. You catch more flies with honey than vinegar, remember? Use it to your advantage.' Her over-whelming magic calmed me—my heart rate eased, and my breaths slowed. I nodded my head and wiped a hand across my face.

Tee handed me a glass of nectar, which I sipped silently —it restored my badly jangled nerves. Once I calmed down, I lost myself in my musings. One: I was stuck here for the next three months. Two: apparently, I was a long-lost goddess, once married to the ludicrously attractive, arrogant god of the Underworld, who wanted me back. Three: some of his fellow gods also fancied me as their wife... As if being trapped in a marriage would be bearable if the man had good cheekbones. Four: if this happened, it would mean having sex with one of them.

I wondered if I could find an active volcano to fling myself into.

But I couldn't lose my cool again. Having a meltdown would work me into an anxious mess, and let's be real—no one needed that, least of all my mental health. I had to keep my head, trust Tee, and figure something out. Reflecting on my earlier conversation with Tee, could I make a difference? Could I help nullify the banishment of witchcraft in the mortal world. Play it smart and behave myself to save the exiled covens?

I could do it. Yes... No... Yes... Yes, I could tolerate these divine idiots for three months, couldn't I?

Fuck. I must be certifiably insane.

Tee's voice shook me from my thoughts. 'The first "event" is in a week. Aphrodite is throwing a welcoming party in your honour.'

'Aphrodite? I'm definitely not into women,' I gasped, and Tee laughed.

'Don't knock it until you've tried it, Sephy. But no.' Tee flashed me a cheeky smile. 'It's a welcome party, that's all. Oh, and you're allowed to bring an escort of your choice.'

I exhaled in relief. Tee might be right. Could I indulge in their silly little game and get something from it? I'd give it my best shot and enjoy being the object of the gods' affections without cringing too much—for a time, at least.

But marry one of them? Not a chance in hell.

'Great,' I muttered, wringing my hands together.

'Hades wants you to have an early dinner with him,' Tee said, observing me. At the thought of seeing him again, my stomach made an idiotic dipping motion, and edgy nervousness washed over me. Knots of apprehension tangled with shame over the dream twisted in my gut. I gave her a curt nod.

'Let's go and burn off some of that rage. Come on. Let's go training and kick Charon and Thanatos's butts.'

EXHAUSTED, I sipped a glass of nectar to ease my sore muscles while Tee prepared omelettes.

'So, tell me about gods having fangs.'

Tee's head turned, her surprise evident. 'He showed you his fangs?' Her brows knitted together, and I nodded. 'Hmm,' she mused. 'Their fangs are retractable.'

I squinted at her, wondering why he'd not concealed

them. 'He said you were behind the whole blood-drinking scheme. Is that true?'

Tee released a throaty chuckle. 'Yeah, I was a bit of a dick in the old days.' I let out a surprised laugh, and she shrugged. 'It's true.' She placed the omelettes on the table and I dove in immediately. 'The custom of consuming blood has always held a magical and mysterious significance. It serves as a symbolic connection to life and death. I drank blood during my feasts—'

'Yuck.' My mouth twisted in disgust, and she laughed.

'I came up with the idea that the gods retain their powers, even without worship, after Titanomachy.'

'The great war between the Titans and the gods,' I mused, and she inclined her chin.

'Zeus despised the concept, but the prospect of possibly losing the cosmos one day was enough for him to agree. After all, no one is infallible. Even the gods.'

'But they're immortal?'

'Nothing that can be killed is truly immortal, Sephy.'

'I suppose.' My hand moved to my divine blade, and a thrum of energy skittered across my palm.

'So they all drank my potion and gained an alternative source of lifeforce. That's part of the reason they lost interest in the humans and the chaos they were causing in the mortal realm. Many humans are driven by arrogance and greed.' She exhaled in frustration. 'And it's a significant reason why Zeus respects me, even though he hates my guts.'

'He's a douche-canoe.' At my words, Tee released a peal of laughter.

'I could brew the potion for you. Do you fancy having fangs?' Tee gave me a sly grin.

'Eww, no thanks. Fangless is good if you don't mind.' I scrunched up my face, and she spluttered a laugh. 'Anyway, I've been swotting up on the gods. Erm, particularly Hades.' I felt blood rush to my cheeks at the mention of sort of being a total stalker over him.

Then, the questions fell out of my mouth in one long exhale. 'He kidnapped me, but he also took the original Persephone, didn't he? Was she like me? Do I look like her? Is that why he kidnapped me? And her poor mother was frantic with worry. What happened to Demeter?'

'You are the original Persephone, Sephy, and you know it.' I wrinkled my nose and the odd feeling that she might be right gnawed at my gut.

'But how?'

Tee gave a half-shrug in response. 'Hades will need to tell you the entire story.' I grumbled expletives at her words. 'Just know, Sephy, your soul is hers; your body and face are hers. You are her.' I scrunched my brows together.

'Even with the remote chance I am her—which is very much debatable—I'm a different person. I'm me.' I squinted at Tee and raised my chin.

'Well, you're certainly more feisty and stroppy than you used to be.' I coughed out a shocked laugh. 'You've been reborn, Sephy.'

'Reborn?'

'Yes. I can't exactly tell you what happened to you... that's down to Hades, sorry.' Tee's brow furrowed. 'But I can tell you that rebirth is a possibility. Souls in the Underworld have the option to reincarnate. They drink from the river Lethe to forget their former lives and are propelled towards new birth; they are reincarnated. Many choose that path. It keeps the circle of life going.'

'Oh,' I muttered. 'But I didn't drink from the Lethe?' Tee shook her head, and confusion addled my brain. If I *were* Persephone, then just... how the fuck? I clenched my jaw as she continued.

'You were reborn to Hermione's daughter, who, as you know, died in childbirth.'

'My mother, yes.' I swallowed roughly.

'Your grandmother at the time was the High Priestess of the New York High Coven.' I gave a brief nod, and Tee hesitated for a heartbeat. 'You're not a witch, Sephy.'

I shot from my seat. 'Of course I'm a witch.' I gritted my teeth. 'This is bullshit.'

'Your flora magic... Your dark power. It's what you had before. You're a goddess... Not a witch.'

'No. No. I'm a witch. My grandmother taught me about magic. Taught me how to manage my dark magic.' I shook my head in vehement denial.

'She taught you to suppress your power, Sephy. She had no idea what it truly was, but you need to be able to control the shadow magic. You're a goddess. A goddess of immense power. The goddess of spring, life, and fertility, among other things.'

I was torn between disbelief and an impending hysterical meltdown as panic sliced through my chest, sending adrenaline pumping through my veins. I wasn't a witch... I was a deity.

'Shadow magic?' She nodded. 'I'm *actually* a goddess?' I muttered in disbelief. 'All this time...'

'You didn't believe me. I know.'

Well, this was just the tip of the fucked-up iceberg. 'What other *things*?' I whispered.

Tee shifted in her seat. 'Your name means Bringer of Death—'

'What? Am I... Was I evil?' I gasped.

Tee smiled kindly. 'You've never been cruel, Persephone. Not once. You've always been fair and kind. But you have a darker side.' My gaze shot to hers, my eyes widening. 'You can heal and create life, but you can also take life away. That's why we need to work on controlling your power.' I nodded wordlessly, glancing down at my clenched fists. 'You are also the goddess of reincarnation and ghosts.'

'I can heal?' She nodded at my question.

'Your powers are growing again, Sephy. I can feel them.'

'I can't even...' I whispered, my mind a spinning vortex. 'And reincarnation and ghosts?' I breathed, frowning.

'And mistress of the Furies.'

'The *Furies*?' Tee nodded with amusement.

'Let's not overload your brain. I'll fill you in on everything you need to know as we train, alright? We have a lot of work to do on this shadow magic of yours. You've got to get it under control.'

'Shadow magic?' I repeated again as I shook my head

slightly; my life was going from crazy-la-la to straight Insanity-land.

'Here.' Tee refilled my glass of nectar, which I sipped. It tempered my jangled nerves and helped clear my spinning head. I sat there, mulling over her words for... I wasn't sure how long, only that it felt like forever.

I'm not a witch; I'm a goddess. A real-life goddess. But that didn't erase the truth: the gods had slaughtered so many with magic.

Tee roused me from my reverie. 'Getting back to what you asked about. Okay, yes, Hades has sort of kidnapped you.'

'Sort of? Really?' I let out a sharp laugh.

'Well, the daft, grumpy bugger rushed into it without thinking it through properly; he was so desperate to get you back, and now look at the mess we're in.'

I closed my eyes, my heart sped up, and as I took another drink, I felt a slight tremor in my hands. It was true; I was in a giant dumpster fire of a situation as far as the gods were concerned.

'But when he lost you the first time...' She hesitated, and my eyes snapped to hers. 'He exploded with rage, Sephy. He killed thousands of innocents.'

'What... what did he do?' The words scraped out of me. I couldn't reconcile the man I'd spent time with as someone capable of slaughtering innocents.

Then again, the gods had never needed a reason to slaughter witches. So what the hell did I know?

'He is mighty, Sephy. He has control over the Underworld, which is essentially the Earth from the crust down.

Because of this, he is also the richest god.' I gave her a 'carry on' gesture with my hand. 'He exploded. And, I mean, exploded. His grief over losing you caused him to lose his mind. His rage caused many earthquakes, killing thousands of mortals. He was absolutely devastated once we managed to calm him down.'

I gasped. 'Holy crap.' Was it my fault so many people had died? A storm of emotions rushed through me—every fibre of my being was swept up in the onslaught.

At times, I could taste his sorrow; it felt almost tangible. Was it due to his anguish over losing Persephone and his ensuing actions? That tug in my chest intensified, threatening to drag my heart from my ribcage. I had an overwhelming urge to see him, but I squished that little fucker back down before I bolted out of the kitchen to find him, like a total creeper.

'And as for Demeter, no one has seen her since you disappeared. We believe, with Zeus's permission, she took herself off to Delos, which was Artemis's court. The original legend of you and Hades isn't true, you know, Sephy.'

'What do you mean?' I tilted my head at the Titan.

A faint smile danced on her lips as she took a drink. 'You first met Hades in Olympus at one of Zeus's gatherings. It was the first one your mother allowed you to attend. She was quite... controlling. You were essentially like her prisoner—'

'Great gods. That's so not cool.'

'Yeah. Demeter kept you on her island for centuries. Your only friends were nymphs, and no one had ever laid eyes on you. She was petrified of losing you.'

'Demeter sounds like she had some major parenting issues.'

Tee huffed a laugh. 'She sure did. Anyway, being able to smell and taste emotions—'

'Which is freaky on so many levels,' I interrupted, prompting her smirk. 'Can any of the other gods taste emotions?'

'Only the big three: Hades, Zeus, and Poseidon. Though, Hades can also see through lies and into souls.'

'Into souls?' My eyes rounded, and she cough-laughed.

'Yup. Anyway, Hades sensed how lonely and miserable you were. When you chatted with him, you opened up and confessed that you wished for your freedom from your mother. He understood, having come from a fucked-up family himself. Zeus has always bullied him.'

'Bullied him?'

'Yeah, he constantly jibes Hades, but he's quite envious of him. He resents how his people adore him and how powerful he is. Naturally, once Hades had you, Zeus's jealousy only grew worse. He's an egotistical prick.'

'That's awful. Why doesn't Hades challenge him?'

Tee shrugged. 'He's gotten used to it over the aeons. He once told me that the only person you can change in your family is yourself, and that comes down to how you choose to interact with them. But he keeps his distance from Zeus as much as possible.'

'Was Zeus really Persephone's father?'

'*Your* father.' She shot me a narrow-eyed look. 'Nope, we don't believe so. Demeter has never revealed his iden-tity, but you've got to remember, Sephy, that the original gods were created, not born. Though they consider them-selves siblings, there's no DNA going on. They're beings of magic and power.'

I mulled over her words for a few seconds. 'Persephone —erm, I—must have trusted Hades to confide in him about Demeter?'

She gave a half-shrug. 'Like I said, he's a nice guy. Anyway, he offered you sanctuary in the Underworld, for as long as you wished. You both staged the kidnapping because Demeter rarely let you out of her sight.'

'Did he really split the earth and come out in a chariot?'

'Yup.' She grinned.

'Like a knight in shining armour,' I breathed, a little bemused.

'Hades knew he loved you from the moment he laid eyes on you.'

'And Persephone?'

'You'—she hesitated—'most probably fell in love with him the first time you met. You were repressed, because of your mother. You weren't accustomed to men. Hades gave you time, but it didn't take long until you and he were—'

'Okay. I get the picture,' I cut in, raising a hand. Hecate grinned, then immediately sobered.

'You ate six pomegranate seeds from the Underworld each time you visited, so you could spend half the year with Hades and half the year with Demeter. You felt guilty about leaving her. When Hades was bound to the Under-world, you had to return here to be with him. You made a conscious decision to divide your time between them both.'

'That must have been hard for Hades?' I squinted at her, and she sighed in response.

'It was, but he would agree to anything to make you happy.' She paused for a beat. 'A bond forged by true fate is unbreakable. It exists between you and Hades, Sephy, whether you want to admit it or not.'

AFTER NATURE, books were the second best thing, so before I had to face Hades, I escaped to the library again for the next few hours. I buried the emotions that Tee's words elicited in me. Now was not the time to throw a hissy fit. I mulled over Tee's words regarding Zeus's relationship with Hades but also suppressed the overwhelming feelings of compassion.

The thought of seeing Hades, after discovering I was truly *the* Persephone—especially following that lust-filled dream—sent nerves and embarrassment slithering through my body. But, I chastised myself; it was merely a dream. He knew nothing of my intense attraction to him. Then I reflected on Tee's conversation and what Hades had done when he lost Persephone—me—but I buried those thoughts deep within the darkest recesses of my mind.

I curled up in a chair and escaped the fuck-upery that was my life as I became engrossed in a fantasy romance book.

Simos's voice broke the spell. 'Look at you, reading your book without a care in the world.'

'Well, nothing cures a bad day quite like reading and escaping into make-believe. Plus, I'm at a particularly spicy part.' I grinned at him, and his cute face flushed adorably.

'I love a bit of spice.' He winked at me, and I let out a splutter of laughter.

'Tell me, Sim.' I set the book down. 'Do you remember Persephone from... from before?'

He shook his head. 'Nope. I lived in Dionysus's realm. I've never seen much of Olympus.'

'So how'd you end up here?'

'I was Dionysus's librarian. He gifted me to Hades to manage his library.'

'Gifted you?' I puckered my brow. 'Gods can't own people.'

'Ah, Dionysus isn't so bad. He asked me first,' Simos replied with a half-shrug.

'And now you serve Hades?'

'I don't serve him. I work for him. Don't believe badly of him; he's a great boss. He cares for and protects those loyal to him. We all love him.'

'Oh.' I didn't know what else to say. That statement intrigued me, along with the story Tee told me about him. He was an arrogant prick, but was he really an okay person? I shelved the thought.

'So!' I jumped up, probably having the best idea ever. 'I've got several, though I'm not entirely certain how many "events" to attend. Like dinners and such, I suppose.' I threw my arms up in an "I haven't a clue" gesture. 'And I'm allowed an escort. I wondered'—I looked into Simos's eyes as he studied me—'if you might be my escort? You'd at least get to see more of Olympus.'

He took a step back as his eyes roamed over me. 'Like a date?'

'No, you moron. As my friend.'

He raised his shoulders and tilted his head slightly. 'Disappointing, but yes. I'd love to be your date.'

'Not a date. Idiot.'

He chuckled wickedly. 'Once you've gone Satyr, you never look back. We're great lovers.'

'Ugh. You're grim.'

He laughed evilly, then sobered up as his gaze met mine again. 'You're a good person, Persephone.'

I hesitated, feeling my heart swell. 'Thanks, Sim. And you're a good friend.'

THE TIME CAME to see Hades, and after my chat with Tee, I dressed to impress—perhaps I could persuade him to free me? He sounded like a reasonable man, after all. Plus, if I were *his* Persephone—that thought elicited a pleasant shudder through me—surely he'd do whatever I asked of him?

I opted for a bold, form-fitting deep blue jumpsuit featuring a sleeveless lace top tied around my neck, with silk noil trousers draping softly against my legs. A pair of ballet pumps in the matching colour completed the look, and I was good to go. I left my hair loose and coloured my lips with pale coral lipstick. I left my divine blade in the room; I couldn't risk angering Hades by threatening him again. Not if I wanted to get the hell out of here.

As my thoughts turned to Hades, anxiety bloomed in my chest. I took a deep breath through my nose and shook out my shoulders, but tension lingered deep in my muscles.

Tee walked in and gave me an appraising look.

'Let's go.' She extended her hand, and as soon as she touched me, we teleported to Hades. I found myself in a lovely, expansive room; the walls were infused with glowing light and painted a soft gold, while plush velvet sofas and chairs encircled an immense fireplace, with sumptuous rugs giving the huge space a cosy feel. The dining table was as black as onyx, embedded with sparkles that twinkled like scattered moondust. Enormous doors filled one wall, standing open and leading to the beautiful terrace where we had dined.

'This room is lovely,' I whispered as I touched the table laden with a massive vase of asphodels.

'It's part of Hades' private chambers.' My head whipped around at her words, and she let out a throaty chuckle. 'Hades will bring you back; don't go wandering off alone again.' She gave me a pointed look, and raised a finger. 'And don't try killing him. Have fun,' she said, winking at me before disappearing again.

Gods and baby kittens everywhere. I was in his private chambers. *If I were Persephone, I must have been here before... and in his bedroom.* The thought made my stomach tumble, but I pushed it aside. I wandered around the space, trailing my fingers over the furniture, when my eyes were drawn to a large screen with intricate designs etched into the metal. As I peered behind, I saw an enormous hole in the tiled floor, filled with what appeared to be sizeable pieces of beautiful black opal. I picked one up and rolled it between my palms, feeling the humming energy of the gem as my gaze fell upon a spectacular eight-foot rose tree—sadly, a very dead eight-foot rose tree.

'Oh, baby! What happened?' I whispered as I made my way towards it.

'You happened.' His voice made me whirl around. The ridiculously handsome, hulking form of the god of the Underworld stood relaxed, resembling some dashing hero from a sexy-as-hell romance novel—and a host of hummingbirds took flight in my belly.

Control yourself, Sephy. For fuck's sake.

'What do you mean?' My throat thickened as I met his gaze.

'When you vanished, life in the Underworld gradually dwindled too, Persephone. Including my vis vitae.'

A tangled web of emotions choked my throat as guilt dug like ice-tipped fingers. It was my fault he was so miserable—my fault that he lost control all those years ago. I wanted to go to him and wrap my arms around him ... comfort him. The pull in my chest was growing stronger.

Instead, I swallowed down the bitter knot of emotions and bit my lower lip as my gaze fell to the floor. After a few beats, my eyes met his again.

'May I?' I pointed to the rose tree, and he inclined his chin. 'You'll be fine,' I reassured as I stroked the thick trunk of the tree. My flora magic pulsed within me, its powerful energy skittering across my skin—it surged, heady and rich through my veins. At my touch, the tree slowly transformed; the bare branches shifted colour as glossy green leaves with toothed edges sprouted, followed by a thick array of rose buds. The sharp thorns contrasted beautifully with the blooms as they unfurled into a mix of very full-bloom purple and red roses. I breathed in their scent and smiled—a magical experience with delicate notes of musk, violet, and lemons.

'I'll never tire of seeing you do that, sweetness. Roses were always one of your favourites.' His voice was hoarse. With the snap of his fingers, the screen vanished, revealing the full splendour of the tree. 'What you have already created in the Underworld'—Hades gestured towards the windows, showcasing the plethora of colour—'is like you bringing the promise of life back to us.'

My gaze met his again as heat invaded my cheeks.

'I have flora magic.'

He sighed. 'Flora magic has always been one of your gifts, among others. Your powers will grow anew while you visit the Underworld.'

The word 'visit' made my heart race... Hope sparked, but I squashed it before it caught fire and spread. At the thought of leaving, though, I was conflicted. Did I want to leave him? My heart squeezed at the prospect of never seeing him again.

'Oh,' I squeaked.

'You are a goddess, Persephone, not a witch.'

'Yeah, apparently. That's what Tee said.' I squinted up at him. In my ballet pumps, I was tiny. He was tall—so big and tall.

'You were reborn and raised to believe you were a witch. To think I was your enemy.'

I didn't know how to respond to that, so I kept my mouth shut. He drew his lower lip between his teeth, and for some weird reason, I couldn't tear my eyes away from his mouth. A heated curl in my stomach made me suck in a shaky breath. I didn't like this feeling at all, for a truckload of reasons. The foremost being that he was king of death and shadows. I might be Persephone reborn, but I wasn't her anymore. I was me. I pried my gaze away and focused on my clasped hands.

'Tee mentioned your fangs are retractable. How come you've not hidden them from me?' I said, lifting my gaze to him again.

He gave a half-shrug. 'I don't want you to be scared of them. And, in certain situations, they are an asset.' One side of his mouth curled into a half-grin. The hidden meaning in his words and the intensity of his perusal caused my skin to heat and my thoughts to muddle.

Dropping my gaze, I muttered, 'Can you... can you tell me what happened?'

'No,' he said, almost commanding, and my temper sizzled.

My head snapped up. 'I beg your pardon?'

He lowered his brows, running a hand over his head. 'I'm sorry.' He looked pained at having to say those words —the arrogant tool. 'What I meant to say is yes, I will, but not today.' The darkness in me rumbled like a slumbering beast, but I suppressed it as I turned back to the rose tree and inhaled the gentle, restorative aroma of the blooms. I didn't want to argue.

'Okay. As long as you promise.'

'You have my word,' he said from behind me. He had moved closer; I could feel his body heat, and his scent swirled around me—it was earthy, like the night air mixed with a fresh, woody, spicy fragrance. I inhaled deeply, like a crack addict taking a hit. My stomach twisted with anticipation, and heat pooled between my legs, making me close my eyes and draw in a shallow breath.

I turned slowly and looked up at him. He was beautiful—a sculptured work of art. His look had a hypnotic, paralysing effect on me; the heaviness and fever in his stare sent flames sweeping over my skin. As I took in the gorgeous hunk of arrogance before me, my gaze returned to his full lips. Gods, I longed to taste them. Something inside me caved. Something foolish that should be stabbed to death, but I couldn't control it. I stared at him, panting slightly, then rose to my tiptoes and cupped his cheek with my hand. A dangerous half-smile flickered on his lips, and my stomach did several traitorous flips.

'Let's eat,' he said, taking my hand, and irritation buzzed beneath my skin like a thousand pissed-off hornets.

I shot him an icy glare as he led me out onto the terrace, pulling a chair out for me. What an asshole.

'You're beautiful.' Hades traced a fingertip down my arm—a featherlike touch that made the fine hairs stand on end, and I almost crumpled into the chair as my knees turned to jelly. The way my body responded to him seriously ticked me off.

He sat opposite me and snapped his fingers. Burgers and fries appeared, accompanied by assorted salads and condiments, plus a carafe of red wine, which I grabbed, filling my glass and taking a generous gulp.

'I've been told you enjoy this food,' he said, filling his glass.

'Mhm,' I muttered, grabbing a burger and biting into it, groaning with pleasure. I slowly licked the cheese off my fingers and ran my tongue over my bottom lip.

'One of my favourites,' I said, peering at him. Hades cleared his throat and shifted in his seat, then grabbed a burger and began eating.

We ate in amiable silence, and once I'd had my fill, I topped up my wine glass and took a sip. 'So,' I began, 'tell me about Persephone.'

'You, my sweetness, were my power, my pleasure, and my pain.' His words made my heart do a weird little dance.

'Your pain?'

He looked down at his hands. 'Yes. When you vanished, I lost myself.' Again, emotion balled in my throat. I could feel his anguish. I could feel him. 'I missed you every second of every minute. Every minute of every hour. The first time, I waited for you for centuries. This time felt even longer. I would have waited another millennium to have you back.' He lifted his gaze to meet mine. 'You were the only one I ever yearned for. The beacon of hope for every lost soul in the Underworld, including me, Persephone.'

It took every ounce of control I had not to weep; dreaded tears clawed at my throat, pricking my eyes as fresh guilt sank its claws into me. I could almost taste his anguish, but I pushed the messy ball of emotion down and took a large gulp of wine.

'I'm sorry,' I whispered, gazing into his pained eyes.

'It was not your doing. I find it difficult to talk about. I apologise.' His eyes turned distant as he drank his wine.

'Are you with Minthe now?' The words escaped before I could stop them, and his eyes shot to my face.

'You're jealous of Minthe.' And he smirked. He actually freaking smirked!

'Am not. I'm not bothered in the slightest.' I narrowed my eyes, giving him a death glare.

'I can see through lies, little goddess.' He raised a brow, and I nearly hurled my wine at him. 'But the answer to your question is no, Persephone.' Instead, I drank my wine, feeling a glow of satisfaction at his words.

'Have you slept with her while I was... gone?' I'm not sure why I asked, but for some strange reason, I needed to know.

After what felt like an eternity, his eyes met mine. 'Once.' Jealousy felt like a bitter pill exploding in my stomach. Totally irrational. *What was going on with me?* But I wanted to knock Minthe's teeth down her throat. I clenched my jaw, my nostrils flaring.

'It was a mistake. I was grieving, and she comforted me. It spiralled out of control.'

'Out of control?' I barked a laugh.

'Are you angry?'

'No! Yes. I'm confused. I don't know why I'm angry.' I blew out a breath and took another gulp of wine, tears misting my eyes.

In a flash, he was beside me. He pulled me to my feet and placed his hands on my waist, lifting me effortlessly to his chest until we were face-to-face. Something raw and primal in his eyes made my breath hitch, and I wrapped my legs around his waist. When I felt his arousal, a bolt of energy surged through my body, filling me with a heady, intoxicating feeling. My lips met his, and he rumbled low in his throat.

The kiss was hot and hungry—he kissed like a man starving for a taste, *igniting* my body. Something inside me thawed and bloomed, like one of my flowers unfurling to meet the sun for the first time. As a thousand butterflies took flight in my chest, a fire burned deep in my core.

The way he kissed me made every kiss before seem like a rehearsal... lifeless, meaningless, forgettable.

This was the kiss I'd been waiting for—a kiss that caused a cascade of liquid heat to pool between my legs. His lips ran fervent kisses down my neck, and when his teeth and fangs scraped my skin, I moaned. As he sucked on the tender skin of my throat, that intoxicating feeling sent me reeling, and when he lifted his head from my skin, I felt bereft.

My eyes widened, and I panted. He was power and shadows, dreams and death, but the attraction was potent.

When that insufferable smirk curved on his lips again, I bristled. 'Do not tell me you cannot feel our soul bond,' he whispered as his eyes locked onto mine—the arrogant prick. I was *not* bonded to the god of the Underworld.

But who was I kidding? I could feel it—that... something, deep within me. Something undeniable. It was a freaking horny nightmare of a bond. Dammit.

I grimaced at him. 'Not really,' I lied, chewing my lip and dropping my gaze.

'I can taste your emotions. Your arousal,' he said in a low, smoky voice.

My brows knitted together tightly. 'Wait. What? I've told you before... That's just creepy!'

'And as I said, I can see through lies, little goddess.' The chill of his voice sliced through me like an ice storm.

'I'm not lying,' I lied again.

'Admit you love me,' he growled.

'What? I've only just freaking met you! And you kidnapped me, you jackass.'

His eyes shone gold as an angry frown marred his beautiful face. The next minute, I was falling onto my ass in my bedroom.

'You *bastard!*' I yelled.

Standing up, I brushed myself off, strode to the cupboard, opened it, and poured more wine, colourfully cursing Hades as I downed glass after glass. His words echoed in my head over and over: *You were the only one I ever yearned for. The beacon of hope for every lost soul in the Underworld, including me, Persephone,* and angry tears spilled down my cheeks.

Was it anger? Or was it something else? Something I couldn't explain, like the 'bond'? I was too confused to think clearly and, eventually, too exhausted. I don't remember passing out.

CHAPTER
TWELVE

HADES

I was furious. I poured another glass of wine and downed it in one gulp. My erection strained against my jeans.

'Fucking Persephone,' I grunted. I'd taken her lips as if laying claim to her soul—a scorching kiss that left me unsteady on my feet; how I'd missed those kisses.

Remembering her taste, her tongue, the soft moans she made against my mouth, and the way her body ignited at my touch almost undid me. My cock grew even harder. I rumbled low in my throat. I should have taken her there and then on the table. I could have, but I knew I must not.

She still denied the bond, though I knew she was lying. The look she'd given me when I'd asked said she'd rather gouge her eyes out with a rusty spoon than admit to feeling it. I needed to get her out of my head. I needed to stop this before I fell any deeper for this stranger. She was getting under my skin like a sweet poison. She wasn't *my* Persephone. I wanted to both fuck her senseless and return her to the mortal world for my sanity, before she and that shadow magic enthralled me completely.

My Persephone had been dynamic and powerful; she took shit from no one, including me—my equal—but she also loved me unconditionally, a love that both comforted and healed me. There is no arguing with the soul bond. She had been made for me—even separated, we would have walked the earth to search for each other. At the thought, I drank another glass of wine and paced the terrace.

Fates, what a mess.

'Went well then?' Hecate's voice made me turn; she had my answer from the scowl I gave her. Her eyes lowered to my crotch, and she smirked. I fisted my hands and squinted at her. 'Not saying a word.' She raised her hands in a surrender gesture but carried on grinning.

'She's sweet one minute and downright infuriating the next. She flat-out denies that she feels the bond, and I know she lies,' I ground out.

'Hades, she's always been the same. You know that. You were married for how long before she—' Hecate stopped as my gaze shot to hers. 'That's one thing you loved about her—her downright feistiness and determination. You're a god, and you expect her to throw herself at you. Stop being so freaking arrogant. This whole situation has turned her world upside down. Give her time.'

'We do not *have* time, Hecate.' My voice cracked despite myself. 'I cannot bear to lose her again, so I must stop this. She denies the bond... our bond.' A crippling pain lanced through my chest, and I forced the next words out like ash. 'She is *not* the same goddess I married. She's not *my* Persephone anymore. *My* Persephone would never put me through this.'

I drew in a ragged breath. 'It's best if she leaves.' Hecate opened her mouth to argue, but I raised a hand to silence her. 'I'm going to see Zeus,' I said, voice low and final. 'I'll tell him Persephone is returning to the mortal realm. I'll dissolve the binding to me. She will be free.'

'Well, I never took you for a quitter—'

'Do not push me, Goddess.' My shadows stirred, curling like smoke as my words sliced the air.

'As you wish.' She shook her head in disgust and vanished, leaving me feeling even more morose.

When I thought of Zeus, my cock softened, and I shadow-walked to Olympus.

He was 'entertaining' two nymphs, and the sight almost made me heave. One was on her knees in front of him, his dick in her mouth.

'Brother!' He grinned when his eyes met mine.

'I'm dissolving the binding to Persephone. She is free to return to the mortal realm,' I said through clenched teeth.

With a click of his fingers, the nymphs disappeared, and jeans now covered his modesty.

'Well, that's you out of the running, then,' he said, offering a smug smile as he approached me.

'What do you mean?'

'Well, Persephone's rightful place is in Olympus,

preferably by my side. The other gods won't stand a chance in the battle for her heart and body. I'll bring her here instead; she can stay as *my* guest while we woo her. I'm salivating, thinking about getting my cock into her hot, wet pussy.'

My shadows enveloped the room, and anger became a living, breathing entity. 'I'll rip your fucking throat out,' I roared.

Zeus bellowed with laughter, wrapping himself in a bubble of clouds and lightning.

'Well, up your game, Brother, and stop behaving like a spurned teenager, you dozy bastard.' Then he vanished, leaving me and my shadows in silence.

What in Olympus's name is he playing at?

I STORMED into my office and kicked a chair. What a fucking mess—Zeus took assholery to an epic level.

Persephone was still caught in the male intrasexual competition for her body, and the thought made me want to destroy them all. The gods vying for her would employ an array of tactics to best their rivals—they were all scum. *She is my fucking wife...* Or had been. If this competition continued, I *had* to win her back. I couldn't allow one of the other gods to have her.

I exhaled a ragged breath as rage swirled within me, mingled with heartbreaking sorrow and a myriad of different emotions that twisted my guts and turned me inside out. Shadows ran rampant around my office, but I couldn't lose control. It wasn't fair to my people. I'd done that once—when Persephone was taken from me—and had killed countless innocents. I was no longer that god.

'Hecate!' I yelled in my mind. No response. Where in the gods was she? *'Thanatos!'* He appeared within a second.

'Highness.' He bowed deeply.

I waved my hand for him to rise. 'Where's Hecate?'

He gave a lazy shrug. 'No idea. Is there a problem?'

'Oh, yes, you could say that. When you see her, tell her to get her ass to me, pronto.'

He bowed and disappeared, leaving me stewing in self-doubt and disquiet—would Persephone choose me in this ridiculous competition for her betrothal? It seemed unlikely. She refused to even acknowledge the bond. The thought of her not loving me caused my heart to ache and my anger to resurface. I took a long, slow breath.

Would she be wooed by another of the rival gods, like Zeus, who had a beautiful realm to offer her, only to be taken from me... again? My heart would be shredded a second time. If that were to happen, I'd likely destroy Olympus and every god within it.

Struggling to rein in my fury, I poured myself a whisky and brooded, with nothing on my mind but my exasperating wife. I needed to see her. She was *mine*.

I called for Morpheus.

THIRTEEN

PERSEPHONE

I was back in the garden and I sighed happily.

The sight of this place elevated my sprits; this was exactly what I needed. I cast aside thoughts of Hades. He was such a cockwomble. He certainly wouldn't be my dream man this time. I willed my dream man as a young Ryan Reynolds during his role in *The Proposal*—one of my favourite romcoms. Plus, he was totally delicious.

'Come on, Ryan,' I muttered as I contentedly settled at the edge of the pond.

'Sorry to disappoint you, Persephone.'

At the sound of his voice, my anger ratcheted to boiling point. 'You? Holy crap, you've got to be joking?'

'You're trembling.' His gaze flicked to my clenched fists.

'It's revulsion. *Not* arousal.' I spat, trying to banish the thoughts of that kiss and the way I'd almost spontaneously combusted—my panties were probably still in the seventh circle of hell.

His voice dropped to something dark and hungry. 'Liar.'

'I'd rather kiss a basilisk.' I glared.

He leaned in, close enough to feel his heat lick across my skin. 'I bite harder.'

Gods. Hand me a fan. My temperature just soared into inferno territory. Damn him.

I stood and placed my hands on my hips. He offered a nonchalant half-shrug. 'You're a total ass-wipe. Oh, my gods, to think I actually wanted to have sex with you!' I seethed. Dream Hades was an even bigger cock that real-life Hades!

'I know. Most women do.'

Damn it, this man's ego must have its own gravitational field. 'Holy fuck, your ego never fails to astound, you arrogant prick.' His eyebrows inched up his forehead. 'Anyway, it's irrelevant now. You're the last man I want to fuck. This is my dream, and I do *not* want you in it!'

'As you wish.' He gave a slight bow and vanished, leaving me more frustrated than ever. That man made me crazy. Why had he just left me? *Because you told him to, you fool.* I stomped and muttered profanities as I considered various ways to slowly kill Hades with my divine blade.

'SEPHY. WAKE UP.' Tee's voice rudely interrupted my murderous dream.

I groaned and clutched the comforter tightly over my head. Gods, how much wine did I drink? 'Quiet down! Someone stabbed me through the eye with a stiletto.' Tee yanked the cover off me, and I growled in frustration. Peeling an eye open, I saw her scowling face.

'Don't get all scary-glary with me, Tee. I feel like shit.'

'Serves you right. You downed an entire bottle of wine, you stupid moron. Get up.'

I jumped up on the bed in anger. 'It was that arrogant asshole's fault—' But before I could utter another word, nausea overwhelmed me; I sprang from the bed and dashed to the bathroom to puke. Ugh. I stared at my face in the mirror and moaned. I was a hot mess of a train wreck. I frowned as I looked down at my silk cami and matching shorts.

Stumbling from the bathroom, I croaked, 'Did you undress me? I can't remember anything.'

'Yes. I put you to bed. You were so drunk, rambling nonsense. I'm not surprised you can't remember.' Her face wore a grim expression. I think she was pissed at me. 'Anyway, I'm taking you home.'

I whispered, 'Oh, I'm sorry—' and then her words sank in. 'What do you mean, take me home? Like, back to London? Am I free?'

'You're free. Come on; you can shower when you get there.'

Confusion gripped me. Free? But I couldn't think clearly; instead, I snatched my divine blade, then took Tee's hand, and she flashed me to my bedroom... my bedroom in Islington.

'I'll be back to check on you later. I need to go to Hades; make sure he hasn't lost the plot... again.' She shook her head and gave me a bitter smile, then flashed out of the room.

Her bitter smile of disappointment left me feeling like shit; my shoulders slumped, and I covered my face with my hands, then staggered to my bed, collapsing into a heap and instantly falling back to sleep.

WHEN I WOKE and opened my eyes, I sat up in shock. I was in my bedroom—my bedroom in Islington. Had it all been a dream? Hecate, Hades, Thanatos, everything? I felt like I'd been beaten over the head with a piñata stick about a thousand times, so I slid from the bed and took a long shower, then pulled on a crop top and yoga pants.

As I brushed my hair in front of the mirror, my thoughts wandered to Hades—the egotistical, infuriatingly gorgeous god who drove me insane. Had I imagined him? Then I noticed the bruise-like love bite on my neck, where he'd seductively sucked on my tender skin. It was him. Hades... and I knew, I knew it had been real. My fingers lingered on the mark, and godsdamn, I craved his lips on mine, his kisses and fangs grazing my skin.

I sat up abruptly, my spine stiffening. Oh, my gods. I was losing my mind. I did *not* want Mr Gorgeous but Deadly. At. All. Nope. But Hades *was* real, just as I knew the strange feeling in my chest—'the bond'—was still there. Without Hades, would it gradually be smothered, and when it had gone, would I have a gaping hole in my chest instead?

Why had he sent me home? And why didn't I feel glad to be free? Free of the gods, whom I loathed. Free of Hades. A horrible, burning sensation churned deep in my stomach, slowly making its way up my throat, while a sinking, drowning feeling threatened to swallow me. Gods, why was I feeling like this? Had Hades chosen Minthe instead of me? At the thought, anger consumed me, but I welcomed it. It was far better than the hurt and that drowning feeling of rejection.

But why, in the world of fucks, did I care who he chose? Even my confusion was confused.

I felt awake, except my will to live seemed to have withered. I smoothed my hair with my hands, clenching my jaw as I colourfully ranted about my so-called 'husband', then walked downstairs to make myself a coffee.

'Hey, Sephy!' Matt's megawatt smile lit up the room. 'Did you have a good time at the club last night?'

I slowed my pace and stopped. Last night? I'd been gone for *well* over a week. I shook my head in confusion, the messy swell of emotions getting the better of me.

'Mhm,' I squeaked, turning my back to fetch a cup. As

the coffee brewed, and after thirty deep breaths, I faced Matt again.

'You okay, Sephy?' He narrowed his eyes at me.

'Peachy.' I smiled and headed back upstairs to drown in my very own sea of turmoil.

FOURTEEN

HADES

I wanted to throttle Persephone.

She dismissed me from her dream after calling me an ass-wipe *and* an arrogant prick! Her disrespect was outrageous. I would allow no one but her to speak to me in that manner. My cock twitched merely thinking of her audacity and what I still longed to do to that impertinent mouth. Regardless of what happened or what I thought, I would never stop craving her. She belonged to me. *She was mine.*

'Thanny said you needed me?' Hecate appeared as I poured my tenth whisky.

'I wanted you an hour ago,' I hissed.

'Ugh, sorry. I was taking Persephone home.'

I spun around, my hands fisted. 'What? Why?'

'You told me to.' She threw her hands up, her brow furrowing.

'Shit. I need to bring her back before Zeus gets to her.' I slammed my drink down.

'What in the gods' names is going on, Hades?'

I gave her a brief rundown on Zeus's plans, and her brows lowered as I spoke. I could feel her simmering rage.

'What the fuck?' she hissed.

I released a frustrated breath. 'I'm worried, Hecate, that if she chooses another, I won't be able to control my rage again. The destruction could be catastrophic.' I ran a hand over my head.

'She'll choose you, Hades. Stop fretting.'

'Will she? I'm not so sure. She's attracted to me but seems to despise me, and I can't blame her. I've turned her life upside down... because I'm selfish and want her back. She feels the bond, I know she does, but perhaps this Persephone will never love me as she once did. As Zeus said, she's a different woman.'

'She's the same person, Hades. The same person with no memories of being your wife or a goddess.' She paused and stepped towards me. 'Allow her to see the real you. Let her see how adorable you are under that grumpy bastard exterior.'

'I am the god of the dead. I am *not* adorable.'

'We all know you're a cinnamon roll, Hades. A pompous spitfire with a heart of gold.'

'Don't push me, Goddess.' I glared, shadows flickering, but she ignored me.

'Listen. You must approach her like a *normal* person this time, Hades. You need to explain the danger she faces, yes, but it must be her choice to return.'

'I'm a god! I'm not a normal person.'

'For the Fates' sake, will you listen to me? You need to court her the *mortal* way.'

'I'm not courting her the mortal way,' I said with exasperation as I crossed my arms.

'You're such an arrogant git sometimes!' Hecate's voice cracked like a whip, startling me into silence. She rarely challenged me... which meant, annoyingly, I should probably listen. 'Fetch your limo from that ridiculous Underworld club and knock on her door, for gods' sake.'

'Fine,' I bit out. 'But it will take ages to reach her.'

'Then go!' She jabbed a finger at the door.

I swallowed the retort burning on my tongue, gave her a hard, steely look, and shadow-walked straight to my nightclub.

Two hours later—bloody London traffic—I finally arrived at Persephone's house, my temper sizzling at this absurd mortal charade. I stalked up the steps, and pounded on the door.

It swung open to reveal an irritatingly attractive man, and my temper almost got the better of me. 'I must speak to Persephone,' I ground out my voice low and dangerous as I locked eyes with him.

The man wrinkled his brow. 'You mean Sephy?' I nodded, and he opened the door wider, leading me to a kitchen area. 'Take a seat.' He pointed to the table, but I stayed where I was, glaring at him. He ran a hand over the back of his neck and dropped his eyes. 'I'll, erm, get her then.'

A few minutes later, she walked into the room and

froze when her eyes locked on mine. 'What do *you* want?' she snapped, arms folding tight across her chest as she scowled up at me.

My gaze snagged the faint mark marring her throat, and I ground my teeth so hard, I was surprised I didn't splinter a molar. Her scent enveloped me—delicate, reminiscent of lilacs, vanilla, and sun rays. And underneath all that? The sharp, undeniable spice of her arousal. A slow, dangerous smirk curled my lips. She could deny me with her words all she wanted—her body told me the truth.

The mortal man looked between us, a furrow forming between his eyebrows.

'You may leave,' I snapped at him as I turned my head.

'Whoa, hold on, buddy.' He puffed out his chest and scowled at me. I raised a brow, and the next second, the man was on his knees before me.

'Do *not* call me buddy,' I said in a low tone.

'Hades!' Persephone yelled. 'Stop it!'

I shrugged, and the man slowly stood. 'Hades? Like *the* Hades?' He stared at me, wide-eyed, and I squinted at him. 'Sorry.' He dropped his gaze. 'I work at your club.'

'You are the miscreant who dared touch *my* wife?' I roared, shadows whipping through the air like living whips. The man's eyes became deep pools of fear, and as his skin drained of colour, he planted face-first onto the kitchen floor.

'Oh. My. Freaking. Gods!' With each word, Persephone shoved me hard in the chest. 'I'm *not* your freaking wife!' I clenched my jaw... She was right; this version of her was a stranger. But she was still *mine*. 'And what gives you the right to waltz into *my* home and act like that? To scare my friend half to death? Why do you gods think you're worth so much more than humans? Why are you all so damned arrogant?'

'We are *gods*,' I grumbled.

'You're a bunch of self-entitled douchebags. And *you're* a colossal prick!' she hissed at me. My mouth quirked into a slow smile. 'Do you find me amusing?' Her eyes darkened, and she jutted her chin up at me. 'I'm about two seconds away from kicking you in the balls.' She pointed a finger at my face.

'I'd rather you didn't, little goddess,' I murmured, fighting the smirk tugging at my mouth. 'It's just... no one but you has ever spoken to me in such a manner.' *And survived*, I added mentally.

She tilted her head at me and squared her shoulders. 'Pick up Matt and bring him to the snug. This way.' She stormed to the door, pausing to glance back over her shoulder. 'Hurry!' I rolled my eyes, scooped up the human, tossed him over my shoulder, and as I followed, I watched Persephone's pert butt as she stomped down the hallway.

I laid him on the sofa and turned to find the tiny, feisty female glowering up at me. 'You make me crazy,' she hissed.

'Good. Then we're finally speaking the same language.' I exhaled an exasperated breath. 'You should be afraid of me, you know.' I narrowed my eyes at her.

'Why? Because you growl like a wolf, Your Surliness?'

The muscle in my jaw ticked at her impertinence. 'Anyway, why are you even here?'

I briefly closed my eyes and opened them to find her scrutinising me. 'We have a problem.'

'What, more of a problem than you kidnapping me?' she snapped, 'and the gods wanting to have a competition to see which one of them is the biggest jackass? I'm not marrying any of you.'

Tension hung in the air like a fine mist as we eyeballed each other, each waiting for the other to break. I knew she wasn't safe—not from Zeus, not from any god—and I would protect her, even if she hated me for it.

'Tell me,' she drawled, her tone pure venom, 'do you always kidnap your soulmates, or am I just special?'

'You're special,' I said without blinking. 'Most of them beg to stay.'

She rolled her eyes, tossing her hair over one shoulder. 'You've got to stop abducting people, Hades!'

She was infuriatingly beautiful—so mouthy. My gaze fell to her lips. Those lips, along with memories of what they could do, sent signals straight to my throbbing cock.

'Well?' she demanded, planting her hands on her hips like a queen ready to pass judgement.

I cleared my throat. 'Yes, um, of course.' Persephone puckered her brow and squinted up at me. 'I freed you from the binding. I believed I was doing the right thing.'

'Oh,' she muttered. 'Why didn't you just ask *me* what I wanted?' I stared at her blankly. 'Never mind,' she sighed. 'Just tell me what the problem is.'

'Well, Zeus is still adamant about holding this absurd competition for you.'

'What?' she screeched. 'No, he can't!' She paced restlessly; her agitation had a citrusy, tart, taste, reminiscent of lemons.

I swore under my breath and scrubbed a hand down my face. 'He can, and he will.'

CHAPTER

FIFTEEN

PERSEPHONE

'I want you to return to the Underworld. You'll be safest there, with Tee... with all of us. We will figure something out, I promise. I shall bestow Xenia upon you,' Hades said as he scrubbed a hand across the back of his neck.

I turned to him. 'Xenia?'

'Yes. It will keep you safe.'

I nodded at his words, worrying my bottom lip.

'So, have you two made up?' We turned slowly to find Matt awake on the sofa.

'Be quiet, human,' Hades thundered.

'Matt,' I barked, pushing Hades in the chest again. 'His name is Matt.'

A muscle ticked in Hades' jaw. 'Did you kiss my wife?' Hades' eyes locked onto Matt's, and as he shrank back against the pillows, Matt's eyes widened to the size of spaceships. I groaned in frustration. Kissing wasn't the only thing I'd done with Matt, but I decided to keep quiet. Given the look on Hades' face, I figured it wise not to provoke him further.

'You're *the* Persephone? I—I didn't know. Holy crap.' Matt's were fixed on me, clearly avoiding Hades' lethal glare, his brow now beaded with perspiration.

'Neither did I, Matt. Don't worry.' I smiled at my friend. 'Anyway, I will freaking well kiss whomever I want, Hades!' I turned and scowled up at him, and at my words, his shadows suddenly danced around us.

'Go to your room, human. You will not mention seeing me.' Matt stood, his posture rigid and his eyes cast to the floor as he walked out of the door.

'Did you just use compulsion?' I glared up at the irritating god.

'No. I think I just scared him.'

'You're such a jerk.'

'I know,' he replied with a tight smile.

'You can't terrorise *every* man I've been with! Anyway, your kisses are decidedly average. So—' My gaze collided with his, and I snapped my mouth shut because the look in his eyes caused me to take a few steps back... but he followed. His proximity sent a wave of liquid fire pulsing through my veins and straight between my legs.

'How many *boys* have you been with?' His voice was a low rumble. Part of me bristled at his demand, but another part of me, lacking functioning brain cells, was weirdly thrilled.

'I've never been with *boys*, Your Majesty.' His blue eyes

flared, swirling with golden aether. 'Anyway, it's none of your business.'

'Oh, it *is my* business,' he all but growled, lowering his head, his breath tantalisingly warm against my cheek. I hated that it made my pulse skip. My gaze dropped to his full lips, and I stepped back again, my back hitting the wall. He leaned in and planted his large hands on either side of my head, caging me in and making the air catch in my throat.

'Explain that faulty logic to me,' I managed to whisper.

A savage smile cut into his lips. 'You're my wife. That makes it my business. *Definitely* my business.'

Fire of a different kind pulsed through me, and I flipped. 'Get out of my face, you asshole!' I shoved his chest, solid as stone. He didn't budge. 'I am *not* your wife. And if I were, you betrayed me...' He flinched, but I was past mercy. 'You fucked Minthe!' I seethed, every word laced with venom. 'You touched *her* while claiming to belong to *me.*'

His nostrils flared, jaw flexing with the force of his restraint. Then his hand wrapped around mine—huge, hot, possessive. The shadows exploded around us like a storm unleashed, curling up my arms, brushing my skin like ghostly fingers, swallowing us whole in that velvety-dark magic.

His voice came rough and low, nearly trembling with the effort to keep it together. 'I never belonged to her.' A beat. 'I've only ever belonged to *you.*'

I HADN'T SEEN Hades since he unceremoniously dumped me on my ass back in 'my' bedroom yesterday.

His words swirled in my mind. *'I never belonged to her. I've only ever belonged to you.'* Was that the truth? And even if it was... it was the original Persphone he meant. Not me.

When I'd walked into my kitchen in Islington and saw him standing there, I was dumbfounded. As his gaze fell to the mark on my neck, his eyes flashed pure gold, and his mouth slammed into a hard, thin line. I'd unconsciously touched the mark, and the memories of him kissing me caused flames to lick deep in my stomach and between my thighs.

As one side of his mouth tilted upwards, I remembered his words: *I can taste your arousal.* That was the point at which I wanted to stab him with my blade... in the eye. Gods, he was such a self-important tosser.

So here I was, back in the Underworld. That annoying, horny, whooshing sensation in my chest was back with a vengeance—which meant he was close, and the anticipation of seeing him infuriated me. I couldn't control the longing, even though he embodied fire, ash, and death. I knew there *was* something real between us. Something real and godsdamned inconvenient.

Tee had been delighted I was back, but she'd also been scarce. I was bored out of my mind—yet apparently 'safe'.

I was trying to read—still swotting up on the gods—but still brooding when a knock at my door jolted me from my reverie. I answered to find Tee standing outside with another woman.

'Sephy, I'd like to introduce you to Hedone. I thought she could have a chat with you about, erm, matters.' Tee appeared flustered. 'And about decorum in Olympus. You know. Preparing for Aphrodite's welcoming party? She's helping me with your makeup and outfit, too.'

The beautiful stranger tilted her head as she examined me from head to toe, causing me to shuffle self-consciously. Wearing yoga pants and a crop top, with my hair loose, I wasn't elegant. I awkwardly ran a hand through my tousled curls.

She had incandescent amber eyes that regarded me warmly, even in my state of disrepair; her skin was a rich ochre colour with warm orange-red undertones. Her hair, black-as-night, cascaded in waves down to her waist, and her sharp, silk trouser suit clung to her curvaceous body. Hedone was the goddess of pleasure, enjoyment, and delight, the daughter of Eros—love—and Psyche—soul, and more specifically associated with sensual pleasure. Heat swept across my cheeks as I scowled at Tee.

'Persephone, charmed to meet you.' Hedone smiled kindly. 'Shall we go and make tea?'

I nodded mutely, glancing between her and Tee. 'But I want to walk, please.'

Tee sighed, and this time, as we walked to the kitchen, I memorised the route. When we entered through the wide grey doors into the expansive space, memories of Hades flooded my mind. Recalling what he'd said to me the last time I was here with him caused me to fist my hands. *You were the brightest star in an endless night.*

Stop thinking about him, Sephy. For the sake of every baby alpaca ever born! But that bond in my chest keened for him like a sulky little bitch. I was missing him. Dammit.

As we sipped tea and nibbled sweet biscuits, we chatted. 'So, tell me about Xenia?' I said, placing my cup down.

'Well, Hades wanted to protect you from Zeus and the other gods,' Hedone replied. 'Now his binding is dissolved... it's only a matter of time before one of them, most likely Zeus, claims you, and believe me, that's the last thing you want.' She pressed her lips together.

'Agreed,' Tee added. 'The goddess Hestia is inherently tied to the concepts of Xenia and generosity. So for Hades to offer it means that you are a guest in his realm—'

'What? I'm not his prisoner?' I snapped.

Tee ignored me. 'You are under his protection, for now, and no one can force you to do anything you don't want to while he invokes Xenia upon you.'

'So, how do I get out of this mess? I can't stay here forever!' I threw my hands up in frustration.

Tee and Hedone exchanged glances. 'Worry not, Persephone. Hades will think of something,' Hedone reassured as she stroked my hair.

Worry not? I was worried sick. Having several Greek gods coveting me for marriage wasn't just worrisome—it was downright menacing. I gulped and clasped my fists in my lap, trying to hide the tremor in my hands.

'We'll get through this, Sephy. I promise.' Tee leaned into me and kissed my hair. I gave her a slight nod and momentarily closed my eyes.

'So...' Hedone interrupted my musings, and I opened my eyes to see her holding a conical-shaped ice pop. 'About pleasing a man.' She gave me a devilish smile and proceeded to lick and suck the offending item like it was a dick, moaning and making guttural humming noises. My eyes widened, and my jaw dropped as I released a short, startled laugh.

Well, this was all kinds of awkward.

Tee snorted behind me, mumbling, 'Subtle.'

'Erm, I'm not twelve,' I said, feeling blood rush to my cheeks. 'I don't need sex ed lessons, thanks.' My eyes darted to Tee, and I bared my teeth in a silent snarl. Tee smothered her laughter behind her hand.

'I only wish to prepare you, Persephone, for when you choose a husband. Have you ever pleasured a man with your mouth?' Hedone lowered the ice pop and tilted her head to the side as she studied me. Heat seared through my cheeks again, and I bristled.

'Of course I have,' I ground out as she gave me a look as if to say, *Really?* 'It was revolting.'

Hedone tittered. 'That's because you haven't been with the right person, Persephone. Oral sex is about giving and receiving pleasure willingly. Executing it well requires skill and practice for both partners. I want to help you.'

'Well, I'm not planning on giving anyone a blowjob, so don't bother.' I jutted my chin at her as I silently screamed.

'Maybe we should focus on the etiquette of Olympus, Hedone,' Tee intervened, eyeing me warily. I shot her a look that said, *Wait until I get you alone later, you grass.* She just smirked.

Hedone's answering smile flickered across her face like a hologram.

'Of course.' She pulled out a chair and sat back down with us. 'We will practice today. I've enlisted a few individuals to assist with the simulated introductions and what you should be prepared for.' I gulped and gave a slight nod. 'A charming woman demonstrates confident and open body language. Her posture is upright, and her hands are relaxed but not crossed or tucked into pockets. She uses gestures when she speaks to liven up the conversation. Eye contact and a genuine smile are how she greets everyone.'

'Okay, I can do that,' I muttered, wondering if I *could* really do that.

'Beautiful women utilise their looks and sexuality to get what they desire from men.'

'I don't desire anything from men,' I grumbled.

'But you do, Persephone,' Hedone answered with a slight smile. 'You must be able to manipulate people in Olympus. It's not like the mortal world. Most people here are arrogant—'

'Bordering on the stupid type of arrogance,' Tee interjected, and Hedone let out a quiet laugh.

'Exactly. You need to use your good looks and sexuality

to get what you want. And why not? All's fair in love and war.'

'The only thing I want is to return to my life in London,' I said as I briefly closed my eyes.

'And we will make that happen, eventually. You need to play the game, for now, anyway,' Tee soothed as she stroked my arm. I opened my eyes to see Hedone giving Tee a curious look. 'Come on, Sephy. Let's go and practice,' Tee said, pulling me to my feet.

Ten minutes later, I found myself in a grand room reminiscent of a ballroom. It was a space fit for a princess; vast, and illuminated by the same magical daylight as everywhere else—staring up at the ceiling felt like looking at a sun-drenched, cloudless sky. Immense columns framed the perimeter, while bejewelled sconces dotted the walls, flickering with a magical glow. Like everywhere else, the entire area was constructed from star-kissed onyx, shimmering with luminosity.

'Wow, what is this place?' I breathed as I stared around the room.

'It's a defunct amphitheatre that converts to a ballroom,' Tee answered.

'Why defunct?'

'Hades has, or had, no desire for gatherings since you left.'

'Oh,' I whispered, furrowing my brows.

'Hey, Persephone!' The stunning Titan, Thanatos, strolled across the room, and I squealed, running towards him, and throwing my arms around his neck. He released a throaty laugh and swung me around.

'That is not the way we welcome guests, Persephone,' Hedone said, quirking an eyebrow. I let out an exasperated sigh as Thanny set me on my feet; he tried, but failed, to stifle a smirk. 'Thanatos, go. Come back in after Charon, as we discussed,' the goddess commanded.

Thanny winked at me and strolled back out through the enormous doors. For the next half hour, Charon, Thanatos, and Tee took turns entering the room, appearing surprised and enchanted to meet me. My awkward smiles and uneasy handshakes were pretty pathetic.

'You are inelegant and sound completely bored, Persephone.' Gods, I was bored, so I gave a half-hearted shrug.

'Watch and learn.' Hedone pursed her lips at me. Charon re-entered the room, a relaxed smile on his handsome face.

'Delighted to meet you,' enthused Hedone as she held out her hand. Charon took her hand, courteously bending to kiss it.

'It's an honour to meet you, Lady Persephone,' Charon's deep voice resonated.

Her eyes remained on his as she spoke. 'May I say you look so regal this evening,' she purred in her sultry tone. 'I hope you have a fabulous time.' Then she turned to me. 'You see, Persephone, as people are introduced to you, it's essential to sound refined and majestic, as a queen should.'

'But I'm not a queen,' I complained.

'Not yet.' She shot me a look as if to say *listen up*, and I clenched my teeth. 'If a man approaches, extend your hand for a kiss. If she's an equal, a woman will air kiss or shake hands; otherwise, they will curtsey; let them lead. Always remember to compliment them on something; flattery will get you everywhere in Olympus. As it's a formal party, it could be their outfit, appearance, or jewellery. Whatever.' She pursed her lips again and gave me a *don't sass me* look. 'Ready to try again?'

After another hour, my fake smile improved, and my level of sophistication met Hedone's approval. 'One more test.' She winked at me, and I groaned softly, much to the amusement of the three Titans.

A strange, statuesque man entered the room. He was as tall as Hades, with a bald head and the face of an angel; his anthracite eyes locked onto mine, and I was transfixed. His skin was luminescent—as black as the night sky, twinkling with pinpricks of stars. He was awe-inspiring.

'Hello,' I whispered as I gazed up at him.

'Lady Persephone, it's a pleasure to meet you; my name is Erebus.'

Erebus, I mused, staring into his eyes and losing myself in those dark pools twinkling with moondust—the god of darkness, and utterly delicious. I flashed him a toothy smile and extended my hand. His touch was cold, and as his lips grazed my skin, shivers danced down my spine, and my shadow magic thrummed.

'I'm so pleased to meet you, Erebus. You are beautiful.' Erebus grinned like the cat who got the cream, and the three Titans erupted into fits of laughter.

'Well, I suppose it will do,' Hedone huffed in annoyance. 'I'll return before the party to help Tee with your outfit.' Then she vanished in a golden flash.

'Come on, you need to eat. It's lunchtime,' Tee said. 'But I have a judging; shall I flash you to the kitchen?'

'Don't worry, Hecate. I'll take Persephone to the kitchen; I could even make her lunch.' Charon's honey-brown eyes twinkled with mischief.

'Let's go.' I grinned at him as he held out an arm. I placed my hand on his muscled forearm, and he led the way.

CHAPTER
SIXTEEN

HADES

I was trying to stay away from Persephone because she was driving me crazy with need—a need to fuck her until she couldn't walk, and a temptation to bury her in Tartarus for that brazen mouth.

I knew she'd lied about the average kisser comment, but it still displeased me.

As I strolled to my office, I heard feminine laughter escaping from the kitchen. It was Persephone. Who the hell was making her laugh like that? I walked slowly to the door as I listened.

'Oh, my gods, it's really hard.'

'I know, my queen,' Charon's silky voice replied with a husky chuckle. 'We need to hurry before the boss catches me.'

My vision clouded with the red mist of fury, and my shadows exploded as I threw open the kitchen door, ready to eviscerate the Titan. Persephone yelped as a pan clattered to the floor.

'Boss.' Charon gulped, shifting uncomfortably. 'You alright, boss?' He could sense my fury and dropped his gaze as he picked up his coffee.

'Charon's been teaching me to flip pancakes.' Persephone squinted at me as she picked up the pan and started cleaning up the mess. I couldn't take my eyes off her as she moved around the kitchen, then perched on a chair, picking up her coffee. Her waves of blonde hair tumbled over one shoulder as she took a sip. Charon smiled brightly at Persephone, but the smile slipped when he caught my eye.

'Erm, I best be off. Duty calls.' Charon gave Persephone a slight bow.

She responded with a dazzling smile. 'Oh, don't forget this!' Persephone held out a small coin to him.

He shook his head. 'Keep it, my queen.'

My brows raised of their own accord. Charon had been with me from the beginning; he was part of the Underworld family, but he could be ruthless when the occasion deserved it, and as the original ferryman who once transported the dead across the river Acheron, he never *ever* gave away his collection of coins from bygone days. Persephone fluttered her long lashes at him and smiled. The Titan blushed. He fucking blushed.

'See you later.' He winked at Persephone as he edged towards the door, then turned to me with a slight bow. 'Your Highness.' I glared at him as he backed out of the door, fighting his smirk. Fucking Titans.

167

'So...' Persephone said, tilting her head.

Those green eyes caught mine, and I cleared my throat, aware that I hadn't moved since entering the room.

'Do you fancy making me another grilled cheese sandwich? Considering you ruined my pancake.'

'As long as you don't try to stab me again, maybe.'

She breathed a laugh, her eyes sparkling, and my cock throbbed.

'And stay out of my way.' I walked towards the fridge and picked up a handful of ingredients.

'You're very uptight about things.'

'I like order. And I dislike people making a mess,' I said unapologetically without turning around. I busied myself with cooking, aware of Persephone's eyes on me the entire time. Neither of us uttered a word.

Once the grilled cheese sandwiches were perfect, I placed them on plates, popping one in front of Persephone and taking a seat in the chair opposite. My eyes fixed on her as we ate, and she stared back at me. The intensity of that gaze sent shock ripples to my dick, and as I felt myself hardening, it was a toss-up between dragging her over the table and fucking her senseless or dropping my gaze. Ultimately, I chose to look away.

'That was delicious,' Persephone said as she licked her fingers, then ran her tongue along her bottom lip. Shit. My eyes were glued to her mouth as I felt my cock begin to engorge even more.

'I should go,' I said, my voice slightly hoarse. 'Minthe is waiting for me.'

'Minthe?' she asked, but I could see fire ignite in her eyes.

'Yes. She is something akin to my PA.'

'I'll bet she is,' she muttered.

'Sorry?' I could taste her jealousy, like burned sugar on my lips.

'Never mind.' She shook her head. 'Anyway, you promised to tell me what happened to the other Persephone. About the war. Why won't you tell me?'

'I will. But I have much to do today.' I knew I was putting it off, but Fates, even the thought of the time made my shadows twitchy. Her anger tickled my nostrils like cayenne pepper, and she nailed me with a 'you're-full-of-shit' look, causing my erection to soften. I stood and paced towards the door.

'Running away again?' I turned to regard her, my jaw tight. She stood with her hands on her hips.

'You should really stop provoking me,' I said in a low voice.

'Or what? You'll scowl me into submission?' Her emerald eyes blazed with anger, and before I could overreact, I took a long, slow breath, turned towards the door and said, 'Enjoy your day.'

'You too, jackass. You're such a prick,' I heard her mumble, and I stopped in my tracks. She was facing away from me as she carefully placed the dishes in the sink. The metallic, bitter taste of indignation filled my mouth. Did she not respect who I was? What I was capable of? This tiny woman was insufferable. Maybe I should let Zeus have her? At the thought, another wave of anger washed over me. My irritation spiked, and as fast as a strike of lightning, I was behind her, my arms wrapping around her body. She yelped and tried to pull free, but I held her firmly against me.

'You need to watch your mouth, little goddess. It will get you in trouble one day,' I whispered into her ear, and she stilled, sucking in a shuttering breath. The smell of her arousal hit my nose and dick at the same time.

Fates. I was doomed.

My hand moved of its own accord, sliding over her stomach, down over her rounded hip, and to the apex of her thighs. I'm pretty sure she stopped breathing. She relaxed into me, and a soft groan left her lips, causing my throbbing cock to strain against my jeans and press into her back. I stroked my hand back up her stomach and slid it into the waistband of her yoga pants, then down over the silk of her underwear and gently stroked her hot pussy, finding the nub of nerves with my thumb. She shuddered and groaned, arching closer to me. Gods, she was wet. So wet.

'You can pick fights with me. Disrespect me. Pretend you don't feel our bond, but *this* doesn't lie. You're so gloriously wet, and it's because you want me to touch you, isn't it, Persephone?' I whispered hoarsely against her cheek.

'Yes,' she moaned, her head tipping back against my chest as her hand reached behind, grabbing my arse. As I stroked her, I was close to losing control, and I couldn't do that. My cock was a long, swollen mass of urgent need, fighting for fulfilment.

I needed her to accept me on her terms. I needed her to love me again, not merely submit to the attraction she felt. If I took her now, I'd keep her, willing or not—and I could not do that. I would not take away her choice.

I withdrew my hand, and she let out a frustrated moan. Then I shadow-walked the hell out of there, her curses bouncing off the walls.

SEVENTEEN

PERSEPHONE

'You fucker!' I growl-yelled as I felt him disappear.

I was sure he was going to fuck Minthe, and jealousy and disgust slithered through my veins like poison.

'You're such an arrogant twatwaffle!' Oh, gods, I was furious. Why had I let him do that? Why *had* he done that? I knew why I'd allowed him. Hades was distracting. Intoxicating. He made me want to simultaneously flee in the opposite direction and rub myself all over him like a fucked-up alley cat. Gods, maybe it was the effect of the stupid bond?

Watching him work in the kitchen—ugh. His body was a masterpiece. Muscles bunched along his broad shoulders and biceps, and his tight butt and muscular legs... I stopped myself before I started drooling. What in the world of all things holy was wrong with me? He was probably banging Minthe as I stood there!

I hated him. He was a god!

But I knew I didn't hate him, even though I wanted to.

Then, the memory of his voice against my cheek—a voice filled with night and dark dreams—and the feel of his massive erection pressing into my back made my nipples harden, which, in turn, infuriated me even more at the response of my rebellious body. He was driving me insane.

I couldn't stop the small smile of victory that he'd lost the stare off, though. Childish, but satisfying.

I needed to go outside and create more flowers. Take my mind off the infuriatingly gorgeous god. 'I'll fill your kingdom with a million blooms, you moron,' I muttered to myself. I stormed outside in a horny huff, making my way through the meadow towards the river. Waterlilies. I needed waterlilies. Or perhaps marsh marigolds and calla lilies?

Outside, the ethereal amethyst and silver sky glistened like star-fire, and as the grasses and blooming flowers brushed against my lower legs, my rage dissipated into 'slightly pissed off' instead of 'I want to punch you in the nuts'. After about an hour, I reached the river and glanced across where the other side still looked desolate. Damn it. I needed to get across. This place needed cheering up so badly.

I shucked off my trainers, and as I dipped my foot towards the water, a soft, melodic voice behind me said, 'I wouldn't do that if I were you.' I shrieked and spun around.

A young girl stood behind me. Her eyes were a deep blue, like lapis lazuli, matching her flowing blue hair and, you guessed it, the same colour dress. She was otherworldly beautiful. As she studied me, I felt all kinds of self-conscious, dressed in my crop top and yoga pants.

'Erm, hi,' I stuttered. 'I'm—'

'I know who you are.' She lifted her chin as she narrowed her eyes.

'Oh, right.' I shifted from foot to foot but felt no bad energy from her; I didn't think she'd harm me. 'And you are?'

'Styx. My name is Styx.'

'Like the river?' My eyebrows creased.

'Yes. I am the goddess of the river. We are as one.'

She definitely wasn't very chatty, but then again, neither was I. I was never good at small talk. 'I was wondering, if you wouldn't mind, if I could create some flowers for the riverbanks. I mean, if you—'

She cut me off as she squealed and clapped her hands. 'Flowers? On my river? Really?'

I nodded enthusiastically as I watched her bounce on her toes. 'If that's alright?'

'Yes!' She nodded back like a broken bobblehead. Her smile radiated pure joy and lit up her face like the sun breaking through dark thunderclouds.

'Let's do it, then.' I grinned, feeling my flora magic thrumming beneath my skin. I knelt, placing my hands in the black sand of the riverbank, where the water lapped gently. My flora magic pulsed through my veins like a symphony of energy as I envisioned an abundance of flowers that loved water. The vibrancy of the magic shimmered through my veins and sparkled across my skin, enveloping me in a euphoric rush. I didn't hold back; I released a burst of pure flora magic and heard Styx gasp. The riverbanks *exploded* into a plethora of colour, and a smile tugged at my lips—no waterlilies, but good enough.

'Fates! That was amazing!' Styx screeched. 'Look at my beautiful river.'

A hum of pleasure pulsated through me as I took in the vibrant array of flora, and, for the first time in a long time, I felt needed—really needed. Then, my mind switched to Hades, and I buried the thought.

'Can I reach the ground on the other side of the river? I can sense life there, waiting to be reborn. It's so desolate.' I turned to Styx.

'Hmm, well, Hades will be very angry if I take you there.' My face dropped, and she relented. 'I can help you cross the river. But you must be careful on the side of the dead.'

'The dead?' I whispered.

'They will not hurt you,' she assured me. 'I will wait for you to call me and bring you back. But it would be best if you stayed near the river. Do not wander.'

'Great! I'll stay near the river. Promise.' I gave her a wobbly smile. I was a tad unnerved, but as Grandma always said, it's the living you should be scared of, not the dead.

We waded into the water, and Styx swam across alongside me, the water cooling my flesh. It was further than I thought, and I was exhausted by the time we reached the riverbank.

'Call me!' Styx vanished beneath the water with a wave of her hand, and I was alone. Plopping down on my backside, I panted and closed my eyes. Gods, I *despised* swimming.

'Excuse me.' I jerked as I opened my eyes to find a man standing before me. 'I think I'm lost. I can't find my wife or child. I don't know why I'm here. This place is strange. Barren. I don't like it. I need to get home.'

'I—' The words died in my throat as the man faded away. Freaked out, I jumped up, and suddenly, I was flying, reeling, falling, and being tossed left and right.

And then there was nothing.

'HMMM, A PRETTY LITTLE SNACK.' The low, raspy voice penetrated my mind. My eyes slowly opened, and I groaned. My vision swam, and the piercing headache felt like a rusty knife scraping at my brain. With a grunt, I pushed myself into a sitting position and grimaced as I touched the back of my head—it was wet. What happened? Where was I? My whole body was banged up; the pain was so intense I couldn't be certain which bones were broken, but I was pretty sure some were.

'You're awake. At last.'

My eyes flicked to the sound of the voice, but it was dark. As my eyes adjusted to the murkiness, I realised I was in a cave. It felt foreboding, and a shudder rippled through me. At random intervals, stalactites and stalagmites joined from the floor to the ceiling. I stiffened, and my stomach flipped with anxiety as the cold air chilled my damp skin.

A flash of flames appeared in my periphery, prompting me to turn my head and look up. The breath froze in my lungs. A tall woman with blazing orange eyes and hair of flames stood within feet of me. She had mismatched legs: one of brass and the other covered in fur, ending in a hoof.

Well, *she* was a bucketful of nightmares.

'Who are you? Where am I?' I slowly inched back on my ass, the body-wracking pain making me wince.

'I'm Empousa.' She gave me a wild grin, showing her long canines, and I groaned. For fuck's sake, why did they all have fangs? I attempted to summon my magic, but nothing happened. I was weak and vulnerable, and the venom of panic gave me a sharp bite. Shit. I didn't want to die in a dank, dark cave at the hands of a freaky-looking demon.

'Wait. You don't want to kill me.' I raised a hand. 'Hades will not be happy. I'm his wife.' I puckered my brow as I said the word 'wife'. I quite liked it, but now was not the time to psychoanalyse my stupid brain.

She laughed, and the sound made my skin crawl. 'I know who you are. *She* told me.' Terror was a bitter taste in the back of my mouth. Then she flew at me, grasping my hair and lifting me off the ground. Searing pain scorched through my scalp, which was nothing compared to the agony of her teeth clamping down on my neck.

A knot built in the back of my throat that tasted of

undiluted rage, and I could feel that slumbering giant in my chest pounding to break free. I was angry. So very angry.

I'd been brought here from my life in London; told I was a goddess once wed to the absurdly beautiful Mr Grumpy and Deadly. Other gods were vying for my hand in marriage. Now I had a freaking donkey-legged demon sucking at my neck, and the pain—it hurt. Gods. It *hurt*. It was the sort of pain that burned as if some invisible flame were branding me—a million tactile nerves felt as if they'd combusted and been replaced with howling torment. I bared my clenched teeth as the thrum of energy in my sternum returned like a maelstrom... and I exploded.

Black scrolling shadows erupted from my hands, writhing like living smoke, coiling thick and merciless around the Empousa. Head to foot, she was bound in my fury, her shrieks splitting the air as she thrashed. Rage wasn't just inside me—it *was* me, a living, ravenous thing, and I was powerless to stop it.

The Empousa convulsed, her eyes wide with terror, and then her body began to wither. In the span of a heart-beat, she crumbled inward, her form collapsing like ash in a storm. A brittle snap, a hiss of air—then nothing. Just dust.

The silence after was deafening. My stomach lurched, bile burning my throat as I gagged, panting hard. My knees gave way, and I crashed to the floor, trembling as the pile of her remains mocked me from the shadows.

I dragged in a ragged breath, every inhale burning as blood from the wound in my neck slicked the floor beneath me. On my hands and knees, my body trembled, my head hanging low, eyes squeezed shut against the waves of pain that rolled through me.

How did I get here? How could I get *out* of here? I kept my eyes closed as shock waves of dull, nauseating pain ratcheted through my whole body.

Suddenly, a flurry of shadows enveloped the space, and I hitched a breath as I lifted my head.

'Persephone.' It was his voice. Hades.

Then blackness enveloped me.

'PERSEPHONE.' The deep voice roused me from the darkness. My eyelids fluttered, heavy as stone, until I managed to pry them open. His face swam into focus—the beautiful god of ash and death. Silken sheets whispered beneath my fingers. A bed. His bed?

I tried to sit up, wincing as pain seared through every synapse in my body. 'Ugh. Ouch. What... what happened?' I whisper-groaned.

He didn't answer. Instead, his fangs elongated, sharp and gleaming, and he bit into his wrist. Two rivulets of purple-blue blood, shot through with shimmering gold, welled from the punctures. I gasped. 'What are you doing?'

'You were dropped from a great height. You're bleeding out, and your powers haven't matured enough to heal you. A normal human would already be dead.' His voice was low, dangerous, but almost tender. 'Please... feed.'

He brought his wrist to my mouth, and I recoiled, wincing again as pain like the fire of a thousand suns sparked through every nerve ending. 'Dropped?' Ugh. I'm not drinking blood!' I rasped.

'You must. It's the only thing that will heal you.' His blue eyes swirled with gold as they met mine. One large hand slid behind my head, steady but firm, and he raised his wrist again to my mouth. I hesitated, but lowered my head to the open wounds and closed my lips around them.

'Suck,' he said. His voice was husky—the word almost sounded sinful. Heat invaded my cheeks, and I did. I sucked. The scent of his blood filled my senses. It was him —the night air mixed with fresh wood and spices. The first taste of him was delectable, and my eyes fluttered closed. The wash of his dark power flooded my senses—a force so seductive, imbued with sin and shadows.

Desire and temptation cascaded over my tongue, igniting a tingling sensation down my throat and throughout my entire body. His taste... It was exquisite: sweet with smoky undertones, reminiscent of smoked paprika. I swallowed greedily, and the warmth of his blood felt like the heat of the sun's rays penetrating sinew and bone. The warmth flowed and ebbed, igniting my insides and rushing through my veins, creating a heady sensation that swept through me, easing my pain and sending me into heavenly bliss.

'Just a little more.' He gently stroked his hand against the back of my head. His voice was thick and deep, and only then did I realise my fingers were fisted tightly into the fabric of his shirt. A swirl of emotions invaded my every synapse: lust, love, craving, and misery, which caused my throat to thicken. 'I think that's enough.' His voice shattered the emotions as he pried his wrist away, and my eyes fluttered open. Hades sat on the bed next to me and swiped his tongue across his wrist.

'Are you well?' His eyes locked onto mine, and my breath caught in my chest.

'Yeah. Yes,' I whispered, somewhat dazed. 'Much better.' The pain was gone, and I exhaled slowly. I felt my neck; the gaping wound had vanished. 'Thank you.'

The effects of his blood continued to run rampant through my body, and I shifted awkwardly, twisting my fingers into the sheets. Molten lava coursed deep inside me, and the swift arousal I felt made me squirm, stealing my breath. Heart pounding, the intense wave of tingling sensations invaded every nerve, every synapse, and every inch of my flesh. My nipples hardened, and my thighs clenched. I throbbed. Yearned. Oh, gods. My eyes shot to him, and his face paled.

He cleared his throat. 'I'll go and get you some food and wine,' he said, his voice like gravel. As he stood and glanced at me with pure gold eyes, I saw the thick ridge of his erection straining against his leather trousers. Gods.

'Kiss me,' I breathed with a heavy moan.

He hesitated. 'It's a side effect of my blood. You are not in control. I will fetch Hecate—'

I launched. Like a damned linebacker, I was on him before he could move—arms and legs locked around him like a desperate tree bear. My mouth crashed against his, teeth clashing, tongues tangling. My fists knotted in his hair as I devoured him, pressing harder, deeper, until there was nothing left between us but need.

He kissed me as if he were drowning and I was his air, and the fire in my belly *erupted* into an inferno. When he tore his mouth from mine, panting, I mewled in protest, dragging him back. He rested his forehead against mine for a heartbeat, before pulling back just enough to brush his thumb across my swollen bottom lip.

When I wiggled my hips in frustration, I felt his long, hard length against my core. Another needy sound broke from me, shameless and aching. His groan was low, tortured, as his lashes lifted, revealing molten gold eyes that pinned me in place.

'Sleep, Persephone,' he commanded, voice husky, frayed.

And then—nothing.

I BLINKED open tired eyes that felt as if they'd been stitched closed. But I was refreshed. Yawning lazily, I stretched my arms above my head. Squinting, I looked down at the bed—I was still in Hades' bed—and my gut tightened.

Scanning the room, my gaze stopped at the sofa by the large fireplace. Hades lounged, feet up on the coffee table, eyes closed, and gods alive—he was stunning. Those mountain peak cheekbones could have been chiselled by artisans—he possessed a vicious type of beauty that made one's breath hitch.

Then I remembered. Oh, bury me alive—I remembered climbing him like a tree monkey on meth, grinding into him, and kissing him with the desperation of... oh, gods, someone truly desperate. I covered my face with my hands. I was losing my mind. This wasn't me.

'Are you well?' The voice made me yelp as I shot upright, my hands slamming down onto the bed. Hades was standing over me, and my heart began to thrum.

'What? How? How do you move like that?'

'Sorry, did I scare you?'

'No. But it made me want to punch you.'

His mouth quirked into a slight smile. 'It's shadow-walking. Travelling through the aether. I'm sorry; it's like second nature to me.'

'Oh.' Yup, that was all I could say as I stared into those spellbinding eyes. My skin felt too tight for my body, as if I was going to burst right out of it, and heat licked at my skin. I pushed the covers down to my waist, blew out a breath, and felt Hades stiffen. Shit! I was naked. Pulling them back up, I felt a blush spread like a fever from the tips of my toes to my face.

'Why am I naked?' I snapped, my gaze flying to his.

He blinked several times. 'Um, it was Hecate. She cleaned you up. You were a little bloody. Would you like me to run you a bath?' He stood and turned slightly.

Was the king of the Underworld actually offering to

run me a bath? 'That would be nice. Thank you.' Well, *this* was all kinds of weird.

He placed an ivory robe on the bed, before gliding with predatory grace into the bathroom. The robe was made of a soft, velvety material, and I shrugged it on, fastening the belt around my waist. I made my way into the bathroom and stopped.

'Wow,' I uttered. 'This place is incredible.' It was opulent, elegant, and enormous. A walk-in shower large enough for six people lined one side of the room, with an immense sunken bathtub at its centre. The tiles were warm underfoot, and the walls were like polished onyx scattered with stardust. The bathtub was deliciously decadent, full of aromatic bubbles; the shelf around the tub was lined with fancy toiletries.

'We should talk,' Hades said, his voice low as he turned to face me. 'After your bath.' My skin tingled, awareness spiking. His eyes met mine, molten and unreadable—but I remembered... His touch in the kitchen. His breath against my flesh. The way he'd vanished like a damn coward. The memory raced through my mind, igniting a wave of prickly anger.

Clinging to my irritation, and thinking about him touching me before likely fucking Minthe, a smile flickered on my lips. Payback time... *Let's see how you like it, sucker.*

If he wanted to play, I could play dirty. I smiled sweetly, sugary venom coating my words. 'Then talk while I'm in the tub... if you'd like to?'

He inhaled sharply, stiffening again, and his eyes

turned that pure golden colour. Shit! What was I doing? But there was no backing out now. Nervously, with my back to him, I slipped the robe from my shoulders, letting it pool on the floor.

Silence.

I snuck a look over my shoulder. He was ramrod straight and hadn't moved from the spot. Shadows curled around his feet like smoke, responding to his barely leashed control. His hands were fisted, and tension whitened the skin around his lips, but the look in his eyes? Gods... Downright. Fucking. Sinful.

I sucked in a heady breath as tiny shivers coursed through every part of me, causing my nipples to harden, and I swallowed thickly. Stepping as carefully as I could, attempting to look alluring and not fall on my ass, I descended the steps, completely submerging myself in the warm water. When I resurfaced, Hades was sitting somewhat stiffly at the side of the tub. I gave him a small smile, washed the blood from my hair with vanilla shampoo, dunked again, and then began to condition. Throughout, I felt his eyes on me, which invigorated me, making me braver.

'Allow me,' he said as he bent over to the taps, brushing the side of my breast with his bare forearm, making my thighs clench tightly. He turned on the attached shower head, and I tilted my head back as he gently ran warm water over my hair. While his fingers soothingly untangled my locks, a thousand butterflies fluttered in my belly beneath the warmth of his touch.

I closed my eyes and exhaled a long, slow breath. That

warm feeling in my chest spread down my body, sitting low in my stomach. I couldn't deny that *something* between us. It was palpable. Was it because he was the most ridiculously attractive man I'd ever met? It was possible... But I knew it was more than that—*much* more.

'I met Styx,' I said as he placed the shower head back onto its holder. The bubbles were just above my nipples, and as his eyes rose to mine, I realised he'd been staring at the swell of my breasts. Heat scorched my cheeks, but I wanted him to look at me that way. Then I tensed. Why did I want that? He was the freaking god of the dead.

His voice shook me from my thoughts. 'Yes, I know. I saw her briefly when she came searching for you in a state of panic.'

'Oh.' I lowered my eyebrows. 'Does she know I'm okay?'

'Hecate will inform her.' His eyes dropped to my breasts again, and I saw his throat bob in a deep swallow. That look sent all kinds of tingles through every nerve ending in my body. 'You should be honoured.' His eyes met mine again. 'Styx is very insular. We don't often see her.'

'She's an oceanid, isn't she?'

Hades nodded in response. 'Yes. And a goddess. She is the guardian of the river Styx. She always liked you.' He smiled, showing a hint of fang.

'Hmm.' I met his gaze. 'Was she like Hecate... My friend?' I pondered the strange feeling of people, whom I barely knew, once being my friends—Hedone, Charon, Thanatos, and now Styx.

'She was.' His eyes flickered between blue and gold. 'You had many friends here, Persephone.' Those words brought me a sense of comfort. I had no idea why.

'Persephone?' Hades' voice jolted me from my thoughts, and my head snapped to where he stood, a towel held in front of him. Garnering as much courage as I could muster, I drew in a deep breath and carefully stepped from the bathtub, my nakedness making me squirm... until I saw the hard set of his jaw, the burning desire in his eyes. He wanted me, and there was something unequivocally empowering in that. The intensity of his attention was like a physical caress. The tips of my breasts tightened, and flickering heat pooled between my thighs. As his eyes whipped with golden coils of aether, his stare scorched my skin. And I liked it.

Okay, I think the fall must have damaged my brain... This is utterly the last thing I need to be feeling right now.

I wrapped the towel around myself, whispering my thanks and avoiding his eyes.

'I shall see you back in the sitting room.' His voice was gruff and thick. Then he turned and left me.

I nodded at his back, and as the door snicked shut, I sank to my knees, trying to control my erratic breath. After a long while, I stood, dried myself off, towel-dried my hair, and detangled it with a paddle brush. Then, I slipped on the soft robe and walked out of the bathroom.

And back into the bedroom of the god of the Underworld.

EIGHTEEN

HADES

Gods alive, I was wound tight.

I had tasted Persephone's arousal on my tongue, like dark chocolate. My cock throbbed in unison with the beat of my heart. Her beauty still struck me hard, like lightning piercing my chest, and all rational thought became almost impossible as I stared at her.

Seeing her from behind, her rounded hips and pert butt, had almost pushed me to the brink, but when she stepped from the tub facing me... *Gods.* Water trailed in glistening rivulets down her full breasts, across her stomach, then down between her thighs—where she was bare, unashamed, utterly divine. I nearly lost it. That perfect pussy—unhidden, unapologetic—short-circuited my brain.

My cock strained against the seam of my jeans, pulsing with a desperation that clawed at the edges of my control. I wanted—needed—to press my mouth to every drop of water sliding over her skin.

What the fuck was this tiny female doing to me?

I was the King of the Underworld. I commanded death itself, and she had me on my knees... without even touching me.

After about fifteen minutes, and a freezing cold shower, I was calm enough to return to my chambers. I found Persephone sitting on the sofa, her damp hair cascading over one shoulder. Her eyes lifted to mine, and she gave me a small smile that tugged at the bond in my chest. I was desperate for her, desperate to fill her in every way, but I'd wait. I had no choice—not if I wanted her to willingly become my consort.

I poured two glasses of wine, handed her one, and sat in the opposite chair. I needed to keep my distance, or else I was close to removing that robe and devouring every inch of her, whether she accepted me or not.

'Did you use compulsion on me to make me sleep when—' She hesitated. 'I, erm...'

'Tried to ravish me?' I sipped my wine and she nearly choked on hers. 'Yes, I apologise if that upsets you, but I thought it best. I didn't want you to regret your actions.'

She gave me a slight nod, her cheeks flushing a pretty pink colour. 'After I saw you in the kitchen—' She paused, averting her gaze. 'Did you fuck Minthe?'

I jerked back, my eyes widening. 'No. Why would you think that?' She shrugged. The scent of burned sugar invaded my nostrils again. She was jealous... jealous of Minthe. 'Persephone. Minthe is a trusted employee; that's all. I promise. She works here as well as in my nightclubs. There is *nothing* between us.'

'Okay.' She met my gaze again, but uncertainty clouded her eyes. 'So, what happened to me?'

'You ended up in Tartarus, in the Empousa's lair.' I came straight out with it; I've always hated pussyfooting around.

Her eyes rounded, and those rosy cheeks blanched. 'How?'

'Someone, we don't know who, teleported you there.'

'One thing the Empousa said—' She narrowed her eyes as if in thought. 'She knew who I was because *she* told her. Who is *she*?'

I hesitated, the smoky tendrils of unease coiling in my gut. 'I will investigate.' She swiped a shaky hand down her face. 'Persephone.' Her gaze returned to mine. 'You must no longer go outside without Tee, Thanatos, Charon, or me.'

Her spine stiffened, and then she exhaled a jagged breath. 'Alright. But I need to cross the river. It's so desolate over there. I think I saw a spirit... of a man.' My eyebrows raised in surprise. 'He seemed lost and confused.'

'Your ability to see and communicate with spirits is normal,' I assured her. 'You were able to before...' I hesitated. 'The ability has always been within you; being here again has stimulated it. It will develop fully, given time.'

'Tee told me about that. It's... weird, but in a nice way.' Her eyes glistened as if she were about to cry.

Before my arms reached out to touch her, I stood. 'We could walk and chat if you'd prefer, and we could go now?'

A bright smile illuminated her beautiful face, making the pulse in my chest purr and, unfortunately, my jeans tighten again.

'I'll go and get dressed,' she said, rising to her feet.

'I have moved you to the adjoining suite.' I nodded towards the set of double doors.

'Wait. What?' Her brow puckered as she eyed me warily.

'For your safety. All of your belongings are already in there. Come.' I stood and held out an arm towards the double doors, then swung one open for her. She hesitated momentarily, then strode through the door, closing it behind her.

I grunted and sank back onto the sofa. We had so much to discuss, and I knew it was time to share the entire story about what happened to her all those years ago.

CHAPTER
NINETEEN

PERSEPHONE

The room was opulent, with a layout similar to Hades', though not as vast.

An enormous fireplace, a plush cream sofa, and chairs arranged around a coffee table filled the space, alongside a small dining table with four chairs. One door led to an extravagant bedroom featuring a large en-suite bathroom with a massive clawfoot tub, while another opened into a walk-in wardrobe brimming with my clothes and shoes.

Like Hades' rooms, fancy French doors opened onto the expansive patio area, where we had dined the night he arrived with Minthe. Jealousy reared its ugly head once more at the thought of her touching him, so I resolved not to think about freaking *Minthe*. Yet, memories of that night intruded upon my mind; it was the night I'd dreamed of him. My resistance was faltering. I desired him, and the feeling was foreign to me. I took a calming breath as I gazed towards the meadows and the life I had created.

I hurriedly dressed in leather trousers, a soft, long-sleeved top, and boots. I left my hair loose, applied a touch of coral lip colour to my lips, and was good to go.

When I walked back through the doors, he was waiting —the king of death and shadows, the king for whom I was falling. He lounged on the sofa in an almost arrogant sprawl. Dressed in leather pants and a black Henley top, his hair half pulled back in a top-knot, those liquid blue pools of flashing fire captured my gaze.

I gritted my teeth and took in a deep breath. 'I'm ready. Let's go and create some life in this dismal place.'

A half-smile adorned that beautiful face, and it took all of my strength not to react and jump him again like a spider monkey on crack. He was Mr Grumpy and Deadly. What in the world was going on with my duplicitous body? I was fighting the inevitable. I knew it, but my inner stubborn bitch held fast.

We walked down numerous hallways until we reached the door I'd previously exited. Strolling through the blooms and long grass while watching the trees sway in the gentle breeze, elevated my soul. A sense of calm enveloped me, and I almost grabbed Hades' hand. I fisted my fingers into my shirt and gulped, glancing down at the path as I walked.

We strolled in amiable silence for a time, then I asked, 'How did you find me? In Tartarus, I mean.'

'I felt you using your shadow magic. Once you used it, I knew where you were.'

'Really? Are we connected or something?'

'Something like that,' he replied without looking at me.

'Are we going to talk about—' Before I could finish, he whipped around, an angry expression on his face, and I took a step away, but when his eyes met mine, he released a weary sigh.

'Let's sit,' he commanded quietly. Planting my butt in the grass, I waited for him to join me. He settled opposite, absently tugging at grass stems as he spoke. He explained the mage's curse, losing the love of his life because of it, and how Zeus had decided to retake control of the mortal realm, declaring war on witchcraft. When our soul bond reignited in his chest, a kernel of hope blossomed within him, leading him to search for me.

'I'm sorry I kidnapped you,' he muttered, his eyes still downcast.

'I'm sorry too, especially about Persephone... me,' I whispered, unsure of what else to say to him. He didn't lift his head; instead, he continued plucking at the blades of grass. 'Where is she now? The old crone?'

'Buried deep in Tartarus.' At his words, an icy shiver tiptoed down my spine.

'Savage,' I muttered. After a few heartbeats, I continued. 'How do you keep the evil souls in Tartarus? Can they escape?'

Hades shook his head, his gaze flicking to mine briefly. 'No. The gates of Tartarus are made from Adamantine—'

'Adamantine?'

'Yes. Your divine blade is made of the same material.

The word is derived from the Greek word "adamas", which means "indestructible". The gods often use it to forge their weapons.'

'But my blade...' *Can kill gods*—the words dissolved in my throat.

'Specific inherent magical powers imbue your blade, distinct from those infused into the gates of Tartarus. Many blades went missing at one time or another. Aeons ago, Hephaestus forged every Adamantine item from meteorites that impacted the Earth... Meteorites saturated with magic.'

'So, how did they destroy the confiscated blades?'

'Hephaestus melded down the confiscated blades.' A loose strand of hair glanced off his cheek, and his eyes looked into mine. 'It is very difficult to kill me, even with your divine blade. I recommend a strike to the heart, then decapitating me with it. See if that works—if that is your ultimate aim.'

I gulped and stared at him, all words escaping me. At one time, I would have revelled in that information. Now, I couldn't begin to dream of really killing him—perhaps strangling him occasionally, maybe.

'The prisoners in Tartarus are also guarded by the hundred-handed giants,' Hades continued as if he were talking about the weather.

'They sound vicious,' I muttered.

'Oh, they are.' He smirked. 'And one of the Furies, Tisiphone, is the guardian of the gates, as well as other things.'

'Other things?'

'The Furies torture wicked souls.' I grimaced at his words. 'They are deserving of such punishment,' he said without a hint of emotion.

After a long moment, I spoke again. 'You know, regarding the banishment of magic. It's really not fair to blame every witch for the actions of one old crone. There's evil in every race: mortals, witches, and gods alike. You can't paint them all with the same brush.'

'I know.' His chest rose with a stilted breath as he scrubbed a hand across his jaw. 'Zeus does not take kindly to threats, and witches became a threat.' He paused, still looking at the ground. 'But eradicating beings with magic wasn't fair; it was a rash solution, and I apologise for the outcome.' The look of pain on his face made my heart crumple. I reached over and covered his hand with mine. He stared down at our hands for a few heartbeats, unmoving.

'Maybe—' I started. 'Maybe we could persuade Zeus to overturn the law. Allow covens and witches to coexist, as they once did. Enable the Council of Magic to flourish in peace, as they used to. Rather than being hidden away like a dirty little secret.'

He shifted his gaze to mine and squinted. 'We?' Blood rushed to my cheeks, but a smile tugged at his lips. 'Perhaps *we* could consult Hecate about that...' My heart skittered a beat, and I beamed.

Then my grin faded; his brows slammed together as he asked, 'Are you worried?'

The nightmare swirled around in my mind. The one I'd learned to suppress and block out, much like my shadow magic—they were locked in their very own Pandora's box. 'Tee told me about... your loss of control when Per... I disappeared,' I whispered. He closed his eyes, tension bracketing his mouth. 'I understand.' His eyes sprang open. 'I—I lost control once.' He didn't speak; he just studied me with those captivating eyes. 'My grandma's sister was murdered...' I swallowed. 'I was there, but I was terrified, and I hid.' Tears stung my eyes and throat. The memories of that day settled around me like a noxious, choking cloud, stealing my breath.

His eyebrows pulled down tight. 'How old were you?'

'I—I was thirteen... I can't remember what happened, but I was overcome with rage. I killed the men. There was nothing left of them; they just shrank and shrivelled into themselves,' I whispered. 'Grandma and I had to move because of it. It was the shadow magic, wasn't it?' He nodded, wiping a tear from my cheek with his thumb. The touch sent a hot, tight shiver pulsing through my core.

'Your darkness is immense, Persephone. It's making you stronger. It's a part of who you are—a facet of yourself that you need not fear. Your wrath has always made people tremble.'

My eyes widened. 'My... *wrath*?'

He tilted his head, one side of his mouth twitching upwards. 'Yes. It is, and always has been, formidable.'

Unease slid through me like slow-moving venom as shivers of apprehension worked up my spine. 'Tee said my name means Bringer of Death, but she assured me I wasn't evil. I wasn't cruel... was I?' I needed his reassurance.

197

His heart-throbbingly beautiful face sobered and his stormy gaze instantly found mine.

'Persephone, your magic embodies everything, both light and dark: death and rebirth, healing and killing. Despite the potential for misuse, your goodness consistently triumphs over the darkness. You relish defending the living and the spirit... Your goodness outweighs all that is dark. You need your shadows as much as you need your life-giving light. Without light, there can be no shadow; it's a balance within you.' I licked my too-dry lips and processed his words. 'Tee told me you are struggling to summon it—your shadow magic. It is buried deep.'

I wrapped my arms around myself. 'Extreme emotions, mainly anger and sometimes fright, are the only times I feel it.'

'Which means it is still not contained. Still dangerous.' He paused. 'I shall assist you in controlling your shadow magic. We can practice.'

I took a shaky breath. 'You will?' He nodded, and the flicker of a smile made my next breath catch.

He helped me to my feet. 'Come on, Lady Persephone. Let's go and fill this world with more life.'

For the remainder of the walk, I was lost in thought about his earlier words: the reason behind the war, his loss, and his pain. I could sense the sadness within him. Sorrow welled inside me, slicing through my chest. He blamed himself for losing Persephone and, most likely, instigating the war. This god was not at all what I'd expected; I was beginning to see the layers beneath his arrogant, grumpy exterior.

After walking in silence for about twenty minutes, we arrived at the river, and his gaze swept over the explosion of colour that my flora magic had created. The smile on his face made him compellingly beautiful. My stomach dipped and curled, and I stared at him for gods knows how long, as if I were nine kinds of crazy.

'You're staring at me,' he said without looking in my direction.

'I'm not.' My gaze turned to the riverbanks.

'You lie so prettily,' he said, his gaze returning to my face. Those bottomless pools of blue flashed with golden aether, and the muscles low in my belly tightened.

'I will shadow-walk you across the river.' Before I could answer, his arms were around me, pressing me against his hard, lean, muscular body. Shadows engulfed us, and in a heartbeat, we were there—no nausea this time. I felt safe, wrapped in the shadows with him. He didn't let me go; instead, he held me for what felt like a small eternity as I fisted my hands in his shirt and breathed in his scent like a total creeper. He released a jagged breath and stepped away from me.

'Work your magic, little goddess.'

'What?' My gaze remained fixed on him, but his jaw hardened.

'Your magic.' He motioned to the surrounding barren and sparse land, his face devoid of emotion. My eyes peeled away from him, leaving me feeling like an utter goober.

Gods, I needed to get a grip on myself, but his rapidly changing signals were giving me whiplash.

Bending down and placing my fingers in the dirt, I

unleashed my flora magic. Tingling sensations rippled through me, dancing along every nerve ending, and the area began to bloom as far as the eye could see.

'Asphodels,' I whispered as I stood, drinking in the sea of blooms: elegant, slender plants, three feet tall, with numerous leaves and millions of starry, white flowers, like windmill sails, swaying in the gentle breeze.

'Yes. You have restored the Meadows of Asphodel, Persephone. When you first arrived here with your flora magic, it was like the first flower blooming after the long vestiges of winter. You promised the warm summer days ahead.' At his words, tears misted my eyes and choked my throat. 'Asphodel derives its name from a Greek word that signifies sceptre.'

'Why?' I croaked.

'It is a sigil of the Underworld, primarily associated with you. Before you came here, most souls were left to wander the barren lands, but you changed that.'

'Me?'

He nodded. 'You decided that not only heroes deserved Elysium, but that every day, upright humans also deserved paradise.'

'I did? I made *that* difference?' I blinked at him momentarily, and he gave a lopsided smile.

'You transformed these barren lands into something beautiful when you first arrived.' His gaze lifted to mine, and I swallowed roughly as tears crowded my throat. 'The souls traverse these meadows; the beauty soothes and calms them, or it did before you disappeared.' He paused for a long moment. 'And shall do so again.' He shrugged unrepentant 'Then they enter Elysium. Well, most of them do, thanks to you. Some, however, find themselves in Tartarus.' I shivered at the thought of that creepy-ass place. 'And some souls remain here to wander, stripped of memories. Those souls do not deserve Elysium.'

'Who decides who is deserving or not?'

'Minos, Rhadamanthus, and Aeacus. These are my demigod ministers, who once established law and order on Earth. Hecate or I occasionally find ourselves summoned to judge.'

'Oh,' I hummed, not quite sure what else to say.

'Thank you,' he whispered, and those pools of sapphire swirled with gold.

I stepped towards him and placed a hand on his cheek as I looked up into those blue eyes, swimming with warm sunlit currents of aether. He lowered his lips to mine—the kiss was long, deep, and languid. A fang grazed my lip, causing my nipples to harden and my toes to curl. He pulled away and took a step back.

I touched my lip. He'd drawn blood. With a smouldering look in his eyes, he grasped my hand, lifted my finger, closed his lips around it, and sucked. The pull travelled all the way to my clit, like molten lava. Holy damn. I inhaled sharply, meeting his gaze, and a fire sparked *deep* in my belly.

I blinked once, then twice, then *launched* at him, wrapping my legs around his waist and closing my mouth over his. I felt his erection against my core, and a heated curl dipped in my stomach and went lower. As his tongue plundered my mouth, a riot of sensations crashed over me like a torrential downpour. Our lips, tongues, and breath entwined as I moaned softly in my throat, feeling him shudder.

'Hi!' The high-pitched voice startled us both, and I jumped down, running a hand through my hair. Heat scorched my cheeks as I looked around and saw a small girl standing a few feet away.

'Are you two married?' She tipped her head and stared up at us. 'My mum and dad do the kissing thing *all* the time.' She rolled her eyes. 'It's gross.' She wrinkled her nose, and I coughed out a shocked laugh.

'Are you lost?' I bent to one knee and gently stroked the girl's tiny face.

'Oh, no. Mommy and Daddy are over there,' she said, pointing. I raised my head, following the direction of her arm, and saw two smiling people. The little girl beamed and raced towards them. They all faded away.

'A whole family?' I whispered, a scalding tide of tears brimming in my eyes.

'Sometimes,' his voice soothed as he leaned down to touch my arm, then helped me to my feet.

'Will they find their way, you know, to Elysium?'

'Yes,' he murmured. 'Those who are destined are drawn to the Gates of Elysium. Let's head back.' I was in his arms again, and within a heartbeat, we were back on the other side of the river.

Before I could utter a word, a loud 'woof' almost caused my eyeballs to rattle. Hurtling towards us came Cerberus. Hades grinned at the sight. Cerberus reached us, nearly knocking Hades over, and that grin deepened until a dimple appeared.

It was obvious how much he adored Cerberus, and when he grinned—my gods, he was devastating. That dimple. That sinful little dent I suddenly ached to trace with my tongue. My gaze flicked between the three-headed hound and the man who owned him, and my chest clenched. Then he laughed— low, dark, rumbling—and it rolled through me like thunder.

My ovaries practically applauded

For the love of everything holy, I was losing my mind. I knew that the feelings I had for Hades were real. *Was* it because he was the *sexiest* man I'd ever met? My stomach clenched with apprehension—I realised whatever 'this' was ran far deeper than mere looks. Something immeasurable—it transcended chemistry; more than desire, although the desire I felt was intense. I could feel it, whatever *it* was, in every part of my being.

It was something tangible yet ineffable... The bond.

The horny bond-bitch had a tantrum in my chest and commanded me to cling to him like a psychotic limpet and take what I needed. I pushed the sexually frustrated little fucker back down—not happening. Nope. I wasn't giving in.

But gods, it was tempting.

I was lost in my conflicting emotions when Cerberus zeroed in on me and lunged, pinning me to the ground and making me squeal with laughter.

'Hi, baby. Oh, you're such a cutie. Let's give the big, proud puppy dog a scritch-scratch. You big soft bundle of fluff.' I buried my fingers in his fur and raked my nails against his skin, eliciting a low groan as he licked my face with all three tongues.

'Stop talking to him like that. You'll embarrass him,' Hades said awkwardly but with a slight smile. I laughed even harder... The king of shadows was trying to be facetious. He took my hand and helped me to my feet but released me as we walked, Cerberus bounding alongside us.

'What does Cerberus mean?' I asked as I scratched the hound's head.

Hades' nose wrinkled, and I'm pretty sure he blushed. 'It evolved from the word "Kérberos", which means "spotted".'

I burst out laughing. 'You, oh mighty Lord of the Dead, literally named your dog Spot?'

He gave a half-shrug. 'Well, he has a spot on his belly.' Tears streamed down my face as I struggled to breathe from uncontrollable laughter. He shook his head. 'Ignore her, Cerberus; she's just rude,' he grumbled.

When we arrived back at the castle, I gave Cerberus a belly rub—checking out his apparent 'spot'—showered him with kisses, and reluctantly left him after Hades refused to allow him to sleep in my bedroom. We sauntered back to my chambers, and he poured two glasses of nectar, handing me one. I was exhausted from using so much flora magic.

'Are you hungry?' Hades asked.

'I'm starving!' My eyes widened at the thought of

food. 'Will you cook or conjure food?' He was about to answer, but I continued. 'If you conjure food, can we have New York-style hot dogs? Please?' I made grabby hands at him.

He rolled his eyes, clicked his fingers, and juicy hot dogs topped with sauerkraut, sautéed onions, ketchup, and mustard appeared inside fluffy buns. I squealed with delight and dove in, downing the feast so quickly, I'm surprised I didn't choke. Hades watched me as he nibbled politely on a hotdog.

I licked my fingers and lips and took a large gulp of nectar. 'May I ask you something?'

He placed his food on the plate. 'Of course.'

'When I drank your blood'—I side-eyed him—'I felt a myriad of emotions.' I hesitated. 'Emotions that weren't mine.'

He stiffened. 'Are you spying on me, little goddess?'

'What? No! I—'

'They were my emotions, Persephone. Occasionally, the recipient of the life force experiences heightened emotions after consuming blood. I'm sorry you experienced that. I should go. Get some rest.'

Before I could answer, he disappeared into the aether, leaving me irritated and confused. What was going on with him? One minute, he was devouring my mouth; the next, his shields were back up. His fluctuating mood swings were worse than PMS. I lowered my brows as I chewed my lip.

The emotions I'd sensed... *Was that how he felt about*

me? Or are those the feelings he held for his original Persephone?

I needed to be cautious, because I wasn't her anymore.

TWENTY

HADES

I stripped off and took a cold shower.

Watching Persephone eat that hotdog, licking her bottom lip, and sucking her fingertips... pure torture. The actions had juiced my brain like an orange, making my cock uncomfortably hard. I closed my eyes as the cold water hit my shoulders.

Persephone affected me in ways no other woman ever had. The image of her sucking her fingers flashed behind my eyelids, setting my skin aflame. I curled my fist around my painfully hard cock and groaned, taking a tortured breath as I stroked myself from base to tip. Bracing my other hand on the wall, I continued fisting my hard length, starting with slow, firm strokes that made me shudder as I thought about Persephone's mouth.

As I pumped harder, my eyes closed with pain and pleasure, and as my fist moved up and down my length, I imagined *her* lips around my cock instead of my hand, causing the base of my spine to gather and jolt. Coming with a roar, I leaned my forehead against the shower wall and rasped, 'She's mine.'

Gods, this woman would be the death of me.

Every part of me—every cell, every molecule—desired, needed, and coveted Persephone. Was it obsession? Maybe... but it was also love. True love. Are they the same thing, I wondered? Regardless, I would do anything to make her happy—anything.

She felt my emotions when she consumed my blood. I allowed her to drink too much, yet I wasn't ready to lay myself bare for her. Not if she continued to reject our bond. Hecate was right about protecting my heart.

Sighing, I readied myself for the Council meeting, wondering what news had Zeus's pants in a twist. But first, I needed to talk to Hecate, Charon, and Thanatos.

'What?' Hecate screeched. 'How in Olympus did she end up in Tartarus?'

'Teleported. By whom, I do not know. But the Empousa mentioned a *she*,' I replied.

'It must be a god... a traitor,' Thanatos mused, his face twisted with fury.

'I think there's more than one.' I placed a finger on my lower lip.

'But why Persephone?' Charon asked. He, too, looked murderous.

I gave a half-shrug. 'We must protect her at all costs. I instructed her to never leave the castle's safety without one of us accompanying her.' All three nodded at me. 'I have a meeting. Hecate, do not let Persephone leave the castle alone.'

'Of course,' she replied.

Ten minutes later, I stood in Zeus's grand meeting room at his New York offices, along with my fellow gods. The room was flamboyant, much like Zeus; plush leather chairs encircled a large silver conference table, while servers offered trays of ambrosia canapés and nectar as the gods mingled in groups.

We had dwindled to ten members due to the disappearance of Hera and Artemis in the war, now presumed dead, and Demeter's self-imposed isolation. I had reluctantly accepted a seat on the Council, despite my lack of interest in politics, to closely monitor Zeus's decision-making.

'Hades!' A beaming Hermes clapped me on the back before slinging an arm around my shoulders. 'How's the lovely Persephone?' he whispered in my ear.

'Exasperating,' I grumbled, much to his delight.

'She always did put you in your place and lead you a merry dance.'

I eyeballed my friend, scowling. He was correct, though—my Persephone had been a force to be reckoned with. Many gods feared her, yet all of them respected her.

'Hades, brother.' Zeus strode in our direction, the trademark cocky smile plastered across his face.

'Zeus,' I gritted through clenched teeth before downing a goblet of nectar.

'We have much to discuss.' A flicker of concern crossed

his face, and a sense of unease wrapped its smoky tendrils around me. Zeus never worried.

Poseidon emerged amidst a burst of seafoam and mist, looking as surly as ever. Many gods dressed in modern human attire, although Athena and Hephaestus still favoured the traditional chiton and himation. Poseidon donned his signature surfer shorts and loud shirt—likely to piss off our brother.

'Hades.' He nodded my way. Poseidon and I were allies to some degree; we had always had each other's backs. People perceived me as the fractious god, but Poseidon was in another league. Hermes suspected he needed 'a good screwing'—typical of Hermes logic. Poseidon hadn't shown interest in the fairer sex since Amphitrite's death centuries ago. Unlike our brother, Zeus, he wasn't the stud of the many legends.

'Welcome to the emergency meeting,' Zeus declared as we took our allotted places. Dionysus winked at me, looking as relaxed as ever, while a few gods offered me respectful nods. 'We have a problem...' At Zeus's words, many gods groaned, but Poseidon and I leaned forward, our elbows resting on the table.

'What sort of problem, Brother?' Poseidon's husky, baritone voice carried an authority that commanded respect.

'Ixion is back, causing problems.'

'Shit,' Dionysus muttered.

The resistance was a radical group of mortals who disrespected and were enemies of the gods. Their name was Ixion, after the king of the Lapiths tribe in Thessaly—

a king with an infamous reputation as mad, bad, and dangerous to know. Zeus had shown compassion for Ixion and recused said asshole, absolving him of the guilt of many crimes. However, behind Zeus's back, Ixion started flirting and pursuing Zeus's wife, Hera. Zeus could not believe how ungrateful and brazen Ixion had been, just as he couldn't conceive the resistance's insolence for disrespecting the gods. When the group of resistors had chosen the name Ixion, the king of the gods had been royally pissed off.

'They are targeting demigods,' Zeus said with a tut. 'A senator fell victim to an attack this morning. He is wounded, but not fatally. At the same time, there was an attempt on the prime minister in Downing Street. We must all remain vigilant.'

Ixion wielded weapons of the gods and posed a significant threat, particularly to the descendants of demigods, who effectively managed mortal politics in our stead.

'Witches are most likely behind it,' Zeus asserted.

'I'm not so sure, Brother.' At my words, his gaze fixed on mine, and he raised a brow. 'Someone teleported Persephone to Tartarus.' A few people gasped, and Hermes cursed under his breath. 'I don't think magic poses a threat to us any longer.'

'You don't?' Zeus squinted at me.

'No. We know that every being with witchcraft has gone underground worldwide, and I believe if we approach the Council of Magic, they may become our unlikely allies.'

'They pose a threat to us!' Zeus snapped.

'Do they?' I pondered as his brows dropped. 'One old crone was the enemy, not the entire race.' Zeus's mouth turned down as he regarded me. 'I believe someone far more dangerous is orchestrating Ixion. The Empousa mentioned a "she" to Persephone. I suspect that this individual is a powerful god with minor gods, demigods, *and* humans working for them.'

'That is ridiculous,' Ares growled.

'Is it?' I held his gaze until he dropped his eyes.

'You mean one of us is a traitor?' Athena frowned.

I raised my arms in a 'who knows' gesture. 'Perhaps. Or maybe some lesser gods are in dissension. Many are displeased with the freedom mortals enjoy under our reign.'

'Whoever it is, we must keep this quiet and remain heedful of the situation. I have assigned additional security details to each demigod in power.' Zeus motioned to a server for more nectar as he stood, bringing the meeting to an end. 'Oh,' he said as he turned back to the table, his eyes snagging mine. 'I look forward to seeing you all at Aphrodite's welcoming party tomorrow, where we will finally meet the delectable Persephone.'

My face betrayed no emotion, but inside, I was a tempest of irritation.

'There will be a strict rule,' he added. 'No god participating in the competition is allowed to use compulsion. Anyone caught doing so will face consequences.'

I stood as Hermes and Dionysus approached me. 'I've managed to discover there are four contenders besides you in this absurd competition,' Dionysus uttered. 'Apollo,

Ares, Zeus, and Adonis.' At the mention of the last name, my teeth clenched so hard that I'm surprised I didn't break my jaw. Apollo sauntered up to us, grinning like a cat that had eaten a roomful of canaries.

'Hades.' He bowed his head. 'Zeus said Persephone is her own woman and can give any man her attention if she wishes. I wanted to confirm that it was true. I don't fancy ending up in Tartarus,' he added quietly.

'Persephone is a goddess capable of making her own choices,' I gritted out, struggling not to give the fucker a slap.

'Great!' He grinned again. 'This is going to be entertaining.' Then he disappeared before I could throttle him.

'It'll be alright, Hades,' Hermes murmured, and Dionysus nodded in agreement. 'One word of advice, though...'

'Do tell, oh wise one.' I rolled my eyes.

'Just don't be any creepier than usual, and you'll do great.' He and Dionysus vanished, leaving me with their raucous laughter ringing in my ears.

CHAPTER
TWENTY-ONE

PERSEPHONE

t was the day of Aphrodite's welcome party, and Tee and Hedone were flitting around like cracked-out hummingbirds, making me more angsty.

I was as jittery as a coffee fiend. I'd spoken to Tee about being teleported to the Empousa's lair, and the only thing she'd said about it was a slightly macabre, 'Thank fuck you're not dead,' and that we'd chat about it another time. But she was on edge; I could tell.

My pale blonde hair cascaded down my back in soft waves, glistening beneath the shimmering lights, and my makeup was nothing short of perfect. The dress Hedone had chosen for me was simply stunning, featuring slender silver straps fastening behind my neck, each widening downwards to cover my breasts, fitting snugly and leaving my upper back exposed. From a thick band just below my chest, chiffon swirled to the floor in waves of midnight blue and indigo.

Slim silver panels flowed between the two, resembling stars peeking through broken clouds in the night sky. A pair of silver Grecian-style sandals and a silver clutch completed the ensemble. Tee dotted my pulse points with a perfume reminiscent of orange blossom and creamy tuberose, and I was ready.

I'd never felt so beautiful, but unease clawed in my gut at the thought of meeting the gods who wanted to woo me. They were probably like a bunch of great whites throwing their maws open, waiting for fresh meat.

Super.

'There's one thing I need to mention,' Hedone said as she fiddled with my hair.

'Mhm,' I mused, looking into the full-length mirror and fingering the soft material of the dress.

'When nectar and wine flow and gods and demigods gather, sex is usually often inevitable.'

My body spun around to face her. 'Is it, like, an orgy? If it is...'

Hedone erupted into a tinkling laugh. 'No. But many will seize the situation and escape for a while. Aphrodite has private rooms...' She pressed her lips together.

I lifted my chin as nausea gripped me, contemplating Hades using compulsion to make me sleep. 'Can gods, um, use compulsion to make someone have sex with them?' I was acutely aware of my unsteady voice while Tee soothingly stroked my back.

'Yes,' Hedone said, 'but it is strictly forbidden to do so.

Don't worry.' I nodded silently. 'And of course, being in Aphrodite's presence fuels this behaviour.'

'What... do you mean?' I squinted at Hedone.

'Well, Aphrodite's presence tends to amplify sexual emotions. However, you wouldn't act against your will. It simply lowers your inhibitions. So—' Hedone gave a half-shrug.

'Excuse me?' I squeak-whispered.

Tee spoke softly, still stroking my back. 'Aphrodite possesses the power to ignite passion and stir desire, but only if it already exists. She embodies the epitome of feminine grace and allure, enchanting all who encounter her. Don't worry, Sephy. She is charm personified. You will adore her.'

Even with Tee's assurance, tendrils of dread sprouted in my gut. I was entering the lion's den, and panic threatened to take hold. *This is seriously worrying. But Hades will protect me, won't he?* Then I thought about Hades and my intense attraction to him. Shit. If Aphrodite ignited my attraction any further, I'd end up becoming a methed-out koala and jumping him again, like I did after drinking his blood. Oh, gods. This could be a complete and utter clusterfuck.

Hedone shook me from my thoughts as she air-kissed me, saying, 'See you soon.' Then she turned to Tee. 'Catch you later, my love.' She planted a kiss on Tee's lips and disappeared.

'Are you and Hedone...?' I tilted my head at Tee.

'Yeah.' Her eyes glimmered like two lodestars. 'We're together. Have been for...' She glanced up at the ceiling deep in thought. 'Maybe two hundred years. She's good for me and great in the sack.'

I let out a shocked laugh. 'But the ice pop.' I frowned. 'When she was trying to give me blowjob lessons.' I grimaced.

'She's the goddess of sensual pleasure, Sephy. She loves men and women. But we're exclusive now,' Tee drawled, winking at me, and my heart swelled at the look of love on her face.

'My shadow magic,' I started, and Tee cocked her head 'Gets excitable when I'm around Thanatos and Erebus. Is that normal?'

'They are ancient creatures of darkness, Sephy. They've always revered you and your magic. Especially Erebus. He is, after all, the god of darkness. They and Hades can feel your magic... It's like a siren call to them. Your magic is the same as Hades', but not as potent.'

'Is that why he wants me?'

She released a frustrated breath. 'No, Sephy. He wants you because he loves you.'

A knock on the door caused Tee to furrow her brows and walk to answer it. 'That'll be my escort,' I muttered as I took deep, steadying breaths, then topped up my lip colour.

She stopped dead and turned around slowly. 'What? What about me?'

'You can be Hades' escort.' I shrugged in front of the full-length mirror.

As she opened the door, I heard her gasp, and I stifled my grin. 'Hey, Simmy, come in,' I called out.

'You've invited a Satyr? What the...' Tee gritted out.

'Charming,' Simmy grumbled as he stepped through the door, looking as cute as ever in a sleeveless, buttoned-up, fancy red waistcoat.

'He's my friend. I like him.' I chuckled at Tee's expression.

'Your Highness.' Simmy gave an exaggerated bow.

'Don't call me that, idiot. Come on, let's go. Move your donkey butt.'

'Hey! It's a goat butt, thank you.'

Simmy shifted his focus to Tee, and his eyes sparkled. Tee, as always, looked like a runway model in her black silk, figure-hugging evening dress, with her midnight-black hair woven into long micro-braids that touched her shoulder blades.

'Lady Hecate.' Simmy winked and gave a polite bow to the goddess, who rolled her eyes hard enough to pull a muscle.

'Let's go,' Tee snapped. So, with nerves cramping up my belly, Tee grabbed us both, and the next moment, we were flashing to Aphrodite's Court of Pafos.

We arrived in what appeared to be a grand courtyard, standing on a raised terrace that overlooked the vast area. Behind us stood the most exquisite mansion, or maybe a palace, constructed from white marble veined with grey. The tall grey roof featured four conical towers, partially visible, capped with pointed roofs. It reminded me of a fairy-tale palace. The evening sky was serene, with the sunset painting the clouds in orange, pink, and purple hues, interspersed with thin lines of silver threading the horizon like melted platinum.

Hundreds of random poseur tables, laden with vases of blooms, filled the courtyard, and tiny lights and climbing jasmine covered the dozens of substantial Grecian pillars around the perimeter—the fragrance of the jasmine drifting to my nostrils on the gentle evening breeze. Torches with enormous pink flames atop each pillar illuminated the entire courtyard, and cleverly landscaped tall flowering trees punctuated the vastness of the area; it was truly exquisite. A string quartet played background music to the hum of chatter, and suddenly, the whole place fell silent.

Everywhere I looked, I saw faces turned towards me. So many beautiful people dressed elegantly, holding fancy-schmaltzy glassware, and gazing at me with expectation. *At me!* Oh, my gods, it was so silent you could hear a fly fart. And, of course, I froze on the spot.

'Own it, Persephone,' Simmy whispered.

'He's right. You've got this, girlfriend,' Tee murmured close to my ear.

So, I inhaled deeply, kicked myself up the butt, straightened my spine, lifted my chin, and smiled widely. My confidence swelled as I gracefully descended the steps to the rhythm of the now-resumed music and moved further into the courtyard.

'Drink?' Simmy uttered softly, and I nodded. A passing Satyr offered him a tray, and he grabbed a drink for Tee and me. I sipped, and the pink liquid fizzled on my tongue, tasting of ripe berries and sunshine.

'Mm,' I murmured, taking another sip. As I walked, people stopped to introduce themselves. For the next hour, I outshone myself—my demeanour radiated grace, decorum, and a warm smile. I caught Hedone's eye, and she beamed at me.

'There's my favourite girl,' a voice I recognised said from behind as large hands spun me around.

'Hermes!' I laughed as I kissed the cheek of the mischievous messenger god.

'My lady.' He bowed, then grinned at me.

'Hey, Dionysus.' The god of wine and pleasure took my hand and kissed it.

'I must say, you look gorgeous this evening,' Dionysus said, making me blush. 'More wine?' I nodded as he handed me a glass of the fruity pink fizz.

'So, how's it going?' Hermes whispered wickedly.

'It's actually fine. So far, everyone has been nice and friendly.' I smiled warmly up at him.

'Where's your husband?' At his words, my stomach flip-flopped. *Husband*. As soon as the words left Hermes' mouth, tiny tingles spread across the nape of my neck, and I took an unsteady breath as the tug in my chest intensified. Hades was near.

When I caught sight of him, my thighs clenched, and I felt my cheeks heat. Even though he spoke to Charon, his eyes were fixed on me. Hades in a tuxedo was... well, everything that a man-parts-loving female or male's wet dream is made of. Every naughty fantasy rolled into one. He maintained his distance, though, and despite his eyes boring into me, he didn't acknowledge my presence, which pissed me off. He stood with Thanatos, Charon, Tee, and Erebus, who all waved in my direction but didn't attempt to approach us.

A passing server offered me a tray of tiny canapés, and because I was starving, I took a few and discreetly stuffed them all into my mouth.

Simmy stuck close to me while I chatted and giggled with Dionysus and Hermes, ignoring the tingles at the base of my neck. I knew Hades' eyes were on me.

People began applauding, and I turned around to see the most stunning woman I'd ever laid eyes on stride elegantly down the steps in our direction, with Hedone by her side. I assumed her to be Aphrodite; with hair a thousand shades of gold married together and pale brown skin, she could have graced the cover of any top magazine.

She was captivating—tall, slender, and ridiculously beautiful. She wore a long, diaphanous dress of pale gold. I could see the darker hue of her nipples and the swell of her full hips, and as my eyes lowered, I choked on a laugh. Well, I could see way too much. Yep, I needed to bleach out my eyeballs. Everybody's eyes were on us as she approached me.

'Persephone, my darling.' Her voice was low and sultry, like honey mixed with gravel. I felt my cheeks warm as I gave her a small curtsy. She laughed, shaking her head. 'Come here.' She enveloped me in a warm embrace, squeezing gently. Hesitantly, I mirrored the gesture, and she whispered, 'I've missed you so much.' Her words caused a lump to form in my throat, and tears pricked at my eyes. I didn't know her, and the guilt of that dug its gnarly talons into me.

'I—I'm sorry. I—'

'Don't apologise, darling. I know you don't remember me. We can reacquaint ourselves and relive all the fun we once had, hopefully.' Her piercing aquamarine eyes held mine, and I nodded, giving her a wobbly smile.

'How is Hades?'

'Fine,' I replied far too quickly. 'He's fine.'

Her smile was as cold and lovely as frost on a window-pane. 'Zeus is an arrogant egotist. Apparently, he's been a wanker since birth. Don't tell him I said that,' she murmured next to my ear, causing me to giggle. 'This competition to woo you is ridiculous. We all know you love our dark god.' She winked at me, and I kept my mouth shut, unsure how to respond. 'Let's catch up soon, darling.'

'Yes. Yes, I'd like that,' I breathed as she air-kissed me and wandered into the throng of guests.

Aphrodite was beautiful, but her proximity emanated so much more than mere beauty—a potent cocktail of lust and longing. She stirred the feelings I was attempting to bury—the desire I harboured for Hades, the infuriatingly arrogant god. Hermes and Dionysus were deep in conver-sation with another person, so I swallowed hard and turned to Simmy.

'Let's have another drink.'

'Oh. My. Gods. Apollo,' Simmy squeaked as we strolled past, nodding towards an attractive man by one of the large pillars.

'Are you fangirling Apollo? I thought you liked women?'

'I do, but you've gotta appreciate beauty in any form, and apparently, he has a huge—'

'Do *not* finish that sentence.'

'What's wrong with you? He's hot!' *Not as hot as Hades.* I wanted to stab that annoying little voice whispering in my ear.

We mingled; I met people, drank wine, and, while socialising, discreetly grabbed and devoured enough canapés to feed a small village. The tingling sensation lingered; I knew Hades' eyes were on me. I took the dress as a success, because every time my gaze caught his, he was staring at me, and a muscle in his jaw feathered lightly each time our eyes locked.

I took another glass of wine as a different god sauntered towards me. I could tell he was a god because he was enormous, beautiful, and a cocky SOB, dressed in a smart, deep blue button-down shirt that strained against his muscled chest and tailored trousers that clung to his massive legs. High cheekbones, a square jaw, and drop-dead gorgeous—in fact, he had the look of Hades. His long, wavy hair was so blond it appeared almost silver, and his eyes were like the ocean on a stormy day—blue-green with tinges of grey and silver. A hum of power radiated from him. I placed my glass on a nearby poseur table and gave him my undivided attention.

'Persephone.' He bowed his head, and I smiled my fake smile, extending my hand. He clasped it, sending a hot shiver crawling down my spine. He turned my hand over and kissed my palm. 'Poseidon.'

'Oh, erm, pleased to meet you. I hope you enjoy the evening.'

'Thank you,' he grunted.

'So...' I hesitated. 'Are you competing in this ridiculous competition to become my husband?' The idea sent another shiver tiptoeing down my spine.

'No. I wouldn't do that to my brother. Unlike some.' His eyes turned to Zeus, and his mouth slammed into a thin line.

'Oh...' I squeaked. Maybe Poseidon wasn't so bad.

'Additionally, I found you rather irritating. Not my type.'

I loosed a cough-laugh. 'What? You don't like strong women with brains and opinions?'

'No. I prefer to be in charge.' He winked.

'At least Hades is confident enough in his masculinity to want a headstrong woman,' I growl-snapped.

'Too much hassle. Subservience is far easier.' He raised an arrogant eyebrow at me.

'Well, aren't you a freaking ray of sunshine?'

'Be careful, Human. I am a god.'

'Yeah, whoop-dee-doo,' I muttered.

'See... irritating. I don't understand why Hades is so obsessed with you. You've always had a bad attitude.'

Well, that was kind of rude. I placed my hands on my hips. 'I'm a goddess, actually.'

'Yes, a goddess who pussy-whipped my brother. And

I'm the king of the sea... a very important god. So, if you break my brother's heart, I'll flood your city.'

My eyes widened, and every part of my being ached to punch him. Hard. 'You may be an important god, but you're still a dickhead.'

Poseidon's eyes flashed like the waves of said stormy sea, and then he bellowed with laughter, engulfing me in a bear hug that almost severed my spine. 'There she is, the ball-whipping vixen.' He let me go, and I grunted. 'Another drink?' He cocked his head, and I shook mine.

'I'm fine, thanks.' I smiled through gritted teeth, and he spurted a laugh as he walked off.

What a cockwomble.

'Persephone.' Hedone's voice made me turn. 'I'd like to introduce you to Ares.' I heard Simmy, who had just returned, groan and then abandon me again. The git. A man who resembled a superhero from a Marvel movie— the enormous type of hero—eyed me with interest. His blond hair was buzzed short, and his shoulders were broad. He was stacked, his muscular arms clearly visible through his white tuxedo shirt. I smiled warmly and extended my hand. His wrist cords bulged like tree roots, and his powerful fingers enveloped my much smaller ones as he bowed to kiss the back of my hand, lingering a little too long to be polite. I gently tugged my hand away.

'Nice to meet you, Ares,' I said in a gracious voice.

'Likewise, Persephone.' Like flames of silver fire, his grey eyes roamed over me, while a smirk danced on his lips. Ares, the god of war, or more fittingly, the spirit of battle —and most probably a jackass. 'Come and stand with me.'

I had little choice, as he all but carried me to a nearby pillar and stood way within my personal space. He threw off testosterone in bucketloads as he eyeballed me. Feeling slightly uncomfortable, I took a step backwards, but he followed. I was screwed because my back now rested against the pillar, and he caged me in when his giant body almost pressed against mine... I guessed he was unfamiliar with the concept of chivalry. He bent slightly and inhaled long and slow, before raising his eyes to meet mine again.

I blinked. Blinked again. And then again. 'Are you freaking *smelling* me?'

'Good enough to eat.' A devilish smile pulled on his lips, and I threw up a little in my mouth, so I took a large gulp of wine. 'I always did like you. Hades was a lucky fucker the first time around. Now I'm going to win you for myself. Just imagine the fun we could have in the sack.' I nearly stopped breathing at the thought, and my stomach roiled. The prick grinned until a godsdamned dimple appeared on his cheek. My anger flared, and common sense went out of the window.

'Has anyone ever told you you're particularly stab-worthy?' I growled softly, wishing I had my divine blade with me. I'd stab him in the cock.

His response? Roaring laughter. 'See! We'd argue and fight, but gods, the make-up sex would be worth it. You've always been a walking, talking siren, Persephone.' He cupped his dick with a hand and grinned at me again.

'You're a rude pain in the ass, and—'

'I'd love to be a pain in your—'

I almost choked on my wine. 'Do *not* finish that! Ugh, you're disgusting.'

'And sexy.'

'Pft.' I glared at him.

'I can't help it. I'm irresistible. You're adorable, even when you're grouchy. Marry me, Persephone. I'll fuck you until you can't walk. You'll love it.' He winked at me. He actually fucking winked at me. 'If Hades can't handle your fire, babe, I'd be more than happy to teach you how to burn.'

Instead of flinging my glass at him, I acted like a lady, curling my lip and shooting him a death glare before scooting under his arm.

'You didn't say no,' he called after me.

'Gods, what a dick,' I muttered to myself. 'And what a dreadful thought. Ugh.' I spotted Simmy again and whinged, 'I need more wine.'

Simmy returned with a glass of pink fizz, and I took a sip. That tingling at the back of my neck made me raise my gaze to Hades, whose eyes were pinned to me from across the courtyard. His jaw was like granite; in fact, he looked murderous. Furious. He was so big.

Furiously... *big*.

Charon, Erebus, and Thanatos gathered around him as Tee whispered in his ear. I gave him a small smile, and my heart sank when he looked away to greet someone approaching them—Minthe. He began chatting with the laughing Minthe, who wore a low-cut, scarlet, sequined gown, and a sour taste filled the back of my throat. I was two seconds away from running, jumping on his back like a monkey, and strangling him. Instead, I exhaled a frustrated sigh and downed more wine.

'How'd it go with Ares?' Simmy gave me the side-eye.

'He's an absolute dick.'

Simmy hooted with laughter and nearly spat out his drink. 'Yeah. He's not very popular. But apparently, he's also got a big—'

'Shut up, you moron.'

Simmy snickered, then cleared his throat. 'See you in a bit. I'll keep an eye on you. Enjoy.' He shot me a wary look.

'What? Where—'

'Persephone.' An icy shiver trickled down my back like a waterfall of spiders. I recognised that voice. I turned around slowly and looked up to meet the violet and silver eyes of the tall, muscular hottie from Kew Gardens. His shoulder-length, dark-blond hair now hung loosely around his jaw-dropping face, and dressed in a tux, shirt open at the collar, he was particularly droolworthy. 'I'm Zeus. Pleased to meet you... again.' He gave me a small wink, a razor-sharp smile cutting across his lips.

'Zee,' I whispered. *Shit. Zee is Zeus.*

Fuck. My. Life.

A kernel of panic took root, and I worried my bottom lip. The last time I'd met him, I had been rude. But, to be fair, he *had* been a complete creepy jackass. I couldn't run. I couldn't hide anywhere. I needed to pull on my big girl panties and face my colossal fuckup like a woman. I inhaled deeply and held his gaze.

'Zeus. How nice to see you again. You look rather suave this evening.' I extended my hand to him.

His large, warm hand enveloped mine, and as his lips brushed against my skin, a hot, delicious shiver ran from my spine to my toes. I tried not to shudder as I withdrew my hand. Power emanated from him, and as he met my eyes again, I tried to remember to breathe.

'You and I, maybe, got off on the wrong foot, Persephone.'

'What, when you stalked me?' I bit out before my brain engaged. Those beautiful eyes swirled with silver again, and then he smiled. A smile that made my heart trip up. His mouth twitched, and I silently cursed. He could sense my attraction.

'I'm not the only one who has been stalking you.'

'What do you mean?' I squinted up at him.

'Well, Hades, of course.'

I fell silent. I tried to swallow, but the lump in my throat made it difficult.

'I'd never seen Hades before I came to the Underworld.' For obvious reasons, I didn't mention the night I fought the Lamia.

'Before he kidnapped you, you mean?' Sugary amusement dripped from his words. His voice the whole time was soothing and melodic, and those eyes—gods, they were spellbinding. 'He has been visiting you in your dreams for quite some time.'

My brows furrowed. 'What?' Then I realised. Oh, my gods. My garden. And I felt my face heat as I recalled *that* dream—the dream when his shadows... Gods. My embarrassment could have probably powered every solar panel in London. I couldn't react, but I was going to stab Hades in the cock, never mind Ares. I schooled my face into a neutral expression. 'Why are you telling me this?'

Zeus smirked. 'Honesty is the best policy.' He raised his shoulders.

'Are you trying to woo me, Zeus?'

His smile turned malevolent. 'Of course, I am.'

'Then stop with the backstabbing and bitching. It's rather off-putting... A little like stalking.' My inclination was to throat-punch him, but that would be a colossal mistake. Instead, I took a long, deep breath through my nose, raised my chin, and arched an eyebrow as I held his gaze.

Zeus smiled; it was a hide-your-kids-and-loved-ones sort of smile, but then he rumbled a laugh. 'Oh, maleficent Persephone. You're quite endearing. It's no wonder my brother is so infatuated with you.' He took my hand, and I flinched at the contact. 'He loves you, Persephone. Don't fuck it up. And do *not* fucking break the bastard's heart.' Then he kissed my hand again and walked away, leaving me utterly bemused.

TWENTY-TWO

HADES

The metallic, bitter taste of anger filled my mouth with every breath as I watched the other gods touch *my* wife.

When Ares had manhandled her, I spat, 'I'll fucking kill him,' as fury consumed me. It took Charon, Thanatos, and Erebus to hold me while Tee spoke to me as if she were trying to calm a wild animal. I knew they were guarding me, not leaving my side, worried about the outcome of Zeus's ridiculous circus.

I watched Persephone stare up at fucking Adonis, and when that scum kissed her hand, rage surged through me like a category-five hurricane. Again, Charon had placed a warning hand on my arm. My burning gaze poured into Adonis's worthless soul like boiling lava. He was an abomination—one of the most tainted souls I'd ever encountered. I'd kill that bastard one day... but she didn't linger long with him, thank the Fates.

Now, Apollo was making his move. The little cock. He was making her laugh, chatting with her for longer than any of the other assholes. I could sense her attraction to him, and my stomach twisted into raw knots as unease blossomed in my gut. I seethed... Was he *singing* to her? Fury coiled inside as red-hot tendrils of rage cascaded through my body. I looked away, my jaw working as icy talons of jealousy dug deep. Closing my eyes, I tried to steady my breathing.

'Are you alright?' my old friend Hermes mumbled as he placed a glass of nectar in my hand. 'You look like you want to kick someone in the balls.'

'He's trying to process his emotions and stop himself from destroying Aphrodite's court,' Hecate said softly.

'Huh?' A somewhat inebriated Dionysus wrinkled his nose as he slurped his wine.

I huffed out a breath. 'I've got to have her. She belongs to me. She's *mine*.'

'Then you're doing a shit job of it,' Hermes growl-whispered as he watched Persephone laughing at whatever Apollo was saying. 'Better figure out if she's worth fighting for, and fast. You have some tough competition, particularly Apollo, and if she thinks you don't want her, she might choose someone who does.'

I growled softly in my throat.

'That's what I keep telling him,' Hecate agreed, and I cast her a withering glance. 'Pull your head from up your arrogant ass.'

'My patience is wearing thin, Titan,' I fumed as Hermes and Dionysus both choked with laughter.

'Well, someone has to push your buttons and set you straight. Now, grow a vagina and go and ask her to dance before pretty boy Apollo makes his move.'

TWENTY-THREE

PERSEPHONE

S immy handed me another glass of wine as yet another god approached.

'Oh, for Fate's sake,' I muttered.

'That's Adonis. Watch yourself, Lady P,' Simmy loud-whispered before making himself scarce. Hmmm, Adonis, the god of beauty and desire.

'Lady Persephone. My name is Adonis.' The god bowed low.

'A pleasure to meet you, Adonis. You look very sophisticated this evening,' I said, my fake smile plastered on like war paint. I extended my hand, and he pressed his lips to it with a long, slow kiss, which made my skin tighten in a way that definitely wasn't pleasant.

His topaz eyes lifted to mine, glinting with lazy amusement, as if he were in on a joke I hadn't heard. He was every inch the sculpted ideal—tall, broad, auburn hair

234

cropped short at the sides and longer on top; his features so classically handsome it was almost offensive. Definitely a man you'd look at twice.

'Oh, we've met before.'

'I know, but—'

'I am aware. It's a shame you can't recall the marathon sex sessions we used to have. Gods, I miss your body, Persephone,' he whispered close to my ear, his breath coasting across my cheek like a winter breeze.

'Sorry? What?' Tiny bumps spread across my arms.

'You and I were lovers, Persephone,' he muttered. 'You adored visiting Phoenicia. You cherished the beauty of my court.'

I released a strangled laugh at the absurdity of the situation.

'No way. There's no way I'd cheat on my husband,' I snarl-whispered.

He completely ignored me. 'If you were to choose me this time and become my wife, we wouldn't have to sneak around.' He flashed me a smile, dimples and all; they were nowhere near as lovely as Hades' dimple, and my heart fractured. Was he telling the truth?

Oh, crap.

'I used to love watching you sleep and—'

'Whoa... back up there, Edward Cullen.' I took a step away and held up my hands as he frowned at me. 'I —I need to go.' I turned around, tears blurring my vision as I rushed away, when Simmy's hand caught my wrist.

'Persephone?'

'I don't like him,' I breathed, swiping tears from my eyes and probably ruining my makeup.

'Good,' Simmy said with a smile as he handed me another pink fizz. I sat there, stewing in silence, Adonis's words echoing in my head, gnawing at me. Guilt twisted my stomach into knots. Gods, what kind of person cheats on her husband? The thought alone made me feel sick—it was the ultimate betrayal. Oh, fuck... I felt like I needed to scrub myself clean with bleach or something.

The music had shifted to slow dance songs, and the dance floor was crowded with boozed-up people, some in rather compromising situations. Many were coming and going, and I pondered on Hedone's words, wondering if they were using Aphrodite's 'private' rooms to get it on. I turned away and exhaled softly.

'Oh, you lucky, lucky girl,' Simmy exclaimed as I saw yet another freaking deity approaching. 'Apollo,' Simmy whispered. 'He's a charmer. He'll cheer you up.' He winked at me and squeezed my hand. Then I turned to face the god of the sun.

Simmy was right—Apollo was like a breath of fresh air. All golden curls, boyish good looks, and that megawatt smile, he seemed to carry the sun with him wherever he went. Just being near him lightened my mood, thawing the heaviness in my chest.

He was easy, effortless—conversation with him flowed like warm honey, and before I realised it, we'd been talking for what felt like forever, laughter and sunlight threading through every word.

'I've researched the gods, you know.' I gave him a wicked smile as he placed a hand over his heart.

'Lady Persephone, whatever do you mean?' He looked at me with fire in his eyes, and a tight, hot shiver curled in my stomach.

'Well...' I took a drink. 'Daphne. If I spurn you, I don't want to turn into a laurel tree.'

Apollo looked appalled. 'That myth is absolutely not true. I assure you. Don't believe everything you read.' He pushed out his bottom lip, and I laughed. 'Lady Persephone, are you teasing me?' His smile lit up his lovely face, and my cheeks flushed, which, of course, he noticed.

'And apparently, you like both men and women?' The question slipped out before I could stop it. It really was none of my business.

He offered a faint smile. 'Yes, I am bisexual, but if you were to be my consort, I would remain faithful.' My breath snagged, and I simply nodded. 'I look forward to your visit to my court.' He leaned close to my ear, his voice soft and low. A flutter in my stomach made me inhale sharply.

I cleared my throat and smiled at him. Gods, he had such beautiful eyes. 'Where, um, is your court?'

'The Court of Cylades. It's an archipelago, a group of large islands; a part of Olympus.'

'Oh,' I muttered, thinking I needed to learn more about the courts of the gods.

'It's lush, green, with lakes and forests, and most importantly, year-round sunshine.' He winked at me as he studied my face.

'Sounds'—I swallowed at the intensity of his gaze—'sounds lovely.'

'It is. And you *would* make a wonderful consort.' He took my hand and kissed my pulse point, causing my breath to hitch.

After chatting for a bit longer, he conjured a guitar out of thin air and serenaded me with Bruno Mars' 'Marry You'.

He was brilliant; his voice so enchanting that I threw my head back and laughed as he gave me a cheeky grin. Apollo officially became one of my favourite gods.

That intense tingling spread across my entire body, and the pulse in my chest went haywire. Hades was near. Very near. I turned to see him approaching, and Apollo's guitar fell silent. Zeus's words about the dream made my temper simmer... Was it true? If it were, I wanted to body-slam Hades against the wall... or attempt to, but that mountain of muscle would be pretty hard to move, I guess. I stared at the massive, muscular chest before me, unwilling to meet his eyes.

'Persephone.'

His voice broke my musings, and I raised my gaze to his. When I looked into those blue eyes swirling with curls of golden aether, I was doomed. The fight drained from me.

'Hades.' Apollo offered a slight bow of his head.

'I'm taking Persephone for a while,' Hades declared in a dangerously low tone that left no room for refusal. Apollo opened his mouth to speak but swiftly closed it again.

'Catch you later, Lady Persephone,' the god of sun and light said as he looked deeply into my eyes, his azure blue orbs twinkling. He then took my hand, placing a lingering kiss on my palm. I sensed Hades stiffen beside me, and his lips tightened in anger. With a cautious glance at Hades and a slight bow, Apollo strode off, leaving me with the god of the Underworld.

Fury poured out of every cell of Hades' tightly coiled body, and I took a wary step away. He exhaled slowly and closed his eyes briefly, but his jaw was hard. 'Would you care to dance? Or perhaps go somewhere more private,' he said in a gravelly voice.

Hedone's words popped into my mind again, and I gulped. My lips pressed together, then opened back up, probably making me look like a goldfish. *Dance, Sephy. Go and dance.*

'Yes, I—I'll dance with you.' And he guided me to the dance floor.

Stupid pulse, please stop racing.

A familiar song began, and he drew me into his arms. I loosened up, the tension within me melting away. We moved together for a while, and then he spun me out, and as I twirled, he grabbed my other hand, pulling my back against his chest—oh, damn, that hard chest... Was he carved from stone? I melded into him, our bodies fitting together fluidly. Then I felt him—his erection—pressing into my back as he wrapped his strong arms around me, under my breasts. I gasped and turned my head. 'It was you.'

'What was me, Persephone?' he whispered against my hair, causing me to shudder.

'In your club. That night...' My voice sounded breathless.

'Would you be annoyed if it *were* me?'

I shook my head, and he turned me around. He bent down, pressing his forehead against mine, and whispered against my cheek, 'Do you want to go somewhere more private? To chat?'

No, say no. I should say no for a multitude of reasons, the main one being my overwhelming attraction to him. I said 'Okay' instead because I'm a raging idiot. He clasped my hand and led me indoors and into one of *the* rooms. My heart pounded so fast, I thought it might jump from my chest and run back outside to safety.

The room was palatial; vases of flowers adorned every surface. Then I cast my eyes towards the bed, my stomach tumbling and clenching at the same time. The skipping of my breath echoed in my chest. For a moment, a wild thrill raced through me, causing heat to settle between my thighs. My pulse thundered.

'You smell—'

'Don't say aroused, please.'

'Why? Does it bother you?'

'Yes. I don't need you telling me I'm aroused every time I see you. And if you *are* reading my emotions, stop it. I've told you, it's rude!'

'I don't tell you every time,' he muttered, and I blew out an aggravated breath. 'I was merely going to say you smell like Ares.' He scowled at the words.

'Oh.' I grimaced. 'He's a complete dick.'

Hades' chuckle was low and throaty, causing goosebumps to prickle my flesh. I turned and walked away, attempting to calm my racing pulse.

'My dream. About my ethereal garden.' I turned, lifted my gaze to him, and noticed him stiffen. 'It was real, wasn't it? And when you...' I stopped. The knot in my throat made it difficult to swallow.

He moved so swiftly that he was suddenly before me, and I jumped.

'Shit! Can you... Can you not do that?'

'Why? Does it anger you?'

'Yes.' I glared up at him. 'You're very fucking annoying.' He smirked, and I wanted to stab him. Like, I really wanted to stab him. I looked down at my feet as the fluttering in my chest buzzed around like nervous hummingbirds.

'It was easier,' he muttered.

'Easier?'

He nodded with a self-deprecating smile. 'The wanting and not having.'

'Huh?'

'When Morpheus found you.' He wet his lips. 'I can dream-walk. It was the only way to see you.' He looked at me—serious and earnest—like the weight of the world rested on his shoulders.

I pressed my fingers into my eyes, then raised my head. 'When you... with your shadows'—I couldn't say it—'was that real?' He briefly closed his eyes and nodded. Hot damn. 'So you and Zeus both stalked me.'

His brow shot up, and his eyes slammed closed. 'Are you upset with me?' he uttered, eyes still closed.

'No,' I whispered, and he released a long breath as his gaze locked onto mine again. 'I recognised the garden.' My eyes searched his.

'It is your garden in the Underworld, Persephone.' At his words, my eyes widened, and a little kernel of happiness took root in my chest.

'Can I see it?'

He nodded again. 'We can practice your shadow magic there.' I grinned up at him, and my breath caught in my lungs. His eyes... they looked close to combusting. 'I would give the godsdamned world to taste you again, Persephone.' His voice was thick with desire.

'My blood?' I squeaked. He shook his head, gaze locked on mine as he slipped off his jacket. 'Oh.' I squeaked again, because apparently, squeaking was my new normal.

Right. Taste me. Gods above, every coherent thought just... evaporated. I swallowed hard. I'd tried it once—with Matt—and it had been awkward as hell. Not exactly my thing. I'd been too self-conscious, too mortified to even pretend to enjoy it.

'May I... taste you?' Shadows gathered in his voice. The air left my lungs in an unsteady rush, and a pulse of desire lit up my veins. Good gods, what was wrong with me? But I knew the answer. Fervent attraction. A haze of throbbing hormones wrapped around me like a fine mist, obliterating all rational thought.

I gave a slight nod, and as his eyes travelled from my face to the tips of my toes, I inhaled sharply. His stare scorched me. My nipples tingled and hardened, and a sensual thrill sent goosebumps across my flesh. He eyed me like he wanted to feast on me as he backed me up against the wall, using one of his knees to spread my legs. Liquid heat spread through my veins, licking at me, and lust pulsed wildly. The still-functioning part of my brain fired off warnings. This was insanity.

'I'm not sure if—' At my words, he stilled, but as my gaze met his, my heart stopped. The feel of his rock-hard chest pressing against my breasts caused my brain to short-circuit. The clothes between us were no match for the heat that rolled off him or the heat clawing within me. The breath I inhaled rattled through me, full of his earthy scent. A tight coil throbbed low in my belly, causing my breasts to ache, and I drew in a deep breath as my lips parted on a breathy gasp.

A small smile twitched on his lips. 'Should I stop?' His dark, brooding voice caressed my ear, and I shook my head. He grasped my wrists, securing them with one hand above my head. Gently brushing my hair from my face, he lifted my chin with a finger, our eyes locking. His look was one of desire—like he wanted to consume me—and a torrent of heat coursed between my thighs, making my legs feel like butter. I was so, so wet. He tenderly cupped my face with his free hand and brushed his mouth against mine, his tongue parting my lips. He kissed me like a man starved. The kiss deepened until we were drowning in each other, and as his tongue licked against mine, my insides liquified.

He picked me up in one swift motion, making me yelp, and carried me to the bed. Hades leaned over me on his elbows. His eyes swirled more gold than blue. His lips and teeth grazed over my neck, making me groan softly, then further down to my breasts. He sucked at my taut nipples through the fabric of the dress, and my back arched as I jolted. Gods, I was overcome with need... desire. My brain tripped and I moaned.

He worked his way over my stomach and slipped the hem of my dress up to my waist, hesitating as he traced the small tattoo on my hip. 'Beautiful,' he murmured at the entwined red and purple roses.

When he slid his fingertips under my lace panties, dragging them down my legs, my heart rate spiked. Once they were off, he placed them into his pocket. Taking my thighs in his large hands, he pushed them apart. I wanted to feel awkward and self-conscious, but I couldn't. As his eyes swirled almost pure gold, I felt want—yearning. Pulses of sublime heat settled in my core, and I arched my hips and whimpered, causing him to growl low in his throat. At the sound, a dipping motion churned in my belly as desire, hot and dark, swelled through me. *Never* in my life had I been so viscerally affected by anything.

He stared between my spread thighs. 'Exquisite,' he uttered darkly as his fangs elongated. His lips brushed the inside of my upper thigh, rasping his stubble across my sensitive flesh, causing me to gasp in response. He kissed, nipped, and scraped my flesh with his lips and fangs, making his way upwards. My breath came in quick pants. When his tongue touched my centre and then danced over my clit, I gasped. 'Gods, you're so delectably wet,' he hummed against my sex. 'You taste like spring flowers,' he purred as his hot, broad tongue danced against me again, flicking, lapping, and sucking, and as he pushed a finger into my tight, wet entrance, curling it and hitting a sensitive spot, I whimpered. He froze as his eyes met mine. 'Am I hurting you?'

'No—no. Please don't stop,' I gasped.

A wicked smile carved into his lips, and as he dropped his head again, that indecent tongue made me *squirm* with pleasure, my fingers curling into the bed covers. When his finger thrust and twisted, I bucked my hips. He held me down with a big hand on my abdomen, letting out a throaty laugh. Feeling myself tighten in little flutters around him, he groaned, '*Fuck,* Persephone, you're so tight.' His hot breath caressed my core, and then his tongue was back in long, broad strokes, licking up my slick centre; when he sucked that sensitive nub, I jerked and whimpered again, trying to buck.

'You're so delicious, Persephone,' he uttered as his fangs grazed the throbbing bundle of nerves.

'I—*oh*,' I panted as he sucked again.

I started to lose focus and closed my eyes. The pressure in me built, and when ripples of pleasure began to cascade through me, I moaned, 'Oh. Oh, *gods, yes*.' I pressed myself deeper into him. Intense rapture enveloped me like ceaseless waves, wracking my body as I felt myself tighten so hard it was almost painful, and I released a guttural moan. Still, he continued that erotic dance with his tongue until I saw stars and broke into a thousand quivering pieces. Hades gave one longer lick, making me twitch, and withdrew his finger.

'You don't know how much I've longed to do that.' His eyes were half-mast, smouldering with lust.

He worked his way back to me and smiled, his eyes never leaving mine. When he put his finger in his mouth and sucked, dark desire ripped through me, and when our lips met again, I tasted myself on his tongue, making me groan low in my throat. The kiss was deep, our tongues gliding over each other. His mouth moved to my lower lip, sucking before his tongue delved deeper into my mouth. I felt the hard length of his erection against my thigh and the feeling of his cock, along with the intensity of coming like a freaking rocket—that kiss tipped me over the edge, igniting a longing within me, a need for something more profound, more palpable. I wanted him—all of him. I needed him to fuck me.

'I—I want you,' I breathed as my hips lifted to him, and he stiffened. The next second, he stood a few feet from the bed.

He chuckled darkly as he picked up his jacket, but frustration marked his features. 'I'm going to fuck you so hard, you won't remember your name. But not today.' Then he vanished into the aether, leaving me alone.

A messy swell of emotions threatened to drown me. Why had he left me? One minute, he was everything I'd ever dreamed of; the next, he was back to being the arrogant king of shadows and darkness. What complicated corner of the universe did he come from?

A scalding tide of tears choked my throat; then anger spread through me like an out-of-control wildfire. I clung to the anger like an old blanket; I was not going to cry over fucking Hades. I jumped up, rearranging my dress as I hiss-growled and stamped my feet. I was going to find Hades, and when I did, gods help him.

Breathless and pantless, I stormed out of the room, ready to eviscerate the bastard.

I stomped down the steps, and luckily, people were too focused on their conversations or conquests to even notice me—well, apart from Charon and Thanatos, who stood together with Hermes and Dionysus, all staring in my direction. *Great gods, where's a hole in the ground when you need one?* Thanatos winked and smiled, but at my returning glare, the smile melted from his face.

'Persephone!' Simmy trotted over to me, studying my expression. 'What's wrong? You look like you want to punch someone in the nuts.' I bared my teeth in response. 'Did you have sex with Hades? You did have sex with him. Has he got a big—'

'Stop. You're gross.'

'Well? Tell me why you're so cranky.'

I stopped, placing my hands on my hips and narrowing my eyes. 'I wanted to, but...' I gritted my teeth. 'I practically begged him to fuck me, but he... Gods, I'm such an idiot.'

'He said no?'

I glared at him and fisted my hands. I glanced at Hermes and Dionysus, who were watching us, looking like they needed a big bowl of popcorn, and it was obvious Charon and Thanatos were gossiping like two nursing home patients.

'Well,' Simmy continued, 'they always want everything on their terms. It's probably god-speak for "I wanna bang your brains out, but I'll make you wait till you're begging me for it".'

My dream flashed through my head. *That's what he'd said in my dream.* I puckered my brow and released an animated sigh—the tosser. 'Let's get wasted. Come on, Sim.'

'I bet Apollo will fuck you,' he whispered as we walked to find more alcohol. I gave him a death glare, and he snapped his mouth shut.

Tee appeared, carrying two glasses of wine, and handed one to me. 'You okay, babe?'

'Peachy.' I smiled grimly, then downed nearly half the glass. 'Where's Hades?' I asked without looking at her.

'He, um, returned home,' she said cautiously. I merely shrugged as if I didn't care a jot, but inside I was simmering.

A beautiful, melodic laugh—an intoxicating sound— caused us both to turn our heads. Zeus, the smarmy bastard. If I didn't know better...

'He's like a giant jackass piñata begging for someone to beat the candy out of him,' I mused, making Tee almost choke on her wine.

Behind him, now chatting with Ares, Dionysus

looked as if he were a second away from faceplanting into a wall. I fought a grin; Ares was as entertaining as a traffic jam.

After finishing another glass of wine, I crossed the tipsy border and stumbled right into drunk land.

'Come on,' Tee said before I could grab another wine. 'I'll get you both back.' Spotting Apollo, I left Tee and made my way over to him. 'Sephy, don't,' she whisper-shouted. Then I heard her curse.

'Apollo.' I grinned up at him, and his mesmerising eyes danced with amusement as I wobbled. He grasped my arm.

'Persephone, are you going?'

'I am. But I just wanted to do one thing before I leave.' He lowered his brow at my words.

'Alright.'

As I rose to my tiptoes and gentry pressed my lips against his, he tensed. But as I ran my tongue over his bottom lip, he groaned softly and placed his large hands on my hips, teasing my mouth open with his tongue. Deepening the kiss, I wrapped my arms around his neck and waited. It felt nice, but not like when *he* kissed me. Ugh. Fucking Hades. I pulled back, smiling. 'Thank you,' I said to a somewhat bemused Apollo.

'Erm, you're welcome?' His erection was evident, and I winked at him before turning back to Tee. She, Zeus, and Poseidon were all staring at me with intense, almost homicidal scrutiny, looking as if they were ready to breathe fire like dragons of doom, and I should incinerate on the spot. Simmy, however, stood behind them with his lips pressed together, looking rather pleased.

I gave them a small wave, and then carefully sauntered back to Tee.

'Let's go, *Hecate*.' I smirked. Her glare? Instant death sentence. Grabbing hold of Simmy and me, she flashed us back to my room.

Simmy skulked out of the room, probably because Tee radiated anger like nuclear fallout.

'What the actual fuck are you playing at, Sephy?' she ground out through clenched teeth. 'Why did you kiss Apollo?'

'Why not?' I slumped onto the bed.

'Do you want Hades to kill him? Because, believe me, if he finds out, he will!'

'He doesn't own me,' I bit back. 'I can kiss whoever I want.'

'Why, Sephy?' Her voice softened, and that messy swell of emotions returned as stupid, damnable tears choked my throat and then leaked from my eyes.

'Hades, he, we—' I gulped. 'He was so sweet. He gave me oral sex. I've never experienced anything like it. The orgasm was...' I placed my hands over my face. 'But he ruined it.' At my words, her eyebrows disappeared into her hairline, and I'm pretty sure she stopped breathing. 'And I practically begged him to fuck me, but he'—I hiccupped —'refused, became an arrogant twatwaffle god again, and left me. Now I feel like a total dipshit.'

'Damn it,' she grunted. 'No wonder he told me to take care of you. Gods, wait till I see him, the dick.'

'Why, Tee? Why did he refuse me?'

And why the fuck was I so upset? I wanted to go back

to London. I didn't want to be with him. Did I? I released a sob, knowing damn well that I did want him. Physically, at least... I yearned for him. The attraction was beyond compelling. I needed the arrogant god of death to want me back, just as much as I needed the air I breathed.

The thought made me cry even harder.

TWENTY-FOUR

HADES

I'm such a fucking idiot. What was I thinking? Touching her. Tasting her. I wasn't thinking; I lost my godsdamned mind.

Eating Persephone's pussy was like burying my face in fucking springtime, causing all clarity to vanish. The need to watch her unravel at my hands and mouth drove me ravenous. I remember how she would fall apart under my touch... before. This time, she responded in the same way —the sweetest, most erotic thing I've ever known. A bad but delicious mistake.

I took her panties from my pocket and clenched them in my fist. I'd give the world to fuck her, but I couldn't succumb to the temptation again—not until she wanted to be my consort. My queen. I needed to be more standoffish with her. I shouldn't have given in to the desire to taste her again. Shit.

Morpheus appeared, and I scowled at him, shoving the panties back into my pocket. 'The dream,' I said, and his face fell.

'I'm sorry, Your Highness.' He stared at the floor.

'Tell me.'

'Zeus demanded I tell him. I have no idea how he found out, Highness.' His eyes rose to mine, and I knew he was speaking the truth.

'Who else did you tell?'

Morpheus hesitated, releasing a worried breath. 'Daeira was the only other person. I'm sorry.'

'Bring her to me. Now.'

'Highness.' Morpheus bowed and vanished.

I paced my office, unease swelling like whisps of acrid smoke. What the fuck was going on?

'She's not here, Highness.' The voice startled me. 'No one has seen her for days.'

I gave him a slight nod, then shadow-walked to Zeus.

Fortunately, Zeus was in his office in the mortal realm. No nymphs in sight. 'Brother,' he said, jumping up from his desk. 'Is there a problem?'

'Yes.' I held his gaze. 'I know you told Persephone about the dream.' He extended his hands, palms facing me, but I continued before he could speak. 'And I know the only other person Morpheus confided in was Daeira. I assume she told you.'

Zeus's eyes lowered, his shoulders slumping. 'Yes.'

'She is missing.' Zeus's eyes widened, and his brow furrowed. 'What I can't understand is why. And how

Persephone was flashed to the Empousa's lair. How did someone breach the Underworld's wards?'

Zeus contemplated my question for a moment. 'The only way in is through the secret entrance in New York that demigods occasionally used, correct?' I nodded. 'However, that would be tantamount to suicide. It leads directly to Tartarus.'

My head snapped up. 'Unless... Give me a moment.' I shadow-walked back to my bedroom. In the closet was a wooden box—one I hadn't opened since the war. The box contained my helm of invisibility. I opened the box... and it was empty. Fuck.

'It's gone.' Zeus spun around at my words.

'What in Olympus... Are you trying to give me a coronary?'

I smirked. 'Your heart is already dead.' He curled his lip at me. 'My helm is missing. Did you steal it?' I squinted as I strode towards him, my temper prickling.

'I swear on the Styx I did *not*, Brother. It would lead to war.'

His words made me pause. *Think.* 'And that is precisely what they want,' I mused.

'Who?'

I lifted my arms in a 'no idea' gesture. 'Someone is plotting against us. They want us to fight. It must involve other gods... We need to inform Poseidon.'

Zeus's face paled at my words. 'Fuck,' he barked. 'Then this stays between the three of us for now. I shall let Poseidon know.'

I nodded in agreement. 'I will close off the secret

entrance immediately,' I replied. Besides, no one had used it in aeons.

Zeus gave a nod, and I went to leave but turned around. 'The Council of Magic would form an unlikely yet powerful alliance. I think you should call off the war on magic. Meet with Hecate. She will liaise with the high priestesses on your behalf. With conditions, of course.'

'I shall ponder it.' His eyes narrowed as if in thought. 'And Hades.' I paused again, my eyes meeting his. Zeus hesitated before he spoke. 'I'm not wooing Persephone. Ask her what I said to her.'

'Then why all this circus?' My voice was low, laced with anger.

He sighed heavily. 'Entertainment.' He offered a half-shrug, and I shadow-walked back to the Underworld before I stuck his head up his ass.

I returned to a scowling Hecate and groaned. 'She told you.'

'Of course she fucking told me. What the fuck are you playing at? You fucking asshole.'

So many fucks; she was livid. I sighed.

'She kissed Apollo. In front of *everyone*,' she seethed, and anger slammed into me like a wrecking ball.

'I'll fucking kill the little—'

'No, you won't.' She cut me off, eyes hard as flint. I set my jaw, but stayed silent 'She was furious at you. And honestly, she had every right to be. It's your fault, you jackass. Tell her the truth, for fuck's sake. Explain why you left before Apollo lays claim on her.' And she flashed from the room, leaving me feeling like a total bastard.

TWENTY-FIVE

PERSEPHONE

My wine-induced headache felt like a psychotic drummer had taken up residence in my brain, and I groaned as I peeled my eyes open. Damn, I'd slept for hours.

I couldn't think about Hades. Of course, my brain switched straight to Hades and, oh, my gods, what we'd done. I groaned in embarrassment and pulled the covers over my head. The image of him—his head nestled between my thighs—took up residency in my mind. It would live in my head rent-free, probably for the rest of my godsdamned life. But the way he'd made me feel. 'Oh, shit.' I placed my palms over my face.

I was so frustrated with myself. Why had I let him do that? I didn't even like it—well, before him. Bah. I couldn't blame him, though; I'd been like a freaking lovesick teenager. Fucking hormones. Fucking Hades and his stupid face. His ridiculous body. Stop! Just thinking about him caused my blood to heat and my lady parts to tingle. Dammit, I needed an anti-sex pill or something for when he was near me. I smacked my forehead with my palm. I felt like a horny, moody adolescent.

I climbed inelegantly from the bed, grunting. That annoying, warm, fuzzy feeling in my chest pulsated. He was in his chambers. I stared at the doors between our suites—the last time I used them, on the day he told me about my disappearance, they had been unlocked... I wondered if they still were. I cursed and stomped my feet. Maybe I'd pop over to Apollo's court. At the thought, that feeling in my chest buzzed like a swarm of pissed-off fire-flies. Crap. This bond shit was unbelievable.

Did I love Hades? I had no idea what romantic love felt like. I was undoubtedly attracted to him. But I couldn't love him. I'd sworn off that ridiculous emotion. Irritatingly, that warm buzzing sensation in my chest still hummed. When would this overdramatic bond bullshit ever end?

I cursed under my breath and trudged into the bath-room. One glance in the mirror—whoa. Red, swollen eyes, courtesy of hours crying into my nectar while venting with Tee. My stomach tumbled, and I blew out a long breath. Argh. I looked like shit. I took a cold shower; but even as the icy water sluiced down my body, thoughts of Hades made my skin burn. Damn him.

I knew he'd avoid me now, and the idea left me both

furious and... weirdly hollow. My emotions were a complete fucking conundrum.

I stepped out of the shower and shivered. 'A bath. I want a hot bath.' I turned the taps, letting the tub fill with steaming water and enough foam to flood a small village. While it rose, I cleansed, toned, and moisturised, pressing a pair of under-eye masks into place to battle the puffiness. I towel-dried my hair and scraped it into a messy topknot.

When I caught my reflection again, I nodded. 'Better,' I whispered. Sliding into the bath, I sank beneath the heat, a sigh slipping free as tension drained from my body. I closed my eyes, and for a blissful moment, I drifted.

My eyes flew open as the door slammed against the wall. Hades stormed in, brow furrowed and lips a hard line. 'I've been waiting ages for you,' he said, then froze when his gaze landed on me.

I growled and hurled my wet sponge at him. Of course, he caught it with one hand, his eyes narrowing; I grabbed the bottle of bath foam next and hurled it with all the force I had—it should've at least left him with a bruise. He caught that too, cool as ever, and I snarled.

His voice knocked me from my temper. 'What's on your face?' My gaze rose to his; his head tilted quizzically as he scrutinised me. Ugh. That *beautiful* face. My temper sparked again.

'What?' I hissed as I remembered the patches beneath my eyes. I deflated. 'Oh, skincare things,' I muttered, peeling them off.

'We need to talk.'

'Right at this very moment?'

'What's wrong with right now?'

Was he daft? 'I'm in the bathtub, in case you're blind.'

'Oh, I'm not blind.' His voice turned husky as his eyes grazed my body before returning to my face. I glanced down; the bubbles were all but gone. I caught his eyes again, and the expression he wore—a muscle ticked in his jaw, and his eyes swirled with gold. Annoyingly, my body went straight back into take-me-now-land.

Damn him.

'Fine,' I gritted out in annoyance at myself and stood. He went completely rigid.

I fought not to cover myself and let him look his fill. The intensity of his perusal ignited my flesh, making my skin flame and warmth pool between my legs.

Double damn him.

'Towel,' I said, holding out my hand. He continued to stare at me, and I smirked to myself. *Here's what you could have had, jackass.* 'Hades!' He jumped, his eyes finally meeting mine. 'Towel.' Shaking his head, he grabbed a towel and placed it in my outstretched hand. Electricity buzzed over my skin as his fingers brushed against mine. I glanced down and raised my brows at the long, hard length pressing against his leather trousers.

'I'll wait outside.' He swung around and closed the bathroom door. I dried off and slipped into my robe, basking in the satisfaction of his reaction to me again. Then I hesitated. No one had ever seen me completely naked, not even poor Matt, but I enjoyed it. I relished Hades perusing my body as if it were a feast to be savoured.

Gods, perhaps I was turning into a harlot?

When I came out of the bathroom, Hades had gone. I took the time to dress. I popped on a pair of shorts, a crop top, and my Nike trainers. I applied a little makeup, mainly to conceal the dark circles under my eyes, and I was finishing braiding my hair when Hades reappeared from his suite, his hair damp as if he'd just showered.

He gave me a tentative smile as I lifted my eyes to his in the mirror, but I glowered at him. 'You're angry with me,' he said.

'No, of course I'm not!' I deadpanned.

'You're not?'

Was this man for real? My hands flew out in exasperation. 'Yes, I'm fucking furious with you, you arrogant, idiotic prick,' I snapped as I secured the final pin in my braid and turned to face him. His jaw tightened, and his nostrils flared. 'You know, your mood swings are giving me whiplash.' Those eyes met mine again, and he cocked his head. 'One minute you're being nice'—and kissing me. Damn it, I wanted him to kiss me—'and the next, you're the arrogant Mr Silent and Grumpy.'

He released a sad sigh. 'The last thing I want to be around you is grumpy.'

'Your emotions are so hard to discern. I need a code-breaker.' He stared at me blankly. *Ugh, men.* He turned to look out of the window at the meadow. 'Like, one minute we're... you know.' I flushed like a fever spreading across my skin. 'Then you're rejecting me.'

His head snapped around. 'I'll never reject you.'

'But you did.' My voice wavered as tears clogged my

throat, and I wanted to smack myself in the face for showing such weakness.

'Persephone,' he said softly as he turned. 'If I fuck you'—His eyes locked onto mine, and the breath froze in my lungs—'Your choice of leaving me will be relegated to when Tartarus freezes over. I shall never let you go.' He swallowed hard. 'I can't do that to you... I can't do what Demeter did by taking away your choice.'

'Oh,' I muttered in a dazed stupor. I shook my head to try to clear my confusion. 'Then why... why did you kidnap me?'

He froze for a heartbeat, scrubbing the palm of his hand along his jaw; then he continued with his stone-strong confidence. 'I was hoping if I kept you for three months'—he swallowed—'you would fall back in love with me.'

I blinked. Blinked again. Then blinked some more. The burn and sting of emotions became a knot I could barely swallow. I felt as if I'd been sucked into a vacuum, aware but confused and disoriented. Long seconds passed before I spoke again, his beautiful eyes swirling with ether, never leaving my face. 'You want me to love you?' I croaked. He nodded. *Could I ever love a heartless god?*

'Do you want me to leave?'

'No,' I blurted, feeling somewhat elated as a happy little seedling took root in my chest. I shook my head. I was sure it was the accursed bond messing with me.

I hesitated; this man was an anomaly. Everything I wanted to despise: first and foremost, he was an arrogant freaking god. Yet I'd seen behind the armour, glimpsed something more. Coming from such a fucked-up family—Zeus being top tosser of them all—must have taken its toll.

No family is perfect, I know, but his was as screwed up as they come. I saw his flaws, weaknesses, and vulnerabilities, and still, that fuzzy knot in my chest swelled when I glanced back up at his face.

I loosed a breath and spoke. 'Your interpersonal skills are worse than mine, great god of the dead.' Again, he lowered his brows. 'Honestly you're doing a dreadful job of trying to make me love you. You need to chill out... ditch the arrogant asshole routine. You know... Less brooding. More personality.'

He grimaced, jaw clenching, and gods help me... even though he acted like a complete dick most of the time, something warm welled in my chest. Was it the bond blindsiding me? Or... was it love? I shoved the thought aside.

'Take me to my garden.' His lips curved, and that damned dimple made my heart skip. I edged closer, slipped my small fingers into his, and he tensed. 'Lead the way,' I said as I squeezed his hand. He stared down at me, confusion clouding his features—then turned, guiding me forward.

After walking down countless wide hallways, we reached another immense arched black door. Hades pushed it open, revealing a vast terrace with broad stone steps descending into my garden. My very dead garden.

I dropped his hand with a whimper, bolting down the steps. My flora magic thrummed violently, and I plunged my hands into the black dirt, unleashing it with the force of a tropical cyclone. The dormant life reacted with delight —the barren landscape gradually transformed into a riot of colour. Jewelled tones ranging from emerald to amethyst, vermillion, and cerulean stretched as far as my eyes could see.

'It was a garden of eternal spring because of you.' Hades' voice startled me. I could feel his body heat behind me, and a grin split my face. The fresh, woody fragrance of the cypress trees drifted on the breeze, along with an explosion of perfumes from the blooms. Jasmine and wisteria clung to the intricate latticework, and narcissi popped up everywhere.

I stopped by the sublime variety of roses and inhaled their heady scent, then strolled along the black marble walkway towards the grassy area and fountain. I trailed my fingers in the water, releasing a burst of magic—waterlilies exploded through the water, and a giggle burst from my lips.

'Persephone.'

I turned slowly to gaze up at the god of shadows, but he let out a frustrated sigh as a swarm of butterflies headed our way.

I gasped and stepped back as the butterflies condensed and morphed into a human shape: a tall, thin man with bone-white skin, ebony hair, and what seemed to be two silver stars peering from his eye sockets. He wore a long black cloak and bowed deeply to us both. 'Highnesses.'

'Morpheus,' Hades said curtly, in an almost bored way, and I shot him a dark look; puzzlement was his response.

Morpheus, the god of dreams, shaped dreamscapes and appeared to sleeping mortals in various forms, often as butterflies. He was a messenger of the gods.

'Hello, Morpheus.' I beamed at the god, causing the bone-white skin on his cheeks to tinge pink.

'My lady.' He inclined his head. 'I merely wanted to say that everyone is delighted with the life you have restored to the Underworld.' I smiled brightly, entranced by his eyes. 'And we do hope you will return to us for good.' My breath hitched, yet my smile remained. 'Have a pleasant evening.' This time, he transformed into a crow and soared into the sky.

'You need to be more friendly,' I said, lifting a brow at Hades.

'Why?'

'Making time for people is important, even for those who serve you. A kind word, or, gods forbid, a smile, will make them feel more cherished. More important. People never forget how you made them feel.'

He stared at me as though I'd just asked him to explain quantum theory. I exhaled in frustration. 'Never mind. Just try to be a little less brusque. Anyway, what were you going to say?' He took a deep breath, opened his mouth, and cursed as we heard Hecate's squeal.

'Sephy, this place looks unreal!' She sprinted down the steps, with Thanatos and Charon close on her heels. 'I think this calls for a picnic. What do you reckon?' I bounced on the spot, clapping my hands. I caught Hades' eyes; his lips twitched minimally, but it was a start.

We wandered to the lush, grassy area surrounding the

pond, and Tee magicked a colossal blanket covered in plush cushions. We settled on the soft fleece material, and my heart lurched as I watched Tee, Charon, and Thanatos chatting. These people were my friends. They cared about me, and I cared deeply for them.

My gaze slipped to Hades. He sat quietly watching me with an unreadable expression. Yet, for once, I didn't feel like an insect pinned beneath a glass. I offered him a smile, hoping—aching—to coax out that elusive dimple; alas, he averted his gaze and the moment dissolved into quiet longing.

'Food?' Tee caught my attention.

'Hm, afternoon tea sounds perfect. With cake. Lots of cake.'

With a flick of her wrist, the centre of the blanket filled with an indulgent spread—dainty finger sandwiches, scones piled high with jam and clotted cream, and an endless parade of pastries and petit fours. Two chilled bottles of champagne appeared beside five crystal flutes, and Charon, ever the gentleman, poured for us all.

We lingered there for hours, laughing, teasing, and trading stories until the air itself seemed lighter. Even Hades, brooding king of shadows, allowed the edges of his severity to soften. After I'd eaten enough to feed a football team, I finished my fourth glass of endless champagne and relaxed back, content to simply listen as their voices wove around me.

Their conversation turned to my teleportation to the Empousa's lair, causing my sense of relaxation to waver. I sat up, and Charon passed me another glass, which I sipped while nestling against a large throw cushion. They discussed a traitor, minor gods, humans, and the resistance, a group known as Ixion. I longed to ask so many questions, but my mind was in a swirl, partly from the champagne. I resolved to ask Tee about it tomorrow; my eyelids felt heavy. Eventually, I succumbed to sleep.

'Let's get you back, Persephone.' A husky voice roused me from my slumber.

'Oh, yeah. Okay.' A large hand helped me stand, and I moved forward, or at least attempted to. My occasional stumble made me wince, but then strong arms swept me into their embrace.

'I've got you, *agapi mou*,' a voice whispered. I liked those words; they felt familiar. *I wonder what they mean.*

I sighed, then closed my eyes again.

I AWOKE WITH A HAPPY SIGH. I'd slept like the dead, and felt incredibly comfortable. This blanket was snug and warm—firm too—draped around my middle and secure between my legs. I released a contented sigh, then knitted my brows together. I peeled an eye open and peeked down —black satin sheets. Shit, I was in Hades' bed. Had we...? The breath stilled in my lungs as I tried to inhale. No. I would remember if we'd... Wouldn't I?

I gently lifted the sheet to find a muscled arm around my bare abdomen and a burly leg nestled between mine. *Crap.* I tensed and breathed slowly, trying to reinflate my lungs. But looking down again, I still wore my shorts and crop top, and that leg was clad in soft grey bottoms, like sleep pants. *Stop panicking, Sephy. Nothing has happened.*

Hades' soft breath whispered in my hair as his slow, steady breathing indicated he was still sleeping. Then I realised there was something long and hard—very long and hard—pressed into my ass. I stiffened with a slight jerk, causing Hades to wake.

'Persephone,' he murmured sleepily. Then he seemed to realise where we were, tensing as he untangled his arms and legs from mine, and slipped from the bed in one fluid motion, like a ballet dancer. I sat up and clutched the sheet in front of me. 'I'm sorry,' he muttered, his back to me, broad and bare, filled with muscles, which extended down to a firm ass, and, my goodness, that derrière. I closed my eyes, gulping silently. 'I intended to take you to your room... I must have dozed off. It's still absurdly early... You ought to get more rest.'

'It's... it's alright,' I whispered as I blinked my eyes. And it was alright, I realised; having him next to me in bed felt... good. He turned slowly, and I exhaled in a rush until there was no air left in my lungs, and my body temperature increased by a degree or ten. Gods, was he sculpted from marble? The smooth, hard lines of his chest were covered with intricate tattoos on both sides of his upper body, from his upper arms and shoulders to his pecs, and I wondered if they were the binding tattoos Tee had mentioned.

Then my eyes dropped to those abs, and I swallowed. He had abs you could do a nation's worth of laundry on.

His pants hung indecently low on his lean hips, and what were those indents? They were by his hips, leading down into the waistline of the pants. I imagined tracing them with my tongue, and my whole body heated—which was when I saw his erection. It looked large—eye-wateringly large.

A ripple of tight shivers shot through me, causing my heart to race and my nipples to tingle and harden. I shifted, kneeling on the bed, and his eyes swirled with gold as his jaw clenched. His shadows swirled and danced around him, yet I wasn't scared.

Holy damn, his body is obscenely delicious.

'Persephone.'

'Sorry, what?'

'Perhaps if you stopped ogling me for a moment, you might actually hear me.'

'I wasn't ogling you.' I was *so* ogling him.

'You're so quarrelsome.'

'I wasn't arguing.' I tore my gaze from the indents and met his smirk. 'And I'm *not* quarrelsome.' My jaw tightened, fully aware that I was most definitely quarrelsome.

'You have zero comprehension of the word "quarrel".'

'And you're a know-it-all.' At my words, a warmer smile flickered on his mouth, and my tongue darted out to wet my lips, causing his pupils to dilate and consume his irises. 'I want to taste you,' I whispered.

The skin between his brows creased, and a keen sense of nervousness invaded me as he stared at my face. 'Sorry... I think I misheard you.'

'I want to taste you,' I said, louder. I was losing my

mind at that point. He drew his lower lip between his teeth, showing a hint of fang, but curiosity marked his face.

'You want me to fuck your mouth?' His words were hoarse. Gravelly. And I nodded. Those words—ugh—would usually be such a turn-off. But when he uttered them, liquid heat swelled inside me like a tide. I actually wanted to do this... an act I'd only ever attempted once before, then promptly quit because I'd hated it.

'O—kay,' he whispered. His dark, soft laugh was smoke and sin. 'I'd *very* much like that.' At his words, I sucked in a shuddering breath, but my want, my need, overcame my nervousness. *Damn, I wish I'd paid better attention to Hedone and her ice-pop lessons*, I thought to myself as I crawled from the bed.

I tossed a few pillows on the floor and stood before him, tilting my head to meet his gaze. His hands were clenched into fists, his jaw was set like granite, and his eyes were closed. He was like a marble statue. He desired this, and I felt empowered. I was in control, and I also needed to do this.

I raised both hands, and my fingers reached up and traced his broad, hard chest, lingering on the tattoos, the contact causing him to jerk. On tiptoes, I licked the ink from his shoulders to his pecs—they were runes, similar to Tee's, but with more intricate designs interspersed with a language I didn't understand. My fingers wended their way down of their own volition to the grooves in his abs and the indents by his hips.

Gods, his bronze-coloured skin stretched taut over

rigid muscle, like silk over steel; it felt firm, warm, and soft. Languid heat made its way down my chest and deep into the pit of my stomach.

I dropped to my knees on the cushions. I felt tiny in front of him, kneeling, but, to be fair, I always felt tiny with him, which was no surprise given that he was built like a Georgian mansion. I pressed my lips against his hip and traced my tongue over one indent, eliciting a low moan from his throat. Then I hesitated. 'I—I've got no idea what I'm doing. I might not be very good at this,' I whispered.

'Gods, Persephone. You're doing okay so far. Take your time. Stroke me hard, but please don't stop.' He turned his face towards the ceiling, his breathing ragged... his shadows creeping closer to me.

Hard. Okay... Hard.

So, I carried on. My hands roamed downwards, avoiding his length, feeling his solid, muscular thighs; then they inched closer to his erection, and I felt him shudder. I gently massaged his massive cock through his pants for a little while, his breathing becoming shallower. Then I braved up and slowly pulled his pants down.

His hard length sprang free, and I almost gasped. It was freaking enormous—decadently so. I studied it for a long moment, wondering how the Fates it could fit anywhere, especially my mouth, before I kissed it. My breath on his skin made his cock twitch, and he grunted.

The length and breadth were worrying, so I wrapped my fist around the bottom, and when I softly licked the head, which was glistening with pre-cum, a strangled moan rattled through him. I liked pleasing him in this way, and when I ran my tongue along his length, he groaned softly, and I smiled, my insecurities melting. He tasted salty but sweet—like mango with a sprinkling of salt.

I closed my lips around him and felt his hands fist in my hair. I flicked my tongue just beneath the head, and he let out a sound of overwhelming pleasure. I began to suck, firmly working my hand up his shaft as I licked and suckled, taking him as far as I could, and at his deep moans, the ache in my belly bloomed into fire. His shadows caressed my bare skin, making me groan.

'Fuck,' he snarled. 'Persephone,' he rumbled low in his throat as he fisted my hair in his hands even harder. 'I've missed this. I—' A ragged sound silenced the rest of his words. My eyes glanced upward and met his. They were pure gold. In a slow rhythm, he began to push his hips, and his cock sank deeper into my mouth, causing my eyes to water. At his soft moans, I took him even deeper, still licking and sucking. I lost myself in the fullness, the taste, and the soft guttural groans coming from him, and I hummed happily.

He jerked. 'I—I'm coming.' His voice was gruff as he went to pull away, but one of my hands grabbed his hard ass, and I pulled him closer, still sucking. He came with a roar, and I felt him release into my mouth... salty and sweet. His orgasm rocked me as I sucked him gently through it.

As his shadows enveloped us, he released my hair, pulling me to my feet, and kissed me like a man dying of thirst. I drowned in it—drowned in him.

'What were you going to ask me yesterday?' I muttered as he ran his fangs and lips along my collarbone.

His hot breath whispered against my ear. 'If I could fuck your mouth.'

And I laughed.

TWENTY-SIX

HADES

Having my cock in Persephone's mouth again was everything I remembered.

I hadn't lasted long because every touch of her tongue was like a surge of electricity, and when she'd groaned and hummed, the vibrations in her throat sent me over the edge.

Watching her swallow me down had almost addled my brain—she had consumed me like an addict. At the memory, my throbbing erection strained against my jeans. I was, and always had been, insatiable around her... I was desperate to fuck her.

It was becoming harder to resist her. Harder to restrain myself.

Our physical love had always matched our emotional love—emotional love satisfying our souls, while physical love satisfied our bodies. I lowered my brows and ran a hand over my head; I couldn't succumb. I couldn't keep her unwillingly, whether I loved her or not.

I needed to maintain a greater distance until she accepted the soul bond.

I was to see her in her garden after I met with Poseidon and Zeus. Taking a deep breath, I shadow-walked to my brothers, to the kingdom of Genesion, many leagues under the sea.

I appeared in Poseidon's throne room—all greys and swirling blues, like the sea he controlled. The glass-like structure above our heads was immense, and marine life swam past, oblivious to our presence. Poseidon's kingdom was vast, as was Zeus's. For obvious reasons, mine was as large as the Earth.

Glass-like structures stretched as far as the eye could see, all connected by covered walkways and roads. It was the only place I ever visited for any period of time. Poseidon was a grouch, but he was my ally—my closest brother.

'Brother,' Zeus said as he slapped me on the back. My jaw hardened, and Poseidon attempted to hide his smirk behind his hand.

'Any further news on Ixion?' I got straight to business, eager to return to Persephone, longing to speak with her, to see her—the extraordinary woman who captured my heart and once loved me enough to become my wife.

As the ocean sparkled overhead, I wondered whether her love for me would reignite and endure the trials ahead, or if it too would crumble under fate's relentless design. I would never love anyone else because my heart would always belong to her—the one who had broken it.

I shook off the thought before the physical pain of her potential rejection brought me to my knees.

'We've not heard anything new,' Poseidon's baritone voice replied. 'But we're making progress with the Council of Magic.'

My eyes widened at Zeus, and my brows pulled tightly together.

'I do listen to you, Hades,' the smarmy bastard said, his eyes glinting with something akin to amusement. 'Hecate has been doing the rounds, and they're considering our offer.'

Hecate. Damn it. I'd scarcely had a moment to speak with her alone since she'd flayed my skin from my bones with her acerbic words about my treatment of Persephone. 'Which is?' I snapped.

'To become our allies. Come out of hiding. However, they must relinquish all divine blades.'

I scoffed a laugh. 'Do you honestly think they will trust us if you make such a demand?'

Zeus frowned. Gods, he was a complete jackass.

'No,' Poseidon replied. 'Zeus's intellect occasionally rivals that of a toddler.'

I sighed as Zeus grew to his divine size, soon followed by Poseidon. I was so tired of the bitch fest that never ended.

'Enough! For fuck's sake,' I yelled. 'I'm sure your dicks are equal in length. I need to return.'

They both morphed into their human forms. 'To the

lovely Persephone?' Zeus smiled with a sinister edge, and Poseidon sighed.

'I know she kissed Apollo,' I seethed. Zeus flinched, and Poseidon shot me a worried look. 'It was entirely my fault. She was angry with me. Don't ask questions.' I pointed in Zeus's face as he opened his mouth, likely to ask questions. 'Rethink your demands with the mages,' I ground out to Zeus. 'They have no reason to trust us. We must demonstrate that they can and that the trust is mutual.' Zeus's face was a picture of confusion.

'That's precisely what I said to the daft bastard.' Poseidon laughed.

With a sigh, I shadow-walked back to Persephone's garden and found her waiting for me. She sat at the edge of the pond, idly running her fingers through the water. She tensed as soon as I appeared, her eyes darting to my face.

'Hi.' She smiled coyly, a rosy warmth blooming across her cheeks.

'You ready?' My mouth twitched at the eager nod of her head. 'Let's practice.' I extended my hand to her and grasped her tiny fingers.

After an hour, Persephone's frustration boiled over. 'I can't do it!' she screeched, stamping her feet for what felt like the hundredth time.

I needed a new tactic, something to cut through her panic. I moved in close, pressing my chest to her back. 'You can. You *will* unlock your power, *agapi mou*,' I whispered in her ear, my arms circling her waist.

'What does agapi mou mean?'

It signified "my love", but I wasn't revealing that information just yet... Not until I knew my love was reciprocated. Instead, I ran my hands down her stomach, into the band of her shorts, and then down to her panties. I pushed them aside, and she moaned low in her throat as I massaged her clit with the palm of my hand. 'Try harder,' I muttered in her ear as she pushed her ass against my engorged cock.

'I need you to...' she whimpered.

I tensed, forcing my eyes closed. 'Persephone. Show me your shadows.'

'I—I'll try,' she groaned, pushing back into me.

I pulled my hand away and licked her neck as my fangs elongated.

She spun around, glaring. 'You're cruel.' I shrugged and bit back my half-smile, trying not to cringe—my cock was uncomfortably hard, and I groaned silently. She resumed her position. 'Here goes. But what if I can't control it?' She glanced worriedly back at me.

'Then I'm here to save you.'

Her power was extraordinary. It made my hard-on even harder. Gods, she was amazing. The black tendrils of shadows pulsed from her widespread hands and enveloped the garden, withering everything under their touch, and she screeched. 'Pull the power back inside you, Persephone.'

'I can't. I can't control it.' Her voice was panicked, so I took her hands, and the shadows dissipated.

'My garden!' she cried.

'Really?' I arched a brow. Her grin was wild, defiant. She crouched, slammed her palms into the soil, and released a torrent of flora magic. Life erupted in a riot of colour, her garden returning even more breathtaking than before.

'Again,' I instructed. We replayed the scenario over a dozen times, and eventually, she gained some semblance of control.

'Your shadows are a part of you, Persephone. A part of you to cherish and welcome. Draw them back inside. Surrender to your magic, and don't panic.' I turned her to me and gazed into her enchanting, vivid green eyes. 'Remember, sometimes, to walk in the light, you need to embrace the darkness.'

She nodded and swallowed thickly as she took deep breaths; then she followed my instructions. Gradually, the shadows receded.

'Gods, I'm exhausted,' she whined after recreating her garden again.

'You're not stopping yet.'

She turned with her hands on her hips, glaring up at me, and I grinned at her until Hecate appeared. My grin withered, like an old memory. Fuck.

'We need you for judging. Like, yesterday,' Hecate barked. I groaned; Persephone scowled, and I vanished into the aether.

AFTER JUDGING two particularly nasty humans to an afterlife in Tartarus and one egotistical demigod whom I'd stripped of his memories and left to wander the Meadows of Asphodel, my mood was dark. I shadow-walked back to Poseidon's realm, to which I had an open entry. I found him brooding in his office.

'Hades.' His gaze looked me over. 'What's the problem, Brother?'

I dropped into his plush sofa and sighed. 'Many things,' I muttered.

'Then let's have wine.' He handed me a large glass of fruity red liquid, and I downed half of it in one gulp.

'Let me guess. Your undisciplined wife is the biggest problem.'

'Of sorts.'

'Of sorts?'

I blew out a ragged breath. 'I want to fuck her so badly —' Poseidon barked a laugh, and I glowered at him.

'Then why don't you? She belongs to you, after all.'

'I can see why you don't have a female in your life. You're a Neanderthal.' I arched a brow at him. 'Persephone is not a belonging, Poseidon.' The words were out before I could stop them—hypocrisy on my tongue. Because she *was* mine. She was *fucking mine*. I had to keep her. A ragged breath escaped me, but I recovered quickly, squaring my shoulders.

Poseidon's eyes locked with mine. He knew bullshit when he heard it, but I pushed on. 'In today's world, we should lead by example. Be civilised.'

'And if you fuck her, you'll keep her.'

I gave the smallest nod.

'That won't stop you,' he muttered.

My jaw clenched as my shadows flickered, writhing from my palms like living anger. Because he was right. I was a hairsbreadth away from taking her—keeping her—whether she wanted it or not.

'Calm down, Brother.' Poseidon's voice rumbled like a storm. 'You're an alpha. You'll have her by any means.'

I opened my mouth to argue, but he raised a hand, cutting me off, studying me for a long, heavy moment.

'Love kills more fucking brain cells than crystal meth,' he grumbled as he shook his head, making me smile despite myself. 'That's why females are a no-go for me. They're nothing but trouble. You won't catch me fawning over one,' he sniped, then pondered for a while. 'Maybe you need to woo Persephone...?' He grimaced at his own words and poured more wine.

'That's what Hecate said to me.'

'At least you'll get to fuck her. It'll be worth the torment.' He drank more wine as he eyed me. 'She's pussy-whipping you again, but this time... I don't know,' he mused, and I lowered my brows. 'But stop being a total schmooze. You're like a spurned puppy, Brother. Make her do some of the fucking work.' I contemplated his words. *Maybe he has a point.*

'Like I said, you're an alpha male. Fucking act like one.' He rolled his eyes, and I bristled. 'Now, tell me. Why did she kiss Apollo? I thought I'd better ask if there was a good enough excuse. Otherwise, I might have to drown the little fucker.'

I half-laughed, groaned, and then told him about what happened. His response? Hysterical laughter. I watched him as he gasped for breath at the hilarity, and I came seconds away from kicking him in the balls.

'Sorry.' He coughed-wheezed as he tried to regain control. 'You're a fucking dozy bastard. Even I know that'd piss a woman off, and, as you say, I'm the Neanderthal.' He carried on laughing until he managed to control himself. 'Anyway, on a brighter note.' He blew out a breath and wiped his eyes—the *dick*. 'Zeus has agreed to new negotiations with the Council of Magic. It's looking promising.'

'Yes, I spoke with Hecate. She's arranging for the high priestesses to meet with us all.'

After discussing politics, Ixion, and the disadvantages of having women in one's life—that part was Poseidon— he decided it would soon be time to return to the mortal realm for his monthly sojourn. One of his many properties was a beachfront hotel in America, boasting excellent surfing beaches, which he adored; another was a mansion in a prestigious area featuring its own private beach.

It had taken Poseidon a long time to embrace the human world and leave his beloved kingdom, but the old bastard was lightening up. When he visited the mortal realm, Poseidon maintained the same level of privacy as I did, adopting an alias as a wealthy and powerful playboy— few were aware of his true identity.

'So, have you returned to the mortal world since you kidnapped your wife again?'

I huffed a breath. 'No.'

'Hmm.' He studied me. 'Maybe you need to see what's going on in those clubs of yours?'

'I have trusted demigods, and Minthe running them. They'll be fine for now.'

'Why don't you bring Persephone to Atlantis hotel? I'll text you.'

I coughed a laugh. '*You* have a mobile?'

He looked affronted. 'I do. Things are changing, Brother. And I think you're right; leading by example is definitely the way to go. But how to get Zeus on board and stop being a philandering asshole?' He raised a finger to his lips.

We both dissolved into laughter at the thought.

TWENTY-SEVEN

PERSEPHONE

I practiced with Hades every day for the following week.

He'd switched up my training regimen and was almost killing me. I was exhausted. But he seemed distant... colder. I tried not to dwell on it, but it stung. Perhaps my blowjob had been too amateurish? Maybe he would turn to Minthe instead?

I needed to get a grip on myself because I was a horny abyss of sexual tension whenever I was in his proximity—my bond was a whiny, sexed-up little bitch. But the adjoining suite doors remained closed, and I was too stubborn to show I was bothered.

The clusterfuck of my life showed no signs of slowing down. I still had to choose a husband, and the thought alone scared the crap out of me. Hecate and I had sketched out a plan: marry Hades, but only in name, keeping my freedom as long as I agreed to spend six months of the year in the Underworld. It was a gamble, but it was all I had. We'd tell Hades when I was ready.

One small silver lining? The longer I stayed in the Underworld, the more my powers thrummed beneath my skin—growing stronger, hungrier—and that felt intoxicating.

That afternoon, we were off to Ares' court in Thrace. He was hosting some kind of trials, and I was the so-called guest of honour.

Kill me now.

As Hecate brushed colour across my cheeks, she launched into a crash course on Olympus politics. 'The big three have their kingdoms, while the others rule courts. Zeus's kingdom, Naxos, and Poseidon's, Genesion, are the largest—though neither compares to the Underworld. The rest of the gods have smaller courts, though "smaller" still means vast—think North America-sized. You know, like Aphrodite's and *Apollo's*.'

She glanced at me in the mirror, but I refused to bite. 'Wow, okay,' I muttered.

'Most of the lesser gods have much smaller courts—'

'Like Adonis? His court is called Phoenicia.'

'Yeah, that douchebag has a smaller court. Probably about the size of Ireland, I'd say.'

'How does it work? I mean, where are these courts?'

'They all collectively form Olympus, Sephy. Olympus is as big as the Earth.'

'Oh.' I squinted at her. 'So, which places am I meant to visit?'

'Thrace, Ares; Naxos, Zeus; Cyclades, Apollo, and, unfortunately, Phoenicia, Adonis.'

'Gods, I need a way out soon, Tee. I can't face going to Phoenicia.' I gulped a mouthful of nectar.

'The asshole told you, didn't he?' she fumed.

I nodded at her. 'Why would I do that? Why would I be... unfaithful? That's so not me.' I sniffed and wiped a hand under my eyes. Tee suddenly became enraptured by her nail polish as she dropped my gaze. 'Please, Tee. Tell me. Did Hades know? And wasn't Aphrodite also in love with him?'

Her eyes rose to mine again, and she gave a half-shrug. 'Aphrodite used Adonis for a while, but she didn't love him. She was... well, a bit of a whore back then.' A startled laugh escaped me. 'Then, out of nowhere, you became besotted with him for a spell. None of us could figure out why. But, I had a feeling that Eros had something to do with it. He was a mischievous little bastard when he was younger, plus he'd had a run-in with Hades. Whether Adonis prompted him or someone else—'

She gave her head a slight shake and grimaced at the memory. 'But the truth is, we'll never know. Anyway, stop freaking crying; you're ruining your makeup.' She scowled, and I let out a shaky little laugh, noticing she hadn't answered my question about Hades. Guilt wrapped its smoky tendrils around me, making the lump in my throat grow larger. I took another sip of nectar.

Tee started piling my hair atop my head into something called a 'heavenly high bun'. A loose updo secured with a pearl hair accessory, while strands hung from the sides and nape, leaving me looking a little boho chic.

'Nice.' I grinned at my reflection as Hedone appeared, giving Tee a long, slow kiss, and then brandished a beautiful lilac dress.

'I love it!' I beamed as I ran my fingers over the material. 'It's lush.'

'Are you bringing your goat friend with you this time?' Tee said, sneering.

'Hey. Don't be a bitch. He's my friend. But no, apparently, he's already busy this afternoon. I don't think he fancies Ares' trials for some reason. He wouldn't tell me why, though.' I frowned. I'd seen Simmy almost every day when I sought refuge in the library, but he'd been a little cagey about Ares' court.

'Anyway.' Hedone interrupted my musings as Tee cleared her throat. 'Let's get you into this dress.'

'I'll be back shortly. Gotta get spruced up and all.' Tee winked at me, kissed Hedone, and flashed from the room.

The dress was more of a cocktail-style, crafted from sheer fabric, and skilfully adorned with glistening beadwork, appliqués, and embroidery. The long, slim sleeves clung to my arms, and the dress ended midthigh, with the hem trimmed with zigzag edging. Paired with silver sandals and a clutch, it looked elegant. The plunging V-neckline showcased my breasts, which I wasn't sure was a good thing if I was meeting Ares.

'Is it a bit too revealing?' I asked, running a hand over my abdomen.

'Be proud of your assets, Persephone,' Hedone replied

as she fussed over me, dotting my pulse points with a perfume that smelled of a floral bouquet—May Rose and jasmine—featuring bright citrus top notes and vanilla.

'I don't want to give Ares the wrong impression,' I grumbled, and she scoffed at my words.

'He will try his best with you, no matter what you wear. He's always lusted after you.'

My head shot around to her, and I groaned. 'Eww.' She simply laughed again.

'Ready?' Tee appeared, wearing a figure-hugging, black silk, off-the-shoulder cocktail dress, and I nodded hesitantly. 'Then let's go.'

We flashed to a vast open-air room, surrounded by enormous, spaced-out Grecian pillars draped in climbing ivy. Between the pillars, I glimpsed a forest, but not much else. The trees looked like Hyperion, a coast redwood. Glancing up at the blazing sun, I took a deep breath and smiled. 'Oh, how I've missed you,' I murmured, my gaze fixed on the ball of orange fire. The room buzzed with smartly dressed people, all sipping fancy drinks and nibbling on canapés. Tee grabbed a couple of glasses of the pink fizz, and I took a gulp. 'I adore this fizz,' I said, staring lovingly at the glass.

'It's champagne and nectar,' Tee answered, and I raised an eyebrow.

I scanned the room but didn't spot Hades. I didn't feel the tingling at the nape of my neck when his eyes were on me. 'Where's Hades?' I enquired casually.

'He's not coming, Sephy. It's killing him to watch the other gods fawning over you.'

I winced, but then I thought about him treating me differently—colder—after everything we'd done, and my temper prickled. 'Good,' I bit out, 'because Lord Deadly and Grumpy from Planet Infuriating is a twatwaffle.'

'Do you know what, girl? Sometimes you're kind, and sometimes you're kind of a bitch,' Tee growled softly before she twirled around and stomped off.

My mouth fell open. Was I? Didn't he deserve it? Yet, uncertainty plagued me.

'Persephone.' That familiar baritone voice drew my gaze to the right. Poseidon. I groaned internally but dutifully smiled and held out my hand, which he kissed. 'I hope you're not leading my brother on a merry dance,' he murmured. 'I vowed to flood your city if you broke his heart, and I meant it.' His lips were nothing more than a thin line. He cared for Hades, and that made me warm to him a little. 'Plus, apparently, he's excellent at oral sex.' He chuckled knowingly, and heat coursed through me like a fever. I wanted to disappear into my hands, but I refused. Standing around him, thinking about it, however, was pretty far up the no-thank-you list.

'You're... You're... ugh,' I seethed as I turned to leave. I was going to gut Hades, the fucking big-mouthed jerk.

He sighed. 'Pearls before swine.'

I spun around again. 'Did you just call me a pig?' He rolled his eyes and walked off, leaving me flustered.

Of course, Zeus found me, and that melodic voice calmed my anger a smidge. We exchanged pleasantries, and as he kissed my hand to leave, he, too, narrowed his eyes at me. 'Why did you kiss Apollo?'

His question took me aback, and irritation buzzed through my veins. 'Why not?' I bark-whispered. 'And what business is it of yours?'

'I'll fucking destroy your city with lightning if you break Hades' heart,' he rumbled softly, then strode away.

Gods. London was set to be not only flooded but also annihilated by lightning. Freaking fabulous. I finished my pink fizz, and a hand placed another in front of me.

'Apollo.' A grin split my face when our gazes locked.

'Lady P, may I say you look stunning?' He bowed and kissed my hand. Zeus and Poseidon stood together, eyeing us both. Feeling increasingly irritated, I placed my hands on Apollo's broad shoulders, and as he leaned down, I kissed him gently on the cheek. Poseidon looked as if he was about to blow a gasket, his jaw bunched and his cheeks rosy, so I smiled sweetly at the god of the sea.

'I can't wait for you to visit my court, Persephone.' My attention returned to Apollo, whose cheeks were now flushed.

'Oh, me too. I'm looking forward to it,' I replied. Apollo glanced over my shoulder, sighed, kissed my hand, and began to mingle.

'Persephone.' I heard Ares' voice and turned. There he was, all broad shoulders and muscles, looking like a mountain ash on steroids.

'Ares.' I extended a hand, and he kissed it for so long that I had to tug it back.

'You look...' he rasped, his eyes never leaving my breasts. 'Delicious.' His gaze finally found my face, and blood poured into my cheeks as my eyes anxiously searched for Tee.

'Thank you,' I muttered, finally relaxing as Tee appeared beside me, offering a plate of canapés. I took several and stuffed them into my mouth, chewing self-consciously as Ares' gaze zeroed in on my moving lips.

'Gods, you're ravishing,' he murmured, gingerly adjusting his crotch. Tee snorted a laugh, and I almost spat the canapés in his face as I spluttered in surprise. 'Let's go.' He offered me his arm, and I placed my hand on his bulging forearm as he led the way. Glancing around, I realised the room had all but emptied.

'You're going to love the trials,' he said excitedly as he led Tee and me to what appeared to be a box like those at the theatre, but much bigger. 'Wouldn't it be funny if I won this competition for your hand in marriage? Gods—' He stared down at my breasts again. 'I really want you to choose me this time, Persephone.' He adjusted his crotch with a wince and then turned away to address the crowd.

'Yeah, about as funny as a Greek tragedy,' I muttered, causing Tee to spurt a laugh. I watched him puff out his chest and wave majestically at the raucous crowd. 'Ugh, he's like a parasitic toenail infection.' This time, Tee nearly choked on her wine as she thumped her chest to clear it.

Tee and I sat in the plush seats. The box was situated centrally, overlooking the enormous amphitheatre, which featured a full orchestra on a stage. Built in a semicircle, the amphitheatre featured tiered seating rising on one side of a central arena.

'Welcome to Thrace Trials!' Ares yelled, and the crowd

screamed in delight. The acoustics of the amphitheatre were superb. 'We have the first soldiers to fight, one-on-one.' Two giant men, who also resembled mountain ash on steroids, strode into the arena, and the crowd went wild. 'Then we will move on to the pairs' battle!' Ares yelled, and the crowd roared.

It was an 'oh fuck' moment. 'They're gladiators?' I turned to Tee with wide eyes. 'I don't do blood sports,' I croaked, starting to panic.

'Calm down, babe. It's simulated warfare. It used to be a major form of entertainment in ancient Greece. Being the god of war, Ares still has a hard-on for it.' She tutted. 'Ares' soldiers are an expensive investment, so it's preferable that they don't die on the field... but they must be strong enough to last more than one fight.'

The orchestra started to play dramatic music, and I took deep breaths as I watched the soldiers come together in a clash of swords and shields. Ares sat down beside me, handed me another glass of fizzy wine, then placed a large hand on my bare knee, making me squirm internally.

'The spear they carry is known as a panoply,' Ares said, leaning close to my ear, his eyes fixed on the arena. As I studied the soldiers, I noticed they also carried a short sword and a circular bronze shield, and wore a bronze helmet, a bronze breastplate, greaves for their legs, and ankle guards.

He turned to me, his eyes zeroing in on my breasts. At the thought of him drooling, my temper sparked.

'Are you completely psychotic?' I gestured with my chin towards the bloodied, battling soldiers. 'I'm about two seconds away from throwing up.' He chuckled softly, shaking his head, then stared at my breasts again.

'Gods, what I would give to get my hands, lips, and cock on your tits, Persephone.'

'Excuse me? You're such a fucking creeper!' I snarl-whispered, and Tee sounded as if she was choking on air.

'I know.' He grinned. 'But I'm a great fuck.' Then the prick winked at me, his eyes turning back to the battling soldiers. He stood and walked to the box balustrade, yelling instructions to the fighting men.

'I'm about two seconds away from sharpening a shiv from my toothbrush,' I whispered to Tee, seething.

'Did you bring one?' Tee cocked her head.

I glanced in my clutch. 'Nope.' I chuckled, and she almost spat out her wine. 'I want you to fetch my divine blade, Tee. Please?' She'd flatly refused several times.

She shook her head. 'Nope. If you had that blade, both Ares and Hades would have been castrated by now.'

I snort-laughed. 'Meh... you're probably right.' After another ten minutes of watching grown men fight, I turned back to Tee. 'Please take me home, Tee. I've had enough of this crapfest.' Tee gave me a furtive smile. 'I mean, to the Underworld,' I added hastily.

We stood to leave, and Ares darted to my side, making me jump.

'We're leaving, Ares,' Tee said gently. 'Persephone isn't feeling too well.'

'Persephone, please don't leave me.' Ares looked close to crying, which made me feel horrible—well, until I realised he was talking to my breasts.

I smiled warmly at him as I took his hand. 'Did I, the original Persephone, like you?' I asked.

He scratched his chin and looked pensive. 'I don't think so. You once called me an egotistical cock.' He tilted his head as if in thought.

Bingo. Nothing had changed there. 'Then, perhaps you need to find someone you're more in tune with. You know? A female warrior. Someone who enjoys hunting and killing things. A woman who revels in torturing and maiming people, perhaps... like a serial killer?' Tee covered her mouth to cough, likely trying to stifle her laughter.

'But Persephone. Apart from Hecate, you're the scariest chick I've ever met. Plus, your breasts are every man's wet dream,' he added quietly.

I took a step back, pointing at myself. 'Me?' He nodded. I shot Tee a worried look.

'Told you we weren't to be messed with.' She grinned. I widened my eyes at her before turning back to the god of war.

'Ares, I have to be honest. You and I—we're just not a good match. I'm sorry.' He pouted as though I'd just asked him to file a tax return. I squeezed his hand, and then Tee flashed me the fuck out of there.

'I'll make us some food. I said I'd meet Hedone and cook with her. Do you want me to bring you some?' Tee asked. I nodded, and then she disappeared.

I poured myself a glass of nectar, kicked off my shoes, and stalked the sitting room. Hades—the arrogant, ignorant tosser—had actually told Poseidon about going down on me. The more I thought about it, the hotter my anger burned. Was it just a game to him? Doubt hissed through me like bitter smoke, sour and suffocating. I downed two more glasses of nectar, each gulp stoking the fury coiling in my gut until I was vibrating with rage. Finally, I stormed to the double doors, slammed them open, and marched inside. There he was—Hades—lounging on the sofa with a book, calm as a cucumber on ice.

Grrr.

'You loud-mouthed tree frog!' I fumed as I stood before him.

He glanced up from his book, and his expression darkened as he looked at me, his eyes fixated on my breasts. 'Did you go to Ares' court looking like that?' he bellowed as he jumped to his feet, still staring at my breasts. His eyes turned into golden aether, and his mouth was nothing more than a thin slash.

'Hey, blame Hedone, not me. I didn't particularly want to get my breasts out for anyone.'

Apart from you, that irritating little voice in my head said. *And you can pipe down!* I growled at the little fucker.

He continued to stare at my breasts. 'Hades.' No answer, his eyes fixed solely on my chest. 'Hades!' I yelled, and he jumped, his gaze finding my face. 'You told Poseidon you'd given me oral sex. How could you?' I gave him a look that should've shrivelled his balls.

He groaned and slumped back onto the sofa. 'He told you?'

'He insinuated,' I barked. 'Is this some twisted game to you? Tell me the truth.'

'No.' He sighed wearily. 'He wanted to know why you

kissed Apollo.' I gulped. *Damn.* 'He was apoplectic. I had to explain how you were well within your rights to kiss him.' His jaw hardened. 'How angry you were when I left you without an explanation. I trust him, Persephone. He's my ally.'

'Oh,' I squeaked. 'Right. Well, no more gossiping about my sex life. Okay?'

'Yes. I'm sorry.' His eyes were back on my breasts. He was focused on them, and I noticed his beautiful *big* cock straining against his jeans. I wanted to taste him again. Gods, I was going insane.

I don't know what came over me... something primal stirred within, but that sensitive area between my thighs tingled and was flooded with wetness and heat. I sauntered over to him, hiked up the dress, and straddled his lap.

'Persephone,' he groaned.

'Hades,' I whispered, nuzzling his neck. His low growl reverberated through me. 'Would you like me to taste you again?' At my words, I felt a shiver roll through him.

'Yes. Or...' He hesitated. 'I could—' He stopped.

'You could what?' I breathed as my teeth grazed his neck.

'Fuck you with my tongue,' he said in a low, animalistic whisper.

Oh, hello, Mamma! 'Okay.'

He lifted me, and I yelped as his hands grasped the front of my dress and tugged. The dress tore straight down the centre, and he pushed it away from my shoulders. As I stood in my lace underwear, he feasted on me with his eyes, then palmed my breasts, making me moan softly. He licked and sucked my taut nipple through the lacy bra, and then did the same with the other. As his fingers rubbed and tweaked and his mouth played erotic games, I felt myself turning to goo—a pile of aroused goo—and I was on the edge of an orgasm.

'More,' I rasped.

'Gods, Persephone.' He raised his head, and I whimpered. 'Your breasts are fucking delightful.' He gave me an indecent smile, then carried me to his bedroom, placing me face down on his bed.

He hovered over me, and I groaned softly. He trailed his fingers down my spine. 'Are you okay?' he whispered.

'Yes.' My voice was shaky and a little breathy. I lifted my head and saw him staring at my ass. Oh, gods. I pushed my forehead into the pillow, biting my lower lip. He pulled my panties down my legs, and I whimpered. He lowered himself and kissed the skin of my neck. My back arched, and my backside bucked into his hard stomach, making him chuckle. 'You want my tongue inside you, Persephone?'

'Yes,' I groaned as he pressed a soft kiss to my shoulder. He placed a hand between my shoulder blades and held me down gently, running his fingers down my spine again, then tilting my hips slightly. I was close to combusting—a trembling mess filled with anticipation. One touch, and I was sure I'd fall. I fisted my shaking hands into his sheets.

'Fates, Persephone. You're so fucking gorgeous,' he rumbled as he pulled my hips higher.

'Oh, yes,' I gasped as his tongue ran down my back, and I jolted when he licked along the crack of my backside.

Then that erotic dance slid over my core, flicking my clit and nudging my opening. He held me open as if I were a feast made to be devoured. That hot, broad tongue had me squirming, and a graze of a fang and his hot lips with deep kisses made me squeeze my eyes closed and arch my ass higher. His tongue circled my sensitive swollen bud, and when he sucked hard, I moaned deep in my throat. 'Oh, my gods, more.'

A low, satisfied growl against my slick folds made me shiver. When the heel of his palm took over, massaging that sensitive bundle of nerves in a slow rhythm, I whimpered, and when his tongue pushed deep inside me, my belly clenched, and I saw stars behind my closed eyelids. My quiet pleading and whimpering made him all the more ferocious in his need to please. As his thumb circled my clit, and that tongue delved deeper, my entire body ignited. Bloomed. And eventually crumpled as I clenched around him and melted into an abyss of pure ecstasy.

'Hades... no more.' As my hips bucked, I begged for him to stop, but he was relentless, licking that swollen pleasure source, and as wave after wave of rapture shattered through my body, he didn't stop. Eventually, I was a boneless mess, and he flipped me over, running his tongue from my pussy over my stomach, stopping to lick and suck each taut nipple, then he bit my shoulder hard; a sharp pain in my skin caused me to gasp and then groan. He showered my neck with gentle kisses, and then his mouth plundered mine.

'Hecate is coming,' he said as he gently kissed my neck

again, pulled my panties up, and went back to the sitting room and his book.

'Oh, alright,' I muttered.

'Persephone,' I heard Hecate call. 'Hades, have you seen—' Tee emerged from my adjoining suite, her gaze landing on me through the still-open bedroom doors. Her stare shifted to Hades, and she narrowed her eyes.

'She's fine,' he muttered.

'Oh, hi.' I sat up, still wrapped in post-orgasmic bliss.

'Whoops, it seems your dress tore.' Hecate picked up the shredded garment and glared at Hades. 'Come on.' She beckoned to me with her index finger.

I rolled my eyes, caught Hades' gaze, and smiled at him, but his expression remained impassive. 'I'll see you later,' I muttered, then followed Tee back to my room, where she closed the doors.

'What in the Fates is going on?' She glowered at me.

'Food!' I shrieked as I stared at the plate on my table and rushed to sit down, picking up the fork and gobbling down the masterpiece of jasmine rice and delicious-tasting chicken. After devouring half the feast without pausing for breath and sipping yet another glass of nectar, my eyes lifted to Tee.

'Sephy, babe. You're in your underwear. You've been with Hades. Tell me what in Olympus is going on. Are you having post-sex munchies?'

I bit my bottom lip, staring down at my hands. Bah. 'Not penis sex.' I looked up at her.

'Oral sex.' She raised an eyebrow, and I nodded, avoiding her gaze. 'He's marked you,' she growl-hissed.

'What?' I wandered over to the mirror and spotted the bite mark just above my shoulder. Two tiny holes were surrounded by a small purple bruise, and I frowned. 'Is that...?'

'Yes. He's claimed you. The jackass,' she growled again.

'Claimed me?' I suddenly sobered up. 'What does that even mean?'

'Any god who desires you will have to challenge him.'

'Oh,' I murmured.

'So no more hanky-panky with him, Sephy. He had no right to claim you without your consent.'

'Argh, but Tee, he's so good at it. So freaking good. I think I'm like a crack addict. I'm addicted to him. And I discovered that Hedone's right! Oral sex each way is good.'

'Sephy, how many glasses of nectar have you had?' I shrugged in response. 'So, you've given him head?'

'A blowjob? Yeah.' I paused. 'Tee... do you think I love him?' Well, that came out of the blue.

'I know you do, Sephy.'

'But how do you know if it's love and not just attraction?'

'You just know, Sephy. You feel like a complete individual when they're in your life. It's the sense that the link you share with them transcends everything. Could you live without them? Want to live without them? From my perspective, the answer is no. I'd be a miserable bitch without Hedone in my life.'

I giggled. Could I live without Hades? My mind was fuddled, so I shut that thought down. 'That sounds... nice. Anyway, I've sworn off love.'

'Why?'

I sobered for another moment. 'Everyone I love leaves me,' I whispered, my lips trembling.

Tee gently stroked my face. 'Come on, let's get you to bed. How many glasses of nectar *have* you had?'

'Hm, about four. Maybe eight.' Tee tutted at my words and cursed under her breath about something or another.

That night, my dream was of Hades. And it was filthy.

TWENTY-EIGHT

HADES

I called Tee to come and fetch Persephone because my restraint was on a hairpin. I was about to lose control and claim her.

Tee's accusatory glare, however, had taken care of my raging hard-on. I'd walked around Persephone's garden when she had left with Tee, then stayed up all night brooding.

The following morning, Hecate barged into my office, looking like she could incinerate me with a single gaze.

'You performed oral sex on her *again,* and she's given you head? She was high on nectar last night, Hades. She had so many glasses I'm surprised she didn't pass out. What in Olympus's name are you playing at?'

I raised my gaze to her and clenched my teeth. 'How come me telling Poseidon about the oral sex is a crime, but her telling you everything is okay?' I spat.

'You what? You told your brother? What the Fates?'

I shook my head in disbelief. 'I had to tell him why she kissed Apollo. I trust him, Hecate. And she seemed fine last night. I didn't realise she was high... Her powers are obviously growing quicker than we realised.' I sighed with frustration, then lowered my eyes.

'You *cannot,* under any circumstances, fuck her. Not until she agrees to be your consort. You cannot keep her unwillingly,' Tee ground out.

I closed my eyes momentarily. 'It's getting harder and harder, but I am aware.'

'And you marked her. You claimed her!' she fumed. 'What gives you the right?'

'I marked her in a moment of lust and madness. I will not act upon it. You have my word.' Those words seemed to pacify Hecate.

'She's still skittish, and you're not doing her any favours.'

'Skittish?'

She didn't elaborate on the statement but continued, 'Maybe I was wrong? Perhaps you ought to lay your heart bare and tell her how you truly feel.' I furrowed my brow in confusion. I couldn't do that. My Persephone had gifted me the most honest, unending love I'd ever known or ever would. The loss of it had been so visceral that it cut me to the bone. Now she was resisting our soul bond; I needed the emotional walls I'd built to shield me from her impending rejection. The pain of her no longer loving me was overwhelming.

'Stay away from her until you swallow your arrogance

and admit your love for her,' Hecate snapped, and my eyes shot to hers. 'I mean it, Hades, for the love of the gods, stay away from her. Otherwise, I *will* take her from you until you calm the fuck down. You're all messing with her head, and I *will* protect her from *all* the gods... including you.'

I glared at her. 'You wouldn't dare take her from me,' I snarled.

'Oh, I would! I'll whisk her away somewhere, and no one will ever find her,' she spat at me before flashing from my office, leaving me with my head in my hands, knowing that, as the goddess of witchcraft, she was more than capable of following through on her threat.

What a mess.

TWENTY-NINE

PERSEPHONE

H ades was avoiding me. Again. I hadn't seen him for over a week and didn't know whether I was coming or going with him.

When he wasn't around, I constantly thought about him, yearning to be near him. I had never experienced anything like it. It felt like a sweet addiction, one I never wanted to relinquish; yet, at the same time, it frightened me. I was rattled, angry, sad, and confused, along with a truckload of feelings I didn't even want to contemplate. It was a precarious mix of terrifying emotions.

Tee mentioned that he was rarely in the Underworld unless necessary, as he was spending time with Poseidon in Genesion and at his nightclubs. Apparently, they had politics to sort out. But whatever. I wondered if Minthe was

QUEEN OF SHADOWS AND ROSES

with him, but buried the thought before I drove myself insane.

She explained about the resistance, a dissident group called Ixion, how dangerous they potentially were, and how Hades suspected they were behind my hideous trip to the Empousa. However, she also mentioned that Hades had convinced Zeus to pardon the Councils of Magic and persuade them to become allies. At that news, my foolish heart performed a trippy dance as I thought of the god of the Underworld. Damn it. Damn him.

Tee was busting my ass... Working me harder than Hades ever had. She was destroying my freaking will to live. The bitch. Even so, without Hades, thoughts of London invaded my mind—when I wasn't passing out from exhaustion. I loved my friends here, but perhaps returning to London, even for a short while, would break my funk and help me move on from the feelings I had for the god of death. Whatever those feelings were, they went beyond the primal and raw sense of lust I experienced whenever I was near him. It was so overwhelming and intense that I often found myself thinking irrationally.

The desire, attraction, and temptation were potent. I was confused... Was it love or lust? I'd gone from disinterested in sex to a freaking femme fatale in the short time I'd been here, and I'd never been irrational. Loss of control was scaring the crap out of me.

'Tee.'

'Yup.' She turned to me. We were in my garden again, practising my shadow magic; she was working me like a dog.

'I need to speak to my high priestess, you know, about covering my demon-hunting duties. So, I was thinking of going home... Maybe just for a few days.'

'No need.'

'Why?'

'I sorted it with your high priestess when you first arrived here. Hades has been sending his men to manage your schedule. Charon and Erebus have returned plenty of the little ass-wipes to Tartarus. Your high priestess is delighted.'

'Oh,' I muttered, confusion clouding my mind. 'Please thank him.'

'Now, Sephy. Use the tiniest burst of darkness this time, then draw it straight back.' I did as she asked and let out a whoop. Tee grinned at me. 'Let's go and have lunch.'

'Thank the gods,' I groaned. 'I think I'll take a nap as well. I've not been sleeping well.'

'Absence makes the heart grow fonder, babe.'

'Well, people who think that should be hogtied and drowned,' I shot back. Tee gave me a curious glance but didn't answer.

After lunch, I wandered back to my room, angsty but tired. I quietly opened the door to Hades' suite, only to find it deserted, and sighed. I was acting like a lovesick teenager, and needed to get control of myself. Pretending I wasn't missing him was draining; pretending I didn't perhaps love him was worse.

I walked to the beautiful rose tree and gently touched the petals, inhaling the magical, restorative fragrance of the blooms.

My eyelids drooped... The tiredness was bone-deep.

I curled up on his bed, clutching the pillow to my face. It still smelled of him—earthy, like the night air mixed with that fresh, woody, spicy fragrance. I inhaled deeply and closed my eyes, wondering if I truly loved him, and, if so, how love could cause such pain—such aching discomfort in one's chest.

'SEPHY!' Tee's frantic voice roused me from my slumber.

'Wh—what?' I grunted as I sat up. I was still in Hades' bed, but the doors between our rooms were open.

'You need to heal someone.'

'Heal? W—what?'

'You're able to heal, or you could, but we're running out of time. Hurry. Come on.'

I scrambled from the bed, my brain still sleepy and fuzzy, as Tee flashed me to what seemed to be a vast throne room. Two black thrones, one huge and one considerably smaller, stood on a large dais. Black marble, infused with sparkles adorned the room, and Grecian pillars, topped with massive golden flames punctuated the walls.

Erebus and Thanatos were in the centre of the room, kneeling over a man I didn't recognise who was prone on the ground. As I walked closer, I halted. The man had a blade in his chest, seemingly near his heart, and the amount of blood staining his shirt triggered my gag reflex.

'Sephy. You were able to heal... before. Can you at least try?' Tee soothed, gripping my hand tightly.

'Heal?' I croaked, my gaze fixed on the man's pallid face. He was struggling to breathe.

'Just try, Sephy. This is Orpheus. He oversees Hades' Underworld clubs. He was attacked in New York; we think Ixion is responsible. It's a blade of Olympus. If they puncture major organs, they are deadly to demigods. It's a bit like a divine blade, but more dangerous. Luckily, another demigod found him, and Thanatos was in the area.'

'Does Hades know?' Tee shook her head in answer. 'I'm not sure I can. What if I unleash my shadows?'

'He's dead anyway if you don't try,' she said matter-of-factly. 'Just try, please.'

'How do I do it?' I was frozen in place, paralysed by fear. Tee shrugged. Great. 'Do I n—need to touch him?'

'No,' Thanny replied. 'You used to, like, shoot out golden vines.'

'What?' My eyes darted to his. 'How do I do that?' He, too, shrugged. 'I think I'm going to be sick,' I groaned as I covered my mouth.

'Persephone.' Erebus's soothing voice drew my attention, and I shifted my gaze to his eyes—those dark pools twinkling with moondust. 'Just try. No matter what happens, if you don't try, he will die.'

'Release it, or try to, when I pull out the dagger,' Thanatos said.

I nodded meekly and closed my eyes. Taking deep breaths, I thought about creating life and healing life and called upon my flora magic. I instinctively knew what to do. I didn't blink or question it. My heart rate slowed as I felt my magic responding—its swamping heat enveloping me, its warmth flowing into sinew and bone.

I opened my eyes and extended my hands towards Orpheus. Thanny nodded once and pulled the dagger from Orpheus's chest, causing him to convulse. My eyes rounded, but I clung to the magic, instructing it to heal Orpheus. I gave a little yelp as golden-amber light illuminated the space; the warmth of the energy felt like the heat of the sun's rays, and golden vines shot from my hands, entwining around Orpheus, but I sensed that the energy was draining my lifeforce. Orpheus coughed and groaned.

'Enough, Sephy.' Tee placed a hand on my arm, and I recalled it to me as I did with my shadow magic. Thanatos let out a whoop of delight.

I wiped my arm across my forehead; my head was spinning, and black dots clouded my vision as I swayed... then I crumpled to the ground and saw black.

'A blade of Olympus? Where in the Fates have they found so many weapons of the gods? Keep it in the vault. I have informed Zeus; I'm off to meet him and Poseidon now. Stay with her... Rotate. She will be unconscious for a while, but do not leave her side. She will require blood when she awakens.'

It was Hades' voice. He was back. My heart rate sped up, and I tried to open my eyes, but darkness pulled me under once more.

THIRTY

HADES

'A blade of Olympus,' Poseidon thundered.

Zeus, Poseidon, and I were in Zeus's plush office in London. 'How many weapons have they got their hands on, Zeus?' Poseidon's baritone voice demanded.

'I've checked the armouries, which haven't been opened since the war. All three blades of Olympus are missing, along with a few other items,' he replied cagily.

'The blades of Olympus that you assured us would be guarded—that you forged with your lightning, from the soil of the Underworld, hermatypic coral, and your thunderbolt? Are *missing?* What other *items* are missing, Zeus? Aside from Hades' helm and the blades.' A vein throbbed in Poseidon's temple. Gods, he was a bad-tempered bastard.

'At least we have one blade back. It's in my vault,' I muttered, and Poseidon released a humourless laugh.

Zeus hesitated. 'Aegis is missing, along with a few other divine weapons.'

Poseidon roared and slammed a fist against Zeus's desk, cracking it in two.

'Calm down, Brother.' I placed a hand on Poseidon's arm.

'To unlock its true potential, an Olympus blade requires an infusion of godly power,' I said. 'Tell me none have been imbued with such?' A vein in Zeus's jaw ticked, and I closed my eyes, releasing a breath. 'If it possessed the power, that blade I have would have slain Orpheus on impact. How many blades have been fortified?'

'Only one,' Zeus replied cautiously.

'Only one?' Poseidon roared. 'They possess a blade that can slay a god?' Zeus bristled, preparing to argue, but I raised a hand to prevent another quarrel.

'Arguing will not change the situation. At least we now know they pose a genuine threat to us. I shall have Hecate ward Naxos immediately. We will not permit anyone to enter without permission. Moreover, as Ixion also has my helm of invisibility, they are well-equipped to attack not only demigods but also gods. Whoever is orchestrating this and Persephone's attack desires that war among ourselves to weaken us. This must *not* happen. We operate as one, but we create the impression we are fighting. This conversation stays within these walls... We do not know who is an ally or a traitor...'

Both brothers agreed.

'Hades, Poseidon.' Zeus stopped us before we could leave. 'I'm sorry.' I frowned, and Poseidon stiffened, giving me a 'Huh?' look. 'I truly appreciate you both. I may have been unreasonable in the past'—Poseidon barked out a laugh, and I narrowed my eyes at Zeus—'but I want things to be different. I want you to be my brothers in the true sense of the word. Things need to change. We need to change.'

Both a little dazed, Poseidon and I left Zeus. 'We will see if the egocentric fucker can change,' Poseidon grumbled.

'Nothing is insurmountable.'

'You're going soft in your old age, you whipped bastard.' Poseidon raised a brow and vanished into a cloud of seafoam and mist, leaving me shaking my head.

THIRTY-ONE

PERSEPHONE

I peeled my leaden eyelids open, feeling like they had fused, to find Thanatos sitting beside the bed. I was still in Hades' bed.

'Ugh,' I groaned.

'My queen,' Thanatos said with happiness. 'How are you feeling?'

I sat up slowly. 'Erm, tired. How long have I been asleep?' Memories of healing Orpheus invaded my mind. 'How's Orpheus?'

'He's fine. You collapsed, Highness. You expended a massive amount of healing energy. And... you've been unconscious for just shy of two days.'

'What?' I all but screeched. I tried to get out of bed but almost collapsed as Thanatos caught me. 'You need blood, my queen,' he said softly. 'It takes a long time for healing abilities to fully develop.'

'Where's Hades?' I whispered.

Thanatos looked uneasy. 'He's, erm, in New York. At his nightclub.'

'Oh,' I whispered. That ache in my chest blossomed, and tears clogged my throat.

'You need blood, my queen,' Thanatos reiterated, biting into his wrist and offering it to me. I recoiled.

'No, no. I can't, I...' I couldn't climb Thanatos like a tree monkey and try to ravish him, as well.

'Don't worry. The reaction to my blood won't be the same as Hades' blood,' he said knowingly, and fire scorched my cheeks. 'Blood of a bonded has a different effect on the recipient.'

When he said bonded, I squinted at him, but he merely shrugged. 'You sure... I won't?' He nodded, so I closed my lips around the puncture marks on his wrist and sucked. He tasted smoky and citrussy, like mezcal and lime juice. He was delicious. I sucked harder until he gently pulled his wrist away from me.

'Sorry,' I whispered as he licked his wrist. 'You taste nice.'

He grinned at my words. 'How do you feel?'

I tilted my head. 'Definitely not horny.'

'Thank the gods,' he deadpanned, blushing. 'Hades would castrate me.'

I snorted a laugh. Gods, I adored Thanny. 'I feel good. Thank you.'

He grinned. 'Excellent. Because you're due at Apollo's court in'—he checked his watch—'approximately two hours.'

I groaned, and he winked at me.

AN HOUR AND A HALF LATER, I was ready; my hair was styled in soft waves, with half in an updo featuring a thick, asymmetric braid that seamlessly blended into the loose curls down my back. The perfume applied to my pulse points enveloped me in a floral and musky scent—like cherry blossom silk embroidered with an almond and musk accord. I sat on my sofa wearing lace underwear, hoping Hedone would arrive with my outfit before Simmy came. Tee had gone to get ready herself.

The goddess of pleasure appeared holding a lush black velvet jumpsuit, which I grabbed and held against myself in front of the long mirror—a square neckline with a jewelled embellished trim, shoulder pads, and an internal corset boning to the bodice. I unzipped and stepped into it as Hedone fastened me up. It fit perfectly, though the cleavage of my ample breasts was glaringly noticeable. Paired with stiletto-heeled shoes, the jumpsuit beautifully complemented my curves. 'I love it, but do I really need to flaunt my breasts?'

'Darling,' Hedone crooned as she stood behind me, placing her hands on my shoulders and regarding me in the mirror. 'Women in the Western world have used their cleavage to flirt, attract attention, make political state-ments, and assert power since at least the fifteenth century. If you've got it, flaunt it.' I wrinkled my nose at her, and she giggled. Tee appeared in a black leather jumpsuit, draping an arm around Hedone's shoulders as they scrutinised me.

'Looking good, Sephy.' Tee winked. 'Pretty boy Apollo will be certainly be impressed.' My face flushed, and I narrowed my eyes while pursing my lips.

'Maybe I'll consider marrying Apollo.' I raised my brow, and her smirk faltered. 'As Hades seems to have lost interest.' At my words, Hedone shot Tee a worried glance. 'Keep your hair on,' I grunted. 'I'm not marrying any of them.' I locked eyes with Tee, and she cocked her head.

'We shall see,' she replied, her smirk returning. I was still mulling over our plan, unsure whether it would work or if I should simply attempt to escape this fuck-upery instead. I had a chance if I could just return to the mortal world. Then, that nagging pain in my chest at the thought of leaving Hades made me curse silently. A knock on the door announced Simmy, and two minutes later, the four of us were at the court of Cyclades.

The area we arrived in was similar to Aphrodite's courtyard: vast and paved in white marble, the obligatory Grecian pillars flamed with burnished orange fire and were adorned with various varieties of Clematis. Instead of flowering trees, the expansiveness of the courtyard was punctuated by Grecian statues, while crowds of elegantly dressed people milled about, sipping sparkling wine and nibbling on canapés.

The colonnade allowed the light and sweet-smelling breeze to reach further into the building. I wandered to the edge of the large dais where we stood and looked up at the shimmering sun, moaning as I felt its rays on my face. The scenery was breathtaking. In the distance, I spied an expansive mountain range with scenic peaks, lush meadows, forests, and lakes.

'Whoa... this place is stunning,' I muttered.

'Isn't it?' Simmy said as he joined me. 'But you'll still choose Hades.' My head snapped around to him. 'Just a fact.' He offered a half-shrug. 'Besides, you can spend time in the mortal world with him.' My insides quivered at the thought.

'I'm not interested in marrying any of them,' I growl-whispered as he flashed me a smug smile.

'Whatevs.' The little shit winked at me, and my jaw hardened.

'Time to mingle, girlfriend,' Tee whispered in my ear as Simmy wandered off to find us drinks and nibbles. Tee and Hedone descended the dais like runway models, and I followed suit.

I mingled and chatted like the goddess I was, serenely and majestically. Hedone watched me like a hawk, with Tee by her side. Simmy appeared with canapés and pink fizz, and I limited myself to two glasses. This place had increased my alcohol intake by fifty percent, and too much of it kept getting me into trouble.

I strolled over to Tee and kissed Thanatos, Charon, Erebus, Hermes, and Dionysus, who were chatting with Hedone and her. We talked as we ate canapés, and Hermes, as usual, lifted my spirits as I laughed at his tales of years gone by.

'So, Ares said to me, "Do you ever want to gently place

your hands on someone's cheeks, look into their eyes, and then violently snap their neck?"' Hermes gave a cheeky grin as we listened. 'Poor Aphrodite was mortified until I replied, "So, I guess you're still pissed off at me, Ares?"'

I almost spat out my food as I laughed. 'What had you done?' I coughed out.

'Probably pulled one of his infamous pranks,' Dionysus replied with a shake of his head, while Hermes pointed to himself in an innocent, 'What, me?' gesture.

As we chatted, I was acutely aware that the tingling sensation I felt in Hades' presence was glaringly absent... once again.

'Erm, is Hades not coming?' I asked Tee as casually as I could. The four men looked uncomfortable, and I squinted up at them. 'What?' I glared at the goddess of magic.

'He might be coming later, but he can't stay. He's swamped at the moment.' I scrutinised her, aware that she was evading the truth. Was he with Minthe? The thought caused coils of disquiet to gnaw at my gut.

Why, in the world of fucks, was I so bothered? I sighed internally... This bond was a freaking bitch.

'Sephy, don't worry. He will be here,' Tee assured me.

'I'm not worried,' I hissed, stomping away as she called my name, with Simmy trotting alongside me.

'Sephy, my darling.' That low, sultry voice made me smile. I turned to face Aphrodite, looking as beautiful as ever in a teal silk gown. Her aquamarine eyes were piercing, but they shone with happiness.

'Aphrodite,' I murmured, embracing her.

'Persephone.' She held me at arm's length, worry clouding her gaze. 'Are you alright?'

'Of course,' I said, managing a wobbly smile, and she narrowed her eyes.

'Come.' She took my hand and led me to a quiet area with a loveseat. 'Sit with me.' She grabbed two glasses of pink fizz from a passing server and handed one to me. 'Spill,' she whispered as she delicately sipped her drink.

I blew out a long breath. 'I'm confused.'

Her tinkling laughter was like wind chimes in the summer breeze. 'Love is confusing, darling.'

'Oh, no, I—' She held out a hand, palm facing me, and I swallowed my denial.

'The complexities of love are so difficult to navigate... Being in love should be clear, not a burden. You are a team that can achieve anything together. You're overthinking your feelings for Hades, darling.' I opened my mouth to argue that I did *not* love the god of freaking death, but the words shrivelled on my tongue. 'Love is simple. It's a force —a bond stronger than death and separation. Don't fight it, darling. And remember, it's essential to seek under-standing; open communication can help navigate these complexities.' She took my hand.

'He's avoiding me,' I muttered. 'And I miss him.'

She squeezed my hand. 'Hecate has warned him to stay away from you, darling.'

'What?' I growled, glaring over at Tee, who had the decency to look at least a tad embarrassed... She knew she'd been outed. 'Why would she do that?'

'Hades is a complex character, Persephone—arrogant

yet just. His love is all-consuming. He does not wish to hold you back by stifling you... He desires you to choose him without lust and attraction clouding your thoughts. Hecate did what she thought was the right thing. Hades is old-school. If he fucks you, he will keep you.'

'But Minthe?' I puckered my brow.

'He does not and has never loved Minthe, darling.'

'How do you know? Has he—'

'I'm the goddess of love, sweet girl,' she said, interrupting me. 'People don't need to tell me.' She chuckled softly. 'The real complication of love is the relationship, which is simple, really. Friendship, emotional stability, trust, and love—relationships devoid of love are tasteless. Then we have passion and sex, preferably the sparklers and fireworks type.' She winked at me, and I ducked my head and blushed. 'So, be brave and tell him. Alright?'

I gave her a slight nod and embraced her again. Was she right? Was it love that I was feeling? Or merely a hormonal haze? Because there was no question: Hades was so, so fuckalicious. Maybe it was a bond haze, if such a thing existed. 'Thank you,' I whispered against her hair. 'And I'd like to spend some time with you soon.'

Her smile was like sun rays lighting up the cloudy sky. 'Absolutely.'

After we chatted, Aphrodite went off to mingle, and Simmy rejoined me. I settled into the loveseat, sipping my wine and reflecting on Aphrodite's words. I could only wish I were able to speak to Granny about Hades—the pang in my chest throbbed at the thought of her. She would have offered me advice on the vortex of baffling emotions within me.

Simmy knocked me out of my reverie when he excitedly grabbed my hand.

'Apollo!' he almost squealed, gesturing at the approaching god like a raccoon on meth. Apollo was pure male beauty, his golden chin-length hair glittering like starfire. Built like a linebacker, kind and funny, he was everything many women would desire. Just not this woman. Damn Hades.

'Lady Persephone.' Apollo bowed as I stood, then he kissed my hand. When his eyes met mine, a fire burned in his gaze, causing my skin to flush. Shit. I'd kissed him out of sheer anger, and that thought made my insides twist. I was a complete train wreck. Oblivious to my internal chaos, Simmy clasped his hands in front of himself as he gazed lovingly at the god.

'Apollo.' I smiled brightly at the god of the sun. 'This is my friend, Simos.' I gestured to the Satyr, who, in turn, fangirled like a complete fruit loop, making Apollo laugh kindly.

'You look as though you're about to head to a rock concert,' I remarked, checking out his T-shirt, jeans, and denim jacket.

'Oh, I am.' He winked at me. 'My band will be performing soon. Just for you, Persephone.'

'Oh.' I narrowed my eyes. 'You have a band? I guess it makes sense, considering you're also the god of music and dance.'

His brow furrowed. 'Have you never heard of us? We sell out venues all over the mortal world.'

'Erm, no, sorry. I'm not really into music. I'm more into books.' Before coming here, I'd steadfastly refused to take an interest in any of the gods or their ventures. I knew Apollo had opened music venues, but I had zero idea he had a famous band. 'What's the name of your band?'

'Thirty Seconds to Olympus.'

I snorted a laugh. 'Like Thirty Seconds to Mars?'

'Yes.' He grinned. 'But we're far better.' He pointed to the graphic on his T-shirt, which clung to his muscled chest: a design of a dreamy sun and multicoloured clouds, with the band's name emblazoned above. 'I need to go and prepare; sound check and the like. But I have a treat for you afterwards. Would you agree to spend some time alone with me?'

I hesitated, and his brows knit together. 'Of course,' I breathed, making his eyes shine with happiness.

'I'll see you later,' he said in a low, sultry voice. He kissed my hand again, wearing his Cheshire cat grin as he strolled away.

Oh, crap on a cracker.

'Oh, Fates. You lucky girl,' Simmy whispered. 'Here.' He handed me another glass of pink fizz, which he had taken from a passing server. 'I know you'll choose Hades, though. And I'm loyal to the god of death, so it's all good.'

'Why, thanks, Dad.' I shook my head at him as he smirked. Did Hades want me to choose him? Or was it the original Persephone he coveted? He was most certainly avoiding me, but at least I now understood why. The thought of best-friend-icide swam through my mind again; I wondered how I might get away with throttling Tee.

'But you have to tell me if you get up close and personal with Apollo and if it's true that he's got a huge—'

'Stop!' I pointed at his face.

'Spoilsport,' he grumbled as he pouted his lips.

'Persephone.' That familiar voice from behind made me groan internally, and Simmy did one—the little twerp.

I turned around slowly. 'Poseidon,' I muttered through clenched teeth, attempting to smile. He cocked his head at me, then took my hand and kissed my palm. I was seriously about to crack a molar.

'You seem uptight, Persephone?' He scrutinised me with those captivating eyes, holding on to my hand—gods, what I wouldn't give to have my divine blade in my fist.

'Do I?' I pursed my lips and pulled my hand free.

'You do. I hope your husband is well. Where is he?' Poseidon's eyes never left my face.

'He's busy.'

'Hm. Is he?'

'Yes,' I bit out. 'Anyway, he's *not* my husband.' I inhaled sharply. 'And I thought he was in Genesion with you.'

Damn my freaking temper and big mouth.

'You're missing him.' Poseidon chuckled darkly, ignoring my icy glare. 'I'm surprised he hasn't just claimed you.' His eyes bore into me, and before I knew what I was doing, my hand slipped to the faded bite mark between my shoulder and neck. I snatched my hand away, but Poseidon narrowed his eyes.

'Hades is a stickler for rules and an arrogant son-of-a-bitch on occasion, but he's a good man, Persephone. Why he hasn't just fucked you and kept you, I'll never understand.' Those eyes seemed to drill into my soul, but I kept an impassive expression.

'Maybe he's not a prick like you. People aren't possessions, Poseidon.' His eyes clouded with swirling storm clouds as a muscle ticked in his jaw. 'Have you ever heard of love? That's why people in my world get married,' I hissed through clenched teeth.

'Love is overrated.'

'Is it? I can't wait for the day you find someone you love—a love that consumes you to the core. If that cold heart is capable, of course.'

He coughed a laugh. 'No woman will ever do that to me; I'm not a sap.'

'Let's have a bet.'

He frowned at my words. 'You always did think with your heart, Persephone,' he replied, rolling his eyes so hard they almost popped out of his ears. 'What are the conditions?'

'If you find love, I want to ride a hippocampus.' I knew Poseidon was particularly possessive towards his favourite sea creatures.

'You'll drown,' he answered drolly.

'Not if I ride it on the surface.' I gave a half-shrug.

He shot me a narrow-eyed look, but a soft grin played at the corners of his mouth. 'Fine. You'll lose because, as you said, my cold heart is incapable of the love Hades holds for you.' At his words, my heart stuttered a beat. '*My* condition is that you make my brother happy... again.' *Again.* That word made the melodramatic bond thrum in my chest and steal the breath from my lungs. My silence thickened the air around us like dense fog.

'Agreed,' I finally managed to whisper as we shook hands. Then, of course, the cockwomble god had to ruin the moment.

Poseidon gave me a shrewd smile. 'I've heard the gossip that Minthe still covets Hades. What if he decided she would make a better consort than you? How would you feel? She does love him, after all.' Ice coated my skin, his words draining the oxygen from the room, and my temper sizzled again.

'I don't know. How would you feel with my fist in your face?' I snarl-whispered as I curled my hand; I could feel my shadow magic pulsing, but I controlled it quickly. A smile twitched on Poseidon's full lips as he cocked his head, and then we both audibly groaned at the sound of Zeus's voice.

'Persephone.' I turned to face the king of the gods, my fake smile plastered across my face and extended my hand for him to kiss.

'Zeus. How lovely to see you again.'

'I hope my brother isn't being bothersome?' he said, a ghost of a smile tugging on his lips.

'No more than usual,' I replied as I side-eyed Poseidon, lifting my chin to meet Zeus's gaze.

'Very good. Well, I feel Apollo has pulled out all the stops to give you a night to remember. Just ensure repayment does not come in the form of sexual favours. Hades would be most put out. As would we.'

My jaw dropped open, and I blinked about a dozen times—*the audacity*. 'We're not all hoe-bags, Zeus. Some of us have morals.' Poseidon roared with laughter, but Zeus's eyes crackled with silver lightning, his jaw working for several seconds until he regained his composure. 'There's one thing I'd like to say.' I flared my nostrils as my irritation ratcheted up another several degrees.

'Yes?' Zeus said slowly.

'You two'—I pointed between the gods, giving them each a death glare—'are both absolute and utter colossal fuck-wits. *And* a massive pain in the ass.'

I growled softly as I stomped away from their rumbling laughter. 'Fucking pricks,' I muttered to myself. Simmy appeared with a glass of pink fizz, and I took a big gulp. The fizzle of champagne and nectar on my tongue eased my mood, much like ripe berries and sunshine. That lasted for about ten minutes, until I spied Ares approaching. My irritation returned, spinning like a high-speed cyclone, but when I saw Hedone eyeing me, I schooled my features. I sighed a moan of frustration, then almost screamed when I saw Adonis walking towards me with Ares.

Fuck. My. Life.

'Dammit,' I whispered to Simmy, who glanced in the direction I was staring. 'Here comes Captain Charisma, who's got nothing but biceps and a degree in lechery.'

Simmy snorted. 'A fitting description for Ares,' he muttered, edging away.

I turned towards him and growl-whispered, 'Come back here, you little shit.' Which he ignored.

I turned slowly, the practiced smile on my face. 'Ares. Adonis. How lovely to see you both again,' I said, trying to mask my 'I'd really like to kick you in the balls' voice. Both men kissed my outstretched hand, and Adonis lingered a moment too long, causing my skin to crawl.

'Well, it seems we're both out of the running to claim you as a wife,' Ares remarked, glancing from my toes to my face, lingering on my breasts for an uncomfortable amount of time. 'So, we've made a wager on who you will choose. Unless you decide to take a lover as well as a husband, then I'm more than up for the job.' He winked at me, while Adonis released a dark chuckle.

'Oh, really?' My face remained blank, but my muscles were tense, and my polite smile never wavered.

'Adonis believes you'll choose Zeus. My money is on Apollo.'

I let out a soft lady-like laugh. 'I see.' My eyes met Adonis's gaze, and at his shrewd look, unpleasant tingles raced down my spine. 'Well.' I inched away. 'Have a marvellous time.'

As I began to turn, Adonis placed a hand on my arm, his eyes sparkling as his gaze locked onto mine. 'I'm sad you won't be coming to the Court of Phoenicia,' he said in a hushed tone. 'You used to love it there.'

'So you say.' I discreetly shrugged his hand off my arm. 'Perhaps I'll visit you with my new husband. One day.' Outwardly, I remained composed, but at his sly smile, my heart started pounding sickeningly fast. I glanced around for Tee, Simmy, or Hedone.

'There she is. My fair lady.' Hermes seized my hand and tugged me towards him. 'Let's get you seated, Persephone.' I gave him a relieved smile. 'Catch you later, Ares. Adonis.' He tipped his head at the gods, both of whom gave him a withering look.

'Thanks,' I breathed. 'Ares is a knob, but Adonis gives me the creeps. He's a one-man egotistical asshole parade.'

Hermes guffawed at my words but sobered quickly. 'Watch yourself with him, Lady P. He's a viper.'

Goosebumps raced across my flesh at Hermes' words. 'I shall do,' I whisper-croaked.

We met with Tee, Hedone, Aphrodite, and Simmy, who handed me another glass of pink fizz, which I sipped carefully while scowling at Tee.

'We can chat later,' she whispered in my ear. I glared at her and chatted with Aphrodite.

Thanatos, Charon, Erebus, and Dionysus joined us as we ascended a broad stone staircase that led into a lavish box of an amphitheatre similar in design to Ares'. The box was central, encircled by tiered seating on each side and in front. Instead of a fighting pit, the arena held an enormous stage adorned with numerous instruments: guitars, basses, pianos, and drums, alongside an area of seats and a sea of instruments belonging to an orchestra. The hum of excited chatter filled the packed amphitheatre as everybody awaited Apollo and his band.

We all settled into our fancy seats and chatted amiably, yet I was in a nervous funk, preoccupied with thoughts of

Hades and his avoidance of me, which both troubled and made me jittery. Did he want *me* or his lost love, the one I knew he yearned for? His hot-and-cold routine was sending me for a loop; Poseidon's words about Minthe invaded my mind and left me feeling uneasy. I fretted over what Hermes had said regarding Adonis, and my gut clenched at the thought of spending time alone with Apollo. I didn't want to lead him on any more than I already had; he was a decent man.

'This is such a treat,' Simmy whisper-shrieked as his little hooves tapped on the plush carpet.

'Hm,' I muttered as I sipped my wine.

'What's with the long face, Lady P?' Simmy murmured.

'I'm fine, Sim.' I gave him a bright smile, but he squinted at me with a knowing look on his face. 'Poseidon mentioned something about Hades and Minthe—' I shrugged, the words dying on my lips.

Simmy blew out a breath. 'Poseidon is a total fucking killjoy. Ignore him.' He rested a hand on my arm, and I turned to him. 'Hades isn't with Minthe. As in...' He made a crude gesture.

A flush invaded my skin, and my stomach tightened at the thought, but I narrowed my eyes at him. 'How do *you* know?'

He tapped his nose. 'The only person he's ever truly loved is you, Lady P.' I let out a humourless huff at his words, but before I could respond, the crowd began to go wild. Glancing up, I noticed the musicians filing onto the stage.

The acoustics in the amphitheatre were extraordinary, and the orchestra and band, along with Apollo's performance, enraptured the entire audience. People stood, danced, and sang; the atmosphere was electric. Apollo was a true rockstar, exuding charisma and sex. I sighed. He would be the easier choice if I ultimately had to select a husband and couldn't escape the obligation. However, I knew the only god I could ever love was the king of death and darkness. I closed my eyes and waited for the knot of messy, raw emotions to climb back down my throat because I knew deep down that Hades didn't want me... he longed for his original Persephone.

At least an hour passed, and the band was still going strong. The concert helped me forget about Hades, and for that, I was grateful. Watching my friends dance, smile, and radiate happiness filled my heart with a fuzzy, warm glow. We were lost in the atmosphere, grinning like fools, while music folded around us like a gentle summer's rain.

'And my final song,' Apollo shouted, 'is for a special lady in the audience.' The crowd erupted, and my heart sank into my pretty shoes. 'It's called "Truly Madly Deeply", originally performed by the fabulous band Savage Garden.

The song was beautiful—one of my favourites. It spoke of being someone's true love; that person being your everything—every fantasy and every need.

And the lyrics continued while I pondered all of this... with Hades on my mind.

'Break it to him gently, darling,' Aphrodite murmured

close to my ear. 'You had always been close friends with Apollo, but he secretly loved you... even back then.'

At her words, things went from crap to double-shit-storms-crap. My life at that point was a mess of epic proportions.

Apollo appeared around half an hour later, freshly showered, wearing jeans, a button-down shirt, and a leather biker jacket. 'Shall we?' He extended an arm, and I smiled sweetly as I took his hand.

CHAPTER
THIRTY-TWO

HADES

I didn't give a fuck what Hecate had demanded; I needed to see Persephone. I had to swallow my pride and take a leap of faith; I needed to beg her to become my consort.

Spending over a week without seeing her had been torturous. I missed the tiny, mouthy, infuriating woman. I loved her even more than I did the first time. How that was possible, I wasn't sure. It was consummate love—intimacy, passion, and commitment—the ultimate, all-consuming kind.

The thought of her being with Apollo was unbearable. My stomach twisted—jealousy, a bitter acid sweeping through my veins. I knew Apollo had loved my Persephone. I knew he still did, and at the thought of her choosing him over me, talons gnawed in my belly and spikes of discord tunnelled into my chest.

My shadows engulfed me, and I appeared before Tee. 'Where is she?' I spat.

She released a slow breath. 'I'm sorry, Hades—' My heart stuttered, and I stepped back. Had she chosen Apollo? 'Don't panic.' She realised her mistake. 'Sephy is fine. She's left with Apollo.' I snarled low in my throat. 'I've spoken to Aphrodite. She had a chat with Persephone, and I'm sorry I stopped you from seeing her. It was wrong of me to interfere.'

'Where. Is. She?' I repeated through clenched teeth as my rage simmered.

'Apollo took her to his stables,' a small Satyr replied. 'I accompanied them to keep an eye on her, but he's taken her off in his chariot to show her his court. He said they'd be back in about half an hour.' I ground my teeth together at his words. 'I'm Simos, Persephone's friend. Come with me; I'll show you the way, Your Highness.'

He bowed, and I followed him.

CHAPTER
THIRTY-THREE

PERSEPHONE

'Oh, my gods!' I squealed, clapping my hands and bouncing on the spot. 'A real-life Pegasus!'

Apollo chuckled at my excitement. 'This is Astra, which means "star". She is one of my most prized possessions. Or maybe I'm her possession? I'm not certain.' I giggled at his declaration as I gently stroked the mare's face. She was pure white, with a small cream star shape between her eyes. 'Poseidon gifted her to me when he was in a good mood.'

I snorted at his words. 'A good mood? He's even grumpier than Hades.' Mentioning his name made my heart clench. 'She's beautiful,' I murmured, planting a kiss on her velvety muzzle. Her wings were tucked in, and a golden chariot secured her in place. 'Are we flying?' My wide eyes met Apollo's stare, and he cleared his throat.

'We are... my lady.' He extended a hand, and I walked around the Pegasus before stepping into the chariot, followed by the god of the sun. 'Here.' He draped his jacket around my shoulders. 'I don't want you to catch a chill.'

'Thanks,' I muttered, heat pricking my cheeks.

Apollo turned to me. 'Hades isn't keeping you... against your will, because—'

'Oh, gods. No,' I gasped. 'I'm there of my own volition.' He studied me for what felt like an eternity, then gave a slight nod.

He took the reins, and Astra's hooves clip-clopped as she pulled the chariot into the open air. 'Hold on,' Apollo said as he issued a command in Greek, and the Pegasus galloped and launched. Her expansive wings took my breath away—a wonderful blend of cream and gold, speckled with white—radiant, like the colours of the warmest sunset. The smaller feathers blended intricately with the larger ones as they rounded the delicate, narrowing curve towards the bottom tip. Her long white mane and tail fluttered in the warm breeze. She soared swiftly and nimbly through the skies—she was majesty personified.

The court was immense and breathtaking. A mountain range in the distance, beautiful lakes, forests, towns, and villages passed us by as we flew through the skies. 'I would love for you to be my consort, Persephone.' Apollo shot me a sidelong glance, and I tried to swallow the boulder in my throat. 'We were close friends before...' He hesitated. 'And the thought of us being more is why I want to be considered.'

'I really like you, but—'

'You still love Hades.' He smiled kindly.

Did I? Love Hades? I didn't respond because, if I did, it would be unrequited. And unrequited love is a bitch. He didn't love *me*—he loved the woman I used to be. The goddess he lost, not the one reborn. I knew he felt limerence and lust... but that was the bond's influence. I inhaled deeply through my nose. I needed to escape this place and return to London and my life.

'Aphrodite warned me, but a guy can hope, right?' He smiled sadly, his eyes holding mine for a heartbeat.

'I'm sorry,' I breathed. 'Can we still be friends?' He nodded and changed the subject as he explained his court to me.

I gasped when a flying ship passed us, the passengers nodding and waving. 'A ship that flies?' My gaze was fixed on the vessel, and Apollo belly-laughed at my wide eyes and slack jaw.

He spoke again once he'd caught his breath. 'Olympus is a blueprint of the Earth, Persephone, in a different dimension. Instead of the sea separating the land masses, we have the sky. Airships serve as a means to travel from one island to another in Cyclades and, sometimes, to different courts. That vessel is a Borasco.' He gestured towards the large flying ship. 'It takes passengers. Some more affluent people possess private vessels, such as a Mistral, which is much smaller. Not everyone can teleport, Lady P.'

'Oh,' I replied, meeting his eyes. 'I have much yet to learn about Olympus.'

His megawatt smile returned, and he whispered, 'Cyclades will always welcome you. I will always welcome you, should you ever need us.'

I dropped my gaze and smiled. 'Thank you,' I said as I touched his hand.

As we returned to the stables, a groom came to take Astra and the chariot, but not before I thanked her again with a kiss on the muzzle.

'That was such fun,' I said as I turned to Apollo. He raised his hand as if to cup my face, and I felt a sharp whirl of tingles ripple across the back of my neck.

'If you touch a single hair on her head, you will find yourself in Tartarus... after I've disembowelled you.' Hades stepped out from behind a pillar. His voice was laced with barely leashed anger. Apollo opened his mouth to speak, but Hades' low guttural growl uttered one word... *'Mine.'*

Hades was possessive and vicious, but also kind and gentle, and my stupid little heart fluttered like it was begging to be ruined. I always thought that a man threatening violence on my behalf would be a turn-off, but coming from him, it made me feel embarrassingly giddy. What the hell was wrong with me? I should have been furious at his assumption, but I wasn't. Go figure.

And, gods, please tell me my nipples aren't tingling.

Apollo stared at Hades as if he'd whipped out his cock and started swinging it around but gave a slight nod, bowed to me, and walked out.

'Persephone.' Hades rolled my name over his tongue as

if he were savouring it, and my legs felt a little unsteady as an intense pulse of desire punched me in the gut. The bond went from a ball of fuzzy warmth in my chest into a raging wildfire.

Our eyes locked, my heart raced, and as I licked my bottom lip, his eyes zeroed in on my mouth. 'I've missed you,' I whispered.

Like a flash of lightning, he was before me, and my breath snagged as his mouth plundered mine, his large hands cradling my face. There was nothing gentle about his kiss... He kissed me as if his life depended on it. The kiss deepened until we were consumed by each other, tongues entwining in an erotic dance, our breaths mingling together. He pulled away, resting his forehead against mine, and closed his eyes. We remained still for several heartbeats.

'We need to talk.' His breath caressed my lips as he spoke.

I met his gaze and nodded. 'We do.'

HADES SHADOW-WALKED me to his chambers, my mind whirling like a softball in a cyclone.

'I want to see my granny,' I said, making him freeze.

He sighed. 'Fine. But one visit is all you can have, Persephone.'

His shadows enveloped us, and we appeared in a scene reminiscent of a quintessential English village: thatched cottages, beautiful gardens, swaying trees, and songbirds. Everything was simply perfect. I spotted a woman tending to one of the gardens—a garden brimming with roses— and then moved closer, unlatching the garden gate. She looked younger, blooming in her surroundings, and I hesitated.

The lady looked up, her eyes meeting mine. 'Persephone, my darling. Oh, how I've missed you.'

'Granny.' I sobbed as I threw myself into her arms, embracing her as I cried. I felt Hades' presence behind me and, reluctantly, let go, gesturing to him. 'This is—'

'I know who he is, darling,' Granny said respectfully, bowing her head.

'Oh,' I whispered. 'Are you... happy?' I held her at arm's length and studied her. That warm smile and the love shining in her eyes made my heart flip-flop.

'I am content, my darling. Yes.' My eyes roamed over her cottage and rose garden. It was like the place she'd always dreamed of.

'How? This place is exquisite.'

She shrugged and smiled. 'It's what I wanted; what I hoped for. Elysium is a beautiful place, Persephone.' That little pulse in my chest felt like a thousand hummingbirds taking flight.

'Hey, Hermione.' A tall, handsome, American Black man waved over the garden fence.

'George, this is my granddaughter.'

George gave me a slight nod, and Hades made his way towards George.

'I'll catch you later, for G&Ts?' George winked, and Granny blushed, causing me to narrow my eyes.

'Sure,' she answered. Then he disappeared inside his house with Hades.

'Are you and George...'

She giggled at my words. 'He's an old flame... He died alone like me. We're rekindling our friendship.' I didn't need to know any more.

'This place seems—'

'It is, darling,' Granny replied before I could finish. 'We have all the necessities of life at our disposal. But here, life is easier. I don't wish to be reincarnated. I'm happy, Persephone.' Her words made my heart do a happy little wiggle, and the pulse in my chest went berserk. 'Let's go and make lemonade.' She took my hand, leading me into her cottage and to the kitchen, a warm and inviting space with creamy white cabinets, a central island, and—typical of Granny—no clutter to be found. She busied herself squeezing lemons, preparing sugar water, and filling the glasses with ice. Watching her brought back so many wonderful memories, and tears pricked my eyes.

'I need your advice, Granny.'

'You don't, darling.' My eyes widened, and I frowned. 'We always knew you were different, Persephone. We protected you, but we loved you more than you could ever imagine. Your destiny awaits you. Queen of the Underworld.'

I gasped. 'How?'

But she ignored me. 'Love is a mysterious creature, Persephone. You cannot change what has happened, but you can change how it ends.' She turned and stroked a hand down my cheek.

'But he's arrogant. He's a freaking god! I have this fear, Granny. What if it's the other Persephone he wants, not me? Maybe this will all crumble, and I'll lose him too. Besides, he's *way* too tall for me.' I brushed a hand under my eyes.

Granny smiled, then sighed. 'Talk over your concerns, darling. What I do know is that Hades loves *you*, and *you* love him. You are part of the same infinite circle. Don't fight it; don't be afraid to admit it.'

I pondered her words as she poured the lemonade.

'I love you, Granny.' I hugged her; tears fell, sharp as heartbreak. I c—can't visit you again. But I miss you so much,' I sobbed.

She held me at arm's length. 'Darling, I'm with you every day... I'm here.' She placed a hand over my heart and smiled. 'Apparently, you and Hades used to visit Elysium regularly. Before...' She raised her gaze to meet mine.

'We did?' I swiped my eyes, and she dipped her chin.

'Yes. When you were his queen. As queen, you will be able to come and go as you please.' My eyes widened. Did I really *want* to be a queen? Granny continued, 'Many areas of Elysium are similar to towns and villages. Depending on what people desire in the afterlife—the sea, the mountains, or, like me, a quaint English village—that's what we have.' I inhaled a breath and stared at her, then started crying again as she laughed and held me.

After chatting and sipping her homemade lemonade, Hades appeared again.

'Go and live a good life, beautiful girl. Make me proud. I'm sure I'll see you again soon, darling.' I gave her a shaky smile, and with one final squeeze of my hand, Hades shadow-walked me back to the castle. He poured two glasses of nectar and handed me one, which I accepted gladly. I sipped the fruity drink, and my trembling nerves settled a little.

'Just let me catch my breath a moment,' I said as I collapsed onto the sofa.

'No.' He moved to stand before me, and I frowned. 'I want it to remain lost. I want to be the man to catch it.' I felt a snag in my breath, and my pulse thundered. 'Please, Persephone,' he rasped, voice rough with need. 'Sleep in my bed. I can't bear the thought of you slipping further away. I want you... need you to want me the way I burn for you. I'd tear the world apart just to keep you here. Please, love me again. I'm begging you—don't walk away from me.'

The force of his need unnerved me. 'I thought you didn't beg?' I searched his eyes. The intensity of his gaze seeped into my gut, settling over my skin like smoke, and I swallowed tightly.

A muscle in his jaw ticked as he regarded me. Our tension was contagious. 'I want to prove I'm worthy of you,' he muttered.

'What? To prove to me you're not an arrogant, egocentric asshole?'

'No. I *am* all of those things. I want to prove I'm much more than just that. I *will* beg, Persephone. If loving you is my ruin... then let me burn in the fires of Tartarus.'

'Me'—I hesitated—'or the original Persephone?' I held my breath when his eyes filled with a caged emotion.

After a long beat, he spoke. 'You, Persephone. You. Only you. I'll beg. I'll lay myself bare for you. I'll do whatever it takes to prove I love you, *agapi mou*.'

'What does *agapi mou* mean?' I breathed.

'My love.'

'Oh.' My breath hitched, and he smiled.

'I don't want to be in the dark anymore. I need your light. Your love. You are the sun's rays that burn through the darkest of nights.' His voice rumbled through me. 'I hunger for you. I crave you. Even if you never accept it, you *are* mine. My queen of light.'

My pulse pounded, my head a swirling mess, and my thoughts were muddied with a sensual haze of confusion.

He hesitated, his eyes downcast. 'Being your friend was all I ever wanted; being your lover was all I ever dreamed. What can I do to make you love me again?'

That pull in my chest was like a riptide dragging me out to sea, threatening to drown me. I didn't care about anything but him; that realisation took my breath away.

Sweet goddess. I couldn't fight it—what scorched through me wasn't just need, it was love, raw and reckless. I craved his body, his mouth, but it was his heart I'd already surrendered to.

I freaking *loved* the King of Death and Shadows.

CHAPTER
THIRTY-FOUR

HADES

The sweet fragrance of roses touched my nostrils, and I gulped. Consummate love. Was my mind playing tricks?

'Don't resist it, little goddess. You're mine,' I said softly as I lifted my gaze.

Persephone rose slowly, pressing a trembling hand over my heart. 'I know, you arrogant fool,' she whispered, her voice catching. Her eyes glistened as she drew a shaky breath. 'I love you, Hades. I tried not to—I fought it—but I do... I love you.'

I dragged my jaw up from the fucking floor. The world momentarily went silent, except for the noise of my heart swelling, stretching, and almost exploding under the pressure of the words she'd just uttered. She loved me. Again. 'I never'—I swallowed the emotion in my throat—'thought I'd ever hear you say that again.'

'Hades.' She was crying as she launched herself into my arms. I kissed her hair and forehead, wiping the tears from her face with my thumb. My mouth travelled the slope of her neck. I unzipped her top, pulling it down her arms and over her breasts as my mouth trailed her shoulder and around her collarbone, lips suctioning and fangs scraping as she moaned softly.

'May I...?' I looked deeply into her eyes.

'Yes. Please... yes,' she answered before I finished.

I placed her on her feet, and she stepped out of her black velvet suit, her a delicate pink warmed her cheeks. As she stood before me in her lace underwear and stilettos, thinking became impossible; her beauty stole my breath, and something akin to Zeus's lightning bolt pierced my heart. She loved me. She fucking *loved* me! Rife, intoxicating lust overcame me, and I kicked off my shoes and tugged off my shirt, letting it fall to the floor. She placed her hands on my chest, and I waited as she slowly ran her palms over my tattoos and stood on her tiptoes to trace them with her tongue.

'Are these the tattoos that used to bind you to the Underworld?' she whispered as I shivered under the touch of her tongue and hands.

'Yes,' I grunted.

Her splayed hands traced the line of my chest and abs, and she licked and suckled her way down until her hands reached my belt. She swiftly relieved me of both my belt and trousers, and gently massaged my cock through my trunks, making me growl low in my throat.

'Your tattoo.' She tenderly traced the tattoo of the

serpent entwined with thorny rose vines encircling my thigh.

'The serpent is one of my symbols, a symbol of transformation, while the roses signify you—embodying spring and beauty.' I whispered into her hair, and her face lit up with a radiant smile when our eyes finally locked again.

Electricity charged the air as I gently drew her closer, and as our skin touched, my senses short-circuited. When our mouths met, Persephone's lips parted with a breathy inhale; my fingers found her bra and then her hips, the lace barrier preventing me from touching her indecent breasts and that hot, wet pussy.

'You'd look so good on your knees,' I whispered as I placed opened mouthed kisses across her breasts.

'Then lower yourself, my king, and show me how it's done.' Her eyes were heavy—hooded—and I guided her to the chair, gently pushing her down.

Kneeling before her, I hooked her right leg over my shoulder, and as my gaze consumed her, a heaviness dropped deep in my gut as desire pierced me. She was mine again. I wanted to savour her. Worship her. And that's precisely what I did with my hands and mouth.

I devoured her until she fell into a million pieces.

THIRTY-FIVE

PERSEPHONE

Great goddess, I was a shaking, whimpering pile of bones and sinew as Hades pulled me to my feet.

'That was...' I gasped, and he laughed wickedly, the sound like melting chocolate. He kissed me gently. I was like a flower seeking sunlight, desperate and parched, and I explored his mouth with my tongue, gently nipping and sucking on his lower lip.

Pulling away, after a long pause, he spoke. 'What do you like?' he said, gripping my hips tightly.

'What?' I asked, a little dazed. I tried to meet his eyes, but he was looking down at my body like I was a goddess —but I *was* a goddess, yeah, and he certainly made me feel like one.

'Persephone.'

'Huh?'

'What do you like?' He played with my nipple like an instrument, and my core thrummed in time with my heartbeat.

My head was a jumbled mess of panic. 'I like oral sex... with you.' I hesitated and took a step back as I pressed my fingers into my eyes. Long seconds passed before I met his gaze again. 'I don't usually experience sexual attraction. Though there's something about Apollo—' I placed a finger on my lower lip, and he stiffened, his eyes darkening. 'I'm joking,' I added quickly. 'Though I'm not sure you can take a joke... That throbbing vein in your temple is a dead giveaway.' He stared down at me, no hint of amusement on his face.

'Anyway... I'm, erm, pretty naïve about sex. I've never...' His smile was feral; his eyes burned with aether, and, glancing down, I gulped. Fates, his erection seemed even bigger, the outline of his hard length straining against his trunks. *How will that fit? I'm not sure it will. Holy crap, will he split me in two?* I stared at the outline of his cock, then up his exquisite body to his face, and a half-smile twitched on his lips.

'Then, we will go slowly,' he said, pressing a kiss to the centre of my palm, and great gods—a shiver erupted along my spine, causing my breath to catch. My want. My need. It almost made my knees buckle.

'You take control.' He guided me to the bed, lying on his back and holding out his hand.

'Okay,' I whispered as I scrambled onto the bed and knelt, one leg on either side of his beautiful body. I pulled down his trunks, freeing his massive erection, and he lifted that toned ass as I removed them. We were both naked. I kissed his chest and down his stomach, then licked the head of his erection, making him groan low in his throat. I took hold of the base of his length and manoeuvred myself over it, my breaths coming in small gasps.

'I'm in control,' I muttered to myself. Hades' body was rigid, his eyes closed. I eased the hard, hot length into my opening, struggling inch by inch to accommodate him, and he moaned softly.

'Don't stop. Please.' His voice was guttural.

It was both pleasure and, oh, gods, pain. So much pain. The sting of pain became so intense as I tried to take him deeper. My thighs and hands trembled as I struggled to fill myself.

'You don't fit,' I panted.

His chuckle was sinful. 'Take your time, *agapi mou*. There's no rush.'

I was shaking and gasping. He was tense, his jaw clenched. I paused for a heartbeat, and he stared into my eyes as his hands rose to my breasts, pinching and rubbing my nipples, and then his thumb circled my clit, making me moan and throw my head back. I opened up and slowly slid down on him to the hilt. He was deep and delicious, and that pain receded, turning into something exquisite.

'Fuuuck, Persephone,' he uttered with a low growl. I could tell he struggled to remain still; he was a picture of coiled restraint. I don't know what I expected from him being inside of me, but it wasn't this. Gods, this was more than fine.

I collapsed on top of him and groaned. 'Hades, your cock is enormous.'

He rumbled a laugh and gently pushed my hair from my face, then, placing his hands on my hips, he showed me how to roll on him. His eyes slammed shut, his jaw set like granite. I started with a slow rhythm and released a guttural groan. His fingers dug into my hips hard enough to bruise... I was so full—stretched to the limit. When his hands returned to my breasts, palming them gently, then running one hand down over my stomach to where we joined, circling that sensitive bundle of nerves with his thumb, I gasped and ground myself against a particularly sensitive spot inside me. As I moved up and down, liquid pleasure pulsed deep in my belly.

'Gods, you're so fucking tight,' Hades groaned. The pleasure inside me built like a boiling pot—liquid pleasure, ready to explode.

'Come for me, my queen. Now,' he said, his voice a soft demand. And I did... As I contracted and spasmed around him, I burst like a freaking piñata.

'You've been testing me since the day I took you—and now, you'll find out exactly how much I can take,' Hades growled, his voice like velvet and sin.

He rose and rolled me in one smooth motion, his body now on top of me, caging mine. He pinned my hands above my head and kissed me deeply. Hungrily. Then he thrust back into me and started pumping, hitting different spots, harder... deeper. As he drove into me, swivelling his hips, I screamed his name.

'Again. Scream my name again,' he commanded as he kissed me roughly.

'Hades... Please. More... *Yes*,' I cried as I relished him. Relished him on top of me. His tongue and fangs scraped over my neck and collarbone, then to my breasts, teasing my budded nipples, sucking and licking. He thrust into me until I was panting and crying his name over again. My nails scraped down his back, along his backside as his thrusts became brutal. Faster.

He watched me with adoration as he fucked me. 'Tell me you're mine,' he commanded again.

'I'm... yours... Yours, Hades. Oh. Mmmm.'

I needed him deeper, so I wrapped my legs around his hips, crossing my ankles on his lower back, and as he pumped his engorged cock into me, I felt the intense pressure building again. His mouth returned to my throat, and a sharp pain in my skin caused me to gasp as Hades closed his mouth around my neck.

Heat scorched my cheeks, and something far warmer and headier slipped through the rest of me. Endorphins rushed through my bloodstream, causing euphoria and something else unexplainably more pleasant. As he sucked, my entire body heated and exploded, breaking apart as I tightened around him in intense spasms, making a throaty moan as my eyes fluttered closed, but he carried on, picking up speed. His large hand grasped my chin.

'Look at me while I fuck you.' His voice was a low and dark demand. 'While I brand you with my cum.' I couldn't look away. I was riding a wave of undiluted ecstasy.

'Hades. *Oh, gods...* Hades,' I screamed as wave after wave of intense rapture ceaselessly rippled through every part of me.

His giant body pumped one final time, his teeth clenching with a moan. Two unexpected smacking thrusts later, as his climax continued, he made a guttural sound, his body shaking and jerking as his cock pulsed. His body dropped onto me heavily, breaths gasping in my ear.

'I've missed you, Persephone. You are, and always have been the only one,' he whispered.

I woke up the following morning sated but sore. We had devoured each other for hours, but I remembered every time with a contented smile. Aaargh, sex with Hades was *so* good. Hades' strong arm was around my middle, my ass pressed into his lap, and his cock was hard... again. I gently turned over, and my eyes roved over his peaceful face and down that indecent body—gods, waking up to a breathing mass of muscle was a joy.

My fingers traced his broad, hard chest, down the grooves of his abs, to the V of his pelvis and that happy trail of dark hair. My cheeks heated as I went further, marvelling at his enormous erection. I lowered my mouth and gently licked him, making him groan softly. Wrapping my hand around his hard length, I dropped my mouth and worked his shaft as I sucked. Hades made a strangled noise, and I raised my eyes to his. 'Morning.' I smiled as I sucked him again. His grin was filthy.

'Shower before my meeting,' he rasped as his strong hands grabbed my waist and pulled me to his chest. He jumped from the bed, making me yelp. 'Your fault, my queen,' he muttered in my ear. I wrapped my legs around his waist as he strode to the bathroom and turned on the shower.

He moved us under the sluicing hot water and kissed me. Hard. He pressed his mouth into my jaw, neck, and chest, and my legs tightened around his waist as my back hit the wall. Desire consumed his expression, and he growled, my breasts against his chest, my backside in his hands. He lifted me and whispered 'I love you' as he lowered me onto his erect cock. I hissed as I slid onto his full length, and he snarled, then moaned against my lips.

'I love you, Hades,' I groaned. 'Claim me... I'm yours.'

At my words, his control shattered, and he pounded into me. I cried out as his fingers dug into the flesh of my ass. Then one of his wet fingers gently rubbed up and down in the split of my backside, dipping in, and my eyes shot wide, but when he touched me there again, I gasped as I clenched around him, making him grunt. He sunk his fangs into the side of my breast, and fireworks exploded behind my eyes as ecstasy enveloped me. I dug my nails into his back and bit his shoulder, and as I contracted and spasmed, he thrust harder, my moans filling my ears. He stretched and filled me with every slam of his cock, and my hips rocked harder, my breathing ragged as I threw my head back, and I bucked, tightening so hard it was almost painful, releasing a guttural cry.

'Yes, my queen,' he whisper-growled in my ear, and I pressed him into me as deeply as I could. My restraint breaking, I tore apart and screamed as I crumpled into him, shaking, pulsing, and gasping as he filled me with his release.

After we caught our breaths, he nibbled my ear and said, 'I would like to take you out.'

'Out?' My brows puckered. 'Are you asking me on a date?' My voice was shaky. Breathy. Post-coital-bliss shaky.

He stiffened and released a sigh. 'I guess so.' His eyes swirled with golden sparks as he met my gaze, and he seemed to be holding his breath.

'That would be... nice.' I grinned. The breath he held released in a slow whoosh. 'Where?'

'A meal, and then a nightclub?' He shrugged. 'You enjoy dancing. You can choose.'

'That would be perfect. Thank you,' I whispered.

I unwrapped my legs from around his waist, and he placed me on my feet. 'I must leave. Before we meet the high priestesses and priests, I'm meeting with Poseidon and Zeus.'

My ears pricked. 'Can I come? To meet them?'

'Yes.' He grinned and kissed my mouth. 'Now, please let me get showered.' He cocked his head. I swaggered from the bathroom and giggled when I heard him mutter, 'Fates, that arse.'

An hour later, after a long soak in Hades' bath, I

slipped on the shirt he had been wearing, which, on me, looked like a circus tent, then walked into my suite. Tee was waiting for me—the table was laden with breakfast for two.

'Hi,' I mumbled, still pissed at her.

'I'm sorry, Sephy. Honestly... I shouldn't have interfered. I—'

'I know.' I sighed. 'It's fine. I know you were looking out for me.' My gaze met hers, and relief softened the taut muscles in her face.

'Breakfast?' She flashed me a coy smile.

'Yes. I'm starving.'

'Sex is a great appetite stimulant,' Tee said with a cheeky grin. I felt blood rush to my cheeks, and she erupted with laughter. 'So, you've finally realised you love him. And you've had sex.' I grinned and nodded. 'Your glow is almost ethereal,' she remarked as her eyes took me in.

'My glow?'

'Yes. He's claimed you, and you've accepted the soul bond. It serves as a warning to others that you're his, and they'd face his wrath should anyone attempt to take you.'

'Oh.' I twisted my mouth to the side in thought.

'Anyway, thank fuck you've come to your senses.' Her grin nearly split her face. 'Come on. Let's eat.'

Once I'd had my fill of waffles and syrup, I sipped my dark-roasted coffee and sighed. 'Love is nice,' I murmured, my eyes locking with Tee's. 'I've fallen hard, Tee.' I'd fallen like a freaking meteorite colliding with the Earth.

'You mean you've finally admitted to loving him, Sephy. You never really stopped loving him.' Tee said with a raised brow.

I responded to her with a smug smile. 'He asked me out on a date. Like a mortal world date. To a nightclub or something.'

'I think he's wooing you.'

I laughed. 'Don't be ridiculous.' I felt a weird, gooey sensation deep in the pit of my stomach. Was he wooing me? 'It *is* me he wants and not the old me, isn't it?' I was still worried. Irrational, but nonetheless.

'Sephy, she is you. You are her. You're no different, babe. Don't fret.'

I nodded and smiled. 'Oh, my gods, Tee. Vaginal orgasms are going to ruin my life. It's all I can think about.' I dug a knuckle into my eye as I released a withering sound. 'Sex with him is just... mind-blowing. It's entirely possible that my brain and ovaries have swapped places. And I'm having improper thoughts about butt-biting. His body is just...' At the thought, my lady parts thrummed in tune with my heart.

With wide eyes, I bit down on my lower lip, and the look on my face caused Tee to melt into hysterics. 'It's not funny! Honestly, he feeds me orgasms like candy. Another, ma'am?' I flung my hands up, causing Tee almost to choke. 'I do love him; you're right. And maybe that's why it's so good?'

'Now you know why Minthe has been trying to seduce him.'

I scowled at her words, jealousy digging its claw into my gut, making me nauseous. I was definitely going to guillotine-choke Minthe one day. The idea of her touching him made rage bubble through my veins.

'But'—Tee grasped my hand—'he only wants you, Sephy. I promise. He spent centuries waiting for you without choosing a consort the first time. He would have spent aeons waiting to find you this time.' I swallowed the grapefruit-sized lump in my throat and loosened my jaw. 'The love Eros is sexual passion. Yours and his has always been potent. These vaginal orgasms will be the start of a freaking great life, honestly.'

I loosed a slow breath, blinked, and tilted my head. Maybe she had a point—but I was still going to ruin Minthe. The intense emotion rattled me, though. I'd never really suffered from jealousy before. Was it fear of abandonment or fear of replacement? Gods, I was a conundrum for therapists everywhere.

Tee cleared her throat and became serious. 'Hades mentioned you want to attend the meeting with the witches.'

'Yes. I definitely want to be there.'

'Fine, I told him I'd meet him at Zeus's office in New York. I'll take you with me. Oh, and when's your coronation?'

'My what?'

'Your coronation. You're not the queen of the Underworld and Hades' consort until he crowns you.' I frowned and shrugged. 'I'll organise it; don't worry. He wants you to become his queen as soon as possible. Come on, let's get ready to meet these old crones.' Tee grinned at me, and I went to get dressed, pondering on how the Fates I'd ended up becoming the future consort of the god I wanted to hate.

THIRTY-SIX

HADES

Pressing into Persephone's hot, desperate body was everything I'd remembered.

Every touch was a surge of electricity, and her soft cries had almost scrambled my brain. Thinking about it caused heat to burn low in my belly like a raging inferno, and my trousers tightened in the crotch area. When I was with her, the world disappeared—when we kissed, fucked, and adored each other, there was only her and me.

All I could think about was her; all I could taste was her lips, and the only thing in my head was her moans of pleasure as I made love to her. Sometimes I fucked her like an animal... which she also liked. I groaned internally.

'Hades!' Zeus shouted.

'Sorry, what?'

'You've fucked her, haven't you?' Poseidon raised a brow.

'Thank the Fates for that,' Zeus muttered.

'None of your business,' I fumed, and the two idiots smirked at each other.

'He's definitely fucked her,' Poseidon grumbled. 'Gods, you're a whipped bastard.'

'What did you say, Zeus?' I turned to my brother, ignoring the irritating god of the sea.

'You mentioned Persephone is joining us for the meeting?' I nodded in response.

'Pussy-whipped,' Poseidon repeated under his breath, and Zeus coughed to muffle his laughter.

'Hecate and she will be here soon,' I replied in a low tone through gritted teeth as Persephone and Hecate appeared. Persephone looked breathtaking; at the sight of her in fitted leather trousers and matching crop top, my cock twitched.

'Hades.' Persephone ran and kissed my mouth, her cheeks flushing slightly as she lifted her head, her gaze catching Poseidon's and Zeus's.

'I need to get you out of those clothes as quickly as possible,' I said softly, for her ears only, standing to hold her tightly. Her pink cheeks deepened in colour, but her green eyes sparkled.

'Fates, I'm going to hurl,' Poseidon mumbled, and Persephone shot him a withering look.

'Are you shitting me? Gods, you're such a jackass.' She arched a brow. At her words, Poseidon clamped his lips together, his eyes swirling with clouds of anger; Zeus bellowed a laugh; Hecate squished her cheeks together, and my mouth fell open. 'I can't wait to ride that hippocampus.'

'Never going to happen.' Poseidon's nostrils flared, a muscle feathering along his jaw. His irritation was evident. In my absence, they'd apparently interacted more than I realised.

'We will see,' Persephone said as she held the king of the sea's surly stare. I puckered my brow, but Persephone simply winked at me.

'Persephone. Hecate. Welcome.' Zeus took charge, as always. 'I understand you have decided to be Hades' consort?' Zeus's eyes met Persephone's gaze.

'Yes, I am to be his consort.' Her words caused a strange sensation to wrap around my heart as blood rushed to my cock. I pulled Persephone in front of me, placing my arms under her breasts, my uncomfortable erection resting against her back. I smiled when I heard her purr of approval.

'Then,' Zeus continued, 'I shall let everyone know, and celebrations are in order. I insist on having a party in Naxos for you both.'

'Oh, absolutely not—' I began.

'Nonsense! I will get it organised.'

'Fuck,' I muttered, making Persephone and Zeus chuckle, and my arousal lessened.

'Now, let's go and meet the twelve most influential witches of the mortal world.' Zeus motioned with his hand towards the double doors. Around a dozen high priests and priestesses were awaiting us as we walked through the doors into a large conference room.

'Lady Hecate.' A chorus of voices murmured as the witches bowed low.

Hecate opened her mouth to speak, but Zeus quickly asserted his dominance. As he stepped forward, a look of frustration passed between Hecate and me. Servers with trays of wine and canapés stood against the walls, but the witches held no glasses. Apparently, trust was still a concern.

'I want to thank you all for taking the time for this meeting,' Zeus said in his melodic voice, a practiced smile gracing his face. 'Who is your spokesperson?'

A beautiful woman with a radiant, rich, terracotta-brown complexion, flowing black hair, and golden-brown eyes stepped forward.

'That would be me,' she replied, her voice like crushed velvet.

She exuded power, a type of power that Zeus might find troublesome. Surprisingly, a reaction I had never witnessed from Zeus almost made me smile. Almost. He stiffened, his eyes swirling with silver aether, appearing at a loss for words. However, I felt no hostile emotions from him—quite the opposite. I released a worried breath, and Poseidon shot me a sidelong glance, narrowing his eyes.

'Bronte?' Persephone breathed as she stared at the beautiful woman.

The woman turned towards Persephone, her eyes widening.

'Sephy?'

THIRTY-SEVEN

PERSEPHONE

I nodded and grinned as Bronte raised a hand to her mouth.

'What are you doing here? With them.' Her head inclined towards the gods, her jaw tense.

'It's a long story—'

But Hades cut me off. 'She is to be my consort.' Hades' face was pinched with a serious expression as he moved closer, almost standing on top of me.

Bronte's eyes raked over my exposed flesh. 'He has claimed you... Is this of your volition, Sephy?' Her fingers twitched, and her golden-brown eyes became worryingly dark as her gaze shifted to Hades.

I rushed forward, placing a hand on each of her shoulders. 'Yes. Yes. I'm absolutely willing.' I stared into those swirling eyes. 'Bronte, I love him.'

'Love... him?' she spat as her scrutiny flicked back to Hades, her brows knitting together.

'Bronte.' Hecate stepped towards us both. 'Persephone is truly Hades' consort in love. They share a soul bond.'

Bronte's breath faltered. 'Hades?' Her gaze locked with his, and a muscle ticked in his jaw.

'I'm a goddess, not a witch, Bronte,' I whispered.

'Your dark magic,' she breathed, and I inclined my head.

'It's shadow magic. I've been reunited with him.' Bronte tilted her head, giving me a confused nod. 'We'll catch up soon. Okay? Hades'—I turned to my lover— 'please meet Bronte. She is my friend and a Dunamis.' Hades politely bowed his head but didn't move.

'A Dunamis?' Zeus's voice sounded wary.

'The most powerful of mages, and Bronte is a Supreme Dunamis,' Hecate answered. 'Only a handful still exist.'

'I see.' Zeus studied Bronte, who lifted her chin defiantly to meet his gaze. 'Bronte...' He seemed to roll her name around his tongue. 'Are they all as beautiful as you?'

'Fates,' Poseidon groaned softly while Hades rolled his eyes so hard that I was sure he saw his brain. I cleared my throat in an attempt to suppress a laugh, but Hecate shot Zeus a death glare.

Bronte's smile was as cold as frost on a winter's morning. 'You want an alliance. Yes?' Zeus gave her a slight nod. 'That's why we're here. We have one condition before we even begin discussions. We will convey the remaining details during the meeting.'

'And what would that one condition be?' Zeus narrowed those violet eyes.

'That the gods behave appropriately. They rule and, as such, should set a positive example for the mortal world: composed, dignified, respectful... and monogamous.'

'We're fucked with Zeus,' Poseidon muttered, earning a slashing look from his brother. I glanced at Hades, whose mouth was twitching.

'Remember,' Bronte continued, 'I am the advisor to the twelve most influential priests and priestesses, who collectively govern the Council of Magic, King of the Gods. So, I suggest you keep your cock in your pants and don't insult me.'

This time, I couldn't hold back my snort-laugh. Poseidon nearly choked on his laughter, and even Hades' lips curved up at one side. Hecate, however, whispered a 'Fates', glancing nervously between Bronte and the purple-faced Zeus.

Zeus's eyes crackled with lightning, if only for a split second, his gaze never leaving the Dunamis. 'Apologies,' he muttered, their eyes still locked. Poseidon's, Hades', and Hecate's jaws dropped in unison.

My gaze switched to Bronte. She was the most badass woman I'd ever met in my life, and my respect for her went through the roof. I was so fucking proud of her.

'Then'—Zeus regained control—'let's talk.' His eyes remained fixed on Bronte as her nostrils flared, but her demeanour settled, and we all took our seats at the conference table. Servers offered wine and nibbles, which both we and the witches accepted. The meeting extended for at least two hours, and Zeus acceded to most of their demands, with Hecate acting as a mediator between Zeus and Bronte. Hecate, Zeus, and Bronte, three of the most powerful beings on Earth.

I CHATTED with my old high priestess from the London High Coven for a few minutes, then slipped away striding towards Bronte.

'Let me explain everything to you. Come to the Underworld with me, even for an hour, Bronte.' I clasped her hand between mine, but her dark eyes startled wide. Hades stood back, giving me space, his blue and golden eyes assessing us both.

'The Underworld? No, no, and absolutely no way.' Her nervous gaze flickered towards Hades, who smirked, and I scowled at him.

'Please,' I whined. 'I've seen Granny.' Bronte's eyes shot back to mine, her smile fragile.

'Hermione?' she whispered, and I nodded. Bronte had been a student of my grandmother when Granny was high priestess of the New York High Coven, and their bond had been strong. Back then, Bronte's magical ability, even at just sixteen, was inconceivable. 'She's happy, Bronte. Really happy.' My breath caught, and Bronte's arms wrapped around me.

'I miss her too,' she breathed next to my ear. 'Witches can live for hundreds of years, but we are still susceptible to rare magical viruses.' She sighed. 'I'm glad she's happy. I will come, but only for one hour.' I bounced on my toes and turned to Hades.

'Hades will shadow-walk us there. Take his hand,' I said. Bronte hesitated as Hades approached us, and with a gulp, she placed her hand on his. 'Take us to my garden.' I smiled up at the god of shadows, and he bowed his head.

We appeared in the soft grassy area beside the lily pond, and Hades left us. 'Wow,' Bronte whispered as she walked towards the jasmine and roses clinging to the trellis. 'This place is the Underworld?' Her gaze moved in a full circle before landing on the fortress behind, which glimmered like star-fire beneath the ethereal amethyst and silver sky. 'This place is... beautiful.'

'This is my garden, but the whole of the Underworld blossoms, Bronte. It's a wonderful place. Well, it is again.'

'Again?'

'Let's sit,' I said with a smile as we sank onto the soft grass. I told her everything—Hades' curse, my rebirth, the cause of the war, how he found and kidnapped me, hoping I'd fall in love with him again. How, somehow, I had. How we wanted a life together, not just here, but in the mortal realm too, now that his bindings were broken.

Bronte listened in silence, her expression unreadable until I finished. 'So, it was all because of a mage's curse that you were reborn...' she murmured, and I nodded. 'Bronagh,' she bit out.

'Who?'

'A solitary Dunamis, low-level, but vicious. Your

grandmother mentioned her once. She vanished around the same time you did. Power-hungry, cruel... dangerous.'

'Well, she's in Tartarus now,' I said, making Bronte shiver.

'Where she belongs.' Bronte stood and walked away towards the lily pond and fountain. I let her go, knowing she needed time to process and reflect. Bronte was an anomaly, but she had been like a sister to my younger self.

'Persephone.' That tinkling voice made me jump up. 'I hear congratulations are in order.'

'Minthe.' I gave her a tight smile. 'Thanks.'

As always, she looked like she'd stepped off a runway— red hair immaculate, makeup perfect, a tailored suit that screamed money. Her jaw tightened as her gaze skimmed over my skin and the bond mark.

'I'm going to Hades' New York club with him soon,' she purred. 'Just so you know, we *are* still fucking. Whether you become his consort or not, I will never let him go. You're not woman enough for him, little girl.'

Bile rose in my throat as my heart slammed into my chest like a wrecking ball. Dizziness swam at the edges of my vision, while a drowning feeling of desolation engulfed me. Was it possible to die from heart failure due to it beating so quickly? My chest was sore with the strain. Was Minthe telling the truth? If she was, then today would definitely be the day I died. My pounding heart would shatter into a thousand shards, but I suppose Minthe would be happy.

Words, though, dried on my lips. My snark and my anger were nowhere to be found. Hades had been nothing... But now he was *everything* to me. Was love supposed to be *so* freaking painful? My mind might have broken if I thought about it too much, so I turned to walk away.

'Liar!' Bronte's shout cut through my turmoil, and I spun.

Minthe stiffened, eyes snapping to the mage. 'I'm not lying. I thought it right to inform our future queen... though it's hardly *your* concern.' Minthe looked down her nose at Bronte, whose eyes swirled and darkened. 'I'd leave now if I were you, child.' Minthe gave me a smug smile. 'Before you get fooled by him again.'

Child? *Fooled* by him? My soulmate? My jaw clenched so hard, and my teeth took the brunt, cracking and grinding brutally together as my temper caught quicker than a forest fire in a drought. I yearned to wipe that smile off her flawless face, hoping to break a few teeth in the process.

I pivoted on my lead foot and delivered a brutal round-house kick, sending Minthe flying with a sickening crunch of teeth and bones. She howled in pain as she landed. Mission accomplished.

I placed my hands on my hips and smiled grimly at Minthe, whose eyes brimmed with hatred as she cradled her likely broken jaw.

'Don't ever tell me my husband is fooling me again,' I hissed at her, feeling my shadow magic sizzling like a pot of dark roast.

'Hades will banish you, you fucking psycho,' Minthe spat, and I laughed—sharp, cold, and without mercy.

Bronte snarled low in her throat as she stepped

towards the bloody Minthe. 'Bronte, it's fine,' I muttered. 'She's not—' I was going to say 'worth it', but I was *far* too late. With a savage smile on her lips, Bronte raised a hand towards Minthe, her eyes now a spiralling tumult of gold and black—shimmering pools of darkness—and the air rippled as a burst of magic, like a swirling constellation of stars, flowed from Bronte's palm. Minthe screamed and began to collapse in on herself, and I shrieked. The nymph vanished, leaving behind a plant in a pot. My eyes were fixed on the spot as my breath grew ragged.

'A mint plant?' I gasped as I stared at the herb, and Bronte laughed.

'Suitable, don't you think? The mint is a resilient plant, much like her. She would have spread her lies, constantly re-emerging to undermine your foundations.'

'But... Zeus hates this type of power. It's something he can't control. He has no idea of your strength... Bronte—' I threw my arms around her, choking back a sob.

'Hey.' She held me at arm's length. 'Tell the king of gods to bring it on. He doesn't scare me.' I let out a watery laugh as she took my hands and whispered, 'She was lying, Sephy. What she said was lies.'

Clapping behind us made us spin around. 'Charon,' I breathed.

'The ferryman?' Bronte whispered. 'Oh, he's delightful.'

Charon's cheeks flushed as he regarded Bronte. 'Nice kick, Lady P.' He winked at me. 'I must tell you that I, like all of us, never cared for Minthe.' He smiled coyly, his eyes zeroing in on the Dunamis. 'Your friend is correct, Persephone. Hades was not banging Minthe. The bitch was lying.'

'I think I need to see him,' I said, trying to temper my distrust and nerves. I knew he was right, but I needed to hear Hades say it. 'Charon, would you take Bronte home?'

'Bronte.' Charon rolled her name around his mouth as if sampling a fine wine, and the Dunamis narrowed her eyes as she regarded him.

'No need. I'll make my own way home. Keep in touch, Sephy.' Bronte kissed my cheek and smiled warmly at the obviously disappointed Titan. We hugged, and she turned away, slicing the air with a finger. The air began to shimmer blue, and then Bronte walked through the gateway, which closed behind her.

'Who *is* that incredible woman?' Charon's voice was gruff, his eyes still fixed on the air that swallowed Bronte.

I patted his arm, then turned to look for Hades, the mint plant in my hands.

Five minutes later, I opened Hades' office door, and he jumped up with a smile; the smile slipped when he felt my emotions and scrutinised my face.

'Persephone?' He squinted at me.

'It's Minthe,' I swallowed thickly. 'She informed me that the two of you are still in a relationship.' My gaze rose to his, and his face blanched as he stepped towards me. I held out a hand. 'Is it true?' I whispered hoarsely, trying to keep my voice steady.

'Fates, Persephone. No. It's not true,' he said, his voice

rough. 'Please tell me you trust me. You don't believe I'd ever do that to you. Just a hint of distrust is enough to potentially tarnish a relationship. I know this.'

My breath hitched. I knew he was referring to Adonis and me, and I wondered if the feelings I'd experienced at Minthe's words were the same as those he had suffered when I'd betrayed him. Gods. I felt like a total bitch.

'Where is she? I'll fucking kill her.' His voice was dangerously low, and his shadows danced around him.

I placed the plant on his desk. 'No need. Bronte turned her into a mint plant.'

His reaction shocked me. He erupted into the kind of laughter I'd never heard from him before, and that dimple appeared, making my heart clench. 'I'm growing fonder of your friend Bronte by the minute.' When he sobered, his gaze locked onto mine.

'Tell me, again, it's not true,' I whispered.

Hades' tormented eyes caused my fragile heart to fracture a little more.

'Persephone. When I lost you—' He paused and swallowed hard. 'I lost my reason to carry on. My raison d'être. But I knew one day you would return to me. Every winter has its spring, and that's what you are to me and the Underworld. You—your touch, your scent, your smile— are my reason for living. Only you. Always you.'

I was breathless as I stumbled towards Hades, the horny bitch bond in my chest throwing a tantrum, demanding that I touch him. I knew every word from his mouth was true. Hades' strong arms enveloped me, holding me as close as possible.

'The only pussy I ever want to fuck is yours. Please, let me show you, Persephone,' he breathed into my ear; his voice was low, like the darkest temptation.

THIRTY-EIGHT

HADES

She gave a slight nod, her eyes hooded, the desire evident.

She kicked off her boots, and I turned her around, unclipping the hooks on her leather top, slipping it down her arms, and gently kissing and grazing the back of her neck with my fangs. I moved her to face me and bent down, taking a nipple in my mouth, making her shudder as she fisted my hair. Flicking it with my tongue, I sucked long and hard, repeating the action with the other nipple, making her back arch slightly as she gasped.

I unbuttoned her trousers and slid them down her legs, then ripped off her panties. My eyes roved over the perfection of her gloriously naked body, and my cock engorged painfully.

I ran a reverent hand down her chest, between the swell of her breasts, and watched in hunger as she shivered, her nipples puckering and pebbling. Every inch of her was open—inviting. Wanting. Wanting me. She bit her lower lip, locking eyes with me.

'Turn around, Persephone.' I grabbed her wrist and moved her until she was where I wanted her to be—braced with both hands on the desk, her back arched perfectly. The sight of her smooth skin and pert ass pulled a low growl from me, bringing me to my knees.

Taking a firm hold of her hips, I kept her where I needed her and feasted on her until her slickness coated my tongue. As I ate her out from behind, her arms collapsed, and her face pressed against the smooth desk. Her hips pushed back against me as she rode my face. When I rolled her clit with my tongue, her thighs clenched around my shoulders as she started rocking back and groaning, her words nothing more than incoherent sounds.

'Hades. Please. Hades. I—I need...'

I stood, slapping her arse, making her utter a low moan, and wrapped my hand around her neck, pulling her head back to kiss her, her back tight against my chest.

'Put your hands back on the desk. I'm going to fuck you,' I said, my voice a low demand as I unzipped myself. She complied immediately—this powerful goddess, my powerful goddess. 'Good girl,' I whispered close to her ear. My shadows danced around us, strands twisting around her ankles, pulling her feet wider, opening her up for me. Lining my cock up to her dripping entrance, I slammed into her. 'Mine,' I growled. She was so wet. So tight. Her moans were like music to my ears, and as I pounded into her, I ran one hand down her spine, the other fondling her breasts.

'Oh, gods, yes... *Yes*,' she groaned.

Grabbing a handful of her hair, I dragged her head back, turning her face to kiss her again. My tongue fucked her mouth at the same pace as my cock slammed into her hot, tight pussy.

Her whimpers and the rhythmic clenching of her muscles on my erection made me grit my teeth, and as my thumb rubbed over her clit, she jerked and yelped—a sound between pleasure and pain—her orgasm taking me over the edge, making me see stars as her pussy squeezed my cock, taking every drop I gave her.

Her whole body trembled as I withdrew. Turning her around, I gently picked her up, cradling her to my chest.

'Now, I'm going to make love to you, *agapi mou*,' I said as I shadow-walked us to my bedroom.

THIRTY-NINE

PERSEPHONE

I awoke sated and relaxed. Hades' slow lovemaking had been cathartic. Beautiful. I'd never tire of his body on mine.

'Morning.' His deep voice rumbled against me as his hand stroked down my belly. He pressed his hard length against my ass, causing my eyes to flutter closed and liquid heat to pulsate in my core. I was definitely turning into a nymphomaniac. 'I've been waiting for you to wake. I want to fuck you again, *agapi mou*.'

I loved the slow-paced lovemaking, but I craved the animalistic side of him, too. The strict, guarded god, losing control over me, was the consummate aphrodisiac. He was like a fairytale prince that fucked like a pornstar.

'Then, once you've cleaned up, I'll bring you coffee and breakfast in bed,' he murmured against my ear. I laughed softly as I turned in his arms.

'Sounds like a good deal to me,' I said, kissing his cheek. He purred low in his throat while kicking the sheet from the bed.

I startled slightly as shadow tendrils wrapped around my ankles, pulling them wide, while two more seized my wrists, pinning my hands above my head. 'Perfect.' Hades' voice was rough, and my heart began to pound unnaturally fast, my breaths becoming erratic. I briefly closed my eyes.

He stepped away from the bed, gloriously naked, and I was splayed out like a sacrifice, just as he wanted me—an object of his desire. The smooth planes of his body were like a vision for me to drink in. His eyes flared at seeing me spread wide for him, a smug smile on his lips as he raked his gaze over me, tethered by his living ropes that answered his every whim.

'Watch me, Persephone.' His voice was a low, rough command, and I whimpered, my back arching involuntarily, straining against the shadows, making him laugh wickedly. His cock was hard, heavy... and mouthwatering, and the hunger in my core roared into something ravenous.

He climbed back onto the bed between my legs, and I squirmed in anticipation. His hot breath against my throbbing clit caused me to almost break before he even touched me. His lips met my sex with long, deep kisses and hard strokes of his tongue, and as he flicked and sucked hard on my swollen clit, I broke into a thousand pieces, squeezing my eyes closed as I climaxed and bucked, wave after wave of ecstasy rolling through me.

When his shadows shifted beneath me, encircling my butt, and he pressed my knees to my chest, my eyes flew open. 'Do you trust me?' he whispered darkly.

'Yes. I'll always trust you, my sexy shadow daddy.' He cocked a brow at me as I smirked and winked.

He lined his cock up and slowly pushed into my slick entrance at the same time as his shadows pleasured my breasts and took my ass. 'You belong to me,' he hissed as he plunged in fully. I was so full, I couldn't breathe—he was consuming me. I writhed and moaned as his cock and shadows moved in tandem inside me. As his hand on my chest held me down, he stretched me to my limit, making my eyes roll into the back of my head, and a long, muffled groan escaped my lips.

When his hand moved down my body, finding my swollen nub again, I came so hard I was temporarily blinded, but he carried on fucking me through my peak. He kissed me brutally, our tongues tangling. 'Every part of you is mine. Tell me you're mine,' he commanded.

'Yes. Yes. I'm... *oh, mmm...* yours,' I gasped as I felt another orgasm build from the tips of my toes, finally washing over me like a tidal wave, breaking me into a thousand sublime fragments as he still pumped into me. He climaxed with a snarl, collapsing on top of me, leaving me a jumbled mess. I closed my eyes, waiting for my breath to steady.

Eventually, Hades left the bed and went to the bathroom to freshen up, and I heard a bath running.

He returned fully clothed and flashed me a half-grin. 'The bath is ready. Don't fall asleep. You have thirty minutes before I bring you coffee and breakfast, and then I'm going to devour you again.'

I shook my head at him and grinned as he turned to leave.

WE SPENT the entire previous day in bed, and gods, it was glorious. Though every part of me ached and certain parts were tender, I wouldn't have it any other way. Gods, as a lover, Hades was better than any of my book boyfriends by a long shot.

Today, though, we had Zeus's party to attend. It was a celebration of our confirmed union, and Zeus was champing at the bit to let everybody celebrate. Hades, however, was the grumpiest I'd ever seen him, which spoke volumes. I had my arrogant, fractious god back; Mr Broody MacFucker was never far away, and I had to bite the inside of my lip to suppress my smile.

I told Hedone and Hecate I'd do my makeup and hair and choose a dress from my wardrobe—a dress that, it seems, I'd worn... before. The cream, sheath-style, chiffon cocktail dress flaunted one shoulder and featured an asymmetrical hemline embellished with ruffles and sparkling beads securing the gathering at one hip. My hair cascaded in curls down my back, and my makeup looked pretty good.

As I entered Hades' office, Tee and Hedone nodded their approval with raised eyebrows. Hades looked like a male model from some steamy romance movie; his stare roamed up my body with enough passion to feel like a physical caress, making my blood simmer.

'Come on, Your Maj,' I deadpanned, and the next look Hades gave me should have made me tremble in my stilettos; instead, I scoffed at him. 'Stop being Mr Deadly and Grumpy.' At my words, Tee, Thanny, Charon, Hedone, and Erebus nearly choked on their laughter, while Hades shot them all a death glare. 'At least look happy to have me as your intended consort!' I pouted at him, still sucking in my cheeks.

He sighed and narrowed his eyes. 'Let's just fuck off somewhere and let Zeus throw his stupid party without us.' His dark, brooding voice caressed my ear as he drew me into his arms.

'Nope. Paste a smile on your face, Majesty.' Tee quirked an eyebrow at Hades' glare. 'Let's go get roaring drunk and celebrate the fact that you two have finally fucked!' Before Hades could utter a word, the five of them teleported, their cackling laughter echoing off the walls.

'They all need burying in Tartarus,' he grumped, but I saw through his surly demeanour.

'I need to say something,' I said, placing my hand on his cheek.

'Yes,' he replied slowly.

'Let's avoid the whole "touch her and you're dead" scenario, alright?'

'What?' His brows lowered as he cocked his head.

'It's a trope from my romance books. The "touch her and die" one is a classic. I'm allowed to kiss men on the cheek, even Apollo, if they're my friends. Don't get all possessive.'

He stiffened, his nostrils flaring, but muttered, 'Alright.'

'Hey, lover.' I stood on my tiptoes and traced my tongue over his downturned mouth, pressing my hands on either side of his face. 'I love you.' He closed his eyes at my words, his breath catching. 'Get through this, and we can pick up where we left off this morning. I have this terrible urge to have your cock in my mouth again.' Even though my cheeks flushed at my unusually forward words, his eyes became a fiery mix of gold and blue, filled with violent delight.

'Deal,' he breathed as his shadows enveloped us, transporting us to the kingdom of Naxos.

We arrived standing on a grand dais overlooking another courtyard. The place was breathtaking, and I sucked in a heady breath. The Grecian pillars encircling the vast area were adorned with a multitude of blooms, while silver flames flickered atop each structure. Everything gleamed in white marble, from the immense palace behind us to the walkways and courtyard.

Outside the courtyard, trellis-covered breezeways wound through the manicured gardens. As far as the eye could see, a vibrant myriad of colours—lakes, meadows, hills—unfolded before us. Everywhere was awash with a plethora of flowers. A host of smartly dressed people filled the courtyard, chatting, sipping drinks, and enjoying canapés. A string quartet played soothing background music, and Tee waved at us to come and join them.

I basked in the sunlight, tilting my head to the sky, where beautiful, swirling purple and pink clouds rolled by, glittering with flecks of silver dust. 'I like Naxos,' I murmured to Hades. His lips smacked together in a thin, hard line, and a muscle ticked in his jaw at my words. 'But the Underworld is just as beautiful, and that's where my heart lies.' I took his hand, and the tension in his shoulders eased.

'Hades. Persephone. Welcome to Naxos.' Zeus's voice boomed as he approached us, Poseidon by his side, and the crowd fell silent, turning to regard us. Holding hands, we descended from the dais to meet the two brothers. Hades was as prickly as ever, so I smiled widely enough for the both of us.

As we exchanged pleasantries with Zeus, a server offered us my favourite drink, the pink fizz, which I accepted happily. 'We have a problem,' Zeus muttered to Hades, who exhaled softly.

'Ixion?' he rasped quietly.

'Nope,' Poseidon replied. 'Demeter.'

I almost sucked wine up my nose, and my stomach hollowed. Hades stiffened, his jaw working overtime, and a perplexed pinch marked his brow. 'How did she find out?' His voice was low, the tension palpable.

'Not me, Brother. We haven't seen her for many years, but you know how gossip travels in Olympus.' Zeus rolled his eyes. 'She's making an appearance today. She wished to reunite with your future consort.'

'Fuck,' Hades mumbled as he squeezed my hand. 'You may need to eat more pomegranate seeds, so she allows you to stay with me.' He swallowed thickly, and I lowered my brow in confusion.

'Allows me?' I huffed a laugh with a slow shake of my head. 'No way, just leave her to me, Hades. No one will ever tear us apart again, not even Demeter. I refuse to split my time between you and her... I'm not that Persephone anymore.' Hades' eyes locked onto mine, and a shadow of a smile flickered on his lips.

'Good luck with that, Persephone.' Poseidon gave me a wry smile, and I scowled at him.

'Stop being a freaking killjoy, King of the Sea,' I snapped, making Poseidon raise a pissy and arrogant eyebrow while Zeus choked on a cough-laugh.

'What's happening?' Tee and Hermes sidled up to us. We relayed the information about Demeter, and Tee groaned softly, sighing so heavily, I'm surprised she didn't blow us away.

Hermes' topaz eyes twinkled with mischief. 'You're a feisty pocket rocket, Lady P. Demeter can't control you any longer.'

'Oh, don't you worry, Hermes. No one is taking Hades away from me. Not ever.' Hades' lips curled in an almost smile as he looked at me.

'Ugh, I'm about to puke again,' Poseidon griped, and I cast him a withering look.

'Let's mingle,' Zeus instructed. 'Everyone is delighted about your forthcoming coronation, Persephone.'

We mingled and greeted people for at least an hour, and I left Hades with his Underworld family before setting off to find Aphrodite.

'Darling girl,' Aphrodite crooned, 'I'm thrilled you've finally embraced your love for our dark king.' She kissed my cheeks. 'You've accepted your bond. You're positively glowing!' She clapped her hands and giggled. 'Come, let's sit.' I followed her to a private loveseat nestled beneath a trellis full of clematis apple blossom. 'Is the sex still as good?' she asked as she sat.

I almost choked on my wine as colour bloomed over my cheeks, but I smiled sheepishly and nodded. 'So freaking good... Sparklers and fireworks aplenty,' I whispered, and she giggled again. 'Can you tell me about Adonis and Eros?' I blurted, causing the smile to slip from her face. She took a sip of her wine, then tilted her head at me slowly. 'I just need to know I didn't willingly break Hades' heart,' I breathed, tears pricking at my eyes. I chewed on my lower lip as she took my hand.

'Oh, darling, you were not complicit. Not at all, I promise.' She paused as if carefully choosing her words. 'I was enraged when I learned that Eros had temporarily beguiled you into loving Adonis. Stories of my jealousy towards Psyche are utterly untrue. I took her away from Eros to complete trials, risking her loss to teach him a lesson about meddling with hearts. He was distraught, and rightly so. They now reside in the court of Hemera and are quite happy, though rather reclusive.'

'Who convinced Eros to do it?'

Her face held an icy calm. 'I have my suspicions, but I don't know for certain, darling.'

'But Hades knows it wasn't my choice?' I asked for reassurance.

'He does, darling.'

I exhaled and nodded, sipping my wine as I contemplated her words. Hades joined us, and we chatted for a little longer until we had to circulate again.

'Cory, my flower!' a crisp, almost musical voice called from behind me, causing Hades to stiffen and an uneasy feeling to trickle down my spine. I slowly turned around to see a beautiful woman with hair and eyes the same colour as mine. She was taller than me, but the resemblance was astounding.

Demeter had arrived.

'Demeter.' I smiled warmly.

'Please call me Mother, flower. Oh, how I've missed you.' She pulled me into her embrace, stroking her hand through my hair. Well, this was a thousand times awkward.

I gently detangled myself from her arms and took her hand instead. 'You know I don't remember you, Mother?'

'Yes, my flower, but it doesn't matter; we have plenty of time to catch up. The Court of Delos is stunning. You will adore it there.' Her eyes sparkled as she cupped my cheek. 'I'm so happy to have you back, flower.'

'Demeter.' Hades gave the goddess a slight bow as he took my other hand.

Demeter's gaze turned to him, her look as cold as an icy winter morning. 'Hades,' she hissed in a tone so chilling that I snapped to attention and drew in a sharp breath.

Frustration marked Hades' face. 'Persephone is her own woman, and as such, she will decide her fate. And her fate is to be my consort again.' His tone was deadly cold, anger tightening his lips as he spoke.

'You cannot keep her this time. I forbid it! I forbid this... this mark!' She gestured emphatically in front of me. 'And I forbid this union.' A small smile of contempt twitched on her lips. Naturally, the entire place was silent, all eyes on us.

'Whoa... Hold up there!' I dropped both their hands, taking a step back. 'I am *not* a commodity to be bargained over... by either of you.' Demeter's eyes widened, a hand pressed against her heart, and Hades' smile was as sharp as a blade. The honeyed rasp of his chuckle caused the icy trickling in my gut thaw a little.

'Mother.' My gaze met Demeter's again. 'Hades will be my husband. I love him more than I ever thought possible. I have chosen him again and accepted our soul bond. He patiently waited for me to recognise our connection, never forcing anything upon me.'

I lifted my chin, gazing into her eyes. 'I chose him the first time too; he didn't keep me against my will then either.' Demeter began to speak, but I silenced her with a raised hand. 'He rescued me. I asked him to take me to the Underworld to escape your control. So, if you want me in your life, you must make an effort with him. We will both visit you in Delos occasionally, and, of course, you can visit us in the Underworld and the mortal realm, too.' The courtyard echoed with murmurs as Demeter, at a loss for words, stared blankly at me.

'Demeter.' Hades' voice shattered Demeter's spell as

her gaze turned to meet his. 'I am over my head, drowning in love for your daughter. I have always been.'

We heard lots of oohs and aahs while Zeus and Poseidon blinked owlishly at his bold declaration. Hades, however, seemed as if he wanted to vanish into the aether, struggling beneath the weight of the guests' attention.

'Stars cannot shine without darkness. We complete each other, Demeter.' His voice was steady, his face devoid of emotion, and I smiled at him as my heart did a little trippy dance. I felt dizzy with a rising tide of emotions.

He stepped towards me, lifting his hand and cupping my cheek. He kissed me—a deep, languid, bruising kiss. Every person in the courtyard whooped and clapped, and Demeter regarded us with a fragile smile.

I turned back to the woman, who was once my mother, and took her hand again. 'Please come to my coronation, Mother.' Her eyes shimmered with tears at my words. 'And once I've settled into the Underworld as queen, I will come to Delos alone and spend a week with you. Okay?' She nodded and embraced me again.

Hades arched a brow at me, but I gave him a no-nonsense look, causing him to huff and clench his jaw. As I hugged her, I smiled sweetly at him over Demeter's shoulder, and he narrowed his eyes at me—a promise of payback. I couldn't wait—maybe he'd spank me again. Getting horny with my 'mother' in my arms felt wrong, but I gave him a sultry smirk, causing his nostrils to flare.

No one is going to control me in this life.

Not even the man I love.

CHAPTER
FORTY

HADES

F ates, the way Persephone handled Demeter was awe-inspiring.

She was stronger than anyone I knew—the goddess of my heart. When I declared my undying love for her in front of everyone, something I had never done before, the smile she gave me was like a thousand suns. I was a lucky fucker.

We'd split up again, but I kept a watchful eye on her from a distance, never wanting her too far away. As she chatted with the other gods, I felt a sense of ease within me this time, even as she laughed and smiled with Apollo. She was mine, and they all knew it. They also understood that I would tear them to pieces and bury them in Tartarus if any of them touched her in a way only I could. This time, the deceit would not go unpunished.

I knew that Eros had beguiled Persephone the last

time. Adonis was not beguiled—but I couldn't prove it. When Aphrodite finally revealed this to me in an effort to ease my pain over Persephone's loss, I lost my shit. The bastard Eros had slipped from my grasp, but the gods forbade me from killing either him or Adonis. We never discovered who was behind the duplicity, and as the war raged on, time passed, but I'd never forgotten.

'Hello, my love.' Persephone's arms snaked around my waist from behind, and I smiled. Poseidon quirked a brow, shaking his head.

'Fucking whipped,' he grumbled, and I smirked at the grumpy bastard as I pulled Persephone around to face me. When she burrowed into my chest, my cock twitched, and she sighed.

'Get a room, you two,' Hecate grunted, nudging Persephone while handing her another glass of fizzy wine.

My queen accepted it with a smile, slipping an arm around my waist as we chatted.

'I'll be back shortly. I need the powder room.' I began to walk with her, but she shook her head. 'I do *not* need an escort, Hades.'

'Quit being overbearing,' Hecate whispered. 'She's fine and probably more powerful than most gods here.' None were aware her shadow magic had already returned and she could wield it flawlessly.

I chatted with Poseidon and Zeus, but my eyes kept scanning the area for her. I couldn't lose her again. Panic gnawed in my gut at the thought. After ten minutes, Hecate frowned and wandered off, causing the panic within me to simmer like an almost boiling pot.

'Stop fretting, Brother,' Poseidon muttered. 'She's probably chatting with someone inside.' I exhaled deeply and nodded, but that unease wouldn't abate. The bond was still pulsing in my chest, so I knew she was still somewhere in Olympus. Most probably in Zeus's palace.

'Gods, you're turning into a worrywart.' Poseidon shook his head, his face wrinkling in disgust.

After another few minutes, I stormed off to find Hecate and, hopefully, Persephone, feeling Zeus and Poseidon at my heels. Taking the broad marble steps two at a time, I burst through the wide, ornate doors and found Hecate in the expansive entrance hall. The haunted look in her eyes and her ashen face told me everything I needed to know.

'Can you still feel your bond?' Hecate's ragged voice whispered. I nodded, and she blew out a relieved breath. 'We'll get her back, Hades.' Hecate wrung her hands together, her lips trembling.

The familiar pain of loss in my chest dropped me to my knees... and I exploded.

It took both Zeus and Poseidon to restrain me. A vortex of swirling mist, sea foam, spiralling clouds, and lightning encompassed me as my shadows ran rampant around me. I lost control entirely—I was like a rabid animal.

'We will find her, Hades!' Zeus yelled at me, and Poseidon looked like he was about to commit bloody murder.

'Whoever has her will die by my hand,' I vowed with an animalistic roar.

CHAPTER
FORTY-ONE

PERSEPHONE

The blinding white light and popping sound sent me reeling, falling, and twisting as nausea gripped my throat. I felt dizzy and confused, throwing a hand over my mouth, trying to swallow the bile on my tongue.

As my vision cleared, I found myself in a bedroom—a bedroom I'd never seen before—and a sharp bite of hysteria flooded my bloodstream like venom.

'Welcome to the court of Phoenicia, Persephone.' The familiar voice sent an extra burst of nervous energy pounding through me.

Adonis.

I turned slowly to see the god of beauty and desire standing by a window, casually leaning against the wall with his arms crossed. The smirk on his face made me want to body-slam him into the floor.

'What are you doing?' I seethed.

'Welcoming you to my court.' His voice touched my skin like a chill wind, sending goosebumps across my flesh.

'This is kidnapping,' I said through my teeth.

'No, beautiful. It's merely taking back what's mine,' Adonis drawled.

I pressed my trembling lips into a straight line. I blinked. Blinked again. Then blinked some more. 'My husband will kill you.' The bond pulsed in my chest. *My husband*. Two words I'd never imagined would apply to me. Two words that I never thought would affect me so deeply.

His laughter rumbled darkly. 'You're not his consort, little goddess. Not yet. But you'll be mine before the hour's done... and no one will find you.' Horror flooded my veins like ice.

His steely gaze locked onto mine, his jaw hard, and as his eyes slowly perused me, from the tips of my toes back to my face, I shivered in revulsion. 'This is where you ought to be.' He smiled wickedly. 'You wore my favourite dress.' He gestured to the cream dress I was wearing. 'You did it for me. I know you did.' His jaw clenched, his eyes flashing. 'You were promised to me. You belong to me.'

My heart pounded against my ribcage like it was about to break bones. He was a freaking psycho.

I sprang forward, poised to deliver a roundhouse kick, but barely reached the window before I was violently yanked backwards by something around one wrist, almost dislocating my shoulder. Landing on my butt, I cursed. Looking down, I could see the outline of a fragile, nearly invisible chain. Adonis laughed, though the smile didn't reach his eyes.

'The chains of Ares. Quite the divine entrapment. Forged from Adamantine and suppressing all of your powers.' He smirked at me. 'I'll be keeping the chain on until I can trust you, but we've always had a penchant for a bit of bondage and dominance, haven't we?' A shiver crept up my spine like a slow-moving vine, and my mind became a whirlwind of fear.

'I can't wait to get my cock back into that hot, tight pussy, beautiful. I've missed you and that delectable body, those perfect tits. Tonight, we will consummate our union.' I'm pretty sure my gasp was heard clear to London.

My skin prickled, the faint golden glow pulsing beneath its surface. The bond—the one tethering me to Hades—flared in protest, searing heat spiralling through my chest. Adonis's eyes narrowed as he took in the shimmer that danced over my skin.

'The King of Shadows might linger in your veins.' His eyes were pure ice. 'But, no matter. He won't find you here. You're mine now. And I intend to keep you... I'll get you refreshments. My handmaidens will soon come to attend to preparations.' He gestured lazily toward the elegant gold gown hanging on the armoire, gleaming like a gilded cage.

I tried to swallow the golf ball-sized lump in my throat as I scrambled backwards on my ass. 'Handmaidens?'

He frowned at me. 'I'm the god of desire, Persephone. One woman is never enough. Though, you have always been my favourite.' He gave a slight bow and strode out of the room.

'Mother freaking hell,' I muttered as I crawled to my feet, nursing my arm. Gods were narcissists, sure—but Adonis was a one-man circus: part sociopath, part lunatic, all asshole. I edged as far as I could towards the window, peering down. Even without the chain, there was no way I'd be getting down there without getting bitten by a radioactive spider and developing suction cups on my hands or breaking my neck. The latter was preferable to Adonis touching me.

Adonis was much bigger than I was—not as big as Hades, but to be fair, I'm about the size of Yoda in a trench coat. If I could get close enough to him, perhaps I could strangle him with the Adamantine chain. I needed to stay calm. Hades would find me; I knew he would. Gods, even Poseidon would help him. I couldn't allow a whole new level of 'what the actual fuck' derail me. *Keep it together, Sephy.*

The bond in my chest keened for Hades; it was a maelstrom of love. I needed to get back to him—back to the safety of him. The door opened again, startling me as Adonis entered carrying a plate of open sandwiches and a glass of amber liquid.

'Nectar will ease your nerves.' He motioned towards the glass and placed the plate on a table.

Shaking my head, I stepped backwards until my back hit the wall. 'Nothing you offer me will pass my lips,' I said through gritted teeth.

He sighed, placing the glass down and pressing his

palms against his eyes. Lowering his hands, he studied me, his eyes boring into my face and body.

'You never had a problem when I was fucking your mouth with my cock, and you swallowed me down.' He gave a dark smirk, and my stomach roiled in response. 'I want to taste you again,' he growled softly, and panic consumed me as adrenaline flooded my system. My thighs clenched together of their own accord—the thought of him touching me sparked disgust that twisted its gnarly talons into my gut.

'No, don't you dare—'

But he was on me in a flash, his hands around my face, and his mouth on mine as he forced my lips open with his tongue in a brutal kiss.

'You're mine.' His breath touched my cheek like a frosty breeze. Then his mouth was on my neck, and he bit down hard, making me yelp. As he sucked on my blood, I started screaming; an obliterating pain tortured my every nerve ending, my skin stabbed by a million hot knives, causing the breath in my lungs to turn to ice. Air slowly leaked from my parted lips, and I inhaled raggedly, trying to close down my mind and call on my shadow magic. *Please, please,* I begged as tears ran rivers down my cheeks. A single shadow rose from my unrestrained palm but went unnoticed by Adonis.

Thick tendrils of shadows spiralled into the room, coiling and rolling along the floor and up the walls. Loud popping sounds caused Adonis to spring backwards, and I crumpled to the ground. 'Hades,' I whispered as my eyes met his god form, and those pure golden eyes locked onto mine, flashing like two lodestars when he noticed the bite on my neck. The power emanating from him drenched the air, and I couldn't tear my eyes from him.

Adonis attempted to teleport but didn't notice Tee behind him, her eyes pure white. Adonis remained motionless as she raised a hand. She then flicked her fingers at my wrist, and the chain snapped, freeing me from the shackle. Two more popping sounds revealed a murderous-looking Poseidon and Zeus, who both rushed to my side. Poseidon gently lifted me into his arms, and Zeus strode to stand with Hades.

My beautiful god shifted form to the man I loved, his massive presence filling the room. As Hades' golden eyes regarded Adonis, deadly violence etched onto his features —a maelstrom of whirling fury. Shadows surrounded Hades like a cloak, swirling around his legs and licking over his shoulders. He really did look like death incarnate. He was cold, stunning, brutal, primaeval—and he was mine.

'You can't harm me. Zeus forbade you from doing so,' Adonis said, his voice steady, but his face was pale. His gaze flicked to Zeus, whose expression remained impassive.

Hades' dark laugh was smoke and ash. 'Shut up,' he roared as his gaze drilled into Adonis. 'You're a monster. You were born a monster. Yet *you* think I'm the monster. You haven't seen what I'm truly capable of... But now you will, you piece of shit. I'll see you in Tartarus.'

Adonis went to speak, but Hades' aether shadows were on him before a sound left his lips. They wrapped around his head and ripped him in two, straight down the middle, as if he were made of nothing more than water. A sickening sound of popping bones and tearing muscle filled the room. Great gods, Hades was terrifyingly beautiful. I think there's something wrong with me because I found it sort of arousing, and a ripple of tight shivers cascaded through me to my very core.

'*Agapi mou.*' Hades took me from Poseidon, cradling me gently, and as I buried my face into his chest, that earthy, spicy scent of him wrapped itself around me.

'Hades,' I whispered again, and then blackness claimed me.

FORTY-TWO

HADES

Persephone slept nestled against my chest all night, her ordeal draining every ounce of energy from her body.

She felt so tiny in my arms. At times, I tended to forget just how small she truly was. Her larger-than-life, sassy, headstrong personality, control, and attitude were big enough for a tribe of Amazonians. Yet when she slept, I saw the petite, beautiful woman with hair like spun starlight and those plump lips that parted with a soft sigh as she burrowed further into my chest. All I could see was her perfection and the way we owned each other.

She is the light in my darkness—my everything.

I slipped out of bed, showered, and put on sweatpants and a T-shirt. My cock was hard with need, but she'd been through enough. If he'd... I couldn't bear the thought of him defiling her. The bite was enough for me to cope with.

I knew it would have been excruciatingly painful, and my teeth clenched tightly at the idea.

An unwanted bite was painful beyond measure; a willing bite was pleasurable, and a bond bite was the most arousing aphrodisiac. We'd all discovered this aeons ago. The thought of her in pain made my shadows twitch... I'd ensure Adonis went through literal hell in Tartarus for doing that to her.

I shadow-walked to the kitchen and brewed coffee, preparing scrambled eggs and toast when Thanatos strolled in and poured himself a cup.

'How is she?' he asked through his teeth.

'Sleeping. She will be fine. Tell everyone not to worry. Please let Simos know; apparently, the Satyr had a melt-down when he heard,' I said as I buttered the toast.

Hecate had stayed with Persephone for a while after we returned to the Underworld, tending to the bite and bruises. Persephone had remained unconscious, but Hecate wasn't worried. Sleep was when our minds were almost free of stress following a traumatic event.

'Sleeping is a normal healing and recovery process after expending so much adrenaline,' I added as I turned to Thanatos. 'Is our guest settled in?'

A cruel smile stretched across Thanatos's lips. 'Oh, yes. Tisiphone and her sisters were eager to get their hands on the piece of scum.'

I gave a curt nod. 'I shall be indisposed today... unless there's a dire emergency.'

'Don't worry, Highness.' The Underworld usually ran like clockwork; my Underworld family ensured it.

I hesitated before continuing. 'I'm taking Persephone to the mortal realm for a week... perhaps longer. Our new schedule will allow everyone at least one long weekend each month for personal time. That includes you, Thanatos.' His eyes widened in pleasant surprise. 'While you rest, Hermes will oversee your army of soul collectors and manage operations in your stead.'

'Great.' Thanatos raised his cup in a salute.

'I'll be in my office tomorrow. Everyone will meet at ten sharp. We'll review the new schedule and assign duties for my absence. I leave with Persephone in the afternoon.'

'No problem.'

I took the tray of food and coffee, and my shadows enveloped me as I returned to Persephone.

'Morning,' she said sleepily, rubbing her eyes with her fists.

'I brought you toast, eggs, and coffee.' I laid the table and smiled as she scrambled from the bed, making excited squeaks.

We ate in silence for a while. Then she sipped her coffee and seemed to force herself to take deep breaths. I could taste her emotions, a blend of mildly spicy fennel and the tartness of lemons—vexation and agitation.

'Do you want to talk about it?' I asked quietly. She raised her eyes to mine; they shimmered with tears, dampness clinging to her lashes. I resisted the urge to go to her.

'He was...' She swallowed tightly. 'Delusional. Deranged. He wanted me to be his consort. He said I belonged to him. That I was promised to him.' She gave a half-hearted shrug.

401

'Promised to him?' I pondered those words, questioning whether the god behind Ixion had any connection to Adonis. 'Did he...?'

'No. He bit me. But he talked about what he would do, and...' Her voice faltered, but selfishly, relief washed over me at her words.

The taste of panic and fear clung to the back of my throat—sharp and sour, like spoiled coffee. She was starting to hyperventilate. I rushed to her, kneeling before and taking her hand. Flattening my palm against her chest, I felt the rapid thrum of her heart.

'Breathe, *agapi mou*. Inhale through your nose for four, hold for seven, then exhale through your mouth for eight.' She followed my rhythm, forcing the air in and out. I counted every breath. 'Again,' I said softly—again and again until the trembling subsided. 'Good girl,' I murmured as the trembling in her body receded.

'I'm sorry,' she muttered, dropping her eyes.

'Don't apologise, Persephone. I'm here for you. You're going to be fine.' A faint shudder rippled through her at my words.

The bite mark on her neck had faded to a faint bruise now that her powers had fully awakened. 'Feeling better?' I asked. She nodded, offering a shaky smile.

'I knew you'd find me,' she whispered. 'I just need to pull myself together and stop being such a damn cry-baby.'

I shook my head. 'You're the strongest woman I've ever known. Even you get to fall apart sometimes.' A small, reluctant smile curved her lips. 'I'm taking you to the mortal realm tomorrow, for a week, maybe longer,' I said, brushing my thumb over her hand. 'We'll travel. Do whatever you want. A change of scenery, and time together, is what we both need.'

'I'd love that,' she said, her voice barely a whisper.

'I'll run you a bath.' She reached out, making little grabby motions with her hands, so I scooped her up, and she wrapped her legs around my hips, her head resting against my shoulder as I carried her to the bathroom.

'I think you can carry me everywhere from now on. Walking is so overrated,' she breathed close to my ear, clinging to me like a koala. I raised my brows in mock horror but continued preparing the bath with her still in my arms.

'I love the sense of safety you give me,' she murmured, and my heart swelled in response. 'I—I need you, Hades. I need your touch. *Your* bite.' My mouth found hers before she could speak another word. A relentless kiss, thrusting my tongue into her mouth as she stroked hers over mine.

I deepened the kiss, and her legs slid down, but I kept her flush to me, her breasts and pebbled nipples hard against my chest, her nails digging into my shoulders, and my uncomfortably hard cock pressed into her stomach. She shivered deliciously.

I caught her bottom lip between my teeth, breathing hard. 'Your wish is my command, my queen. I'll hold you, kiss you, and suck those beautiful breasts the way you like.'

'Yes,' she whisper-groaned, lips swollen and trembling.

I kissed her again—hard, hungry. 'Shall I kiss and lick your wet pussy?' She nodded, eyes dark with need. 'And bite you while I'm fucking your pussy... and your arse?'

'That sounds really nice,' she breathed, dragging her tongue over her lower lip. The sight nearly undid me, and my erection became a stone monument.

'But first, I'm going to bathe you.' Her eyes were like two jade moons, and a soft smile graced those plump lips. Persephone's gaze held mine, and her breath caught as I stripped her bare, lifting her into the water. Slowly, deliberately, I bathed her, my hands and the warm water gliding over her skin in a rhythm that felt like worship. I lingered on her breasts, then between her thighs, circling her clit with my thumb until her moans filled the room, sweet and broken.

When I finally lifted her from the tub, she clung to me, water dripping from her body like liquid moonlight.

'Now, Hades,' she whispered, voice trembling with need. 'Please.'

'Patience, Persephone.' I gave her a half-smile, and her eyes narrowed. By the time I'd dried her body and wrung out as much wetness from her hair as I could, my cock was pulsing—hard and heavy, demanding her. Every inch of her gleamed like temptation incarnate.

I lifted her, and she wrapped her legs around me. Our gazes locked as I pressed her against the wall. 'I can taste your need,' I murmured, my voice rough. 'Sweet and warm as syrup.'

'Yes. Need. Hades, please...' she groaned.

Holding her with one arm, I freed myself, my erection springing against her slick heat. Shadows coiled around us like living silk as I sucked her taut nipple into my mouth, then thrust into her with one driving stroke. 'Fates,' I growled.

'Holy gods,' she gasped, arching as my shadows teased her nipples and slid lower, exploring her ass. I filled her entirely, lost in the tight, pulsing heat of her body. Her moans turned ragged, wild, as I thrust deeper, harder—each movement a promise, each sound a prayer. She spasmed, meeting each grind of my hips, my cock pulsing with fierce, unrelenting need.

'I will never disrespect you,' I whispered fiercely against her ear. 'No one will ever harm you. Your every desire is my command.' I gripped her chin, forcing her gaze to meet mine. 'In a world filled with nightmares, you are my paradise.' Each declaration fell in time with every deep thrust. 'I would do *anything* for you... You are my power, my pleasure, my everything. I will love you until all that remains of us are memories... and our bones are returned to the stars.'

Then I set a brutal rhythm—fast, hard, relentless. Her nails tore at my shoulders as my mouth devoured hers, wild and desperate. She shuddered, her voice growing hoarser with every cry. The tremor in her lower body turned into spasming contractions as she writhed and bucked, and when I bit her, she arched and screamed my name, pleasure breaking her apart. My hips drove into her over and over as she orgasmed again and again, until the tension coiled at the base of my spine exploded, and her spasming pussy milked my cock.

'I love you, Hades.' Her soft breath brushed my lips. 'You are my every desire... wrapped in the safety I never knew I needed.' A slow smile curved my mouth as I pressed a kiss to her damp forehead.

Our breaths came in jagged gasps as I carried her into the bedroom, laying her gently on the bed. We devoured one another—hungry, reverent, insatiable—until the world beyond us ceased to exist, and love became the only thing left between our shattered breaths.

Her head rested on my chest, and our limbs intertwined. Persephone slept, her languid breaths steadying my own as sleep pulled at me like a tether; yet even in rest, I held her close. I wasn't letting go. Not now. Not ever.

She is the sun that blazes through my darkest night, my muse, my distraction—my reason for enduring this immortal life.

She is my salvation; she is home.

She is my one and only, and she is mine again.

At last.

SERENDIPITY

TEASER FROM BOOK TWO—QUEEN OF TEMPESTS AND SIN

LONDON, ENGLAND.

Elias Drakos was a cunning man.

Cruel and opportunistic, his criminal pursuits had earned him a stench no wealth could mask. Not even a Savile Row suit, Burberry shirt, or pristine Prada dress shoes could disguise the sewer rat beneath the polish.

The woman twisted her mouth in distaste as he entered the room. Drakos, despite his vices, was a valuable contact—for her and for Ixion, the insurgent group seeking to wrest control of the human world from the gods. Drakos wouldn't recognise her because of her ability to shapeshift; she was literally hiding in plain sight. The woman would conceal her true form until the right moment.

The three primordial gods stood in her way, but she was patient. She had aeons of life experience to cultivate such patience. Fortunately, the divine were divided. Her sources told her the three primordial gods were at war, which worked in her favour. Hades would eventually side with her. He loathed his brothers almost as much as she did.

A bodyguard stood beside the oak door as Drakos approached the desk—an imposing mahogany monolith dominating the luxurious Mayfair office. He was aware of the danger, aware of her connection with the Resistance, but they needed him and his services, so fear was dulled by necessity. He concealed his nerves with a confident swagger.

'Madame Basilissa,' he said with a shallow bow, trying not to recoil under her icy gaze. 'A pleasure.'

She watched him with predatory calm... beautiful, yes, with long dark hair and steel-grey eyes, but there was an energy to her, a power that curled around the room like smoke.

'Sit, Mr Drakos,' she commanded, her voice husky, laced with a faint accent.

Drakos complied and tried not to fidget. He never bowed to women. In his mind, they were the lesser sex, but he was not a fool. This one, he sensed, outmatched him.

Drakos ruled his empire through fear and manipulation, but sold loyalty to the highest bidder—and if Ixion won, he intended to be on the right side of history.

'You have a worthy assassin, I believe.' Madame Basilissa looked up from the papers she was studying.

'The best,' he replied, allowing a smirk. 'No one better.'

'Very good.' She held his gaze. 'The target will not be an easy kill. This dagger...' She raised a blade encased in a clear silver-edged scabbard. The hilt was ornate, forged of intricate silver filigree, a blue crystal glowing from its bolster. The double-edged blade shimmered with strange patterns—like star-fire frozen in crystal.

Drakos's breath caught in his throat. This appeared to be a weapon of the gods.

'...is lethal to all life,' she continued, 'except humans. The assassin must pierce the target's heart with the dagger, and then they must decapitate them with the blade. I want the head.'

'The head—' Drakos echoed as he carefully picked up the blade. 'The head—' he repeated again as he eyed the weapon.

'Yes. Do not fail me, Drakos. You have one month to achieve this.'

He blinked. 'One month?'

'One month,' she repeated. 'You will receive more details from my assistant in the morning. You must destroy the documents once the assassin is clear on the details. Depending on which country the target is in, I will arrange the collection of the head. We believe the subject will travel to America, but one of my minions will confirm this with you first.'

She narrowed her eyes at Drakos. 'The assassin will need to drug the victim with this. Don't worry, it's odourless.' The woman handed him a small vial of white powder. 'And give the assassin this phone.' She passed a phone to Drakos. 'The assassin will receive a call once the target is in place, and we know for sure how long they will be in the area.' The woman then produced a black lacquered box. 'This will grant invisibility. The assassin may use it as they wish. Do *not* open the box until they need it. And I want it back afterwards.' Madame Basilissa's shark-like eyes sharpened. 'Understand?' He gave a slight nod and tried not to gulp. Basilissa's smile was like a knife's edge.

Daeira had done well—stealing the helm of invisibility with Minthe's help. The nymph's jealousy made her predictable. She was so desperate to become Hades' consort that she would do anything once Madame Basilissa had promised to dispose of the irritating new Persephone. And when Hades discovered the theft? He would blame Zeus. He always did.

Suppressing a smug grin, Basilissa turned back to Drakos. 'The assassin will fly privately. Diplomatic immunity has been arranged. Details forthcoming,' she stated, and Drakos nodded again, a feeling of foreboding choking his throat.

'Ten million has been transferred; the rest will be sent when the contract is honoured.' Drakos resisted the urge to grin. 'But be aware, Mr Drakos.' Her gaze chilled. 'I do not tolerate failure. It would be unfortunate for those you care about to bear the brunt of my wrath.'

A razor-sharp panic clawed at Drakos's insides, and pressure clamped down on his chest. He forced a tight smile, schooling his features. 'Do not worry, Madame

Basilissa. My assassin is... unmatched.' He inhaled deeply through his nose, trying to calm his racing heart.

'Good.' She returned to her papers.

The meeting was over. Drakos ground his teeth at the abrupt dismissal. He placed the dagger, phone, and vial in his briefcase, tucked the box under his arm, and left the office.

Once in the elevator, he pulled out his phone and dialled.

'Hello, little flower. I've got a job for you,' he said, voice low. 'Start packing. It looks like you're going back to your motherland... Meet me as soon as the plane lands—we'll go through the schedule. You'd better not let me down...' He paused, inhaling deeply. 'I'm afraid there will be consequences if you don't succeed. Failure is not an option.'

He ended the call and, swallowing his worry, strode from the offices, stepped into his waiting limousine, and tried not to think about Basilissa's cold eyes.

No—his assassin wouldn't fail.

She couldn't.

She had too much to lose.

THANK YOU FOR
READING 🤍

Every time you leave a review a baby unicorn is born ... 😉
Please leave a rating if you can.
I'd be eternally grateful. Helena xoxo

ACKNOWLEDGMENTS

If you're reading this—thank you! I hope you loved *Queen of Shadows and Roses* and Hades and Persephone's journey of rediscovering their eternal love.

I'm endlessly grateful for the support of my fellow authors, especially the amazing Eva Lauder, Eva Alton, and Liana Valerian.

But most of all, thank you to you—my readers. Your love and encouragement means the world! And to my street team... you are LEGENDARY. I adore you!

Keep an eye out for *Queen of Tempests and Sin*—Book 2 in the Brothers of Olympus series—coming early 2026.

Poseidon is about to meet his match.

Big love always, Helena xoxo

THE BROTHERS OF OLYMPUS SERIES 🦅

You can find me on SM, mostly Instagram @craggshm.
The link in my bio (linktr.ee/helenamcraggsauthor) will
take you straight to my permanent ARC team for Brothers
of Olympus.

Make sure to sign up for my newsletter at Helenamc.co.uk
and get the goods: spicy book updates, early reveals,
exclusive sneak peeks, artwork, and the occasional chaotic
ramble—straight to your inbox. Low pressure. High
drama. Total vibes.
You'll also get chances to enter **exclusive giveaways!**

About the Author

I've been a voracious reader ever since I was a little girl wandering the library aisles, letting my imagination run wild in fantastical worlds. These days, I'm still a devoted bibliophile, forever enchanted by the escapism of swoon-worthy romances and faraway realms. I believe books hold infinite possibilities—and mine are no exception. Expect magic, sharp banter, morally grey heartthrobs, fierce and witty heroines, and more than a little passion.

I live in rural West Yorkshire, England, with two ridiculously gorgeous pups, two perpetually cynical cats who very much run the household, a chicken with attitude... and a husband. When I'm not writing, I'm either devouring fantasy novels (the more romance, the better), laughing with friends, or rambling through the countryside with my dogs.

ALSO BY HELENA M CRAGGS

BROTHERS OF OLYMPUS SERIES. **A New Adult** series—
Badass heroines. Swoony romance. A fierce, addictive ride.

Book 1 **Queen of Shadows and Roses**

Book 2 **Queen of Tempests and Sin**—Due spring 2026

Book 3 **Queen of Starlight and Salvation**—Due 2026

THE YOUNGLINGS. **Young Adult** Urban Fantasy with
magic, danger, and super-hot supernaturals.

Book 1 Shadows & magic

Book 2 Fire & magic

Book 3 Mayhem & Magic

Book 4 Storms, Starlight & Magic

TRIGGER WARNINGS

STALKING & ABDUCTION
ALCOHOL CONSUMPTION
DECEASED FAMILY MEMBER
VIOLENCE
OPEN-DOOR ROMANCE SCENES
MATURE LANGUAGE